Covered Bridge Charm

Covered Bridge Charm

Dianne Christner

SHILOH RUN PRESS
An Imprint of Barbour Publishing, Inc.

Print ISBN 978-1-63058-897-7

eBook Editions:
Adobe Digital Edition (.epub) 978-1-63058-901-1
Kindle and MobiPocket Edition (.prc) 978-1-63058-900-4

All scripture quotations are taken from the King James Version of the Bible.

For more information about Dianne Christner, please access the author's website at the following Internet address: www.diannechristner.net

The author is represented by and this book is published in association with the literary agency of WordServe Literary Group, Ltd., www.wordserveliterary.com.

Cover design: Kirk DouPonce, DogEared Design

Published by Shiloh Run Press, an imprint of Barbour Publishing, Inc., P.O. Box 719, Uhrichsville, OH 44683, www.shilohrunpress.com

Our mission is to publish and distribute inspirational products offering exceptional value and biblical encouragement to the masses.

Printed in the United States of America.

Chapter One

Sweet Home, Oregon

Carly Blosser's curvaceous body lifted and sailed airborne for a full two seconds. She whipped the handlebars in both directions, causing her tires to crunch against asphalt and her round rump to smack the bike's pink seat.

The ribbons of her prayer cap streamed, and her skirt flapped, revealing too much black stocking as she picked up speed going downhill from her small cottage on Hawthorne to the back entrance of Sankey Park. Taking a shortcut across Ames Creek and Sweet Home's Weddle Bridge, the washboard turf of the historic covered bridge jarred her humming where Dot's lyrics had hitched an unwelcome ride.

Poor demented Dot. Eighty-two and stuck on lamb nursery rhymes that unintentionally drove a cruel spike into Carly's heart because she felt like she was a black sheep in her Conservative Mennonite flock.

With years of practice, she pushed back her regrets and loneliness. Today her thoughts fixed on something more crucial. She churned her legs and picked up speed on Long Street where, in spite of an errant blond curl, a shadow caught her vision. She leaned over the handlebars and groped inside her basket as the shadow materialized into a black dog, snarling and baring its fangs.

Her tires skidded and met flat surface. A practiced whip to the left straightened them. Just in the nick of time, she hurled the dog's decoy.

It sank its teeth into the flying object. A glance over her shoulder caught the animal limping away with its prize, and she turned her gaze back to the road's shoulder.

The first time, she'd been caught unawares and tossed the attacker her entire sack lunch. After that, they'd come to terms—a fat stick from a woodpile her brother kept stocked behind her cottage. The dog had grown old now, and that's exactly why she humored it.

Honk! Honk! She acknowledged the truck's horn with a wave. Adam Lapp, a godsend and burr rolled into one masculine package, and probably the only Lapp who didn't hold a grudge against her for spurning one of their relatives. Too bad his uncle Simon wasn't more like him.

Simon Lapp was director of the Sweet Life Retirement Center where Carly worked as a caregiver. The center was owned and operated by Mennonites of varying sects. Members of the Old Holley Conservative Mennonite Fellowship Church, which Carly attended, drove plain cars and used electricity and some modern conveniences. The women wore white head coverings. About six of the women wore strings on their coverings, and Carly was one of them.

Simon's wife didn't wear a head covering because he attended a more liberal Mennonite church, and they didn't wear plain clothing either. But doctrinal issues hadn't caused the wedge between Simon and Carly. Her very presence reminded him of his lost son and his personal shortcomings. As a result, he instinctively put the kibosh on her ideas. But it didn't stop her from voicing her opinions.

Carly met Simon's gaze with earnest appeal. "As the residents age, they need more care."

He blinked jaded brown eyes. "These things run in cycles. Right now our average resident is nearing ninety. But when the older ones pass on, a younger bunch moves in. Evens out in the end."

Indignation stiffened Carly's shoulders. These were lives, not to be replaced like farmed trout. She clutched her armrests to keep from swatting his patronizing smile.

"Now I've offended you. Look Carly, the elderly decline. That's life. We try to afford them their dignity, but there's only so much we can do. According to state requirements, we're well within the normal range of caregivers."

After careful research, she was also informed. "Two is a bare minimum. Did you know Dot Miller fell yesterday?"

He tapped some paperwork. "Yes, I have the report. But remember, this is an assisted-living facility, not a nursing home. There'll be some accidents." He raised a condescending brow. "Why, I heard you even took a spill the other day."

She ignored the disparaging remark, long past defending her lifestyle. The residents' welfare was the issue at hand. "That's my point. Volunteers could fill the gap. They'd provide more hands and eyes to prevent accidents."

"I agree. And we've already implemented that idea with our two V. S. workers."

Carly frowned at his reference to the Mennonite Voluntary Service women who served as regular caregivers, not additional help. "I work with Miranda. She's a hard worker." She wasn't as familiar with the woman who worked the night shift. "But that's not the kind of volunteers I mean."

"And there's Adam in woodworking and Betty in exercise."

"Yes, but they're in independent living. What about assisted living?"

"There's the bingo lady." His finger whipped the air. "And what's her name, who delivers snacks?"

Loneliness was a silent killer that stalked many of the elderly. Carly identified with loneliness, and it made her more determined. "I picture volunteers who read and write letters." Her voice cracked, "Hold their hands. And the more hands—"

"I get the concept," he said, his voice hardened with impatience. "Realistically, families need to pick up the slack. It's more important for me to focus on keeping the electricity running. Hiring a new dietician." He glanced at the wall clock. "Not to mention we need a new roof, and there's a leak in the laundry room—"

A scratch at the door stole their attention.

It creaked open a few inches, and a hairbrush poked through the crack. Next an arm appeared, and soon a head popped into view. Carly bit back a smile at the intruder's cockeyed hairdo, partly bound in curlers with a tangle of purple clips.

The aged face lit up. "Am I late for my appointment?"

Si buzzed the receptionist. "Get somebody from the hair salon over here pronto." Meanwhile, he ushered the intruder to an adjoining waiting room and returned.

"Who was that?" Carly asked.

"Don't worry. She's not an escapee. The salon started taking outside customers." He scooted his chair into place. "Now where were we?"

She looked away from his amused expression and lifted her gaze over his peppered hair to the '80s popcorn ceiling. "It won't cost you anything. And you won't have to lift a finger. I'll recruit all the volunteers."

His eyes widened in terror. "Whoa." He shook his head. "Hold off on that idea. You'd need the board's approval."

Her hope burgeoned. "When can I meet them? I have other ideas, too."

He pointed at the clock. "Which must wait since I have to prepare for a meeting."

With no intention of leaving without his support, Carly watched him shift his attention to an open file. She tucked a strand of hair beneath her prayer cap and cleared her throat. "When is the next board meeting?"

Si slapped it closed. "Complaints and wispy dreams won't stop the aging process. You need to let this go." For the first time, she felt a spark of sympathy for him. Something in his tone hinted at a purposefully hardened heart, one that hadn't always been that way. She studied him carefully, surprised when he finally relented. "Next time, at least bring a detailed, viable plan."

She rose, with lips itching to thank his cheek. "When's next time?"

Doing his name justice, he exhaled deeply. "Next Monday. But don't put the buggy in front of the horse."

"I won't."

He spun his chair away and punched the buttons on his cell phone. His rude dismissal didn't matter. With her toe in, the door would soon be dangling by its hinges because the safety and well being of Sweet

Life's elderly depended on her success. She had one shot, with only a week to prepare.

Adam Lapp brushed sawdust from his pants and sank into Uncle Si's vinyl armchair, staring at the mess. "Sorry 'bout that."

With an indifferent wave, Si got to business. "No shame in being a working man. I need a favor."

"Sure." Adam's gaze scanned the room, wondering what sort of project Si had in mind. Bookcases?

"You need to rein in Carly Blosser."

Adam's curiosity dove for cover. "I thought the library matter got settled by using book carts."

"If only. Now she's found a new way to upset Sweet Life's applecart." Si leaned forward and twisted his lips. "She wants to recruit volunteers for me."

Adam caught a frightening glimpse of Carly zipping her pink bike through the countryside, knocking on doors. Only that would be too ordinary. "She means well."

"Hah."

Adam shifted his gaze because his good sense waved a red flag. "Sorry, I don't have time to recruit."

Si studied him carefully. "What I need is a distraction."

He wasn't falling for it. Adam already regretted his promise to keep an eye on her for Jimmy—Carly's brother and his best friend. Once she'd been his cousin Dale's girl. Adam had always admired her from a distance. But impervious to drop-dead gorgeous and entertaining, he'd managed to stay single all these years and wasn't ready to change matters. Anyway, Carly possessed attributes that killed a man's curiosity. Distract her? He'd take a beating before he tried something so harebrained.

"How about some innocent flirting? Take her on a picnic down by Foster Lake."

Adam's objection erupted like a dying man's choke. He couldn't believe his uncle would try to pawn Carly off on him. Had he forgotten she was responsible for breaking his own son's heart? "That's crazy talk. Uh-uh. Not getting involved."

"She likes you."

Unbidden heat rushed to Adam's face. "Only because I'm her ride every time her bike breaks down."

Si hardened his jaw, and Adam cringed at the familiar expression. "You refusing me?"

He nodded.

"Too bad. Thought we'd nip things in the bud this time. Make it easier for you later."

"She's not *my* problem."

Si's voice turned reflective. "Funny. You're turning me down, yet you allow your dad to lead you around on a sissy's leash."

Adam clenched his teeth and stared at the manipulative face. Si and Dad were identical twins. One as maddening and stubborn as the other.

On her way home from work later that Thursday, Carly disembarked and walked her bike up the steep hill to Aunt Fannie's century-old home nestled in tall evergreens and tangled bushes, picturesque with autumn flower beds. Auntie played dual roles of mother and sister, otherwise lacking in Carly's life. She snatched a large paper bag from her bike basket and was soon pressing it into Auntie's inquisitive hands.

The slight woman, clad in plain Conservative Mennonite clothing, pulled out a wrinkled garment and ran her finger along a ragged tear. "My, my. Another hem's bit the dust." She met Carly's eyes. "Heard you took a nasty spill."

Carly gave a sheepish smile. It wasn't her fault that skateboarders had converged upon the hill by her house and she'd had to hit the ditch to avoid them. Wishing to skip the futile lecture, she asked, "Can you fix it?"

"I'll have to raise the hem. You want to show that much leg?"

"You know I don't." In fact, she always had Auntie add extra cloth to her capes—the modest layer of fabric the Old Holley Conservative women wore over their bodices. She added it for bicycling ease. But she also prided herself, for what she lacked in female submissive qualities, she made up for in modesty and generosity. She kept the strings on her head covering because the prayer cap symbolized male headship. It was the stick she threw to the church to remain in good standing and remain at peace with herself.

Carly followed the scent of chicken and dumplings to the stove and lifted the lid. "If you raise the hem, I'll wear it around the house."

"And if somebody knocks on your door?"

Replacing it, she shook her head. "Believe me, nobody will."

Auntie's voice softened. "Your closet's about the size of my bread box. And now you need a new dress."

With a reluctant nod, Carly sank into a ladder-backed chair, eying Auntie's mousy characteristics, feeling comforted in spite of any criticism. Auntie defended the ways of the church, but her prim facade belied a game spirit.

"Will you make it soft blue?"

"Sure, sure, the color of your eyes. But if you ask me, there's nothing economical about that bike. I still can't believe you ordered a pink one."

A complaint that would follow her to the grave. But it was her personal symbol of freedom and a reminder to stay true to her heart in spite of peer pressure. She'd ordered it after she'd stood up against Dale. She shook off the painful memories and smiled. "You can borrow it anytime."

"Ach! Such sass." Auntie turned away and returned with two heaping plates of food.

"Thanks." Steam fanned Carly's face, making her mouth water as Auntie blessed supper. The dumplings melted on her tongue. "This is good. By the way, I met with Simon Lapp today."

Auntie's spoon clattered. "When will you learn to quit nagging that man? It's a wonder you still have a job."

"Learn?" She shrugged, having learned plenty in twenty-seven years. After Bishop Kauffman's sermon on inner beauty, Carly had turned herself inside out looking for it. She'd shaken her soul with spring-cleaning vigor. But her inner self remained as contrary to the plain ways as her outer. She couldn't help it if her honey-colored ringlets exploded in volume as each day progressed. Or if they refused to take a part unless wet. Carly wasn't big on wet hair or restraint. She didn't even try to hold back her smile. "He's gonna let me recruit volunteers."

"What? You're joking."

"Wanna help?"

Auntie shook her head. "Nagging sure never worked with your uncle. Bless his departed soul."

Carly laid aside her spoon. "But I only have a week to make a plan. I need to purchase supplies, and I'm already short on funds."

"God will make a way, child. Now start at the beginning."

CHAPTER TWO

The next afternoon at Sweet Life, Carly stood outside the elevator and tapped the down arrow while thinking, *I need an inspirational slogan to recruit volunteers.*

"Look." Widow Martha Struder sucked a shallow breath that left her lungs hungry for air and waved a birth announcement. "Isn't my great-granddaughter the cutest?"

"Yes, she's sweet." *Make life sweeter at Sweet Life.* "Better use your inhaler, Martha."

The widow fished in her pocket for the small breathing device and sent the card and several candy wrappers sailing. While Martha inhaled the medication, Carly knelt to gather the fallen objects. *Helping Hands.*

The recent controversy over the library excursion left her personally responsible to get the readers, Martha and the Millers, safely returned. It was the asthmatic who worried her. She tapped the button again.

Meanwhile, Dot Miller's eyes fixed on the candy wrappers. "If we don't hurry, we'll miss supper."

Carly turned her gaze on the bit of a woman. "We had supper."

Her lip pouted. "I'd remember if I ate."

"Meatloaf and baked potatoes," Crusher reminded his wife. The plain people loved nicknames, especially amusing ones. The name Dot described his tiny wife, but his own nickname belied his gentle character. He got it from working at the quarry.

Martha's inhaler hadn't eased her breathing, but a *ding* brought the elevator to their level. The doors groaned open in tune with Carly's weariness. Her recruiting plan had gobbled both time and sleep. She was anxious to call it a week, get home, eat leftovers, and take a long bubble bath. That was the catch. Because of her drab existence, she drooled over a bubble bath made from dishwashing detergent. Discouragement settled over her. Could she really head up a volunteer program?

The elderly couple shuffled into the elevator while Carly slipped the fallen objects into Martha's coat pocket. In confusion, the older woman stalled in the doorway. Carly grabbed her arm and pulled her inside the elevator, but the inhaler took three bounces and rolled into the hall just as the doors closed.

Martha Struder panicked. All her life, she'd fought to breathe, but lately it was becoming worse. She clawed the door, "My inhaler!"

But the caregiver restrained her. Carly Blosser didn't understand what it was like to struggle and feel your windpipe closing. To feel the tightening, gurgling wheeze that squeezed her throat like an intruder wanting to snuff out her life. Frantic, she shoved Carly away and thumped the Stop button. The elevator jerked. She pressed the Open Doors button, but nothing happened. Frantic, she tapped all the buttons.

Trapped! She was trapped in an old woman's body and stuck away in an assisted-living facility. A place people put you when you weren't good for anything any longer. Her family never came around. The photo she'd shown Carly was as old as the hills. They probably all hoped she'd croak. And she would if she didn't get out of here.

Carly gasped as the struggling widow nearly took them both to the floor.

"My inhaler!" Martha Struder punched elevator buttons in an attempt to reopen the doors. Carly finally contained the distraught woman's arms and urged her toward a grab bar. But Martha remained uncooperative and agitated. "I need my inhaler."

"I know." Carly glanced at the numbered lights. "I'll go back for it."

But the elevator bucked.

"Eeeks!"

With sudden concern, Carly whipped her gaze to Dot.

The elevator shuddered. In seemingly slow motion, it catapulted library books that scuffed her black oxfords and littered the carpet. Frozen, Carly watched Dot slide to the floor with a soft thud and a loud squawk.

The elevator started again, but abruptly halted. Finally, it remained still.

Stumbling across strewn books, Carly gasped, "You all right?" Another fall was the last thing Dot needed. The tiny woman moaned. Her wild gaze searched for Crusher, who was slow in peeling himself from the wall. Eventually, he staggered toward them.

"Careful, now." Carly grasped the waistband of the retired quarryman's broadfall pants, helping him to Dot's side.

"You better look at this," he said.

Carly dropped to her knees and examined an almond-sized knot on Dot's temple, hoping it wasn't a concussion.

Meanwhile over by the doors, the portly widow poked her tongue through pinched lips and punched buttons as if methodically annihilating a trail of ants.

No wonder. Carly lunged and carpet-surfed on a slick magazine. "Stop!"

Martha flinched. She shrank back from the panel and lifted a defiant chin.

Carly realized the widow's intensifying emotions could trigger a full-blown asthma attack. Taking a moment to think, she resituated her dress and made a calm gesture. "I apologize. Now let's get you safely settled, before the elevator starts up."

The widow peered at Carly through the bottom of her bifocals and let out a raspy breath. "The elevator's not going up, young woman. We're headed down."

"Well, of course. You're right."

After settling her beside the Millers, Carly turned her attention to the elevator panel—detergent-bottle boring seeming lovelier by the moment.

Her eyes lit on the alarm button. She gave it a sound rap, imagining the receptionist calling Sherie, the manager. Sherie would set a fire under Rocco, the Italian maintenance man. He'd fetch his toolbox and hurry to help. Rocco could fix anything and do it from less than ample funds or materials. He kept the facilities functioning.

When she noticed the riveted gazes of the elderly trio, she forced a smile. "Help will soon be on its way."

"Good, cause I need my inhaler," Martha wheezed.

"I know. Try to remain still. That'll help."

Darkness seeped through the elevator's hairline cracks. Carly surmised the compartment was suspended somewhere between levels two and three of the four-tiered building. Her gaze darted around the purple confinement. Was the breakdown another of Simon Lapp's low-budget moves?

Carly wasn't green. She knew tennis balls descuffed walkers and the importance of storing the super glue away from the eye drops. But this was her first elevator crisis. How long would it take for a repairman to arrive and fix the problem?

"I'm scared and cold." Dot shivered.

Martha nodded. She wore her long silver hair swept up and fastened beneath a prayer cap. "According to the paper, we're getting frost." When it came to news, she was the Mennonite version of the Internet.

Dot's haunting voice lifted into a nursery melody: "Baa baa black sheep. . ." Crusher looked anxious. Carly knelt and buttoned the singer's coat, glancing at the lump on her forehead and wishing for an ice pack. "Better?"

She quit singing. "Think we'll miss supper?"

A few miles from Sweet Home, a black truck rumbled past flanks of fir and hit a cab-rattling rut that sloshed coffee onto Adam's passenger.

"Ach!" The stricken man said, "Slow down, would you? You'd think Christmas is tomorrow."

Time and family revolved around a holiday three months away. Not because of the holy birth, but because Roman Lapp owned and operated a Christmas tree farm.

Tugging a hanky from his pocket, Roman blotted his pants. "What's got you all fired up? You didn't lose our Portland account?"

Adam lowered his window and took a frustrated draft of piney air. It wasn't the account, not the birthday party his six alphabetically named sisters were—secretly—planning, nor the card from Cousin Dale that read: *Remember when we thought thirty was old?* It was the handwritten message on the card that caused his turmoil.

Reaching back for his coffee, Dad stared through the windshield at the evergreens ready to be individually priced for the upcoming harvest. "Did you hear your cousin Dale's having another baby?"

Adam nodded. *And here we go.*

Right on cue, Dad said, "Don't you want children?"

"You have grandkids."

"It's your kids who'll carry on the family name. That is, if you ever settle down."

"I'm settled. Got my own great place." He met and held Dad's gaze, wondering whether he'd ever get the recognition he deserved or even a partnership in the business.

Dad put his coffee in the cup holder, holding his peace until Adam steered the truck down a grassy side lane. "You seeing that woman you took to the Oregon Mennonite Festival?"

"I didn't take Carly. We ran into each other."

"Good. Cause she's one woman I don't want you bringing home. Stubborn and independent, that one. You need someone like your mom, who doesn't cause a big to-do." Dad snickered. "I hear Carly's a real thorn in Si's side."

The Lapp twins were two noble firs crowding each other for sun, roots embedding deep to possess the soil. In such cases, a horticulturist removed the weaker tree. In humans, the contest went to the end. And heaven help those, like Adam, caught in the fray.

Their newest rivalry appeared to be gaining control of his love life, or lack of it. He pulled off the lane and steered the truck between two rows of nobles. He hit the brakes and inwardly grinned when Dad's hands slapped the dashboard.

Once outside the truck, his gaze rested on an ax in the bed of his vehicle. Now was the time to lop off his sissy leash. "You can't tell me who to date. Keep it up, and you're going to run me off." *Like Dale.*

At first Dad stared at him with mouth agape. Then he gave a harsh laugh. "In this economy?" He spread his arms to include the fertile land and well-groomed trees. "When you have all this?"

His cousin's handwritten birthday note came to mind, offering him everything but the sky. "Dale's expanding his carpentry business in Nappanee. He asked me to join him."

"Indiana?" Dad shook his head in disbelief. "So that's what this is about?"

Adam's phone buzzed. He glanced at the screen with frustration. "I need to get it." Turning his back, he replied, "Stuck in an elevator? You can't be serious. Uncle Si, it's not Carly's fault." He ended the call and explained, "It's Sweet Life. I gotta go."

"On my time? Si hollers. You jump. And that's the woman you took to the festival, ain't it?"

The questions made Adam's head spin. "Sorry. I'll send one of the girls to pick you up."

"Jah," Dad waved. "Just go."

With a dismissive nod, Adam hopped into the cab, gunning the engine to life. He envied Cousin Dale's freedom, living away from his family. Though he longed to join him, he'd never leave Dad in a bind. But it would be interesting to check out Nappanee after the Christmas harvest.

Chapter Three

Time passed, and the small group at Sweet Life remained stuck in the elevator.

"What if the lights go out?" Dot asked.

Carly wasn't sure if Dot's recent fears stemmed from being separated from Crusher, who remained in an independent-living apartment, or if it was her increasing dementia. But she hoped the lights continued to operate.

Martha drew in a wheezy, shallow breath. "What worries me is crashing to the bottom of the shaft."

With only a half-stitched notion of an elevator's workings, Carly tried to console them. "That won't happen. We're probably near the bottom, anyway."

Determination lit Dot's eyes as she lurched forward. "Crusher, get something to pry the door."

He placed a gentle hand on her shoulder.

"It does so happen!" Martha argued, turning to Carly. "A woman in New York City got crushed and died. When she stepped into the elevator, it took off and she got caught in the shaft." She broke into a fit of coughing and wheezing.

Crusher frowned. "You should quit reading the paper. It's depressing."

Carly gently touched Martha. "Please relax. Try to talk less and breathe more. Think of this as a grand adventure. A story for your grandkids."

"Who never come to visit."

Ignoring the sarcasm, Carly sorted and stacked books. "I think we should read."

"Hold up on the reading, I gotta go pee." Dot struggled to rise, but Crusher tugged her arm and whispered. Dot's gaze widened and darted around the small room. Shoulders slumping, she sank back to the floor. "I'll just hold it."

Carly hoped she could. After three mistakes, a resident was required to wear protective underclothing. Dot didn't need an additional nuisance. In Carly's mind, this was extenuating circumstances. But she hadn't worked ten years at Sweet Life without learning its rules and regulations.

Opening a women's magazine, she read, " 'French country style is a marriage of ruffles, distressed woodwork, and both vibrant and subdued hues.' "

Martha's eyelids instantly flickered. Hoping it stabilized her breathing, Carly continued, but her mind drifted away from French country. Surely elevators had fresh air? Would artificial respiration help asthma? Was it ten or twelve breaths per minute?

A sharp jab to the ribs brought her back to task. A second jab dug into her side. "Ouch!" She speared Dot with irritation. "What?"

The tiny woman pointed at Martha's soft snoring.

Crusher's stomach growled. "Sorry."

Dot laughed. "You're always hungry."

"And you eat like a canary," he teased.

Dot's delicate face softened, and her blue gaze turned glassy. "We should've bought us a canary. That would've been nice."

The soft snores drew Carly like a catchy yawn. She'd never fallen asleep on the job, but she hadn't slept for so long. Technically, she was off duty. Definitely not off duty. The library excursions had been eliminated until she volunteered to do them on her personal time. After several minutes of fighting drowsiness, her surroundings faded away, and she dozed.

In what seemed like the next instant, a hellish scream erupted in her left ear, awakening her to confusion and utter darkness. A touch on her right arm sent her to the moon before she came to her full senses and remembered she was stuck inside an elevator. A pitch black elevator. *Oh, no*. She groaned before she thought better of voicing alarm while she was the care *giver*.

"I knew it!" Dot said, "We're gonna crash."

Carly reached for the frightened woman, but her hand brushed air and carpet. She crouched, crawling toward the voice, when something sharp clamped her calf. A sudden prickle zipped up her leg, Martha's fingernails snagging her new stockings. "Please let go of my leg."

"That's your leg?"

"Well it better not be Crusher's," Dot snapped.

Carly tried to disengage Martha, to no avail. Willing herself to remain calm, she took roll call. "Everybody okay? Crusher?"

"Yep. Dot's with me."

"Good. Now let go of my leg, Martha."

"I can't."

"For heaven's sake! Why not?"

"My fingernail's caught. And you gave me a hangnail. It smarts like crazy. So quit squirming until I get loose."

Dot's voice panicked. "Where are we?"

"Just stuck in an elevator," Crusher reminded.

"Stuck in a stocking, over here," Martha wheezed. "I saw the sale in the paper. You can't skimp on stockings."

"I don't." Carly yanked. The tear disengaged Martha, and the older woman jerked her hand away. It sounded as though she put her finger in her mouth. Regretting her loss of temper, Carly softened her tone. "You're right. I got them on sale."

Martha drew in a short quivering breath. "You should ask for a raise." She coughed. "You deserve it."

The outrageous comment reminded Carly of her meeting with Si. His nephew would know how to handle Martha or any other difficult situation. But Adam wasn't volunteering today. Or was it night? She'd lost track of the hours. "Please hush, Martha. You must quit talking while you still have breath."

On hands and knees, she crawled toward the widow, blinking furiously when a sudden flood of light encompassed the tiny compartment. She squinted. Crusher and Dot nestled safely in one corner. In the opposite, Martha sucked her finger.

Carly jerked her twisted skirt and pressed to standing. Martha's face appeared pale. Her eyes wide and breathing critical. She needed medicine. Feeling helpless, Carly glanced around the purple compartment and sprang when the phone suddenly rang, snatching it to her ear. "Jah?"

"All fixed, ma'am. Make sure everybody's set to move."

Her voice gushed, "Thank the Lord. Can you get us help? Martha's having an asthma attack. And Dot fell and has a lump on her head."

"The nurse is here, too."

"Good." Carly hurried back and slid next to Martha. "Everybody stay put. He's starting it up."

This time Martha didn't argue; she just slipped her hand into Carly's. Across the elevator, Crusher hugged Dot protectively. The tender scene flooded Carly with love. She wouldn't trade the moment for a thousand squirts of dishwashing detergent.

The elevator glided smoothly, and Carly wondered if Si had been right to question the library excursions. When the doors yawned, a small crowd of concerned onlookers looked in. Supervisor Sherie and Rocco from maintenance rushed forward to help the residents. They guided Dot and Martha toward waiting wheelchairs and the resident nurse.

After thanking the elevator repairman who'd rescued them, Carly gathered books and stepped into the hall, surprised Crusher had remained behind.

"You did good in there."

"Thanks, Crusher. You, too."

"You think they'd allow me to get her a canary?"

"Oh, I don't know."

"I'd take care of it."

Softening, Carly replied, "I'll find out." *Soon as I finish my recruiting plan.* She looped her free arm through Crusher's, hoping he didn't look down and notice his wife's wheelchair had left a wet trail on the floor.

Beneath the parking lot's floodlights, Carly watched Adam's muscles bunch as he easily hefted the pink beachcomber into the bed of his truck. He whipped out a packing blanket and shoved it beneath the front wheel and handlebars.

"Thanks for the lift. I'm exhausted. What're you doing here, anyway?"

A touch at her elbow urged her into the cab, and his masculine rumble grazed her ear. "I could ask you the same question."

"We're both softies, aren't we?"

With a grunt, he slammed her door. The cab heaved as he got behind the wheel.

"Why so irritable on your birthday? You'd think you were the one stuck for hours in an elevator."

He started the truck and eased into traffic. "Sorry, it's been a long day."

She eyed him curiously, remembering she still needed to buy him a birthday gift and was at a complete loss for an idea and funds. In a forced cheery voice, she asked, "What do you want for your birthday?"

His masculine square jaw flinched. "Nothing. Tell me about your elevator ride."

"Not until we finish this discussion." She had no idea when she'd be able to corner him like this again. "I can't show up at your party empty-handed."

His head nearly swiveled off its stocky neck. "You're coming?"

Hurt at his shocked tone, she forced her gaze to the window. Adam was God's angel, sent to lend her a helping hand by her brother's arrangements. She shouldn't expect more from him. Obviously, friendship was stretching the perimeters of their relationship. She raised her chin against the personal onslaught of resentful attitudes which had seemingly struck every male in her congregation. Now Adam had caught it, too? Just because she hadn't submitted to Dale's plot to move to Timbuktu. Sure it had crushed him. Especially since their engagement had already been announced. But the breakup was just as hard on her.

He cleared his throat. "That sounded wrong. It's just that I hoped they were planning something small—as in only family." He gave her a sheepish grin that was irresistibly endearing and almost believable. He could be quite charming when he tried. But his brown eyes remained skittish. His gorgeous smile resembled Dale's, but the two men were nothing alike. Still trying to read him, she muttered, "Sorry to disappoint, but I'm invited to your party. Your sister isn't reading more into our relationship than there is, is she?"

He pulled onto Hawthorne Lane. "Nope. She knows we're just friends." In her driveway, he killed the truck's ignition and draped a chiseled arm over the steering wheel. "Heard you had a meeting with Uncle Si."

"Jah. I'm working on a plan to recruit volunteers. He's taking it to the board. This is big. You know how bad we need volunteers." She blinked dreamy eyes, surprised to catch his black brows in a judgmental V.

"Don't do that."

"What?"

"Judge me. Don't act like you don't care about the residents as much as I do. I meant it earlier when I said you were a softie."

"I wasn't. I was thinking about something else."

"Like what?"

He shrugged. "It's not important."

As his gaze went to her mouth, she stirred uncomfortably.

"If you must know, I was stuck on your earlier question. What I wanted for my birthday. It got me thinking. You have a nice mouth. But it would be better suited to kissing than arguing and nagging with Si. Sometimes you talk so much I can't even keep up with our blasted conversation."

"Well that's plain rude. You're right. Birthdays don't suit you." She jerked the door handle. "Just get my bike."

With a curt nod, he jumped out of the truck.

Normally, she went inside while he took care of her bike, but she had instantly regretted her harsh remarks. It wasn't his fault she was having a rough day. She moved toward the tailgate to make amends. But on the way around the truck, a wild idea flew into her brain. It was crazy, but. . .

He unlatched the tailgate and easily hoisted down the bike. "You forget something?"

"Just curious. Were you thinking about kissing me in particular, or talking about all women in general?"

His dark, deep-set eyes lit with interest, but he quickly schooled his expression to one of mild curiosity. "Both, I guess. Guys usually wish women would talk less and *you know,* smile more."

She hesitated, wavering between the practical and the indecent. With one easy stroke she could move some meager funds from the birthday column to the recruiting column. The clock was ticking, and she didn't know what to buy Adam. A friendly kiss might finally remove Dale's lingering ghost.

He toed the kickstand and faced her so close she could smell his piney scent. His eyes were two deep pools. "Carly? I know that look. What are you scheming?"

She studied him, taking in the thick black hair and masculine square jaw which now sported an evening shadow, and deemed it risky but practical. "Adam, would you settle for a birthday kiss?"

He couldn't hide his shock. "Is this a trick question?" She tucked her full bottom lip between her teeth and smiled in that fetching way that deepened her dimples and made her likable. But he couldn't let down his guard around her. "Now Carly, you're either overtired or not thinking clearly."

Miffed, she turned and blasted him with a parting shot. "Well just great. Last night I didn't get a wink of sleep worrying about my recruitment plan. And tonight I'll lay awake worrying about your dumb birthday present."

Drat Si. It was his fault he'd stared at her lips and blurted out his thoughts. Now he was in a no-win situation. With no strings attached, he was for it. Only with women, there were always strings. And unlike his sisters, this fetching creature even wore them on her covering. "Wait a minute."

Shoulders slumped, she turned rejected and pathetic. But that didn't mean she was harmless. Not this woman who'd caused such a family stir. He knew first-hand from Dale how this curvy woman was anything but yielding. If there was kissing involved, he needed to set some boundries. "I don't like being manipulated."

Her eyes narrowed. She pushed his shirt. "Just go. But don't complain if I buy you a pair of socks."

He caught her hand. "Wait. I don't want a gift. Your friendship's enough." Her pained gaze struck him. His rejection had hurt her. Softly, he said, "Just the same, I would like to claim that kiss." He tipped her chin and whispered, "Tilt your head, Carly."

"I know that."

"Be quiet, please."

He felt her quiver beneath his touch. It sent a jolt of unexpected pleasure through him. He was wrong. She was soft as she looked. . .to the touch. Entranced, he lost himself until he felt her hands lightly pushing against his chest. When he opened his eyes, he was thankful to see she wasn't regretful. More like perplexed.

He gently tugged one of her curls, hoping the gesture would pass as thanks. He was a gentleman, after all. Then he set her aside and grabbed up the beachcomber.

When he returned from her backyard, however, he discovered she *still* hadn't gone inside, but stood there, wearing a vulnerable expression. Had he really distracted *the* Carly Blosser? Sudden fear leapt through his heart. This independent woman always got what she went after. Surely, she wasn't after. . .

She flashed her dimples. "So, happy birthday then."

A smile tugged his lips. "Sure. By the way, you have a gigantic tear in your stocking." With that, he hightailed it to the truck. In his rear-view mirror, he saw a light go on inside the cottage. Happy Birthday. Merry Christmas, and every holiday all rolled into one.

When the pleasure faded, however, he realized that kiss would instigate something terrible. He could feel it in his bones. Sheer terror. Nappanee beckoned stronger than ever. Snatching his cell phone, he punched in speed dial.

"Hey, Jimmy. I'm worried about Carly."

"Why? That crazy old dog didn't attack her?"

"No, nothing like that." *Unless he was the dog.* "She thinks Si gave her permission to recruit volunteers for the center. Only, he's stalling until she forgets about it."

"Fat chance she'll forget. All right, I'll talk to her."

"Great. She's coming to my party. Maybe you can give her a lift?" If she came on her brother's arm, it might not cause such a stink with the family. He wondered if he should tell Jimmy about Nappanee. A guilty thought struck him. He'd kissed Carly, knowing full well he might be leaving. A more disturbing thought followed. Carly's kiss was chaste-like. For some reason, that bothered him more than the fact she'd only kissed him to pinch a few pennies.

Chapter Four

Carly flipped on her living-room light and almost stepped on the soft creature dashing circles around her feet. Dropping her purse on an end table, she eased back the curtain enough to watch Adam's taillights disappear around the corner. With a sigh, she sank into the sofa's saggy spot and touched her finger to her lips, which were still warm from his kiss. "Oh Cocoa, what on earth was I thinking?"

Resting her forehead in her palm, she tried to reason with her anxious heart. "It meant nothing." To him, anyway. Sure, Adam was always her brother's *good-looking* friend. The dark brooding fellow who attracted female attention. Every brother has one, right? But she'd never been interested in him until he started instructing the retirement center's woodworking shop, and he'd earned her admiration with his compassion for the elderly. So different from his gregarious, ambitious cousin. But Jimmy was mostly responsible for her budding friendship with Adam.

When her brother had taken his trucking job, hauling Oregon fruits to the Midwest and picking up loads there that often kept him away from home for days at a time, he'd enlisted Adam to keep an eye on her. At first it embarrassed her to have Adam taking Jimmy's place, keeping her woodpile stacked, hauling her bike around, and fixing her garbage disposal. But she'd grown accustomed to it—a lopsided friendship to be sure. And she'd never entertained thoughts that he was actually interested in her as a woman. Wasn't that what he'd hinted at tonight? It came as a surprise, then, that his free birthday kiss could stir up something which long lay dormant. She should have known free was too good to be true.

His kiss came with a cost. A sad longing settled over her. She was playing with fire, and she'd surely get burned if she wasn't careful how she handled this situation in the days to come.

Thump! Thump!

Uh, oh. "Cocoa, no-no," she warned.

Again, *Thump! Thump!*

Two thumps too many, too late. The chocolate-and-white rabbit lunged at her legs and started digging furiously on her stockings. "Careful, sweet. I know you need attention. You're lonely, too." She reached and gently disengaged its claws from the ragged mess on her calf. Lowering herself to the floor and leaning her back against the couch, she rubbed Cocoa's head until the offended rabbit settled down and became a fat, furry puddle. Adam's snide remark leapt to mind, *"By the way, you've got a gigantic tear in your stocking."*

Laughter bubbled up. Following that, she remembered Martha's fingernail getting caught in her stocking and the older woman's stern reprimand about buying stockings on sale. Bits of the irrational conversation that had taken place inside the elevator soon had her laughing hysterically. It felt good to release the tension from the whole elevator episode. It must have affected her more than she'd realized. That's probably why the kiss didn't turn out to be the joke she'd intended.

"Oh Cocoa, what a day." The bunny was doing its tooth purr. His gentle tooth grinding was a sign of rabbit bliss. She rubbed beside his long, lopped ear. The plump bunny was a unicorn lop with one ear up and one down. It was what had attracted her to her mixed-breed pet. He was a rescue bunny and had always been on the nippy side when he didn't get his way.

"Okay, lazy. Let's get us some dinner." There was fresh hay and a raisin treat for Cocoa and leftover spaghetti calling her name. She loved her tiny cottage, even if she was the youngest resident on the street. It met her needs. The kitchen was at one end, providing a window over the sink, which looked out at her flower bed. The one Jimmy unenthusiastically helped to create. From the window, she could watch her neighbor Imogene uncoil her gray hose and water her colorful zinnias. On hot days, she watered Carly's garden, too. Sometimes she even refilled Carly's hummingbird feeder.

There was another window by a square table big enough for her pressed flower crafts and an adjoining living room with a ratty, green-and-white-striped sofa and matching armchair. The large bamboo plant was a gift from her aunt. While she couldn't sew, Carly was great with any green living thing. Well, practically any living thing. Except men.

Next came a hall and bathroom. Her bedroom was at the back of the cottage. The yellow quilt that graced her bed was her mother's. She liked to think she slept inside her mother's hug. A mother long gone, yet the quilt bridged heaven and earth. Long ago, it had helped her decide that sunny yellow was her favorite color. Mostly dressing in dark plain materials, she enjoyed her cheery room. She went with a more Conservative Mennonite traditional look in the kitchen. Same as the living room, bright green and white.

As she washed her plate, she watched Cocoa move toward his litter box.

Carly finished in the kitchen and started her bath. With a squirt of dishwashing detergent, the bubbles exploded, a few popping against her cheek. Instantly her mind recalled Adam's touch, the way he'd gently tugged her hair. At that moment, his unguarded gaze had held a smolder she'd never witnessed in him. She frowned, wondering what it meant. How quickly it had been replaced with a twinkle. Then the snide remark about her stockings. Was it his way of covering his feelings? Why had he stared at her legs? She broke off her thoughts, remembering she wasn't ready to get back into a relationship. Because of Dale, her trust toward men had been wounded. He'd chosen his career over her. Best not to think about the kiss she'd shared with Adam.

In the upset of the day, she'd forgotten all about her volunteer program. With a sigh of comfort, she turned off the faucet and sank deep into the water. Tomorrow was Saturday. She'd go to Auntie's and find a way to turn her grandiose idea into a viable recruitment plan. She'd been given a chance to do something great for the residents. And she wasn't going to let them down.

Stretching on his hind legs, Cocoa peeked over the tub to lick water droplets.

"Hi, Sweetie. Tomorrow we're going to Auntie's. And while we're there, I'll tell her to make my new dress extra long so Adam doesn't ogle my legs. That'll teach him."

Late Saturday morning, Carly jumped off her bike and lowered the kickstand, taking a few moments to catch her breath. They'd gone the long way since Cocoa couldn't tolerate barking dogs. It felt good to work off the adrenalin surging through her veins over Simon's upcoming board meeting. She hoped Aunt Fannie could help her organize her frazzled thoughts into an engaging, workable plan.

Grabbing a yellow legal pad and tiny bell—which kept Cocoa in line when away from home—she eased the rabbit out of his soft bed in the bike's woven-reed basket. Cocoa snuggled tight, put his ears back, and grunted with displeasure.

Aunt Fannie's house could use a coat of white paint, but the porch smelled sweet from the autumn clematis that trailed along its railing. The latch clicked, and Auntie swung the screen door open with a smile.

"I was expecting you." She pet the rabbit. "And I'll put up with it."

Inside, Carly released Cocoa and waited while Auntie prepared a litter box. Cocoa raised up on his hind legs and scoped the room, then nose twitching, hopped away to investigate the small dining room where patterns were strewn across a slightly dusty table.

"A new design?"

"Jah. I'm calling it 'autumn paisley.'"

Carly rustled the thin tissue paper as she examined a drawing done in colored pencils. "What a fascinating design. It's different."

"Ach, it's simple." She pointed. "Just pears and leaves."

"Jah. I see it now."

The older woman with gray-streaked, dull brown hair took joy in creating colorful new quilt patterns. Some were tested on the Old Holley Fellowship sewing circle, but many were never revealed, awaiting her dream of publishing a pattern book.

A quick glance sent Carly scurrying from the room with her aunt soon at her heels. The women ran down the hall, and Aunt Fannie brushed past Carly, entering the tiny bedroom on the right. "Cocoa! You naughty rabbit!"

Auntie bent and tried to pry a pattern from the rabbit's mouth. Cocoa spit it out and nipped her hand. Pulling back, Auntie screeched, "Ach! Why did I forget to close the door?"

While the older woman made repairs, Carly moved past the multicolored quilt that covered the bed and stood on tiptoe to peer onto a closet shelf. She lifted a shoe box lid labeled *Rabbit's Toys* and withdrew an empty toilet paper roll. "Try that instead, Sweetie."

Cocoa snatched the offering and hopped under the bed.

"Sweetie," Auntie mimicked sarcastically.

Carly used the rabbit's bell to lure Cocoa back into the main part of the house. Auntie closed the bedroom door and got Cocoa a raisin treat for obeying the bell. "Not that it deserves it." She glanced at Carly. "How do you get yourself into such trouble? Keeping a spoiled rabbit for a pet. Riding a pink bike. Tearing your—"

She interrupted with a nod. "That reminds me. Make my new dress a couple inches longer than normal, will you?"

Aunt Fannie lifted a brow but remained silent.

Let her figure that out, Carly thought. "Speaking of trouble. That's why I'm here. I need your help with my volunteer plan."

Auntie sighed.

"Will you?"

"Jah. Just bring your yellow pad to the kitchen. I'll make tea. You always drive me to drinking."

Carly grinned, having heard that line many times. "I've made a list of places we can advertise for recruits. The library, farmer's market, restaurants, newspaper, radio, places of business around town and church."

"What about Salem's Quiltopia?"

"The quilt festival's too soon. At least this year."

"Jah, probably. It's only two weeks away." The tiny woman cranked open the antique window near her sink. "That feels better. Cocoa got me heated up."

Carly scribbled, *Need script for radio, article for the newspaper, fliers, posters, brochures.*

Auntie poured tea. "What do these volunteers do?"

Carly whipped to the next page. "Why they can do anything: crafts, singing, games, Bible groups, sharing talents like painting or teaching computers."

"Computers! Ach. Scratch that off."

Ignoring her, Carly continued, "Hand massage, needlework, bring pets, exercise classes, visitor companion, reading, phone companion, taking residents to get their hair done, swimming."

"Swimming?"

Carly shrugged. "I'm just brainstorming."

"How about scenic drives? Something to get them out of the center?"

"Good idea. But I wonder if legalities are involved. I'll have to find out. The volunteer would have to be trustworthy. A good driver. Too bad Sweet Life doesn't have a van."

"You'll have to interview them."

"So I'll need questions, applications that include reference checks, and I might as well come up with duties and responsibilities."

Auntie glanced at the clock. "They'll want to know how much time it requires."

Carly scribbled. "And they'll need supervision and accountability." She set down her pencil and sipped her tea. "This is going to be a big job."

"But all you need now is the plan. When it comes to implementing, you delegate."

Gazing into the distance, Carly wondered if Sherie would get involved. What if nobody wanted to be involved? She couldn't do everything. First, she needed someone with artistic talents to do the posters. And she didn't have much spare time, except weekends. She worked some Saturdays. Worry traipsed up her spine. She needed to outline a timetable with phases. Her train of thought was broken when

Cocoa zipped through the kitchen and back out again.

"Ach. What's it up to now?" Auntie asked.

"Cocoa's just playing. He's happy."

"Humph. It's spoiled."

"You're an artist. Can you do my posters?"

"If I can find the time. I wasn't going to say anything, but I'm taking some of my designs to the Quiltopia."

Carly leaned back in her chair. "That's great."

"Now don't tell anybody."

"Of course not."

"So what else you need?"

Carly shrugged. "I need a slogan to make this plan sparkle. I've racked my brain, and I can't come up with anything good. I couldn't sleep last night and won't be able to sleep again until I have one. *Adam's kiss hadn't helped any.*

"The gift of time is priceless."

"You're on the right track," Carly nodded.

"Volunteers make each day brighter."

"That's good." *But not quite right.*

Auntie patted her hand. "Don't worry, dear. It will come to you. Maybe on the ride home."

Carly recognized the brush off, which meant Aunt Fannie was eager to get back to her project. She had her own goals and hadn't been able to come up with the magic slogan. As she tucked Cocoa under her arm, she thanked her aunt for the help she'd given.

"You're welcome. I hope that rabbit doesn't jump off and break its neck."

Chapter Five

Carly had avoided Adam since the kiss but would see him within the hour. She'd donned her Sunday best for the birthday party, a pink floral made in the same modest design as her solid-colored clothes. She wished her new solid blue had been ready and hoped she didn't appear overly zealous wearing the print.

"Penny for your thoughts, over there."

She glanced across the truck at Jimmy. Normally he wore jeans, but tonight he looked handsome dressed in loose black slacks and a white button-down shirt. It was the male uniform of Old Holley Conservative Mennonite Fellowship members. While his wavy blond hair and tall, wiry frame attracted females and his gregarious personality had filled their homes with friends, it was his protective care that was so endearing. Most of the time. "I'm just a little nervous. I've never been to the Lapp place."

"You and Adam friends now?" His voice held a cautious note, probably because of the initial contention he'd stirred up with Carly when he'd asked Adam to keep an eye out for her.

Her head swiveled, "Why?"

Jimmy shrugged while turning off of the Halsey–Sweet Home Road and steering onto a narrow road with Christmas trees in neat rows on either side. "You've never been before, and now you're invited."

"Ann invited me. His sisters threw a big party since it was his thirtieth. She must have heard we were. . ."

He grinned. "You see my point."

She hoped they were still on friendship status. "You're right. Guess

I never gave it much thought." *Until lately.*

"Adam warned me you've been getting Simon Lapp riled up over some volunteer program."

Feeling a flash of anger that Adam had tattled, she snapped, "Sometimes that's what it takes to get things accomplished at Sweet Life."

"Look. I know improvements are needed, and you're doing a good thing. I just don't want you to get hurt. Simon wields a lot of power."

"I know. But better I get hurt than the residents."

Jimmy reached over and squeezed her hand. After that, they rode in companionable silence until they pulled into a long winding lane with a tall white farmhouse, bigger than most. She'd always admired it, and now her curiosity renewed.

"My goodness. Everyone we know must be here." Carly crooked her neck to take in the scene. Across an impeccable lawn, people assembled in small clusters, some walking from a row of cars and carrying gifts. Jimmy parked at the end of the row.

Outside, Jimmy reached behind the seat and pulled out a small package. "You want me to put your name on this, too? It's a knife."

Her face heated. "No. I gave him a gift earlier."

As they moved toward the house, the chatter and laughter grew louder.

"Jimmy! Over here!" Adam called from a group of guys.

Jimmy looked at her, and she motioned, "Go. Want me to take your gift inside?"

"Thanks." He handed it to her and fled.

She saw others entering the front door and followed, stepping into a large living room where some older men were gathered. The Lapp twins sat at opposite ends of the room. She could tell them apart by their clothing and hairstyles. When the more progressive twin's eyes lit on her, their gazes locked. Simon paused his conversation and nodded at her. Adam's dad Roman seemed surprised to see her but motioned to a doorway. "The women are in the kitchen."

"Thanks."

In the kitchen, she tossed out a question in the general direction of Adam's many sisters, "Can I help?"

Ann paused, platter of food in hand. "No, but let me show you where to take your gift."

"You weren't kidding when you said you were throwing a big bash. This is huge."

Setting down the platter in the dining room, Ann grinned. "Gigantic. Isn't it? You should have heard Adam's groan when all the cars started arriving." She giggled. "He never wants a party, which is exactly why we always have one. But he had no idea it would be like this."

Carly placed the gift on a folding table against a wall. "In other words, you like to torture him."

"We sure do."

"Mama. Mama." A four-year-old girl ran into the room and tugged Ann's dress. "Jacob told us we can't play tag with the boys."

"Then start your own game with the girls."

"But. . .okay." Little Mary skipped away.

Ann shrugged. "And Jacob likes to torture his sisters. Gets it honest. I'll deal with him later tonight." She studied Carly a moment. "Actually Adam and I are close. I'm usually defending him because I'm the family peacemaker."

Carly thought she was also the most beautiful of the sisters. While Adam took after the Lapps' dark, good looks, Ann took after her mother, Sissie Lapp. Their brown hair had just enough waves in it to make it manageable and enhance their faces. Their blue eyes were like the ocean on a sunny day, both playful and inviting.

"He stops by my place often, letting off steam." Ann tilted her head. "He talks about you and your work at Sweet Life."

Carly laughed. "Let's off steam about me?"

"I didn't mean it that way. He admires your work." Ann was open spirited, and her expression easy to read.

"But?" Carly urged.

The other woman leaned close and whispered, "He tells me you like to ruffle Uncle Simon's feathers, and he has to smooth them down again."

Carly felt like ruffling Adam's feathers. Possibly wringing his two-sided, tattletale neck.

Sissie Lapp popped into the room. "We're ready. Girls, get Adam inside, and everyone else will follow."

Carly forced a smile when Ann enthusiastically looped her arm through hers, cementing her to the spot where Adam's family would assemble and become the party's focal point. Adam strode into the room like a man going to his own hanging. His sisters hovered and turned him to face the crowd.

He raised a hand, and everyone quieted. "And I thought you were my friends. I turn thirty, and you all come to gloat."

"Over the hill," someone called.

He ruffled his thick, ebony hair. "But not bald yet."

"Flirty thirty," another teased.

He shrugged. Titters filled the room. "Just remember. Whatever happens tonight, there will be paybacks." He pointed to the food. "Help yourselves. I'm so choked up, I can't pray. Dad, you want to do the favor?"

Roman Lapp replied, "Jah, sure."

After the prayer, Adam asked Ann, "Happy now?"

She released Carly's arm. "Very. But I don't think Carly is. I let something slip. Oops. Gotta go refill drinks."

It annoyed Carly that, up to this point, Adam hadn't acknowledged her presence.

"Why does this not surprise me?" Amusement creased his mouth and eyes.

"Flirty thirty, huh?"

His gaze pinned her to the spot. "You would know."

She struggled not to blush. "So Ann tells me you're always smoothing down Simon's feathers after I ruffle them."

Adam shrugged brawny shoulders, his eyes brimming with amusement. "How do you do that?"

"What?" she asked, tentatively.

"Most people show their dimples when they smile, but yours deepen most when you're angry. It's an enigma." He ran a hand over his freshly shaved jaw. "I've been trying to figure it out for a while now.

Sometimes I make you mad just to observe. Do it again."

She rolled her gaze and grinned. *Godsend and burr rolled into one.*

Sissie motioned impatiently, "Adam. Please start the food line."

"Sure, Mom."

He touched her elbow, nudging Carly in front of him.

She shot a dagger over her shoulder. "Don't make it look like we're together."

His warm breath tickled her ear. "Don't make a scene."

He had a point. When they reached the center of the laden table, graced by flowers and black balloons, he whispered, "It's my party so I can do whatever I want."

"Jah. It *is* your birthday."

"Let's find a table." While she knew most everyone at the party, she didn't have any friends clamoring to her side. Over the years, friends had drifted away because she preferred to pour all her energy into Sweet Life. He led her outside to a picturesque tree with a rope swing. Beneath it was a white-clothed table.

"You're lucky to have a family who cares enough to throw you a party like this."

The lantern cast a warm glow on his thoughtful face. "Don't you get parties?"

"Well, sure. That sounded wrong. But it's just Aunt Fannie and Jimmy. Nothing elaborate like this."

He bit into a pulled-pork sandwich. "Would you like something elaborate?"

"Maybe under the right circumstances." She blotted his chin with her napkin.

His chewing stilled. He met her gaze, forcing her to be the first to look away. Then he forked mushrooms to the edge of his plate. "Love my family. Even if Mom adds fungus to the salad on my birthday. But sometimes they're suffocating." His gaze looked into the distance. "And I wonder what it would be like to break free."

His comment startled her because it mirrored conversations of long ago. Dale's need to make a break from the family. It brought back those arguments about moving away from loved ones. It wasn't that she had resented Dale's dreams or ambitions. She just hadn't loved him enough to follow. And he hadn't loved her enough to stay. But what hurt was his betrayal, the way he'd put all the blame on her, spreading the rumor she wasn't submissive enough to be a good wife. He'd tarnished her name. Even insinuating—

"You look miles away."

"I'm sorry." She broke from her thoughts and studied the man sitting across the table. "You're not that kind of guy."

He frowned, "How do you know?"

"You're too kind to hurt your family." *Dale and Simon didn't even speak anymore.*

His voice softening, he argued, "You're kind. And free spirited."

"But you're"—she grinned, knowing she'd rile him—"passive-aggressive and maybe a picky eater."

He smiled. "I may surprise everybody. You inspire me."

"Because I like mushrooms?"

He made a face.

From what she knew of Adam, a soft-spoken brooding type, she understood his struggle. Roman controlled the entire Lapp family except for Simon. All the Lapp men were hard headed. Poor Adam. It was a shame Roman resented his work at the center.

"At thirty, a man should be able to make his own way," she encouraged.

His hand closed over hers, and she stilled.

"That's exactly what I told Dad."

Her heart sped from his touch and the intimate turn of the conversation. "You did?"

He withdrew. "He doesn't get it."

"Don't let him stop you. Dreams are God given."

"Some are. But a person shouldn't go with every idea that pops into her head."

"Her?"

He grinned. "Yes, her head. I've been cleaning up your messes for a while now."

She argued, "Have not."

"What about the time you got your bike stuck up in a tree and Jimmy and I had to—"

"I was only fifteen."

"Old enough to know better. Or the time you talked Sherie into the assisted living picnic under that beehive, and the nurse had me run to the store after Benadryl?"

"That was horrible. I'm thankful someone didn't have an allergic reaction." She knew he often came to her rescue—just never considered his perspective: cleaning up her messes.

He gave her a crooked grin. "I could mention a dozen more times, but I won't because that would kill the mood."

"Mood?"

His hooded eyes dared. "Remember it's my birthday, and I can do whatever I want."

She nodded warily.

"And I'm wanting to take a walk behind the barn to collect the rest of my birthday gift from you."

She leaned forward and arched a defiant brow. "You've already gotten your entire nonrefundable gift."

"How about returnable?"

Biting back a smile, she shook her head.

"A birthday gift should be given on a birthday, don't you think?"

"I think a guy shouldn't go after every idea that pops into his not-so-bald, thick head."

Jimmy plunked his plate down beside Adam's. "This a private party?"

"No," Carly replied triumphantly. But Adam's gaze promised otherwise, and later it would haunt her as she lay awake, wondering about it.

A glow still flickered from the bonfire the Lapps had built to stave off the autumn evening's chill. As the last guests trickled across the lane to their vehicles, Adam stacked chairs and leaned them against the tree where he'd flirted with Carly. The moment he'd laid eyes on her standing beside Ann, he'd felt something mutinous quicken inside him. An evil insurrection which set him on a stubborn, rebellious course. Using

Carly allowed him to revolt against both Simon and Dad. Neither liked her. One warned him to be rid of her, and the other coaxed him to get close and influence. Or did Simon want to use him to get even with Dale?

Regardless of their motivations, he chose to charter his own course. Whether anybody liked it or not. It was his birthday to do as he pleased. Turning thirty was the real source of the uprising. Carly a convenient weapon to swath a path toward freedom. Except Mennonites were peacemakers, and he didn't know how to wield a weapon. It hurt to hear her call him passive-aggressive. But she was right.

Yet beyond an innocent flirtation, what was his choice? Drop her and run like Dad warned? Or get close to see what happened when one camped around a free spirit? What mattered most was that the course was his own. Not theirs.

While he knew from experience that Carly frequently attracted trouble that spilled over onto those encamped about her, the princess also wore courage like a crown. And he needed courage to break free. He needed it because he didn't want to hurt Dad or the rest of the family. Was it possible to be independent without hurting anyone? Usually for Carly, it backfired and hurt her, he reasoned.

Then there was that confounded kiss. It wasn't what he'd expected, given her reputation. As humorous as she'd intended it to be, it had promised spoils that taunted him daily. She did tantalize, the way her free spirit broke forth into a riot of blond curls and curves that wouldn't stay confined by plain clothing and prayer caps or rules and regulations. But what if the real spoils awaited him in Nappanee? The stakes were high. He didn't want to leave any devastation behind. Didn't want to march forward without certainty and at least one more kiss.

"Quit daydreaming and help me fold up this table," Dad grumbled.

"Sure." His sisters had already removed the tablecloths, so he lifted the nearest table and folded its legs.

"Let's stack them on the truck and haul 'em to the barn. We can return them later."

Adam had missed the rental set up, as Dad had sent him to

Portland after some farm supplies. "Thanks for the party."

"It was your sisters' doings."

As far as mechanics went, Adam and his dad worked like a well-oiled machine. It was almost like one was an extension of the other. If only their minds could sync the same way.

"What's the deal with the Blosser woman?"

"We're just friends."

"Then why'd you flaunt her in front of everybody and treat her like your girl?"

They slid another table onto the truck's bed. "What if she was?"

"Looked like she was playing hard to get. And even if you caught her, what then? You wanna get dumped like Dale?"

"If I wanted to get her and keep her, I could." The truth of his own words struck him with knee-buckling force. He possessed the power to sway her. He'd seen the attraction in her eyes, the way she fought a blush. And that's why he shouldn't pursue her just to irritate his uncle and dad. The situation was entangled enough already with the thrill of the hunt and the enigma of those dimples.

"I'm telling you, she's trouble. If you married her, she'd run all over you. Just like her aunt did when she was married to poor old Bob. Open your eyes and look at what's going on around you at Sweet Life. Even Simon and I can agree she's one headstrong woman."

"I also possess the stubborn Lapp genes. If I was looking for a wife, I'd be looking for someone with grit. Otherwise, life wouldn't be any fun."

"That kind of fun doesn't last. Running this tree farm is hard work and stressful. When you marry, you need somebody to fit in and make life easy for you at home."

"I love Mom, but a different type of woman interests me."

Roman softened. "Jah, your mom's a good woman." He drew out a hanky and rubbed the back of his neck. "Listen, Son. I've been thinking about that talk we had. That nonsense about Nappanee. I'm wondering why you would want to leave just when I'm offering you a partnership in the farm."

Adam involuntarily braced himself against the truck.

"You heard me. I'm offering you a partnership. I think sixty/forty's more than fair."

"Dad." Adam straightened. "I wasn't expecting this."

"Why not? It's your birthday, isn't it?"

Though Roman rarely expressed his emotions, Adam could see his pleasure. Moved by his father's gesture of approval, he shifted to initiate an awkward embrace. "Thanks, Dad. I don't know what to say."

Roman patted his back, then released him. "Jah. Say, Jah."

"Of course. This has been my dream."

"Mine, too. We'll change the sign to read Father and Son."

Adam thought about the Lapp's Tree Farm sign at the farm's entrance. Happiness burgeoned within to think that all the world could see Dad's trust in him. "I won't let you down."

"I know you won't. There's just a couple of stipulations. You know this is our busy time and how hard it is to get away. So let's wait till after Christmas to do the official paperwork."

"Sure." Adam nodded. "A birthday and Christmas gift rolled into one."

"Great." His dad pounded his back with shared enthusiasm. Adam's eyes burned, and his chest expanded at his dad's touch. "Let's finish up here so we can go tell your mom."

He hoisted another table and helped shove it onto the truck's bed. Never had Dad seemed so cordial. Life had turned a corner.

"And the other stipulation," Dad said as they grabbed the last table. "Quit chasing that Blosser woman. I don't want her doing anything to upset our family business. Surely you understand that now. *Father and Son*. It's gonna be great."

Chapter Six

Absentmindedly, Carly watered a tiny basil herb and set the clay pot back on the window sill. In the early dawn, a rufous hummingbird danced in the spray of neighbor Imogene's hose, then darted to her zinnias, causing Carly to do a double take. She'd thought they'd all have migrated south by now.

Cocoa, having received his fresh alfalfa hay, sprinted from the hall to the kitchen and back. All around her, nature awakened, but Carly felt like crawling back beneath her yellow quilt, weary from staying up late to finish her proposal for the Sweet Life board. She topped her coffee, turned away from the window, and shuffled across the wood floor to the kitchen table.

It held one potted purple moth orchid, one granola bar wrapper topped with an apple core, an empty raisin box, and six copies of her proposal neatly stapled and stacked. Taking a deep draught of coffee, she imagined herself standing in front of the four-man, one-woman board and reciting her spiel.

Handwritten in neat strokes, the proposal outlined everything Sweet Life would need to start and operate a volunteer program. But she'd worked into the wee hours trying to create a working title and a slogan. And gotten nothing. She'd have to pen Aunt Fannie's suggestion of "Volunteers Make Each Day Brighter." Only her gut told her it wasn't right.

The board held meetings on Monday evenings, but a conflict had shifted this one to early morning. She'd gotten the call Sunday afternoon while weeding her coneflowers. A task she'd hoped would stimulate her creative-writing juices. At first, she'd thought Simon had changed the time purposefully to shorten her preparation or in hopes she'd arrive late. But the theme of Sunday's sermon had popped into her mind: Turn the other cheek. Bishop Abe Kauffman preached Matthew 5 at least twice a year to remind his flock they were peacemakers. For Carly's sake, it should be more frequent.

Cocoa followed her into the bathroom and nestled between her feet. It was their morning ritual of rabbit-human affection. Normally it was the perfect send-off to start her day. But one glance in the mirror, and she forgot about Cocoa altogether. Of all mornings to look like a wild woman. Meticulously she smoothed every hair. Auntie Fannie always said every little bit helped, and she needed a lot of help this morning . . . *every little bit she could muster*, she thought poking bobby pins here and there. Then it hit her.

Bolting, Carly fled for the kitchen, causing Cocoa to squeak in terror. "Sorry, Sweetie." She plopped into a chair and picked up her pen. *Everybody can do one little thing to stamp out loneliness.* The perfect slogan. It wasn't trite or derogatory. Didn't allude to anything that would make Simon look bad in front of his board members. It spoke what was on her heart. It was the goal of her campaign.

She tapped her pen, looking at the proposal's blank title space, then neatly penned, *Every Little Bit Helps: Recruiting Volunteers.* It was so simple. Why hadn't she seen it sooner?

Sooner! She glanced at the clock, scooped everything into a bag, kissed Cocoa, and hurried outside to her bike rack.

"Morning, Imogene."

The older woman waved from her white plastic lawn chair. "Morning. You're off early. Want me to water for you?"

"Oh, could you? I'm in a rush."

"I can see. But aren't you forgetting something?"

Carly checked. She had her proposal, her sweater, and her purse. "I don't think so. Why?"

Imogene tapped her head.

Following suit, Carly tentatively touched her own head, always careful not to displace her head covering. Only, her head was bare!

"Oh, thank you!" With time slipping away, she darted back into the cottage.

Carly would be late unless she took the shortcut through Sankey Park across Weddle Bridge. But Long Street would be busy with early morning traffic, so she'd have to keep to the sidewalk, which could be treacherous with its bumps and cracks. Grabbing a stick for the dog and waving at Imogene, she peddled decorously down Hawthorne Street. But as soon as she was out of Imogene's sight, she hit the hill and picked up speed. Too much speed. A car was turning into Sankey Park, blocking the road.

Whipping the handlebars and skidding her tires, she had no choice but to head for the deep ditch with the wild blackberry bushes. Again. "Oh, no!" She held tight, but her wheels slid out from under her and she landed in a thorny tangle. "Ouch."

A man jumped out of the car and ran to the ditch. "You all right?"

"Jah, I think so."

"Wait there."

He ran to his car for gloves and returned to help her out of the ditch. He set the bike upright. "Don't you have any brakes?"

Ouch. She brushed at her skirt. "I was late and didn't see you until it was too late."

"I wasn't paying attention, either. Can I take you someplace?"

"No. Thanks. I just live up the hill."

She finally convinced him to go but had no intentions of returning home. She kicked the tires and thought the bike would still get her to work. She pulled her skirt loose where it was pinned to her stockings. *Ouch!* Ignoring the pain in her palms, she placed her bike back on the path. Stickers pierced her back. Ugh! She was too old for this. With a groan, she retrieved the bag and stick and set off for the bridge. From past experience, she knew her tires would be flat before she reached Sweet Life if she didn't work fast.

Today she'd sacrifice her rims, if need be. It took several tries before her skirt was situated so that her bottom didn't feel like a pincushion. Commiserating that Martha would be on her case about her ruined stockings, she almost forgot to have her stick ready. The old dog ran too close, and she jerked the handlebars away and tossed the stick clumsily in the other direction. The dog loped off, snatched the stick, and looked back at her with satisfaction.

As she continued, a dull pain throbbed in her neck. One of her tires soon deflated and riding grew more difficult. By the time she'd reached the center, her neck was extremely painful. She parked outside the maintenance man's shop and knocked on the door.

"Hey, Carly."

"Morning, Rocco. I need your help."

She felt his gaze, starting at her head and quickly assessing down to her black oxfords. Without condemnation, which is why she adored him, he knelt to examine the bike. "One tire and a rim. I have 'em in stock for you. Just don't forget to replace 'em again."

"I will. Thanks." Good it was payday. "I don't know what I'd do without you."

"Today's your big meeting with the high ups?"

She nodded, retrieving her bag and purse from the bike's basket. "Are you a praying man?"

"Yep." He pulled a chain with a crucifix out from beneath his shirt and kissed it.

"Then pray for me." Rocco always gave her a listening ear.

"I will. Getting volunteers is a good idea. But we also need funds. This place is falling down, and one of these days I won't be able to put it back together again."

"If anybody can, though, it's you. Every little bit helps. That's my slogan."

"I like it. But you'd better head to the lady's room and fix yourself before your meeting."

She gave him a sheepish smile. "I'll try."

Rubbing her neck, she was just coming out of the public bathroom when she saw Adam striding toward her.

"Hey, Carly. You're in early."

"Today's the board meeting. What about you?"

"It is?" He sighed. "I was returning the tables and chairs we rented for the party. Since I was nearby, I wanted to see Uncle Si. But if he's busy, it can wait till Thursday."

She nodded and turned to go.

"Uh, Carly?"

She paused. "Jah?"

"Can you follow me?"

"Now?"

"Believe me, you'll want to take the time."

Curious, she followed him around the corner of the building.

His eyes held concern. "You fell again, didn't you?"

She dropped her hand from her neck. "Jah, but I'm fine."

"You don't look fine. There's grass in the back of your hair and stickers on the back of your dress."

"Oh?"

His mouth twitched with amusement. "Turn around. Let me help."

She couldn't go into her meeting looking like she'd slept in a barn. "Fine." She stood still as he fiddled with her hair and even replaced a bobby pin.

"You know what you're doing?"

"I have six sisters. Okay, don't take it personal, but I'm going after the stickers on your dress now. Just trying to help, you know. Clean up another one of your messes."

Carly felt her cheeks burn yet appreciated his humorous attempt at distraction. She felt a couple pats and pressed her eyes closed in humiliation. "Hurry, please."

"There. Good as new."

"Thanks. I gotta go."

"Good luck," he called as she hurried away.

Not wanting to meet his gaze, she rounded the corner and almost ran into Miranda—the voluntary service caregiver, who'd taken the trash outside.

When Adam came around the corner right behind her, the other caregiver's eyes widened.

"See you gals." Adam winked at Carly.

She ignored him and hurried inside, meaning to take a shortcut through the assisted-living facility to Simon's office. The wheeled garbage container rattled behind her, and she felt a tug on her arm.

"What was that about?"

"Nothing," Carly replied. "He was just helping me with something."

"Are you guys a thing?" Miranda probed.

"No," Carly said too quickly. "We'll talk later."

Simon's secretary motioned Carly toward his office. Breathing a prayer, she opened the door and closed it behind her. They hadn't started the meeting. Rather, they formed a semicircle around his desk, eating doughnuts and drinking coffee. Mrs. Nissley, the other female present, patted the chair next to her. With a grateful nod, Carly slipped into it, placing her bag on the floor beside her.

"We're still trying to wake up," Mrs. Nissley explained. "Have a doughnut and some coffee?"

"No coffee, but maybe a doughnut." Carly met Simon's smug gaze from across his desk as she placed a powdered doughnut on a napkin and returned to her seat. She hadn't realized how dry her mouth was until she took a bite and choked. She coughed and tried to suppress it by snatching another napkin and pressing it to her mouth. Her eyes watered. Finally she shot up and darted from the room. She guessed the walls were paper thin because Simon's secretary pressed a paper cup into her hand as she rushed to the bathroom across the hall.

"Oh, Lord," she prayed. "Why is this so hard?" After several long minutes, she had the choking under control. Still fervently praying, she returned to Simon's office.

"Are you all right, Miss Blosser?" Simon asked.

"Jah, fine."

"Good. Let me introduce the board."

She concentrated on each unfamiliar name and face—for they all attended Simon's church. Mr. Coblentz, a heavy-set man wearing jeans and a black T-shirt, winked at her. Mr. Moseman, a more scholarly type, nodded his head and folded his hands. Frank Ebersole lifted a sugar-coated finger in acknowledgment.

Simon nodded at Carly. "We'll begin our meeting with your idea, Miss Blosser. Then you can leave while we discuss other business. So if you're ready, why don't you take the floor?"

"Yes, sir." Fumbling, she withdrew her proposals and passed them around the room. "I'm sorry they're not typed, but I don't have a computer."

She received some smiles. "No problem, your handwriting is a work of art," Mrs. Nissley reassured.

She heard shuffling papers as she moved to face them. Mr. Coblentz tilted his bald-shaved head and smiled. She smiled back. " 'Everybody can do one little thing to stamp out loneliness.' Being a single person who works with the elderly"—her voice broke, and she cleared her throat—"I understand how loneliness can grip the residents, making what could be a good experience a miserable and even frightening one. No matter how excellent Simon and you all do your jobs, loneliness creeps in to cause problems that become cancerous to the atmosphere of our facility. I'm proposing a campaign that inspires people to get involved by doing things for the residents that the employees don't have time to do. I want volunteers to realize that every little bit helps.

"As you will see, I've detailed a plan that includes defining tasks and roles, responsibilities, time requirements, skills and qualifications, the recruiting process, the application process, and training and supervision and rewards. I've identified some risks involved, along with the need for policies and procedures in those areas.

"On page five, where it begins with 'Singing, reading, and writing letters,' you'll see a list of the many ways volunteers can use their own talents and gifts to enhance the life of residents at Sweet Life. And I'm sure the list is not exhaustive." She paused and rubbed her aching neck. "Please take a moment to look over the proposal. Then I'd be happy to answer any questions."

"You can take your seat, Carly," Simon said.

She didn't wish to sit because she felt it gave her an inferior position, but she also didn't want to oppose Simon in front of his board so she returned to her chair and quickly realized that Adam had missed a sticker.

Mr. Moseman cleared his throat. "Your proposal seems thorough, although I'm not familiar with this type of thing. But this project would be huge. It would be extremely time consuming to get it rolling. And our staff is already stretched thin."

Before Carly could respond, Mrs. Nissley replied, "Oh, Moseman, you always pooh-pooh everything. This plan follows a logical design, and if it was followed step by step, I can see how it could work. It would add some excitement to the center."

Carly cleared her throat and stood again. "If I may address Mr. Moseman's concern, recruiting someone with office skills first, I could train them to do much of the work without adding to the other employees' workload." She sat back down.

"Delegating the organizational work to a volunteer under your supervision," Mr. Coblentz repeated. "I like that."

"Me, too," Ebersole echoed.

As they continued to discuss the proposal, Carly fielded their questions. Throughout, Simon remained strangely quiet as the group's enthusiasm toward the project increased. Finally, Mr. Moseman—who pooh-poohed everything—pushed his glasses higher on the bridge of his nose. "I make a motion that we take a vote. But I propose a stipulation that places Simon overall in charge, meaning he can appoint the positions to run the program, that is, if Miss Blosser's proposal meets with our approval."

Carly's pulse quickened. She always expected Simon's involvement in the program, but emphasizing his leadership sent a shiver down her spine.

"I second the motion and the stipulation," Simon said, casting another smug look Carly's way.

"Then let's take the vote," Mr. Coblentz said. "Two no's and three in favor. I guess that means that Simon has a program to head." He chuckled, "One he voted against."

"Won't be the first time," Simon joked. "Congratulations, Carly."

Breaking into a huge smile, Carly addressed the committee. "Thank you. For your time and for all you do for Sweet Life."

Then Simon cleared his throat and waved his proposal. "Miss

Blosser, could you get me another copy of this. I'll be needing one for Sherie. As general manager of assisted living, she's been seeking some kind of promotion. This is perfect. I'm putting her in charge. She's the key to making Little Steps a success.

Every Little Bit Helps, Carly mentally corrected, her world crashing down around her. Simon's betrayal felt worse than if the board had rejected the idea entirely. She stared at him, realizing where Dale had gotten his betrayal genes. Or was this revenge? She felt a hand on her shoulder and cringed from her neck injury.

"I'm sorry. You didn't see that coming, did you?" Mrs. Nissley whispered.

"No, ma'am."

Simon glanced at his watch. "Perfect timing. Your shift begins in five minutes, Carly. Thanks again for coming."

She snatched her bag, took one more look at the board, understanding then that Mr. Moseman and Simon had their backup plan prearranged. Blinking back tears, she slapped her copy of the proposal on Simon's desk. "For Sherie."

As she started from the room, Mr. Coblentz stuck out his hand. She took it, and he clasped it between both his a bit too firmly, but she appreciated his silent support as she fought back tears and fled the room.

Chapter Seven

After work Carly iced her aching neck, then took Cocoa to Aunt Fannie's for a preplanned celebration/commiseration dinner. The new tire and rim worked perfectly per Rocco's expertise, and the ride worked off some of the anger she'd stuffed in order to fulfill her shift at the assisted-living facility. Thankfully, Sherie wasn't at work. It would have been her undoing.

Jimmy saw her arrive and swung open the door. "Aunt Fannie's making fried mush."

Carly lowered Cocoa to the floor. "Thought you were going on the road today."

"Not until tomorrow."

She followed her nose to the kitchen and kissed Auntie on the cheek. "Thanks for making my favorite."

"Ach. It's so messy, splattering my countertop and making everything greasy."

The heavy smell of frying filled the kitchen—mush was one of those foods like broccoli that tasted great but smelled bad—and Jimmy moved to crank open the window.

"I brought Cocoa. Are the bedroom doors all closed?"

"Jah. And the litter box is ready."

Feeling at home in her aunt's kitchen, Carly opened a pantry door and snatched an apron. "Want me to fry the eggs?"

"Jah, and Jimmy you can do the toast."

When they'd first arrived to live with Aunt Fannie—after their parents were killed in a car crash—she'd put them to work. Over time

Carly discovered it helped with the grief. Aunt Fannie would know, because she'd also lost a husband and son to an accident. Working together bonded them into a family unit.

Since Auntie didn't have a farm for Jimmy to work, she provided him with chores most men in their congregation considered women's work. Now her brother had the skills he needed to live a bachelor's life.

The Old Holley Conservative Mennonite Fellowship was more conservative when Fannie first arrived with her late husband. As it progressed from Beachy-Amish to the more liberal Conservative Mennonite, Aunt Fannie clung to the old ways, such as wearing her stringed prayer covering. Carly found no problem following Auntie's plainer style of dress. Anyway, the cap helped control her bushy hair.

Now Aunt Fannie wielded her spatula, slipping the crisp brown strips of fried mush onto a platter. "Bring everything into the dining room where I cleared off the table"—she shot Carly an accusing look—"so it would be special for tonight."

A renewed sense of failure sagged Carly's shoulders as she carried a platter of fried eggs into the dining room. The table was dusted and set with Fannie's best dishes, increasing her humiliation. Jimmy prayed and they passed the food before Fannie posed the questions which would steal Carly's appetite. "What happened at the meeting today? You don't look so good. And why are you rubbing your neck?"

Fiddling with her fork, she explained, "They liked my idea. Vote was three in favor and two opposed."

Fannie appeared startled. "Ach! That's good. I suppose Simon voted no."

"Jah. And the man he has in his pocket."

"What! Surely not."

"No, I shouldn't have said that. I'm just angry."

"Spill the beans, girl."

"This Mr. Moseman added a stipulation to the proposal before the vote. It put Simon in charge of the program."

"Ach my," Auntie said.

"But Simon wouldn't want the responsibility if he doesn't support the program. Would he?" Jimmy asked.

Carly steepled her hands. "At that point in the meeting, I was thinking the same thing. But I knew something wasn't right."

Fannie waved her hand. "Well, what happened?"

"He congratulated me."

"That's hard to believe. So why so glum?" Fannie frowned. "Did you fall off your bike again?"

"Jah. But back to my story. I was admiring Simon for it until he asked me to make a copy of my proposal for Sherie. Said he was putting her in charge of the entire program. He bumped me out."

Fannie slammed her fist on the table so hard it rattled the china passed down from her mother. "That rat!"

"That does it!" Jimmy pushed back his chair. "I'm gonna go talk to him."

"No!" Carly grabbed his arm and flinched at the sudden pain that shot through her neck. "He knows how I feel. I slapped my proposal on his desk so hard it rattled his teeth and told him to give it to Sherie."

She dropped her hand. "I've thought about this all day. It was preplanned that Moseman would add that stipulation. And everything was legal. I could tell some of the committee didn't like it." She thought about Mr. Coblentz's firm handshake and Mrs. Nissley's attempts to help her. "But they didn't call him on it. It hurts that he doesn't think I'm capable." Her voice broke. "Sometimes I think he hates me." She didn't add what they were probably all thinking, because of Dale.

Jimmy pulled her up into the embrace she'd needed all day. She dug her fists into his shirt until her sobs subsided. When she pulled away, she feigned a smile, "Watch the neck."

"Sorry."

"The rat," Fannie mumbled.

Carly sat back down and started to cut her mush into bite-sized pieces. "I'm fine now. But I don't understand why he doesn't just fire me."

Fannie puffed with indignation. "Because you're the best caregiver he has."

Jimmy gripped the back of his chair. "I still think I should talk to him."

Fannie argued, "Even though I think he's a rat, it wouldn't do a bit of good. Sit down, Jimmy. Let's think this through."

But he moved behind Carly's chair and gently massaged her shoulders. "You're the best caregiver there. He doesn't deserve you. But the residents do."

"That's right." Fannie wrung her hands. "Jimmy. Get my Bible from my bedroom. And be sure to close the door and check on that rabbit."

"You just told me to sit down."

Carly giggled in spite of the situation and felt her appetite returning. "I'm sorry you went to so much trouble when—"

"Shush now."

Jimmy returned. "Cocoa was on his belly, sleeping with his legs stretched out behind and in front. What a life. Now he's chewing on his toy."

Fannie thumbed through the Good Book and cleared her throat. "Here it is. And it ain't pretty. Proverbs 25:21–22. 'If thine enemy be hungry, give him bread to eat; and if he be thirsty, give him water to drink: For thou shalt heap coals of fire upon his head, and the Lord shall reward thee.'"

"Sounds like we should've invited Simon to dinner," Jimmy stated sarcastically.

Carly considered the verses. "I guess if he hates me, he is the enemy?"

Auntie nodded. "And the best way to embarrass your enemy is to treat him with grace and respect. Even if he isn't shamed into repentance, others'll see who is right, and the Lord will bless your desire to help the residents."

Carly grew thoughtful. "I suppose I could show him more respect."

Jimmy shook his head with disgust. "I'm still mad. Why should Carly take the blame?"

"Because it's our way. It's God's way, and I've seen it change people. Nothing Carly has done up to this point has changed Simon's attitude."

"She's right, Jimmy. I only want the best for the residents. And

I got the program approved. It's just my pride hurting that I can't administer it. Maybe my job is done."

"Maybe," Auntie replied. "We'll see."

"I'll try to be kind to Simon and Sherie." Carly cringed. "But I'm not ready to apologize to Simon."

Auntie nodded as if the matter were resolved. "Ach! The food's getting cold. And we're here to celebrate the best caregiver at Sweet Life. Everybody eat up."

Carly felt Cocoa snuggle in-between her feet, and the love of her family overwhelmed her. They'd provided a plan. They always stuck by her. They'd helped her get through the rumors buzzing around church after she'd split up with Dale. Rumors he'd spread. And now she had to forgive his dad. Given her temperament, the plan wasn't going to be easy to implement.

Carly placed her bike in the stand and greeted Rocco as she passed the maintenance building. Her cheery countenance masked conflicting emotions, dreading her first encounters with Sherie and Simon. She punched numbers into a keypad, and sliding-glass doors opened to admit her into Sweet Life's assisted-living facility.

"Hello! Hello!" Magnificent the cockatiel pruned its feathers from its cage. The lobby resembled a living room filled with second-hand sofas and out-of-date armchairs. It sported a round recreational table and television, though not a flat screen. Some shelves contained books and hideous knickknacks. Next to a stone fireplace was a wooden cradle filled with dolls and stuffed animals, which the senile residents could hold and rock.

Light bathed the lobby from its double doors and a side door that led to a walled-in flower garden with patio and benches. There a circuit sidewalk provided exercise for the residents. Carly glanced at the clock. Seven fifteen. Her shift was 7:30 a.m. to 4:00 p.m., Monday through Friday with an occasional Saturday. She headed to the receptionist's desk, noting several residents were finishing breakfast. Klepto, their wanderer, turned her back to Carly, trying to hide the fact she was fiddling with the staffroom's door handle.

Since Miranda had come to Sweet Life, the residents were dubbed with nicknames. Names solely used by the caregivers. It wasn't malicious. Miranda had a hard time remembering names, and when needing to quickly identify a resident, descriptive nicknames flew out of her mouth. They'd stuck. The staff didn't mean to demean anybody. It just happened.

For instance, Nines—the woman who always dressed to the nines for dinner and who used impeccable manners—could often be found sitting in the lobby with an outdated hat and purse in her lap as if waiting to go someplace. Since she wasn't at the moment, it meant she was in her apartment with Teacup—her cat.

Carly stuffed her purse in a bin behind the receptionist counter and glanced down a long, carpeted corridor. Hall Patroller was working the wheels of her chair, headed to her room for her morning television shows. Television was the only thing that kept her out of the hall.

The hall. It was a real showcase, decorated with a mishmash of welcome plaques, photos, wreaths, and nameplates that identified studio apartments. Carly removed her keys from a hook and attached them to her clothing. While some of the residents kept their doors open, others were closed and locked. She had the master key. Each room was a mini version of the resident's former homes. And each resident had unique daily routines and interests.

Miranda popped out of Dot's room and approached with a glint in her eye. Carly waited for the inevitable. A Mennonite Voluntary Service worker from Goshen, Indiana, Miranda was on a one-year stint. While working at Sweet Life, she lived in a V. S. apartment in nearby Albany. Her wages went directly into the V. S. unit, and they reimbursed her a tiny salary, enough for necessities that the unit didn't supply. Although Miranda was cheery and kind to the residents, she had a man-tracked mind. And she was younger than Carly.

Stepping behind the counter, Miranda pulled out a chart. Her focus, however, remained on Carly. "So we never got to talk about what I saw the other day."

"Is Kelly room-picking again?" Klepto often invaded others'

properties, and the staff would find stolen items hidden in her drawers.

Miranda shrugged with irritation. "I don't know about that. I'm talking about you and Adam coming out from behind the building. Are you two seeing each other?"

"You know he's my brother's best friend, right?"

"No-o!" Miranda's eyes lit with excitement. "I didn't know you had a brother. Is he single? If he is, maybe he'd like to go hiking with the V. S. unit sometime."

Carly grinned. If anything, Miranda was consistent. She tried to imagine Jimmy hiking with Miranda. He'd probably be attracted to the stunning Spanish woman with black bobbed hair. Thin figure. Red lipstick. But when she latched onto him with those painted nails, he'd bolt and never stop running.

Carly chuckled. "Jimmy's a confirmed bachelor with a hunger for adventure. I don't think he'll ever settle down."

"Our V. S. group's adventurous. Ask him if he likes hiking. Or bring him around. I'll ask."

"He drives a truck and is gone most of this week."

Miranda closed the file she'd been using and opened a drawer, letting it drop. "Back to Adam. . . So you don't care if I flirt with him?"

Carly placed her hands on her hips and tilted her head. "You're asking me this now?"

Miranda's dark expressive eyes looked repentant. "I know. I'm obvious. But I don't want to move in on your territory, that's all."

"Thanks. To answer your question"—Carly shrugged—"sure, I like Adam." Let her stew over that one. Meanwhile she'd try to figure it out herself. "Anything I should know?"

Frustrated, Miranda replied, "Yeah, Sherie's in the staff room and wants to see you."

Dread fell over Carly. "Thanks." *Let's get it over with. Act nice.* She opened the door Klepto had finally abandoned. The assisted-living manager was typing at a computer.

"You asked for me?"

Sherie spun her chair and smiled. "I did. Please, sit down."

Carly took an armchair situated next to a mini refrigerator topped with a droopy artificial plant and attempted some small talk about Sherie's extended weekend.

Crossing long shapely legs, Sherie leaned back in her chair. "Congratulations on getting the board to pass your proposal."

Heat rushed up Carly's neck and face. *She's not my enemy.* "Thank you."

"You never cease to amaze me. This isn't a job to you. It's your life."

"Jah. It is."

"I understand."

Carly searched Sherie's blue eyes and saw approval.

"We're alike." The forty-something woman from Simon's church wore a knee-length pencil skirt and scoop-necked sweater. A long necklace hung from her neck. She ran a hand through her short, perky hairstyle. They were nothing alike. "I've got my eye on a seat on the board. Mrs. Nissley leaves in six months, and I've talked to Simon about it. Your. . .uh. . .volunteer program—"

"Every Little Bit Helps," Carly interjected.

"Yes, exactly. Your Every Little Bit Helps will help *me* to obtain that chair."

"And stamp out loneliness."

"What?"

"That's the slogan, *Everybody can do one little thing to stamp out loneliness.*"

"Oh. Don't worry, I understand the goal. I'm just trying to explain why heading this program is so important to me. I know you had your heart set on running it. I can only imagine your disappointment. But I think Simon made the right choice. You're still young. Your time will come. You're valuable, and I need your support. Do I have it?"

Carly glanced at the floor, then back at Sherie. *What kind of support?* "I have to be honest. Yesterday you didn't. But today, my focus is back. I only want what's best for the residents."

Sherie's eyes widened with surprise. "I appreciate your candor."

Carly knew her manager had hoped for more enthusiasm. She wished she could act as though she hadn't been stabbed in the back. When she'd left home that morning, she'd had good intentions.

But now *kind* words wouldn't form. Guiltily, she remembered Aunt Fannie's plan. If she couldn't follow through with Sherie, how could she forgive Simon?

"Let me see. There was one other thing." Sherie tapped her finger on her skirt. "Oh, yes. Martha's daughter is planning a surprise birthday party for her in December. I told her about the dried flower cards you make, and she'd like to buy some to use for invitations."

"I'd be happy to bring in some samples."

"Great, thanks."

"I'm glad she's throwing a party for Martha."

Sherie smiled. "Helen said Martha's mentioned turning eighty-five about eighty-five times."

Carly laughed. "Jah, or ninety."

"So she's decided to make it memorable. They're pulling out all the stops. But in the meantime, Helen keeps brushing Martha off as if it's no big deal. She thinks Martha's getting offended, perhaps depressed. Have you noticed any depression?"

"Perhaps more irritable than usual."

"Good description. She was grumbling at breakfast about nobody caring, so you might want to give her some extra attention."

"How's Dot doing?"

"Loves that bird. That was a good call. Especially since Crusher takes care of it."

"Is that it then?" Carly stood.

"Yep. Just bring in card samples and leave them at the receptionist's counter. Thanks." Sherie spun back to the computer.

Carly left the room, her heart weighed down with resentment.

Chapter Eight

Hoping to cheer up Martha, Carly grabbed the newspaper, but Miranda intercepted her. "Harry lost his teeth again."

"Oh, no. Did you check the trash?"

"His or everybody's?"

Carly placed the *New Era* on the recreational table and glanced toward the hall. "I'd start with his room. Next Kelly's room. Check her mouth. Then work your way down the hall searching all the trash cans. If they didn't get tossed out, we may come across them before we have to call his son again."

Martha had been eavesdropping. She interjected, "Harry's son's not going to be happy if he has to buy another pair. This will make the third time this year."

Miranda nodded and left them. Unfolding the newspaper and giving one section to Martha, Carly skimmed for topics of interest. "Last weekend was the Covered Bridge Festival in Cottage Grove. Have you ever attended?"

"Oh sure. Who hasn't? That town's so quaint with all its murals."

"I know. Says here it was held at Bohemia Park and there were fiddlers, Ukranian dancers, bluegrass music, a historic auto parade, a timber competition, postage stamp collection, wine tasting, a pumpkin catapult, and kids activities. Goodness, I think it must get bigger every year."

"Pity's sake. A pumpkin catapult? Can you imagine the mess that made? What are people thinking?"

Carly laughed. "Anything to draw a crowd."

"In my opinion the best thing about covered bridges happens without a crowd."

"What do you mean?"

"You know. The kissing."

Widow Martha slipped back in time to the summer she'd turned sixteen. Her heart beat rapidly as she remembered how she'd met her first love. She'd leaned over the bridge and dared to speak to the handsome Englísh boy flirting with her.

"No, I don't want to bait your hook."

His warm laughter compelled her to stay, even though she knew it was wrong.

"Wait. I'm coming up." He laid aside the pole.

Her heart raced. She was crazy to wait for him but couldn't make her feet move.

Panting, the tall blond leaned against the bridge and studied her. "You Amish?"

"No. Mennonite."

"You got a boyfriend?"

John Struder's image popped into her mind, but they weren't really committed to each other. "No, why?"

"Wondering if I should bother to teach you to fish."

Martha grinned. "Well I'm a quick learner." He grabbed her hand and led her to the bank. She looked at the rugged path down the steep embankment.

He laughed that infectious laugh of his. "Don't worry. I got you."

His muscular build supported his words. She recalled the thrill of his hand.

"Martha?" Smoothing the article, Carly shook her head. "Doesn't say anything about a kissing booth."

Martha sighed with impatience. "I'm not talking about the festival. When I was young, it was a place to go with your sweetheart."

Dropping the paper in her lap, Carly asked, "You ever do that?"

Quiet for a long, reflective moment, Martha nodded. "I sure did. I had a secret boyfriend. We used to meet there."

"How old were you?"

Her voice carried a loose asthmatic-rattle as she replied, "Sixteen. Seems like forever and also like yesterday. I can still see him. Tall. Handsome. Blond."

Leaning forward, Carly asked, "Why was he a secret boyfriend?"

She wheezed, "Because I was Mennonite and he wasn't. It would've been forbidden." Martha smiled. "He was my first love. We even carved our initials on the bridge."

Entranced, Carly probed, "How'd you meet?"

"I was walking one day and ended up at the bridge. He was fishing. He introduced himself. We had a good time that day. After that, I headed out there as often as I could. Guess he did the same thing, 'cause we met again. Pretty soon we were planning to meet."

"How long did this go on?"

"That whole summer. My friend Ruth Stucky sure was jealous." Martha's face saddened. "Until he went off to war. Then I never saw him again. I always wondered if he made it back."

"Were you heartbroken?"

Martha nodded. Though time-wrinkled and framed in gray, her face was still touched by emotions from years earlier. "After that, the bridge was the loneliest place to go. I wanted to stay away. But I kept thinking I might meet him again. I had to keep trying. Mostly I got over him. But I did go back one more time. Stared at that big old tree where I had my first kiss. It was the week before I got married."

Riveted, Carly's eyes misted. "You must have loved him."

Martha adjusted her glasses on the bridge of her nose. "I did. But he wasn't there, so I married John."

"Were you happily married?"

She sniffed, then used her inhaler. "You know I was. I talk about John all the time. He was the best man a woman could ever have." She hardened her voice and snapped, "The other relationship never would've worked. And now I have such a nice family. Until they put me in this place. Now they forget I exist. Helen doesn't even remember I'm going to be eighty-five."

At least the distraction had worked for a while.

Martha continued, "Don't you think that's a big birthday? Kinda like a fiftieth wedding anniversary? I don't know how many times I've mentioned it, but Helen hasn't said anything about celebrating or even asked me what I wanted."

"What do you want?"

"A cake, for one thing!" Martha's chest rose and fell laboriously.

"When is it?"

"December 12," she wheezed.

Carly tried to calm the asthmatic woman. "There's still plenty of time."

"Not so long if you want to plan something."

"I'll bake you a cake."

"Do you bake?"

Carly laughed. "Of course. Not very often, since I live alone. But I can."

"Well I sure don't want no burned cake for my birthday. But you could order one from that cute little bakery in Halsey."

"If that's what you want."

"Well good. I'll tell Helen. Maybe it'll make her jealous and she'll get on the ball."

"We found them," Miranda called, approaching them.

"Where?" Martha demanded.

"When I checked his room, I saw leftovers from last night's supper in his teeth container in the bathroom. That made me wonder if he put his teeth in that little plastic container he keeps in his refrigerator. You know, got them switched. Sure enough. There they were."

"Pity's sake," Martha exclaimed. "That actually makes sense."

Carly asked. "Does he have them in now?"

"Yes, I helped him. I'm off to sterilize his teeth container now." She waved the little plastic butter dish he used.

"Good thinking," Carly said. Once Miranda left, she patted Martha's hand. "I don't think you need to worry about your birthday. You're going to be celebrating many more. Now ninety, that would be one worth celebrating."

"You just make sure that cake is chocolate, you hear?"

"Okay. I gotta go make some rounds now. Why don't you finish up the paper, and if you come across anything juicy, we'll discuss it after lunch."

"It'll be old news by then," Martha snapped.

"Better than no news. I'm glad I have you to keep me up on things."

"I know one thing I won't be reporting."

"What's that?"

"Any stocking sales. My finger's still sore."

Carly grew concerned. "Let me see."

"No." Martha shoved her hands beneath the table.

"I'm sorry that happened."

"I know, I shouldn't have brought it up. But I'm still not telling you about any stocking sales."

Biting back a smile, Carly went to look up a chart and missed a step when she glanced back at Martha. Her head was downcast and her cheek was wet.

On Thursday after her shift, Carly went to the woodworking shop to catch Adam before he left the center. She needed a lift, but mostly she was excited about her new idea. He was expert-extraordinaire at pointing out the negatives so she could make a clear-headed choice. Passing the goldfish pond, she heard a familiar hum rise above the splashing water feature. Stepping to the side of the sidewalk she waited.

A red scooter puttered up next to her carrying a thin, wiry man with a holstered gun.

"Hi, Aesop. How's it going?" Carly didn't know his real name. He liked to be up front with his speech impediment to set people at ease. The first time they'd met, he'd told her his wife dubbed him Aesop because of his stammer.

"Not—not very good. I think I made a mistake when I broke up a fight between the Masts and the Yoders."

She tilted her head, wondering what had transpired. Aesop was sensitive for a security guard. "That sounds like a necessary thing."

"You—you know how the Masts always let their little chi–chi–chihuahua dog run loose, and he pees on the Yoders' bushes, and the neighbors. . .they—they stand in the yard and argue. So I told the Masts they could lose their little guy if they didn't keep him on a leash."

He referred to a pair of neighbors who resided in independent-living homes. Although she worked in assisted living, the center was small enough that she knew many of the residents in independent living. She'd heard of the little dog that barked and snapped, and the Masts had been warned to keep their feisty pet on a leash. "That's true. And they should know better by now."

"But—but you should've seen. . .saw the daggers they gave the Yoders. I'm afraid I made them enemies. . .bitter enemies."

"Why don't you write up a report and ask for some mediation sessions."

"Good—good idea. That's—that's what I'll do."

"But don't feel bad. You're not trained in that area. You did the right thing telling them the rules and sending them on their way."

"I hope so. You—you leaving?"

"Yes."

"Be careful. I—I worry about you." The scooter purred away.

Carly continued briskly toward the woodworking shop. She only had to move aside three more times—once for a wheelchair and twice for walkers—before she arrived. She popped her head inside the shop's open door. "Hello!"

"Hey." Adam motioned with a grin.

She smiled back. "Can I hitch a ride with you?"

The tan, virile woodworker leaned on a push broom. "Sure. I'm almost finished."

Tearing her eyes away from his toned physique, she explained, "My fall into the blackberry bushes had repercussions. Rocco replaced a tire earlier. But now the other one went flat."

"You ever get all the stickers out of your dress?"

"Jah. Of course." She ignored his teasing and remained thoughtfully quiet while he closed shop. As they drove through Sweet Home, he brought up the meeting. "Did the board approve your idea?"

"Jah."

"They did?" She could hear the surprise in his voice. "That's good."

They passed the library and approached Sankey Park. The cottages on the residential streets at the top of the hill displayed an array of colorful pastels. Carly had fallen in love with the yellow one at first sight. Only this afternoon, she wasn't focused on the picturesque. "But Simon took it away from me. He put Sherie in charge of the program."

Adam's chiseled jaw flinched. "That's gotta hurt." His eyes softened. "I'm sorry."

She shrugged. "It's getting easier. At least they passed it. It's going to do good things for the center."

"I suppose."

"Actually the last couple of days my mind is turning over a new idea."

He grimaced.

She'd seen that expression too many times before to be dissuaded. "Martha told me the most romantic story the other day about the boy she met when she was sixteen. They were forbidden, so they snuck out and met on an old covered bridge." Her voice turned wistful. "All summer long. They fell in love, and then he went to war, and she never heard from him again."

He scowled. "That's sad. But what can you do about it?"

"Her daughter's giving her a surprise birthday party because she's turning eight-five. Martha's been depressed lately. After she told me that story, I saw her crying. What if I—"

"No." He pulled the truck into her drive. "You don't want to get involved with that."

Irritated that he hadn't even allowed her to finish explaining her idea, she argued, "What harm can it do to find out if he made it back from the war? I think she's sad because she doesn't think he did."

Adam turned off the engine, and his face became a dark thunderstorm. "What harm? Because if you find out he's alive, you won't let it stop there. After that, you'll be trying to matchmake."

"Jah! Wouldn't that make the best birthday surprise ever?"

He shook his head. "You have a tendency to see the rosy side of things. You forget that matchmakers usually stir up more trouble than they can handle."

She arched a blond brow. "And you're the love expert?"

"Are you?"

Frustrated, she got out of the truck. Before she closed the door, however, she looked into his turbulent eyes. "I thought we understood each other. That night at your party. . .I got a glimpse of the real you. Guess I was wrong."

"Wait right there." He jumped out and came around to her side of the truck. "It's not fair to get mad just because I bring up a couple what ifs." His voice softened. "You're right. Things are changing between us."

Breathless at the sudden change in the virile man facing her, she said, "Okay, I'm listening."

He gave her a flirty grin. "I'm getting attached to you. Want to protect you."

"Jimmy *asked* you to protect me."

A touch on her arm sent hot lava flowing through her veins. His voice rumbled, "These aren't brotherly feelings."

She rubbed her tingling arm. "What then?"

His eyes narrowed, settled on her mouth. "Feelings that should wait until I have a few major things sorted out in my life."

She swallowed. "Fair enough." Better than falling in love first. Like last time. She didn't want that to happen again.

Then his mouth quirked. "Though another kiss might help me sort things out quicker."

"Kissing should wait. Until you know what you want."

He studied her curiously. "So you ready to listen to my what-ifs?"

With a sigh, she crossed her arms and listened to him count off his reasons.

"One, digging up the past exposes secrets that hurt people. Two, it wouldn't be easy to dig up the old rascal. Especially if he's dead. Even if he didn't die in the war, at their age he most likely is deceased."

"What a horrible thing to say."

"I know. But I'm not finished. Three, what if they fall in love again and her family objects? And four"—he touched her cheek—"how do you get that dimple to do that?"

She pushed his hand away. "You're a burr."

"You would know about stickers."

"Exactly."

"What happened to 'Adam, you're such a godsend'? Speaking of, do you need a ride tomorrow?"

"No Rocco's dropping my bike off later tonight."

With a nod, he closed her truck door. "Later then. I know you'll do the right thing."

CHAPTER NINE

Carly thrust her gloved fingers into the soil and pulled out a thistle. As she worked, she thought about Adam's warning and Martha's newest outburst. She'd been playing bingo with Dot Miller—the old friends once enjoyed an ongoing, hearty competition. Only with Dot's growing dementia, Martha was easing up on the friendly jabs. But today, she'd gotten angry when Dot won. She'd snapped, "You have a canary and a loving husband. Do you have to win, too?"

"You want a canary?" Dot had asked Martha. "I'll have Crusher get you one."

Carly had quickly intervened. They couldn't have an entire ward of canaries. She'd worked hard to get the staff to make an exception for Dot's. But Martha's depression had to be deepening for her to turn on the friend she most dearly loved. Now Carly was torn between Adam's advice and her desire to improve Martha's state of mind.

Nearby, Cocoa nibbled at ferns that clustered around the porch. The fatso hardly needed nourishment. Thankfully, her pet didn't favor the pink coneflowers which made such a striking show against Carly's yellow cottage. She didn't mind a little grazing, but Imogene across the street would. While her neighbor adored Cocoa, she loved her garden more.

Suddenly Cocoa went on alert, arranging his unicorn-lop ears to catch sound. Soon Carly heard a familiar rumble. "Jimmy's back!" She started toward the truck, with Cocoa hopping behind.

Jimmy jumped out of his truck and gave her a quick hug. "Brought you some sticks for that crazy dog of yours." He opened the bed and carried armfuls to a stockpile behind the cottage. As he worked, he kept an eye out for Cocoa, who hopped about his feet, nose twitching.

"Thanks. My supply was getting low. I'm taking a ride tomorrow. It's Saturday, so I thought I'd join that bike bridge tour."

He let out a whistle. "That's a long ride. And the weather report isn't good for tomorrow. You could get into trouble."

"Really?" she replied, disappointed.

"I'd take you, but they're sending me right back out on the road."

"I wish you didn't have to be gone so much."

"I asked for this gig. I haven't been to the Dakotas yet." His gaze softened with yearning. "Wish I could take you along."

"Sometime I'll take a few vacation days."

"You've been promising that for a long time."

"I know. Things never calm down at work. Right now, Martha Struder's depressed, and I'm trying to figure out how to help her."

"What's going on with her?"

"Probably a lack of mental stimulation. She always enjoyed conversations with her late husband, and now her best friend, Dot Miller, is slipping into dementia. Martha's about the sharpest one in assisted living. She's only there because of her asthma."

They sat on the steps, and Cocoa nestled between them, sniffing Jimmy's jeans. His hand moved to stroke the pet. "So nobody wants to listen to her anymore?"

"Exactly." She darted a skittish gaze at him. "I have a reason to take the bridge tour. I need to make a decision. While he quietly listened, she explained about Martha's long-lost love and her new idea. She repeated Adam's warnings "So you can see how I'm torn. I want to stand on one of those bridges and pray. But I don't want to stir up more trouble with Simon. Yet if I can help her, I need to do what's right."

He squeezed her hand. "You always do what's right. But it usually takes people out of their comfort zone. That's what causes trouble."

Their personalities were similar, but he had the luxury of being a man where assertiveness wasn't viewed as a personal flaw. "How'd we get to be so different than everyone else in our congregation? You're traveling, seeking adventure." She tugged off her gardening gloves and set them on the porch decking. "Auntie refused to marry after Uncle Bob and little Bobby were killed in that accident. She was still young, but she moved into Sweet Home and lived like a recluse."

"Until we came to live with her." Jimmy took up the story. "Then all three of us became our own little rebellious clique."

"I guess."

He shoulder-bumped her. "That's why we gotta look out for each other."

"Except. . .apparently, I'm the only one who really needs looking out after, right?"

He gave her a contrite grin. "Why not go to Weddle Bridge to do your thinking? That way you won't get stranded in a storm."

"Really? I see that bridge every day, and it doesn't have anything to do with Martha. Anyway, if I get caught under one of those bridges, it might be kinda fun."

"There's water under those bridges, too, you know. Your bike could get stuck."

She rolled her gaze heavenward.

He tried another tactic. "How you going to pray with all those other bikers staring at the plain-dressed girl on the pink bike?"

He made a good point. "Maybe I should just ride out to the Crawfordsville Bridge. The tour won't get there until afternoon. I'm pretty sure that's the one Martha was talking about anyway." She shrugged. "I'll make sure my phone's charged."

"You're not taking Cocoa?"

Carly scratched the bunny, and he licked her hand. "Of course not. I'll toss my phone in my bike basket. And everything will be fine."

"Be sure to call Adam if you get into trouble."

Adam thanked the waitress for his third cola refill and leaned his head on the back of the red vinyl booth.

"Sorry I'm late."

He straightened as Jimmy slid in across from him. "I almost ordered without you."

"You should've. I stopped by to check on Sis, and things got complicated."

He gave his friend a sympathetic grin. "I was picturing something like that."

A waitress flirted, then left with their orders.

"So you're heading to the Badlands?" Jimmy could have been a Christopher Columbus or a Ferdinand Magellan in another life, one where he wasn't born Conservative Mennonite. His adventuresome side always made him fun. Only now his thirst for exploration had expanded beyond the hills and rivers of Linn County, where they used to play as kids. His sharp mind was fascinated with the history of the places he traveled. He had no interest in settling down.

Over the years, Jimmy's attitude had rubbed off onto Adam. Though women were attracted to them, they'd both managed to remain single. Lately, they'd been moving in different directions. Didn't see each other as often. Jimmy's new job allowed him more freedom, but Adam's world remained confining and controlled.

Jimmy grinned. "I'm going to Deadwood Gulch. I've been reading up on Wild Bill Hickok and Calamity Jane."

Laughing, Adam replied, "Maybe you'll get some tips on how to keep up with Carly."

"Regarding my sister, you may be getting a phone call tomorrow. She's riding her bike to Crawfordsville Bridge, and there's a storm moving in. I told her to call you if she gets in trouble."

Adam caught a vision of Carly wet and muddy, mad and dimpled. Then a flash of Dad's newest stipulation. He narrowed his eyes. "Is this about finding Martha's old boyfriend?"

"It's about thinking the idea through. She's considering your opinion, but my guess is that she'll end up getting involved in some kind of matchmaking scheme." As they discussed their concerns over her latest plot, Adam grew restless. He'd been keeping too much from Jimmy on what was happening in his life. "You know I've always got your back. I care about her, too. But things are getting complicated."

"Busy time of the year, heading toward Christmas?"

"Jah, but that's not what I meant. Dad offered me a partnership.

He's drawing up paperwork after the holidays."

Jimmy leaned forward. "Hey, that's great! It's what you always wanted."

"I know." Adam fiddled with an empty straw paper. "But he's using it to control me. He wants me to settle down, but he wants to tell me who I can date, too. And it's not Carly."

Jimmy flinched. "That's harsh. Am I off limits, too?"

The waitress returned with their burgers but didn't interrupt their conversation. "No, nothing like that."

Jimmy nodded and downed a couple fries. "Wait a minute. You want to date Carly?"

Adam squirted ketchup on his plate, then met Jimmy's waiting gaze. "I don't know. But I hate Dad's interference so I can't find out. And it's not just him. It's Simon, too. Only Simon's pushing me to pursue Carly. He thinks it'll keep her from being overly involved at the center. He wants me to distract her. It's a real tug-of-war, and I'm so sick of their manipulations. No offense, but I probably wouldn't have even started thinking about her that way if Simon hadn't been goading me. Before she was always just your little sister. Dale's ex. Besides all that, Dad wants me to quit volunteering at the center."

Jimmy doggedly returned to his earlier question. "So you and Carly? And I've been pushing the two of you together. Look I'll figure something else out with Carly so you can back off. I don't want her getting hurt."

"I'd like to let this play out. For both of us."

Jimmy's eyes darkened. "You mean she's interested in you, too?"

"I think so."

"Well I don't like it." He pushed his empty glass away. "I assumed it was a given that we wouldn't chase each other's sisters. You have six pretty ones I've always respected." He shook his head. "After this haul, I'd better stick around for a while."

"Don't make me sit on you." Adam had always been the strongest. "I'm not going to hurt Carly. But I'm not going to let Dad control me, either." He knew his next statement would take Jimmy over the edge, but he wanted to come completely clean. "Besides that, Dale offered me a job in Indiana."

Jimmy slammed his back against the booth and ran a hand through his blond, wavy hair. "What are you thinking? You know Carly won't move to Indiana. Did you tell her?"

"You think I'm crazy?"

"Kinda. Bet that made your dad mad, too, with the feud he's got going with Simon."

"Now you're getting the picture."

Jimmy sighed. "I'd hate to see you go. But if you do, it better be soon before you drag Carly into this. I don't want to see her hurt twice."

"I have to stay long enough to finish the Christmas season."

Jimmy's expression hardened.

"Trust me."

Carly kissed Cocoa on the head, donned a warm black sweater, and tossed her lunch and phone into her cruiser's basket. With a wave for Imogene, she set off past the row of pastel-painted cottages, breathing in the crisp autumn smells. She headed west out of Sweet Home, hitting a leisurely pace. For once, she had plenty of time and intended to bathe herself in nature, hoping to feel a little closer to God and to straighten out her jumbled thoughts.

She crossed Ames Creek, and the road curved south. The Santiam River sparkled blue against its mountainous backdrop until it meandered out of sight. A logging truck whizzed by her, and she had to keep to the shoulder until she veered off the divided highway onto the less traveled Holley Road. As her gaze took in the rural landscape, which bore the marks of logging, she thought about the conversation she'd had with Jimmy. After he'd left her cottage, she'd made up her mind not to call Adam unless it was a last resort. She'd gotten so dependent on the both of them that she'd almost forgotten she was capable of taking care of herself. Pure foolishness!

The chilly air brushed her face and she felt the pleasant rush as she coasted down the slopes and peddled up inclines on the two-lane road, which curved past horses and picket-fenced homes. Cows circled a feeding trough, and sheep dotted the landscape. As the area grew more agricultural, the wind increased. Alongside deep ditches, sword ferns waved, rooted in rich soil tucked under blankets of gold. Sudden gusts swirled brittle leaves from nearby trees, temporarily blinding her.

Spitting leaf debris, she stopped at a place where blackberry vines intertwined in an old wire fence. She secured her prayer-covering strings and drank some water. The wind indicated a storm was on her heels. The overcast sky wasn't exactly ominous, but she wouldn't want to be under the power lines when it hit.

Making a quick decision, she continued onward. It took some muscle to get started again, and even though she had to lean forward and work harder to keep her pace, she immensely enjoyed the exercise.

She passed Old Holley Church and Greenville Road, on which Adam's tree farm was located, able to see some trees in the distance. Her breath caught when three elk burst from the woods and trotted across the road. The last one, with a dark mane and velvet antlers, paused to stare at her before it disappeared into the trees on the other side.

The Crawfordsville Bridge was off the main road, picturesquely situated in a tangle of blackberry bushes and trees. She walked her bike around the gate. A white board fence heralded its entrance, and she crossed the bump where the bridge's wooden floor met the road. In the center of the bridge, she lowered her kickstand and peered out one of its many windows overlooking the Calapooia River. She tried to imagine Martha's old boyfriend fishing from a rock below. They would've had to yell extremely loud for their voices to be heard over the water's rushing and the cackling of Canada geese.

The bridge, however, had been moved since Martha was a girl, so she had no way of verifying Martha's account of that first meeting. *Lord, please give me direction. I don't want to meddle, but to bring joy back into Martha's life. Except for the promise of heaven, her joys are diminishing with each day. Please reveal Your will to me. I'm not concerned with what people think about me. But I care what You think about me.* She took a deep breath of the cold moist air. *I long for peace.*

"Forgive."

As the idea downloaded into her mind, she was convicted about her resentment toward Sherie and Simon. "Jah, I know. But I need Your help with that."

She moved along the walls and looked at the rafters. Ran her hands over the carvings of lovers' initials. What had happened to all those relationships? A severe pang of loneliness shot through her so that she could relate to Martha. And she knew she would pursue the quest. *Thanks, Lord. If my loneliness serves others, then living the single life is good enough for me.*

Overhead the sky darkened and churned. She decided to eat her lunch at a picnic table, with the river to her back. She watched rotten apples drop from a large hanging tree. Suddenly the rain began, pelting hard from its onset. Grabbing her peanut butter sandwich, she spotted a huge tree and wondered if it was the tree where Martha got kissed. She lingered there, gazing through the downpour to see if there were any other big trees in the vicinity. But a loud clap of thunder had her tossing her sandwich and running for the bridge.

As she drew her sweater tight, the rain deluged her, flattening her prayer cap. She fled. Jimmy was right. Again. She jumped over water rivulets and reached the bridge's shelter. With the open sides of the bridge, water spray still reached her.

Her phone rang. She snatched it and stared at the screen, a smile forming as she answered. "I'm at the Crawfordsville Bridge. Not swimming, but almost. Okay, bye." Adam was on his way, and she didn't regret it. Fickle heart.

Although the bridge had been restored, she watched puddles form under a leaky roof. By the time Adam arrived, she was drenched and cold. She made a dash for his truck as he handled her bike. When he jumped inside, water dripped off his dark hat. He grinned at her, and they both broke into laughter.

"Too stubborn to call," he chided.

She shrugged.

The truck windows grew foggy. "So was it worth it?"

"Jah. I had time to think. I'm going to do it." She raised her hand to stave off any determent. "I was standing on the bridge, praying about it, and this deep loneliness swept over me." She let out the part about needing to forgive. "It was like the loneliness is a calling so that I can empathize with the residents. I think it's God's plan for me."

He frowned. "Loneliness?"

She nodded. "I can't argue with God's plan, can I?"

Amusement crinkled his mouth. "Well you could, but I wouldn't advise it."

He leaned close, and his rugged form filled the tight space. "Did you get any other insights? Like maybe your lonely years are about to end? You don't have to constantly eat pie to remember what it tastes like."

Her heart sped as it always did when he flirted. She untied her prayer cap, smoothing its wet strings. "I don't know. But I felt God on that bridge."

"Carly."

She looked into his wistful eyes. "Jah."

"I wish I felt that kind of certainty. I want to fill that lonely spot for you, but I'm afraid that if it wouldn't work out, I'd hurt you. Jimmy's afraid of that, too. He warned me away from you."

Her jaw dropped. "But how did he even know about us?"

Adam shrugged, wiped drops of moisture from her cheek. "We're close."

Her voice broke, "So are you taking his advice?"

His expression reluctant, he asked, "Do you want me to?"

She stared at the foggy window. If they got closer and it didn't work out. . .if Adam's friendship was somehow removed from her life, she'd be devastated. She knew he had some kind of issues to work out before he could commit to her. If she waited, he might even change his mind. And Jimmy was usually right. "Jah. We should listen to reason. But first"—she clutched the front of his shirt and trembled.

Adam didn't need instructions. His arms quickly embraced her and his virile lips sweetly caressed. She could tell he felt the same, grasping for a taste of heaven and what might have been. Or what could destroy them both. Warmed from within, she touched his cheek. "You're a good man, and I'm fond of you. But I'm set in my ways. Jah. It's probably best if we take Jimmy's advice."

His eyes dark and hooded, he ran a rough thumb over her lips. "Maybe." He sighed and drew back. "You're shivering. For now, I'll take you home."

Chapter Ten

Adam gazed across the humble sanctuary at the women's pews and watched Carly, unawares. All he could think about was their recent kiss. Usually he was the initiator, but she'd kissed him twice now. Her passion had ignited a strong desire in him. He admired her both for claiming it and for afterward being strong enough to say no to the possibility of pursuing a relationship with him. The things he'd heard about her from Dale weren't jiving with the woman he was getting to know. He'd never had the nerve to ask Jimmy about Dale's accusations.

He'd been disappointed when she pushed him away. Had hoped she would take the risk. Hoped that she'd be strong enough to carry them both through new territory, to fight for him like she fought for her residents. It hurt him to watch her taking Bishop Kauffman's sermon on family relationships so intently. He could read her mind. She'd use it to strengthen her resolve against him, to take her brother's advice to heart. To push him away, just like with Dale.

It soured his stomach to think of his own family situation, the way he allowed his dad and uncle to use him as a pawn to fuel their private feud. Every time he stood up to them, the stakes were pushed to a higher level. He always strove to be a peacemaker as their faith dictated. Would he find peace if he moved to Indiana? Even if he didn't want to leave his family or Carly?

That afternoon, his confusion drove him to her cottage, and he had every intention of telling her about Dale's offer. He needed to get the Dale thing out in the open and persuade her he wasn't like his cousin.

If the information leaked out by other means, it would only complicate matters. But when he arrived at her cottage, her bike was missing, and she didn't answer the door.

Sunday after church, Carly kicked off her shoes and stretched out on Aunt Fannie's sofa, one leg dangling leisurely, thinking how the service had confirmed her decision. The songs and even the scripture, Psalm 68:6, called her name. "God setteth the solitary in families." She'd never considered that verse before. But she felt He was telling her to seek solace in her family. That it should suffice. And that she could be like family for Martha and the other residents.

Adam had made it clear that he felt the same attraction she felt, but that he wasn't ready to commit. He was giving her forewarning that if they moved forward to explore their feelings, he might pull away. There was an obvious risk in any budding relationship, but the fact that he'd alluded to it twice now meant something deeper was troubling him. A definite red flag. She ran her finger across her lips, remembering and wishing it could be different.

A rustling sound alerted her to move her leg. Cocoa was futilely digging at Fannie's wood floor, and Carly's leg would be the rabbit's next target.

"Ach! Make that rabbit quit. It's ruining my floor!"

Carly moved onto her side and rubbed the rabbit's fur. He treated her as his personal groomer and got angry when she didn't comply. "Settle down, Cocoa." Though her rabbit was usually silent, that didn't mean he didn't have anything to say, and as any good bunny owner would do, she'd memorized his body language. He soon mellowed into a chocolate-and-white puddle.

Aside from her outburst, Fannie had been unusually quiet. Carly had hoped to tell her about her plan to help Martha or maybe even feel her out about Adam. But she wasn't even talking about the quilt show she'd just attended. "I wish you'd tell me more about Quiltopia."

"I told you about the Quilted Cottage Tour."

"I know, but it feels like it didn't meet your expectations this year."

"I just got my hopes up over nothing."

Carly gave Cocoa a final pat and sat upright. "Did you talk to someone about your pattern book?"

Auntie pursed her thin lips, then opened up to Carly. "Two people. First I talked to a woman in a booth. A national quilt designer. She gave me tips on how to organize my work and got my blood a-rushing. She told me she'd introduce me to a man from a Mennonite publishing house on her break. So I brought in some samples from the car, but he wasn't interested in taking on that kind of project."

Fannie swiped her hand across her eyes, and Carly's heart broke. She hurried across the room and knelt in front of her aunt's chair, placing her hand on her knee. "I'm so sorry. How devastating."

"Jah, well." Fannie patted Carly's shoulder as if she was the one needing support. "Now you know why I didn't want to talk about it. Didn't want to go spilling my tears all over you. Now get up and get me a hanky off my dresser."

Carly quickly did as bid. When she returned, she reassured, "There are other publishers."

"I know. And the tips I got about organizing will help me for the next time. It's just that I'm tired. I think I'll go take a long nap."

"I wish I was as good at giving pep talks as you are."

Fannie chuckled. "You are, in your own way. I'll rest, and then I'll get up and give myself a pep talk."

"Good. And the next time I drop in, I hope to see that dining-room table covered again. And you can explain more about the new stuff the lady at Quiltopia taught you."

Fannie stood and straightened her skirt. "Jah, I'm just too tired today." She sighed. "But not too tired to see something's troubling you."

Carly saw that Auntie wasn't going to let her go until she confided so she blurted out, "Do you think Adam is like all the other Lapps?"

Auntie's eyes widened. She dipped her head for so long that Carly thought she might be falling asleep. Then she lifted her gaze. "He doesn't seem to be. If you've got your heart set on a Lapp boy, then there's something I should tell you. Should've told you before. When Bob passed, Roman offered to marry me."

"What?"

"Like you, I couldn't help but be attracted. But it had only been a year since Bob and Bobby passed. It was too soon, and I was scared because he wasn't taking no for an answer. Just like your Dale, he had everything planned out his way. So I went for his Achilles' heel. I told him I wasn't the meek type. And that I still loved Bob. Then he left me alone."

Carly bit her lip, imagining Roman's reaction.

Auntie shook her head and said in a weary voice, "It never would've worked. I've no regrets. I've had a good life. Especially since you and Jimmy came to me."

Carly's heart expanded with love. "Thanks for sharing that."

"So given both our histories, tread careful."

"I will." She kissed Auntie on the cheek. "Get some rest." Then scooping up Cocoa, she headed outside. The sweet smell of jasmine filled the air, but sadness and disappointment filled Carly's heart.

Adam played a scenario through his mind: he went home and confronted Dad, told him he was pursuing Carly. He imagined the threats that would follow. Dad would withdraw the partnership offer and dare him to go to Indiana. He wasn't ready to do that, couldn't because he needed time to repair the damage he'd caused in his relationship with Carly. To fight for her. He could confront his uncle over the way he'd treated her. He should have done so as soon as he'd learned of Si's devious tactic.

So he found himself rapping on Simon's door instead. His aunt answered.

"Adam. What a nice surprise."

"Is Uncle Si handy?"

"He's in the living room. Come on." Following her, he saw Simon napping in his favorite chair. His aunt tapped him on the shoulder. "Adam's here."

"Hmm?" Simon stirred and then motioned for him to take a seat. Adam glanced at the television and hesitated.

While Simon didn't understand his reservations, his aunt took the remote and turned it off, honoring Adam's religious views against it. "I have cake. Want some?"

"Sure," Simon said. When she'd left the room, he arched a brow. "You look serious. What's my brother up to now?"

Sitting on the edge of the sofa, Adam quickly replied, "Nothing new. But I heard what happened to Carly when she took her volunteer plan to the board." He felt Simon studying him.

"Surprisingly, she did a great job with it."

"Then why did you take it away from her?"

"It's not personal, if that's what you think. Strictly business."

Adam shook his head. "It wasn't fair, and you know it."

Simon's hand swept through the air. "You don't understand how things are done. Sherie was in line for a promotion. I'm sure she'll find a way to include Carly and keep an eye on her at the same time."

Not liking Simon's condescending tone, Adam argued, "Carly cares more about the residents than anyone else at Sweet Life. Doesn't that account for anything?"

Simon grinned. "Well this is a sweet turn of events. You standing up for Carly. I'm pleased to see you've changed your mind about her."

Bristling, Adam asked, "And what if I have?"

"It's a good thing. You're levelheaded. I trust you like my own son."

Only Simon didn't trust his own son or have a good relationship with him. Adam wondered if he even knew that Dale was expanding his business, given the bad blood between them.

"I do appreciate her. With Sherie's supervision and your guidance, we can channel Carly's energy in a productive way. It'll be best for everyone involved. Including Carly."

"She's changing. Just give her a chance."

"I think you're the one whose changing, Adam. What does your dad think about all this?"

"It doesn't matter. I'm not going to allow either one of you to manipulate us."

His aunt entered the room, and from her expression, she'd caught his last statement. She set the dessert tray on the coffee table and glared at Simon. Then she smiled at her nephew. "It's so nice of you to drop by Adam. We miss Dale."

Adam saw a painful look pass between husband and wife, then Si's expression hardened.

"I miss him, too," Adam said, resolving not to let anyone drive him away. If he went to Nappanee, it would be his choice.

Thursday afternoons, the residents of Sweet Life Assisted Living assembled for their weekly bingo game. Carly helped Shirley, the bingo caller who resembled an avocado with her gray-green hair, plumpish figure and pitted skin, to round up her troops. At the same time, Miranda brushed past. "I'll take the floor if you take bingo."

"Sure." It was a routine they'd fallen into weeks earlier. Less than half of the residents actually played bingo, but it was still more than Shirley, gregarious as she was, could handle without incurring some incident.

Carly passed out cards and scooted in next to Martha, hoping to keep her mood elevated and ward off any heavy competition such as had occurred the previous week with the unsuspecting Dot. Shirley started the mechanical ball blower and called the first number.

After B-12, Dot interrupted. "I'm worried about Birdie." She stared at the glass double doors across the center's lobby. "Where's Crusher? Birdie needs his cage changed."

"He'll be here like he always is," Martha replied. "Can you repeat that last number Shirley? Dot's blabbing in my ear."

Shirley smiled and repeated, "G-50."

"Got it!" Dot grinned and placed a yellow piece on one of her cards.

"Should've kept my mouth shut," Martha grumbled.

Widow Martha knew she was being unreasonably surly, but she felt bitter. Ever since John had died, life had taken a bad turn. Nobody understood her or treated her with the respect she needed. Sticking her in a facility with half-demented people. It was an insult to her sharp mind. At first she'd been excited to learn that Dot was moving into the facility. But she'd quickly discovered her lifelong friend was but a shell of the woman she used to know. She remembered a day when the aged body sitting beside her housed a feisty woman who loved a good challenge.

"I planted a row of eggplant."

"But I thought Crusher didn't like it."

"He just doesn't know he likes it. But come the end of summer, he'll find out."

Martha shook her head. "John would have a conniption."

"That's the fun of it," Dot replied.

For a moment, Martha wondered if she was too boring. But she had a good life with John. They shared their love of books and politics, even though getting involved with the latter was forbidden in the church. No, she decided that day. She'd never make him eat eggplant. While she admired Dot for her grit, she felt sorry for Crusher come the end of summer.

She pulled her thoughts back to the present game. Martha was bored to her gills. Beside her, Dot acted as though bingo was the hottest thing since the Internet. The Internet. Martha's fingers itched to explore the world of knowledge that the forbidden pleasure surely possessed. The Sweet Life library was dull as its meals. Just before he died, John had decided to install the Internet at their home. Said they'd put it inside a cabinet so nobody would find out. The library had a computer, but she'd been too depressed to explore it. With her asthma worsening, she figured she was too close to death to risk playing with the fires of hell.

But she missed that part of her that took risks. James had ignited that fire in her. Challenging her to think outside the Mennonite box.

"This old tree will keep its secrets," he'd breathed into her ear. His eyes, so full of life, beckoned. "Dare you."

"Just be quick. They can see us from the road."

But he wasn't quick, and she hadn't wanted him to be. And they'd kissed many times after that. She was lucky she hadn't lost her virginity, but she'd drawn the line there. He seemed to respect her for it. And she was glad for it when she later married John. It was bad enough that she carried the guilt of loving someone else. At first. But then John, wonderful old John, had become her life. And she was a foolish old woman now to be thinking of James again. If only Carly hadn't stirred up those memories. It made her feel grumpier than ever.

Carly relaxed when Shirley called about a dozen bingo numbers without any interruptions. But then Repeater, the resident who had a habit of losing his teeth and often repeated what other people said, started taking it upon himself to repeat every one of Shirley's calls. Martha glared at him.

"G-45," Shirley said.

"That'll be G-45," Guy echoed, placing a token on his card.

Martha clamped her lips tight, and Carly whispered. "I love how you're showing restraint."

Before Martha could reply, Klepto pushed back her chair and stood. "I've got a headache. I'm gonna go lie down."

"I'm so sorry," Shirley said. "Take a candy bar for being a good sport."

Klepto's eyes lit, and Carly helped her claim her prize and took her to her room and helped her to bed. She returned just as Repeater called, "Bingo!" with such exuberance he had to push his teeth back into place.

She slid in beside Martha, who said, "We'd be better off if he lost those things again."

"You know that's not true," Carly chided, before helping everyone rearrange their chips and cards.

Evidently Repeater thought his previous strategy was working and so continued to repeat every number. Martha leaned toward Dot. "I wish he'd stop." When Dot glanced at Guy, Martha's hand shot out and removed one of Dot's chips.

Carly's mouth gaped.

Before she could decide how to handle it, Inez the hall patroller suddenly whipped her wheelchair around the corner and decided to take a spin around the bingo table. Of course, the space was too tight for a wheelchair, and she banged into the chairs and caused a ruckus. Carly shot to her feet to assist as Shirley called a recess and whipped out a list of jokes that she read to ease the tension.

Interrupting Shirley, Dot exclaimed, "Martha you cheat. You put that token back on my card right where it was on N-45."

Martha crossed her arms.

"You told Inez to cause a ruckus so you could take my token."

"I did not."

"Some friend."

Carly was relieved to see Adam and Crusher enter the room. Crusher stood behind Dot and massaged her shoulders. Adam leaned his back against the receptionist's desk and crossed his arms to observe the game.

"Martha cheated," Dot tattled. "And you're late. Birdie needs her cage changed."

"This can be easily settled," Shirley said. "Just put the token back, and I'll verify for accuracy after the game. Now, let's start again. Carly, can you give Guy a candy bar for his help. But I'll repeat the numbers for the next game, all right Guy?"

Carly placed a candy bar in Repeater's shirt pocket with a wink and turned from his grinning face to join Adam. He nodded toward the empty staff room, and they left the door ajar.

"Now Martha's cheating?"

"I wouldn't have believed it if I hadn't seen it with my own eyes."

"Bingo!" They heard Martha's gleeful cry.

His face creased with amusement. "Maybe that'll help."

She shook her head. "I feel like I'm losing another friend. I hate to see the changes they go through as they age. Dot with her dementia."

He grew serious. "I'm sorry. I hate it, too. Though most of my residents are in pretty good shape or they couldn't take woodworking."

"I'll talk with her this afternoon. And unless she says something that makes me change my mind, I'm going to hunt up her old boy friend."

He moved close and gave her a melting gaze. "How can I help?"

Carly read the depth of desire in his hooded brown eyes. If she spent the extra time with him, they'd cross the line they'd recently set. But his truck would be convenient to canvas the neighborhood. "I'll think about it. You're a good friend, Adam."

Frowning, he teased, "Not a godsend?"

"Friend," she verified. "Consider it a step up."

He shrugged. "Can I pick you up on Saturday?"

Before she could reply, a wheelchair banged into the door. Its driver exclaimed, "Kelly is at it again!"

Carly bolted out of the room, but saw Miranda striding toward Klepto's room.

"I'd better go," Adam replied. "Ten o'clock?"

"Sure. Thanks." Their gazes followed Dot, clinging to Crusher's arm as they walked down the hall to her room. "He's amazing," Carly remarked.

"He's hurting, too."

Carly watched Miranda return and intercept them. "Hey, Adam. You like to hike?"

Burning with jealousy, Carly moved behind the receptionist desk, turning her back to them. She fiddled with a file. Even though she strained, his masculine rumble was too low to comprehend. But Miranda's flirtatious laugh wasn't.

"I'd like to see that." There was another low rumble, and Miranda's voice grew intimate. Closing the file, Carly left them to their flirtation. She had no right to be jealous.

She found Martha sprawled across her bed, sobbing into her pillow. Moving to sit beside the tall woman, Carly patted her back. "I know you're sorry about what you did."

The older woman sat up and covered her face with her hands, and Carly noticed her struggle to breathe. "Where's your inhaler?"

Martha motioned to a table beside her recliner. Carly retrieved it and waited while Martha administered the life-sustaining vapor. She rubbed the widow's back. "You know Dot won't remember it. You can ask God to forgive you and start brand new."

Setting her jaw, Martha wheezed, "I don't think God's answering my prayers. John was always the strong one."

Carly squeezed her hand. "Changes are hard. Would you like me to pray with you?"

Martha nodded. "And a breathing treatment, please."

Chapter Eleven

The second week of October, Adam was pricing trees for sale, discounting the crowded ones. Lapp's Tree Farm raised both full and layered noble firs. Today they worked in the layered nobles, which were favorites with many people because they held heavy Christmas ornaments. Most of the competitive farms had small shops that also sold ornaments, but Lapp's Tree Farm didn't because Old Holley Fellowship didn't believe in decorating Christmas trees.

Given that fact, it was remarkable that a Mennonite family even sold trees. Originally, Adam's grandpa bought the farm to grow vegetables, but it came with a small tree crop. In order to be a good steward of his resources, he got permission from the bishop to sell off the trees. But with the trees in various sizes, it took a decade to bring them all to maturity. During that time, the bishop passed away, and Lapp's Tree Farm had become a popular place for young Mennonite men to find work.

At one point, his grandfather made the decision to keep growing the trees because they provided for the livelihood of several church families. Nobody confronted the Lapps at the time, and now it was accepted. They'd always taken care not to make a profit off the ornaments or promote the glitz of Christmas.

Adam leaned into a fir, tying a yellow plastic ribbon. His light jacket was saturated with the distinctive piney scent. He propped a measuring stick against the evergreen and brushed off his sleeve before going to the truck for more colored ribbons. Saturday was Tag Your Own Tree Day at the farm, and although his sisters would take care of the customers, Dad expected him to help. He hated to spoil the prevailing peace—since he hadn't contested Dad's stipulations. Yet. But he needed to fulfill his promise to Carly.

With that in mind, he fixed a cup of water and went to his dad. "Need more ribbon?"

Dad gulped down the water. "Not yet." He toed the rich soil. "Last night's frost was just in time."

Adam nodded. Some farmers believed that frost before harvest made the trees dormant and improved needle retention. "Right on schedule. With Mother Nature cooperating, now would be a good time for me to take some time off. The girls love Tag Your Own Tree Saturdays. In fact, they're making their farm-famous Amish sugar cookies today. And you've already got extra help."

"How much time?"

"Half a day or so. It'll only get busier."

Dad eyed him speculatively. "Simon need you at Sweet Life? Now that you're a partner, you need to establish priorities."

Adam shook his head. "It's not Sweet Life. But as a partner, I shouldn't have to ask. You know I always make up for any time I take."

"*Humph*. Forgive me if I still think like a dad. If it isn't Simon, then you must have a date?"

"Just helping a friend."

"Jah? Who?"

Although Dad wasn't one to talk much, he stayed up with the latest gossip between Mom and the sisters. And Adam knew he wouldn't let it go until he had all the facts, especially if it involved family. "Helping Jimmy. He took a long haul to the Dakotas, and he asked me to watch over Carly. So I need to help her with some things. Don't know how long it'll take." He hated resorting to a half truth.

Dad gripped the empty cup. "I thought we came to an agreement about her."

A sudden breeze whipped through the trees, and some straggling reddish cones littered the ground at their feet. Adam kicked one across the lane.

"You're stirring up trouble," Dad warned.

"Why does my friendship with Carly have to come between us?"

"You're fooling yourself to keep referring to her as a friend."

"Jah. My feelings are mixed."

"She's causing a rebellious spirit in you." Dad shook his head. "Can't you see I'm meeting you more than halfway? I know I should've loosened the reins earlier, but why do you keep pushing for more? You still have Nappanee in your blood?"

Adam sighed. "I know you're trying, Dad. We make a good team on the farm. But I believe my love life should be private."

"In this small town? Nothing's private."

Adam hardened his voice. "Well, I'm helping Carly on Saturday. And honestly, I don't know what else to say because she's got me confused."

"And that's just the beginning of what a woman does to a man. I'm telling you she's just like her aunt."

Startled, Adam asked, "What do you mean?"

"They aren't wife material. Fannie told me so herself."

Confusion slowly turned to understanding. "You dated her?"

"Jah. About a year after Bob was killed. She led me on, then all of a sudden she decided she didn't want the accountability that went with marriage. Told me point blank she wasn't the meek type and that she still loved Bob. I think she figured out I wouldn't let her boss me around like she had Bob. Do you see the similarities?"

He couldn't deny it. Carly had led Dale on and then pushed him away because she couldn't fit in with his plans. Dad pointed his finger. "You think good and hard about it. You have until after Christmas to make up your mind between her or the farm. Do the smart thing."

"Dad—"

A rickety green truck rumbled down the lane and pulled to a stop in front of them. One of their hired hands rolled down the window. "We're done in the southeast field. What next?"

"Go up to the house and help Ann set up tables. Do whatever the women want, and then start in the back ten acres."

"Sure, Boss."

When they'd driven down the lane, Dad pushed his cup at Adam.

"Been standing here long enough. You still have some paperwork on that Portland account?"

Adam nodded. "I've got scheduling to do."

"Well, go on."

"Fine. I'll see you in a couple hours. I'll bring some cookies back." Adam put his tools away and jumped in his truck, grateful for the separation.

At the house, he passed the kitchen and snitched a cookie on his way to the office. "Smells great." He groaned with pleasure as the sugar melted on his tongue. "This is how we sell Christmas trees in October."

"Flatterer." Ann winked at her sister Eve and brushed crumbs into the sink.

He playfully tugged the hair of his youngest sister, Faith. "Where's everyone else?"

"Mom and Beth are out telling the men where to put tables. Charity's nursing, and Dee went into town for supplies."

"What are you doing here in the middle of the day?" Eve asked.

"Dad got mad and sent me to the office."

Ann rolled her blue gaze toward the ceiling. "Honestly. What now?"

"Carly."

"Oh." Ann grinned. "I like her. She'd add some spice to our family."

"I'm already outnumbered in sugar and spice."

"We'll take that as a compliment."

Eve shook her head and moved toward the ovens. While Faith wiped down the counters, Adam lowered his voice and continued his conversation with Ann. "I'm helping Carly with a project."

"Oh?" she arched a brow. "At her place?"

"No. Right now she's into covered bridges."

"Sounds romantic."

"I hope." *But should he?*

Trees swayed in the howling wind, and dark clouds dimmed the midmorning sky. A dead bush tumbled across the country road and bounced into a deep ditch. Carly wiggled stocking-clad toes inside her black oxfords as Adam's heater finally warmed the truck's cabin.

"This is not looking good for Tag Your Own Tree Day," he mumbled.

"A drop in the temperature might put people in the mood," she encouraged. His brow wasn't creased in worry, but their conversation served as a reminder that the holidays would soon make him unavailable to her. "How'd you get away?"

He grinned mischievously. "Used my charm."

"You may need some of that for today's venture."

"Don't worry. There's plenty to go around."

Good looks, too. Best not to dwell on those in such close quarters. After flashing him a smile, she noticed they were nearing Martha's childhood homestead on the Halsey–Sweet Home Road. Supposedly, a cousin lived there.

"Dad kicked up a bit. But I'm used to it."

"Is he like my aunt? She's kindhearted but puts on a brusque front. She won't even call Cocoa by name. Always says 'that rabbit.' But when she thinks I'm not watching, she plays with him. I think Auntie's afraid to love again since she lost Bobby. I can't imagine losing a child. Can you?"

"No. It would be hard."

"Auntie loves us. She's just afraid to show it."

Adam laughed sarcastically. "If Dad has a gooey side, I've never seen it."

Curious about his family, she asked, "Is he different toward your sisters?"

"More like indifferent."

"The grandkids?"

Adam wrinkled his dark brow in thought. "Gentler. But between Mom and my sisters, he doesn't need to spend much time with them. When the family gets together, it's one big noisy mob with the kids running in and out. Faith often entertains them."

Carly tried to imagine family gatherings so different from her own. They pulled into a long gravel drive and parked beside an old two-story farmhouse. There was no activity outside that she could see. She didn't know the occupant, so with heads bent against the wind, they trudged to the front door.

Adam shouted over the wind. "You ask the questions. I'll pour on the charm."

She rang the bell, and a middle-aged English woman opened a door that would have banged against the exterior siding if Adam hadn't caught it with a gloved hand.

As strangers, it was encouraging to be invited inside. Whether their hostess trusted them because of their plain clothing or pitied them for the cold, Carly wasn't sure. But she made quick introductions while a small yapping dog bounced up and down around her skirt. From the entryway, she glimpsed modern renovations and heard the hum of a television.

"I work at Sweet Life Assisted Living, and one of our residents is Martha Struder. I understand this is her childhood home."

The woman looked skittish. "The house belongs to my husband's family. What's her maiden name?"

"Stutzman."

"Yep. Follow me. You'll want to talk to him." A hall led into a cozy sitting room where her husband was watching some brightly clad men huddling around a ball. When he saw them, he muted the game. His wife offered them seats and filled him in about the situation.

He tapped his chin, considering their question. "I believe Martha would be a great-great-aunt or something, but we fell out of touch with the Mennonite side of the family." He looked curious. "Why do you ask?"

"She'll soon turn eighty-five." Carly tucked her feet under her skirt, trying to keep Cocoa's scent away from the sniffing dog. "The center is helping her family plan a surprise birthday party. I'm trying to locate some old friends and neighbors. She mentioned a Ruth Stucky?"

He knew a Stucky about Martha's age and gave them directions. Thanking them, Carly and Adam returned to the truck. The address they were given belonged to Ruth's brother, but he gave them Ruth's Halsey address about twenty miles away.

On the way into Halsey, Adam asked, "Hungry?"

"Jah."

"We're going right by the bakery."

Adam stopped at the familiar shop run by a conservative woman, bought two cinnamon rolls, and hurried back to the truck. Thanking him, Carly placed a napkin on her lap and pulled her pastry out of a small paper bag. "When Martha told me she'd lost track of Ruth, I wasn't sure we'd be able to track her down. We're lucky she still lives in the area."

Adam slowly licked his fingers. Carly looked away and stuffed a bite into her own mouth.

"*M-mm*," he groaned with pleasure. "Even if we hit a dead end, this makes the excursion worthwhile."

Men and their food. Jimmy was the same way. She cast him a glance, assuming he referred to his pastry. And he did. But for her, the day was worthwhile just because they sat together snug and protected from the weather and world. She'd love to prolong the intimacy, but she was also anxious to proceed with the hunt.

"Delicious. I have high hopes Ruth will remember the boy."

Finishing his pastry and stuffing everything back into a paper bag, Adam replied, "You romanticize, thinking of him as a boy."

"I suppose. Martha was sixteen at the time. But he was old enough to go into the military."

"Good grief. If he's living, he could be close to ninety. Most men don't live that long."

"I realize we probably won't find him. But wouldn't it be great if I could find one of his relatives and get his life's story? I'd write it in one of those nice journals and give it to Martha for her birthday."

"What will you do if—never mind."

"I'll satisfy my curiosity and think of another way to cheer up Martha."

He flashed a warm gaze. "You're one of Sweet Life's best assets." Then he put the truck in gear and pulled back onto the road. "I told Uncle Si that last Sunday. He told me what a great job you did on your volunteer presentation."

"He did?"

Adam nodded. "Just so you know, I confronted him about the way he treated you."

Melting with gratitude, Carly felt her cheeks heat. "Thanks. You're a good friend."

After that, Adam quietly brooded until they reached Ruth's home. The elderly woman was quick-witted and in good health for her age. She lived with her daughter in a small steepled house in the heart of town. Neither of them dressed plainly, which was probably why Martha had lost track of her.

They assembled in a room with a crackling fire in a corner fireplace. Ruth sat in a rocking chair with a blanket draped across her lap. But the warmth of the room caused Carly to unbutton her coat.

"I'm happy to hear Martha's still alive. I've thought of her over the years. Wondered if her asthma ever got the best of her."

"She continues to struggle with it."

After offering one of her pressed-flower invitations to the party, they got down to business. "Did you know that she had a secret boyfriend when she was sixteen?"

Ruth's eyes lit with merriment. "I remember. Actually, it was the summer we both turned seventeen. We'd talk about it at church. I was kinda jealous. I never met him, but according to Martha, he was a handsome, charismatic young man."

Carly held her breath, almost afraid to ask. "Do you remember his name?"

"Let me think." She tapped the rocking chair's wooden armrest. "Was it John?"

"That was her husband's name."

"Oh, yes. John Struder."

Carly urged, "Martha told me his first name was James but she couldn't remember his last name. I was hoping you could."

"That's odd. Does she have dementia?"

"No," Carly replied, wondering if Martha had really forgotten or continued to hide her secret.

Ruth strained. "It was something foreign or fancy. I believe it was the name of a country. No, it's not coming to me." She stopped rocking. "Why do you ask? Is she still mooning over him?"

Adam gave Carly a tread-with-caution look.

She folded her hands. "No. She loved John. Just mentioned that she always wondered if James made it back from the war. I wish I could tell her he did."

"That's kind of you. All this talk stirs up a lot of memories. It'll be fun to see Martha again. But sometimes it's best not to know some things. If she kept him hidden then, she might not want you to dig up the past now."

A niggle of doubt troubled Carly. Was she doing the right thing? But she'd felt God's leading that day on the Crawfordsville Bridge. Not venturing a glance Adam's way, she replied, "Perhaps."

When they returned to the truck, Adam remarked over the obvious. "You look discouraged."

"A little."

He studied her with his deep brown gaze. "So where next?"

"I wish I knew." Carly sighed. "Probably won't help to stop at the bridge. Given the renovations, I'm sure their initials are gone. At least, I didn't see them the other day."

"Let's swing by there on our way home." Adam's smile reached his warm eyes.

"Really?"

Half an hour later on the bridge, with her covering strings securely tied and her coat gripped tight, they searched the carvings that were deep enough to have survived renovations. Shuddering, she said, "He probably wrote his name first so it would be J something plus M. S.

Adam moved his brawny form to shield her from the wind. She felt his hand squeeze her shoulder and warmed from his touch and nearness.

"Better?" he asked, his masculine breath close to her ear.

She nodded, and he hugged her close as they moved along, exploring the walls. Highly aware of his protective chiseled body, she found it hard to concentrate on the initials until one jumped out at her. "Look!" She pointed. "It's J. H. + M. S."

Adam ran a finger over the carving and hugged her. It was barely visible beneath the layers of paint, and with a good imagination, it could be a J. Or an I. Even an L. But she looked so hopeful. "This might be it."

Elated, she replied, "Now if only we could find an old phone book."

"Simon's computer would be faster. Let's go." He took her hand and drew her toward the truck.

But she dragged her feet regarding the use of Simon's computer. "Oh, I don't know. He probably wouldn't approve. And just because we found a likely match doesn't mean it's *their* initials."

"I've been meaning to call Dale. He has a computer for his work. I'll bet he'd search it out for us."

Unease rose up and stole her breath. She stared at the ground. "I didn't know you stayed in touch."

"We were close as kids."

"I don't know."

"Carly?" He halted, tipped up her chin, and searched her gaze, and she felt as though this was about more than a computer search.

Her mouth went dry. *Let it be,* she inwardly moaned.

Adam squeezed her shoulder. "Let me handle it."

At the truck, she turned to face him. "Thanks for everything. This may turn out to be a wild-goose chase, but your help means a lot to me."

He chuckled. "Believe me, Carly. Today was way more fun than Tag Your Own Tree Day."

"It was," she replied, only she was positive their time together meant more to her than it had to him.

Chapter Twelve

As she stepped into Dot's room to administer morning meds, Carly's mind was occupied with Martha's former sweetheart. She'd have to find a tactful way to jog Martha's memory again. She automatically checked the thermostat as Dot couldn't remember how to adjust the mechanism and often had the temperature set at some extreme. It was a cycle with Dot. She grew uncomfortable, then fiddled with the dial, again, having no idea whether she was setting the heater or the air conditioner.

In general, Mondays at Sweet Life could be difficult as residents needed to recover from the weekend's visitors or lack of them. Dot was up and dressed, sitting at a small table with two chairs. In her elderly throaty voice, she repetitiously sang "Little lamb, little lamb, little lamb." Next to her, the bird's cage remained covered.

Spying a new coloring page attached to Dot's magnetic calendar—which reminded her which day they took her laundry and which days they helped her shower—Carly asked, "Did your grandchildren visit?"

" 'Little lamb.' They sure like Birdie, but it's almost too much for him the way they poke their little fingers into its cage. The little lamb will probably sleep all day."

"Shall we remove its cover and see?"

"Yes, let's give Birdie a choice."

The comment reminded Carly everyone needed to maintain a sense of dignity, even when they needed others to care for them. As Carly removed the cover, Birdie chirped gratefully. Shredded candy wrappers covered the floor of the birdcage, and she figured Dot was right about the grandkids. Next she unlocked the medicine drawer and got the meds and water ready. "You're up early." She waited for Dot to take the meds.

"Really? I was afraid I missed breakfast."

"Why don't you take these pills? It's still a little early for breakfast."

Dot gulped the water and coughed. "Yuck, one melted in my mouth."

"Let me see."

Dot opened her mouth wide.

"Lift your tongue. I think you got it all. Drink some more water."

"Just a little. I'm full from breakfast."

When Dot started cooing at Birdie, Carly slipped out of the room. After she finished her rounds, having helped several residents dress, she moved to the receptionist's desk to update their files.

Sherie popped her head out of the staff room. "See me when you get a moment?"

"How about now?" Carly followed her in and took a seat beside the mini fridge.

"Did you see the roof?" Sherie asked.

"No. What happened?"

"Wind blew off some tile. Simon's in a snit."

"They should replace the whole thing," Carly remarked.

"If the money was there, I'm sure the roof would get replaced. For now, it's getting repaired. How did your rounds go?" When it came to Simon, Sherie always played the middle road.

"A little slow. Repeater was missing the new puzzle his daughter brought him on Sunday. I found it under Klepto's bedcovers. She clawed me good." Carly displayed her forearm.

Sherie gasped. "Be sure it's noted in the files and better have the nurse look at it."

"It's fine. Anyway, I took her one of the house puzzles, but she wasn't satisfied. She wanted the new one. I'm going to bring one in for her. It'll keep her in her room for a while."

"Good idea. If she likes doing them and it keeps her from roaming in and out of everyone's rooms, I'll personally see that we keep her well supplied." Sherie stretched out her slack-clad legs and crossed her arms. "You like making phone calls, Carly? I mean I've seen you carry a cell phone, and you handle yourself nicely when you answer the center's line."

She felt irritated at her supervisor's patronizing manner. "I don't use it much. The church doesn't exactly endorse it. It's one of those gray areas. But living alone, it comes in handy."

"This would be strictly business. I could use your help making some cold calls for volunteers. I'd write the script for you."

It hadn't occurred to Carly to make cold calls. She'd envisioned riding her bike to call on people from her church, talking face to face and putting up posters. Not reading somebody else's script. "Would there be a lot of calls?"

"Yes. And it would be after hours, of course."

"*H-mm.* I have another project going. I'll have to think about it."

Sherie's lips parted in surprise. "This volunteer program was your idea. I thought you'd be all over this."

Carly stared at the carpet as bitterness welled up in her heart. The Lord's admonition to forgive came to mind. Could she help with a tweaked plan, confined to a script? Would it be easier to forgive Simon and Sherie if she stayed away from the program altogether or joined in to assist them? *Lord, help me here.*

"I'm sorry. That was out of line. Go ahead and think about it. But please, don't take too long."

Standing, Carly met Sherie's eyes. "Okay, thanks. Anything else?"

"No."

Eager to be out of the room, Carly almost ran into the resident nurse, Linda Lehman. "Oh, sorry."

"No it was my fault."

"Is somebody ill?" Carly asked. "Yes, Miranda's cleaning up a mess in Kenneth's room." Kenneth was the resident they referred to as the General. An ex-air force pilot, he had also worked for Intelligence. "He has a fever. We'll have to keep him secluded. I gave instructions to Miranda and will check back on him."

Poor woman, forever bustling here and there, needed everywhere.

She thought about showing her the scratches on her arm but, noticing the dark circles under Linda's eyes, thought better of it.

Next the caregivers rounded up the residents for breakfast, and Carly paused at Martha's chair. "You want to read the paper together later?"

"Not today, dearie," she wheezed. "I think I'm allergic to Dot's bird."

Dot gasped. "That's absurd. I'm clear across the hall."

Martha's voice wobbled, "I'm not blaming you. Just not feeling good."

Dot got up from her chair. "I'll take breakfast in my room." She stormed away.

Carly slid into the empty chair and patted Martha's hand. "It's been so windy. Must be pollen got inside."

"I'll be fine. I didn't mean to make her mad."

"Music!" Repeater shouted. "We need music."

Carly smiled. "I believe you're right. Put on something cheery, Miranda."

On Thursday after working her shift, Carly felt unusually weary and cold and was looking forward to turning in early and snuggling beneath her mother's yummy yellow quilt. It was leftovers night, so dinner would be easy. Then a nice bubble bath and an evening with Cocoa and a book.

First, however, she needed to check out her arm, which had gotten some red streaks. She popped her head inside the nurse's office, pleased to see Linda sitting at the computer, looking somewhat composed. When she looked up, her eyes widened. "Everything all right?"

"With the residents. I've got a couple scratches I want you to see."

"Sure. Sit down."

Carly pushed up her sleeve to reveal the red, swollen marks.

Linda instantly went to work, cleansing with an antiseptic wipe that burned. "It's good you came. Those are infected."

"Sherie warned me to come in when it happened."

After taking Carly's temperature, Linda asked, "When was that?"

Carly thought a moment. "Three days ago."

"Yes, next time don't wait so long. You've got a slight fever. Use this ointment on it, and I'll get Dr. Rink to send an antibiotic to your pharmacy."

"Thanks." Carly eyed Linda's tropical calendar. "Ever been to any of those places?"

"No. But as soon as I retire—in exactly 751 days—hubby and I are traveling. It's what keeps me going."

"Sherie's working on a volunteer program. Could you use that kind of help?"

Linda's eyes brightened. "You bet I could. Where do I sign up?"

Chuckling, Carly said, "Just ask her about it. Maybe she can do something for you."

"Are you going back to assisted living?"

"I can. What do you need?"

Linda smiled with relief. "Can you get this inhaler to Martha? She might need it tonight."

Nodding, Carly agreed. Her arm stung, and she felt even wearier as she returned to the assisted-living building.

Miranda, who had an occasional night shift, looked up with surprise. "Forget something?"

"Linda asked me to give this inhaler to Martha."

"I was about to check on her. She just darted through the hall looking disturbed. Let me know what's going on before you leave."

"Sure."

As Carly stepped into the hall, Martha burst out of her room. "Carly! Where's Dot?"

"I don't know. What's wrong?"

"I can't find her."

"I'll help you look."

Together, they checked Dot's room. She wasn't there. Next they tried the kitchen since she always thought it was meal time. Martha's breaths came too rapidly from the exertion, and Carly had her wait in the lobby while she alerted Miranda. Sherie covered the floor while the caregivers checked the library and returned to Dot's room again.

They even looked under the bed. They searched every room in assisted living. Dot was nowhere to be found.

Sherie alerted security and Simon. The alarm was carried to all the parts of the retirement center.

Growing worried, Carly thought Crusher should be notified. Dot could have left the building and gone to his apartment. With the night staff in place, Sherie released her to pursue that avenue of the search.

Grateful, she shrugged into her coat, pausing to give Martha a few comforting words.

"It's all my fault," Martha moaned. "I drove her away."

"That's not true. You're her best friend."

"Not lately."

"Please try to relax so your asthma doesn't flare up."

Miranda joined them and put her hand on Martha's shoulder. Carly eased away as Miranda spoke soothing words to Martha.

Shivering, Carly stopped by the woodworking shop first and was relieved to find Crusher there working on a project. Alarmed by the news, he grabbed his hat and fled toward assisted living as fast as his eighty-year-old legs could take him.

Carly and Adam sped after him.

"I've got to find her," he panted. "She counts on me for everything since—"

"I know," Carly puffed, while tugging his shirt sleeve. "Please stop."

Crusher halted, looking frantic and old.

"You must go home," Carly reasoned. "If Dot's outside the building, she'll go home. Stay there, and we'll search. The police are on their way."

Adam volunteered to walk Crusher home and close up the shop before he helped search.

Nodding, Carly ran to the assisted-living entryway. She hesitated. If Dot was visiting Magnificent by the door and someone happened in, she might have slipped out while the door was open. Though the entire center was on alert, it wouldn't hurt to check out the exterior grounds.

Chapter Thirteen

Carly searched, working her way to the front of Sweet Life Retirement Center. Though her heart was pumping with fright, the grounds seemed quiet and deserted, situated in a picturesque setting of aged, droopy-limbed evergreen and mature vegetation. She hurried down the sidewalk that edged the parking lot, past the visitors' benches, and halted at the twenty-foot, twin evergreens shaped like giant Hershey's Kisses. Which way?

To the east was independent housing and the community garden, quaint with birdhouses and picket fence. Not a creature stirred within her sight. Just to the right of the garden, a wide path beckoned. It led through wild vegetation and dark canopied trees to a steeply embanked river. On either side of its clover-trodden path, blackberry, old man's beard, fern, and grass tangled menacingly up to seven feet in height. Enough to swallow Dot. Carly could hear the rushing river beyond. Her heart pounded. *Deadly.*

Staring at the redbrick independent-living homes, she reasoned surely Dot would be afraid to take that path.

Heading west, she hurried into the nearest neighborhood of cute, prim, cookie-cutter track homes. She made a quick loop through the neighborhood and arrived back at the main entrance without a single sign of Dot. At a sudden blast of a car's horn, Carly shrank back and clutched her bodice. She felt a vice grip on her left arm as Adam drew her back to the safe confines of the sidewalk.

"Did you find her?" she gasped.

He shook his head. "No. You all right?"

She shrugged away and blinked at the leaf-littered gutter, allowing her sudden fright to subside before she spoke, "I'm fine." But she wasn't. She was shaking, and despair had clouded her thinking so that she'd stepped off a residential curb, oblivious to oncoming traffic.

"It's getting dark, Carly." At his husky reminder, she realized it was a miracle the driver of the automobile had even seen her.

Hopelessly, she considered their surroundings as she tried to gather her thoughts. Newly planted angels of conifer and maple spread sheltering wings over middle-income lawns. Shadows replaced the chrysanthemum and asters' colorful splash against driveways teeming with economy cars. All around them, people were returning to the haven of family and loved ones—except for Dot. Where could she be?

She buttoned her black wool coat in an effort to ward off the dropping temperature. Had Martha's changing behavior provoked Dot's disappearance? "If only I can remember something to help us see the situation through Dot's eyes, then we might know where to search."

"She could be a thousand miles from Sweet Home."

Considering the city limits of their small Oregon town, Carly frowned up at her friend. "You think someone abducted her?"

He shrugged shoulders sculpted deep and broad from manual labor. "Dot could be miles from reality. Nobody understands dementia." Belying his bleak statement, his quirked brows gave evidence he was trying to puzzle it out, too.

A squirrel skittered up a tree, and a street light blinked on. There was no stopping the encumbrance of nightfall once the sun dropped behind the hills. "I can't bear the thought of Dot spending the night outside, cold and alone. I didn't want to think about the river, but what if she went that way?"

Adam touched her shoulder, and she longed to curl into the comfort of his arms and draw from his strength. He whispered, "Then we'll find her."

Carly straightened her shoulders. "We must." She glanced in both directions and started across the street, back toward the river.

Adam fell into step beside her. "But I can't concentrate, worrying about—"

Her temper flared for no reason and she lashed out in confusion. "What? One car honks their horn and now I'm a worry?"

"No," he said. "Crusher's frantic. If you're not going home, stay with him or at least go back to the center and help field calls. Talk to the police. The other residents need you now, more than ever."

Of course she wouldn't go home. Her heart sank just to think how the appearance of a police officer would alarm the elderly residents. Crusher's tender expression flashed into her mind. Even with the test of living in separate quarters, his love for Dot endured.

Every day, he walked from his independent-living facility on the edge of the retirement community to the assisted-living building to bring his wife fresh-squeezed orange juice because he'd heard it helped with dementia. And he'd gotten her the canary. She blinked back threatening tears. Crusher wasn't the only resident who would be devastated. Poor Martha.

Adam was right. By now the staff would have notified all the proper authorities. Dealing with calls and police officers would make them shorthanded. The evening shift was busy with visitors, medications to administer, and residents to assist with bed preparations. She understood how a single event could send a virus of confusion throughout the elderly group. Reaching the other side of the street, she fought against the pressure mounting at the sides of her temples.

With a nod that caused a curl to slip from her bonnet, she turned abruptly to face him. His shoulders were rigid, and concern shone in his soft brown gaze. "I'll go back." Still she protested, "But what if she went down to the river? Those cliffs."

"I'll fetch a flashlight. Volunteers from church are probably already assembling. We'll get organized and search the woods and the river. But it's not the place for you. You'd be snagged and pinned to a blackberry bush within minutes."

"Oh."

Adam sympathized at Carly's wavering, "Oh." It wasn't often that anyone rendered her hesitant, much less speechless. Her blue eyes swam in pain, and some of her blond curls had escaped her covering.

As they returned to the center, his gaze darted everywhere, hoping to spot the tiny missing woman. Crusher always teased, "Temper and all, Dot weighs in under a hundred pounds." Adam figured a puff of wind could have lifted her out of Linn County and carried her across the Pacific Ocean and Asia, back to the land of their Swiss German ancestors by now.

Uncle Si wouldn't be happy about the missing person incident. He expected things at Sweet Life to flow orderly and efficiently, like everything else within his touch.

His mind ran along a well-oiled track. Dad and Uncle Si were reincarnations of the biblical Jacob and Esau. Only difference was they were identical twins. Uncle Si was Esau because he'd married outside the Conservative Mennonite Church and soon quit worshipping there.

Carly brushed past him to punch a code into the pad that opened the center's glass doors. He followed her in. But when she made an uncustomary pause, he plowed over her foot.

"Ouch!" She shot him a dark look and proceeded into the fray before he could apologize. She headed straight to Crusher, who apparently hadn't stayed put at home. He sat slumped at a table that displayed a partly assembled jigsaw puzzle of an old covered bridge. He looked up expectantly.

But she shook her head, touching the wrinkled chambray shirt. A black suspender slipped down his sleeve.

"I told my neighbors to keep an eye out for her. But I couldn't sit there alone, not knowing what was happening. I had to come here."

With one quick feminine gesture, she had the suspender strap back in place and was whispering something soothing.

Crusher nodded, his gray eyes lighting with hope.

Though Adam ached for Crusher, he figured there was more comfort in Carly's feminine touch than any awkward attempts he could manage.

Disappointed that Dot was still missing, Adam strode to the caregiver's station. "Hi, Miranda."

"Awful, isn't it? Your bishop's rounding up a search team. We called the Alzheimer's hotline, and the police are on their way." Tucking her short bobbed hair behind her ear, she leaned forward. "While normally I'd love hanging out with you, could you assemble the troops outside, away from the residents?"

"Sure." He turned away to follow her instructions, when she called him back.

"Adam? Don't forget my invitation."

"Invitation?" he teased, wondering what Dad would think if he caved in to Miranda's suggestive flirtations and brought *her* home.

Outside, the temperature had plummeted several degrees, a chilling reminder that Dot probably wasn't wearing a coat. He'd only gone a few steps when a red scooter rolled around the corner of a brick building, its rider braking in front of him.

"Hi, Aesop." Even though the other man's expression was grim, Adam asked, "You heard anything new about Dot?"

"No. . .nobody's seen her." The facility's security guard raised a bright red glove, designed to allow his fingertips to poke out, and pointed toward the lamp-lit parking lot. "There's a—a group. . .meeting over there."

Adam followed the security guard's gesture and recognized the bishop and several other men from his congregation as well as some strangers. "Thanks."

With a nod, Aesop continued his patrol.

Adam strode toward the row of black cars. Nothing made sense. They should've found Dot by now. She'd only been missing a half hour before they'd initiated a search. Someone within the Sweet Life Retirement Community should have seen her. Though unlikely, if she'd made it to the outside and knocked on a stranger's door, they should've called by now. It wouldn't take long to discover she had Alzheimer's and wore a medical bracelet with the facility's phone number. He didn't want to think about the possibility she'd wandered to the river or lay injured on the forest floor.

Picking his dad from the group of black coats, he hurried to his side. "Thanks for coming."

"Dot still missing?"

Uncle Si answered, "Yup."

Adam nodded at Dad's mirror image, who was clad in jeans and a ball cap. "Inside, they said the police are on their way. And some volunteers are here from the Alzheimer's hotline."

The bishop cleared his throat, and the crowd quieted. His white bearded face shone eerily silver in the lamplight. "They've searched inside?"

Uncle Simon replied, "Yes, sir."

Bishop Kauffman gave a brief nod. "It'll take the police time to go through their hoops. Meanwhile, I've divided the brothers and volunteers into two groups. One will knock on doors within the bounds of the retirement center, and the rest will fan out in the woods. The Lord's our helper. Let's pray." The bishop removed his black broad-brimmed hat, and the others promptly followed suit. "Dear Lord, we ask for Your direction as we search for our sister and for Your mercies to keep her unharmed."

Glittering hate-filled eyes forced Dot to cower and bury her face in her arms. *Go away*, her mind begged. *Leave me alone.* But the menacing thing remained, dark and evil. Her heart thumped with terror, and she knew she was trapped. But she couldn't remember how she'd come to be in this awful, godforsaken place. She lay immobilized in suffocating fear until she dared to raise her face for a gulp of fresh air. Her throat constricted. She took several short breaths. Her nose tickled. She swiped at something, and the demon vanished.

She relaxed and rested her cheek in the soft cup of her hand. As her fears receded, her breathing grew easier, and her mind floated far away. She landed in a slant-ceilinged room. She saw a small, cast-iron bed with rumpled covers. She sensed it was her job to put them in order. But before she could do that, she had to find something. What was missing? As her hands groped, she struggled to remember.

Inside assisted living, Carly plumped a pillow next to Nines, who as usual was dressed as if prepared for an outing and clutching her purse. Carly was positioning a lap blanket when the entrance alarm engaged.

With frustration over the constant string of misfortunes, she hurried toward the door.

A police officer with a handgun strapped to his belt stared at her through the glass pane. When the door slid open, he stepped into the building, filling the room with authority. He brushed his blue gaze over Carly, and his expression softened. "You in charge here?"

She pointed him to the caregivers' station and watched him stride toward Sherie.

"You in charge here?" Repeater said. "Who's that?"

"I didn't catch his name."

Repeater turned his attention back to the television, while Carly kept her own eyes averted from the electronic evil. She glanced toward the desk. Sherie spoke to the officer who curved a finger, summoning her.

When Carly stood in front of the officer, he asked, "You were on duty when Dot Miller was reported missing?"

"Just going off duty, sir."

He took paperwork from a clipboard and pushed it across the counter toward Sherie. "If you fill out this missing person's report while we talk, it'll save time." His gaze shifted back to Carly. "Miss Blosser, when was Mrs. Miller last seen?"

"At dinner. Around 4:30."

"Do you have any idea where she may have gone? Any clues at all?"

"Jah, maybe. Dot has a routine. She usually visits Magnificent before heading to her apartment for the evening. The cage is by the door."

When the officer gave her the same expression as those who couldn't understand Pennsylvania Dutch, she clarified, "The birdcage." He still didn't get it. "Sometimes when visitors come and go, they don't watch for residents who may slip through the automatic doors. I don't know how else Dot could have disappeared."

"Does she have endangering health issues?"

"Dementia," Carly explained as her fears escalated. "She's very fearful, and she's tiny and wasn't wearing her coat."

His eyes widened with alarm. "Do you keep a visitation log?"

"Jah." Carly moved behind the counter and opened the ledger. "Donna Weaver checked out at five thirty. Does that fit with your scenario?"

Nodding, Carly replied, "I'm afraid so. But we already called Donna, and she didn't remember anything. Here's her phone number."

Sherie interrupted, "You want me to sign this?"

"Yes. Before I can initiate a search, I'll need a photo and Dot's medical records."

Sherie handed him Dot's file. "It's all in here." They watched him rifle through the file and click an electronic device over the paperwork.

"One more thing, Miss Blosser. Can you describe her clothing?"

Carly thought for a moment. "Jah, a green dress with tiny flowers."

"Thanks, that's all for now." The officer turned his back to use his phone.

Sherie had finished the report. "I know you're off duty, Carly, but would you mind distributing meds?"

"Not at all." Still shivering and nearly sagging with weariness, she left the caregivers' station and worked without incident for several minutes. She was directly across the hall from Dot's apartment when the officer reappeared. He pointed toward Dot's open door, and Carly nodded. Her curiosity drew her to follow him inside the apartment.

Crusher had fallen asleep in Dot's recliner. Carly crossed the room and woke him with a touch, explaining about the officer. His sad eyes followed the officer's movements as he opened closet doors and asked pertinent questions.

"Is there any possibility that your wife could be at your apartment?"

"When I got the news, I asked the neighbors to watch for her and call if she turns up."

"Good thinking." The officer verified the address, his gaze continually scanning the room, when suddenly he stopped speaking. His eyes narrowed to focus on something across the room.

Carly's heart sank at the officer's grim face. "What?"

He raised a palm, warning her and Crusher to stay put as he moved purposefully toward the dresser.

Chapter Fourteen

Carly clutched Crusher's arm, her gaze following the officer as he moved across the small apartment. Alarm slammed her heart to wonder what had his attention so riveted. When he reached the antique piece, he sank to his knees and disappeared out of sight.

With an understanding gasp, she flew after him and saw a solitary shoe protruding from beneath the bed. But the officer blocked her view from Dot's body.

Soon he raised his head. "I believe we've solved the mystery."

Eyeing the immobile shoe, Carly gasped, "Is she—"

"Breathing."

With a sigh of relief, she cried, "Crusher, we found her."

"Bless the Lord." The older man shuffled toward them, muttering a stream of thanks.

Meanwhile the officer remained prone on the floor, limiting Carly's vision. "Mrs. Miller? You all right under there?"

At Dot's slight groan, Carly implored, "Please, Officer, let me talk to her so she isn't frightened." In affirmation, the officer backed away. Behind her, she heard Crusher telling him that they'd checked under the bed earlier. "Guess all her blasted storage containers hid her. She collects quilt scraps and patterns. She doesn't sew anymore, but she won't give 'em up."

Dot stirred at Carly's gentle nudging, "Why don't you come out where it's more comfortable."

"Nope."

"Why not?"

"Sh! I'm hiding," she whispered.

"But there's no need," Carly reassured.

Dot exclaimed, "It's the Death Angel. He's pure awful and stalking me."

Placing her arm around Dot as best she could in the cramped quarters, Carly said, "He's gone now."

Dot's head swiveled, and her eyes darted. "Jah. He can't find me here. His eyes are so evil."

"Crusher's here."

"Crusher?" Dot moved and banged her head against the bed's bracings. "I'm trapped," she panted.

"You're fine. But it's tight quarters. So keep your head down and scoot backward. I'll help." As Dot got the hang of it, Carly inched back, bumping into Crusher.

When Dot rolled out, she lay on her back and gave Crusher a contrite smile.

He exploded. "What are you doing under there?" His unusually sharp tone told Carly he'd been frightened to the core.

Carly saw a flicker of confusion in Dot's eyes, and she replied in sing-song, "Tommy's tears and Mary's fears will make them old before their years."

Crusher exchanged a disheartened look with Carly and softened his tone. "You had us all worried."

Carly started to help Dot to her feet but suddenly felt faint herself and clutched the bed while the officer rushed forward to help Dot. The older woman tottered uneasily at first. She took a deep breath and rubbed her head. "That hurts."

Crusher placed one hand at Dot's waist and plucked a dust bunny from the side of her misshapen covering.

The officer asked Carly, "You all right?"

"Yes, just dizzy for a moment. I'm fine." But she felt anything but fine.

He smiled wide. "Good. We don't always have happy endings. I'm glad this one was. I'm going back to the front desk. We'll need a nurse to check her out before I can close the case."

Carly watched him disappear. Happy ending? Though she was thrilled to find Dot, her heart broke to think she'd been hiding all those hours from the Death Angel. In her confusion, she must have forgotten that she was a Christian headed for heaven's happily ever after. Would she forget her faith altogether? Is that what was causing her fear?

Her grim thoughts fled when Martha stuck her head inside the room. "Is it true? You found Dot?"

Blinking back an unexpected rush of tears, Carly smiled. "Jah, see for yourself."

"You foolish woman. I'm never going to say a cross word to you again," Martha blurted.

"About time," Dot huffed.

"How could you hide so long?"

"I fell asleep."

Dot's admission gave Carly some relief that Dot might not have been fearfully hiding the entire time. She swiped her sleeve across her eyes. Perhaps she'd only awakened from a bad dream.

Following right behind Martha was the staff nurse. "Oh Carly, you're still here? Shoo now. I've got this."

"All right. Thanks, Linda." Feeling exhausted and shaky, Carly moved toward the caregivers' station. At Sherie's affirmative wave, she fetched her coat and passed through the vacant lobby. The television was turned off and the lights dimmed. Magnificent's cage was covered. Everything seemed in order, but her heart remained heavy.

If only she could do more to help her elderly friends finish their lives with grace and confidence. She'd talk to Martha and see if the two of them could come up with ways to help Dot overcome her fears and substantiate her faith. Horrible as this had been, she hoped it could be a turning point for the elderly women's friendship. She punched in the exit code, surprised to see Adam standing outside the building. His hair was tousled, and his coat covered in burrs.

"Was she really under the bed?"

The soft question drew her gaze to his eyes. They held no criticism, and the kindness she saw drew out her confession, "I feel so inadequate."

He softly chuckled. "You're anything but that. I saw the way you handled Crusher. You're a natural with them. You anticipate their needs before they even know they have any."

"Thanks."

"Crusher still in there?"

"Jah." She smiled. "But they'll kick him out any minute now." Cold air penetrated Carly's coat, and she gave an involuntary shudder. All she could think of was her soft warm bed. A melodic peal sounded throughout the courtyard, interrupting their conversation. They waited as the chapel's steeple clock chimed nine times.

Adam frowned. "It's late, and you're cold. Let me take you home."

At that moment, Aesop came around the corner and killed his scooter's motor. "Here—here to meet Crusher. Good thing they found his lady."

Carly nodded as Crusher appeared.

Aesop handed Crusher a helmet. "Hop—hop on."

Their eyes widened as Crusher drew his finger to his lips to silence their objections and slid behind the thin but sinewy security officer. Aesop must have been assured they liked him too much to tattle. In fact, by Crusher's expression, it hadn't been the first time they'd ridden together.

Laughing, Adam drew his arm around her.

As they drove through Sweet Home, dead this time of night, Carly replayed the evening in her mind. She'd been shocked to see Dot's foot sticking out from the bed. Then when she'd seen Dot's wide-eyed fright, she'd wanted to wrap her arms around the little woman and hold her forever.

She rubbed her arms, dimly aware of pain emanating from her scratches. "She told me she was hiding from the Death Angel."

Adam's startled expression saddened. "What? You believe her?"

She leaned her head back against the headrest. "I don't know. She could have seen an angel. Or maybe a demon. She said its eyes were evil."

Turning onto Hawthorne, Adam replied, "It's possible, but with her dementia, her mind's most likely playing tricks on her."

Carly shivered. "I suppose. But it's real to her."

"I know."

"What about her faith? Is she forgetting about God?"

"We can trust God to keep His own."

Carly nodded. Trust God. Could she trust God with Dot? Trust Him enough to forgive Simon? When Adam hopped out of the truck to take care of her bike, she meant to follow him, but it felt so good to just rest a moment. She closed her eyes, startled when the door suddenly burst open.

"Carly?"

She shook her head. "I'm sorry. I was so comfortable, I drifted off."

"Poor thing. You're exhausted. Let me help you."

He touched her arm, and she shrank back with pain. "Oh, no."

"What?" "I forgot about my prescription. One of the residents scratched me, and it's infected. But Linda called in a prescription."

His gaze lifted from her arm and shot to her beaded forehead. He touched her brow with the back of his hand, and she leaned into his touch, shamelessly.

"You've got a fever. Let's get you inside, and then I'll go for the prescription."

"Don't want to trouble you," she mumbled.

Cocoa greeted them and went to his food box and started thumping.

Carly grabbed the back of a chair to steady herself. "Cocoa won't settle down until I feed him. I'm late, and he's hungry."

Adam helped her out of her coat, replying. "Just sit down and tell me where the food is. I'll take care of him."

Unable to argue, Carly slumped into the nearest chair. She'd never make it outside to get to Cocoa's hay, and she was too sick to give Adam those instructions. "Just fill his dish with pellets. There's a bag in the laundry room." She listened to the scuffling and drifted off again, awakening to Adam stroking her forehead.

"Can you take this pill?"

She blinked and stared at the bottle in his hand. "You already went to the pharmacy?"

"Jah. And Cocoa seems nervous."

"Jah, prey animals sense when others are anxious or things aren't right." She glanced at the floor to see the rabbit next to her and smiled.

"You need to take this."

She nodded, accepting the pill and water he offered. "Thanks. I can't believe I'm suddenly so weak."

"I'm taking you to your room." She pushed up with her arms to stand and flinched at the pain. "Like this." Suddenly he swept her into his arms.

She gave a small gasp but didn't argue because she needed his help. She would be immensely enjoying this if she wasn't so sick.

"Sweet Carly," he whispered near her ear. "Always helping others. Never taking care of yourself."

"That's not true," she smiled, savoring his closeness.

Feeling protective, Adam lowered Carly on top of a yellow quilt, turned on the light and looked around the room.

"You shouldn't be in here."

She'd read his mind. For he was thinking about stretching out next to her and cradling her. "Probably not. But you know you're safe with me."

"Am I?"

He sank onto the bed beside her and started untying her shoes. He placed them on the floor, and when he returned, she'd removed her covering. Using restraint, he pulled back the covers for her and helped her get settled.

"Cocoa," she mumbled.

He lifted the distraught rabbit to the foot of her bed. It grunted and hopped up to check out Carly's face. After licking her, it hopped back to the foot of the bed and began nesting. Knowing he'd never get this image out of his head and relieved she hadn't loosened her hair, he quickly stood. "I'll fetch you a glass of water." When he returned, she stirred.

"Thanks."

"I'm going to lock your door and take your key. I'll give it to your aunt when I stop by to tell her you're sick. So don't be alarmed if she lets herself in during the night."

"Late," Carly sighed. "Better go."

He hesitated. Then leaned down and kissed her brow. "Get better, sweetheart."

Carly drifted in and out of sleep, trembling and unable to find warmth even beneath the pile of covers Auntie had piled atop her yellow quilt. Wild dreams of anything but sugarplums danced through her head, one reoccurring. There was a chasm, and Sweet Life was perched on a cliff on the other side. It was too far for her to leap across, and she knew the only way to reach the other side was to fly. A myriad of winged sinister beings and beautiful beings offered their assistance to fly her across the gorge. She knew she needed to choose wisely, and she struggled with this decision throughout the night chills and sweats. The residents needed her, and at times they cheered her on, but she knew she was failing them. Until one of the winged beings took on Adam's image. She ran to him. "Are you sure we can fly?"

"Trust me."

But always she awoke before flying across the gorge.

At last she awakened to the touch of a cold wet cloth on her brow. Slowly, she opened her eyes. "Auntie."

"Here, drink this."

The cool water felt good against her cracked lips. "You came."

"Of course. When Adam told me how sick you were, I came right away. But you had a rough night of it."

She pushed damp hair away from her face. "What time is it?"

"About nine o'clock."

"I'm late for work."

Auntie chuckled. "I called Sherie. Don't think I'm letting you go to work. Not after all that mumbling about the Death Angel."

Bits of her jumbled dreams came to mind. "Thanks. I kept having this weird dream." She shared the bits she could remember.

"How dreadful. I'm thankful it was just a dream. You had me worried. Let's look at your arms."

As she stretched them out for Auntie's examination, she was amazed how weak she felt.

"They don't look good."

Carly understood the reason for her frightening dream. "Did Adam tell you Dot was missing?"

"Jah. That she was just under her bed."

"She told me she was hiding from the Death Angel. That his eyes were evil."

"Of all things!" Auntie exclaimed.

"I don't know how to help her."

"You must remember that we all choose the paths for our lives. Dot's had a lifetime to deal with her fears. Everything intensifies in old age. Now it has her in bondage. That's why a person needs to grow in the Lord along the way."

"But you can't blame Dot. It's her dementia."

"I'm sure it plays a big part in Dot's problems. I'm just saying you can't fix everything."

"She has always depended upon Crusher. Now she lives alone."

"The Lord was good to allow Crusher to be there for her."

Carly nodded and took the pill that Auntie offered.

"That rabbit's been a mess. Thumping. Nudging and nipping me. Tell me what it needs."

Carly laughed. "Cocoa's worried about me, and he missed his hay last night. But he should be satisfied with pellets."

"Well it isn't, because I tried that."

After explaining that the hay was in a box between her bike and the woodpile, she snuggled against a fresh pillowcase, feeling drowsy.

The next time she opened her eyes, she was alone. But she could hear the clattering of pots and pans, grateful Auntie was making herself at home. She slowly sat up and moved to the side of her bed. In the kitchen, Auntie was bent over the stove.

"That smells good."

"You want to lay on the couch?"

Carly nodded, and Auntie rushed to get her a pillow and covers. "Your neighbor lady saw me outside this morning and wondered if you were all right. So I told her you were sick. We got to talking, and she ended up bringing me this chicken to make soup."

"She keeps an eye out for me. Waters for me sometimes and tells me when I forget to put on my covering. That kind of stuff."

Auntie gave her a horrified expression which quickly turned into a grin.

"Sorry if the cupboards are kinda bare. I only get what fits in my bike basket. But it's enough for me."

"Not that bare. I found the noodles!" Auntie smiled. "You've got it nice here. Except for that pesky rabbit."

Later, after having some of the soothing chicken noodle soup, Carly told Auntie how Sherie wanted her to make cold calls using a script. Auntie slapped the counter with a dish towel and mumbled under her breath. Then she joined Carly at the table.

"Do you want to be involved with the volunteers?"

"Jah."

"If you do as she asks, maybe she'll give you the responsibility you want."

"I suppose. I've tried to forgive, but it's hard."

"Always is. But I've never known you to hold a grudge before. It's not like you."

"I've never wanted anything so badly before."

Auntie laughed. "You have. The difference is, you usually get your way."

Shocked, Carly asked, "You think I'm spoiled?"

"Jah. We both are."

"I'm selfish, too. Have you been working on your quilt patterns?"

"Of course. I'm not letting one measly editor quash my dream."

"Then I'm not letting one measly director quash mine."

CHAPTER FIFTEEN

On Sunday, Carly stayed home from church to recuperate, determined to return to work on Monday. Though she'd rather tend her garden, her weakness kept her inside. She dug out the cozy mystery novel Miranda had loaned her. She'd started it one evening when she couldn't sleep but had put it aside because she wasn't sure if solving a murder was appropriate reading for a nonresistant believer. But boredom had driven her to get it out again. Now she was into the story and had to find out who had killed Lady Elizabeth and stuffed her in the maid's trunk.

Cocoa suddenly stilled, alert and listening. When the doorbell rang, he leapt off the couch and hopped under the table, one of his favorite hiding places. Setting aside the novel, Carly went to the door.

"Adam!"

He wore an irresistible but sheepish grin. "You're looking better."

"Come in." She felt suddenly self-conscience with the memory of him carrying her to her room and tucking her in bed.Kissing her forehead. Had she dreamed he'd called her sweetheart? She quickly turned so he couldn't read her expression.

He went to the couch, and she took the chair. "I'm much better. Thanks for everything the other night."

"I've been worried about you."

She shrugged. "No need. Auntie filled me with pills and chicken soup."

"Your arms?"

Her face heated. "Better."

"I talked to your aunt in church." He appeared restless.

"Did I miss anything good?"

"Just a sermon on forgiveness."

Carly sighed. "I should've been there."

"Jah. It was one I needed for sure." He seemed introspective, then turned his dark gaze on her and spoke with tenderness. "Just wanted to see you, I guess." Her breath caught as they looked into each other's eyes and read the yearning. Then he shifted his gaze across the room. "You have a nice place here."

"I'm lucky the owner let me fix it up."

"My sisters try to fix up my old house. They take turns cleaning it."

"I'm sure they spoil you. Must be nice."

Grinning widely, he said, "It is. I like to be spoiled."

She wondered how a wife would ever compete with that or if she would even want to, then she quickly cast the thought away. Cocoa had hopped over and now sniffed his shoes. Adam gently lifted him to the couch beside him.

"He doesn't usually like people to lift him."

"We made friends the other night."

"You have any pets?"

"Nope. I like animals, I'm just not home enough to care for them."

"Rabbits are easy. They have some sort of hierarchy. Cocoa thinks he's higher than me. I'm his slave, and he gets impatient when I don't respond quickly."

"I noticed. You spoil the rabbit like you do the residents."

"I suppose." She'd probably spoil Adam, too. Her cheeks burned as she tried to shake off the thought.

He picked up the mystery novel with a sinister-looking baron on the cover and grinned accusingly. "What's this?"

"Miranda loaned it to me. Said I had to read it because the hero was such a hottie."

He chuckled. "That sounds like her." He studied the cover. "So she likes them dark and handsome?"

A pang of jealousy sharpened her tone. "I guess."

"And you?"

"Jah. And mysterious," she added.

"Guess that leaves me out. You read me like a dog-eared prayer book."

"Hardly." But she could solve one mystery right away. "Miranda asked me if you were off limits."

"So? Am I?"

"You weren't when she asked," she replied softly, embarrassed by the hope that strained her voice.

"You don't need to worry about her. Anyway, right now I'm too busy to think about anything but work. That's one reason I stopped by. Simon's postponing the woodworking classes until after Christmas."

Her heart sank to think she wouldn't be seeing him around the center, but it sang joyfully to hear him downplay Miranda. "At least you have Sundays off. Don't most tree farms stay open on weekends?"

"Jah, but we make up the sales by our good name."

"Everybody knows Mennonites are hard workers." Amusingly, she referred to an old Mennonite saying.

"Jah, but I meant the Lapp name. Our farm's been around for several generations. Our customers know we don't sell diseased trees that prematurely shed needles. Like some farmers."

"What do you do with the bad ones?"

"We don't tag them and later toss them on a burn pile."

"You roast hotdogs and have a party?"

"No, but that sounds fun." He studied her carefully. "Dad offered me a partnership in the business. Said after Christmas, he's even changing the sign out front."

"Adam! That's wonderful."

"I know. If only he wasn't using it to control. . .some other things."

"Oh," she said with sympathy. "You'll work it out."

His expression softened. "So if you need anything, there's still Sundays."

"I'm stuck regarding Martha's old boyfriend. Did you talk to your cousin?"

"Jah. But he didn't come up with any leads for us."

Carly voiced a concern that had been troubling her. "How can somebody forget a boyfriend's last name? Especially when she only had two boyfriends. James and John."

"That you know of. Maybe she intentionally blocked him out after she married John."

"Maybe. I guess we're at a dead end. Now Dot has me worried, too." She didn't want to tell him about her own feverish nightmare.

"Maybe the volunteer program will help."

She nodded and grew reflective.

After a moment, Adam stood. "I should go."

She followed him to the door where he gave her hand a gentle squeeze. "Just keep being you, and everything will work out fine."

"Thanks."

"Remember to call if you need me." He teased, "I can always send one of my sisters."

She stood at the door and waved as he backed out of the drive.

Afterward, she found it hard to get back into her novel. Instead she rehashed their conversation. When she came to the part about the volunteers, she realized God was making it clear by verifying His will three times. First Auntie encouraged her to get involved in the program, then the sermon was on forgiveness. Now Adam brought up the volunteer program. Frustrated, Carly knew what she had to do.

The black dog bared his teeth but, instead of picking up momentum, seemed to be falling back. A thunder clap rent the air just as Carly sent the stick flying. It leapt and caught it midair, but when it landed, its hind legs collapsed and it sank to the ground panting. Skidding her bike to a stop, Carly stared at the dog. It wasn't attempting to rise. Another thunder clap cracked. But the dog didn't move. Oh, no. She saw something new in its eyes. Fear? Pain? Lowering her kickstand, she ventured a few steps closer. "Nice dog. Good doggie." She needed to get it back on its feet.

He lay growling, but more of a warning growl than a vicious one. "This exercise is getting too strenuous for an old pup like you." She went back to her bike and got her sandwich. Then she slowly advanced. It gave another warning growl, then sniffed the air. She stopped and lay it on the ground, hurrying back to her bike. She rode several yards then stopped to watch. It dropped the stick, wobbled to its feet and inhaled the meat in one swallow. Then it retrieved its stick, gave her a triumphant look and limped slowly back to its porch.

"You did good," she called, then muttered, "Poor thing. At least it's back to its porch with the storm coming." Gazing at the black sky, she peddled harder and wondered if in the future she should poke the stick through some meat before she tossed it. But this fragile relationship had started with her tossing him her lunch. She'd be foolish to get back in that routine. Poor old dog. Still, it looked well fed even if she'd never seen any interaction between the dog and its master.

As she reached the center, it began to rain, and she walked her bike under a covered sidewalk past the maintenance room, stopping to chat with Rocco.

He grinned. "I brought two rain jackets today. One for me and one for you. I see you came unprepared."

He was right. Her wool coat wasn't waterproof. "Thanks. You're a godsend."

He tossed an unopened bag containing the raincoat into her bike basket. "I know how to take care of my girls."

"How's your wife and your daughter?"

"Very good. My Trish, she loves school this year. And Dana is happy with her housecleaning jobs. She cooks me a fine meal every night, and I'm happy." Then his face turned stern. "Except not so much today. The laundry room's leaking again. Something always leaks around here when it rains. I'll be busy."

"But not wet," she joked. "That's good to hear about your family. But this rain will probably affect the residents' moods. I'd better go."

"Make it a good day," he called.

"You, too, Rocco."

Placing her bike on the rack, she grabbed her lunch and rain jacket, punched the code in the double glass doors, and hurried inside.

Besides the usual "Hello! Hello!" a gravelly voice greeted her. "Wondered if you'd get caught in the rain."

"Oh! You scared me. How's Magnificent this morning?"

"She's sad it's raining. I came to cheer her." Dot whispered, "She's jealous since I got Birdie, so I visit her as much as I remember." She looked contrite. "Sometimes I forget. What are you carrying?" Dot trailed after Carly as she took her supplies to the staff room. She placed her apple in the refrigerator and hung up her coat. "You missed it. We had gravy and biscuits this morning for breakfast."

Knowing they hadn't had breakfast yet, Carly smiled. "Bet that was yummy."

Dot got a faraway look. "Yes, Crusher's favorite. Where'd he go anyway? You seen him?" Holding up the packaged bag, Carly tried to divert her attention. "Rocco gave me this rain jacket. Wasn't that thoughtful? Did you know I ride my bike to work? You'd like it. It's pink with a wicker basket."

Dot tried to assimilate all this new data. "I missed you."

Carly loved the moments when Dot spoke with clarity. "I was sick."

"I know. Martha and I prayed for you."

Her eyes stung. "You did? I guess God answered, because here I am."

Thunder shook the building, and Carly noticed the wary glances of those gathering for breakfast. Dot moved to the glass patio door and peered at the downpour. She started to sing in an eerie voice: "Water in the gutter. Water in the street. Water, water, water, wetting people's feet."

Carly sighed. It was better than "Baa Baa Black Sheep," but she wished Dot sang Christian refrains instead and wondered why she didn't.

She approached Sherie at the receptionist's desk with a smile. "Good morning. Looks like everything's back to normal."

"Now that you're here. How's your arm?"

Involuntarily crossing her arms to touch them, she replied, "Oh fine. Healing nicely now."

"Probably wasn't smart to get all wet. Everybody worries about you. Some of the residents prayed for you at mealtime."

She rubbed her wet sleeves and fought back her emotions. "I heard. That's special." She hesitated briefly, then said, "I'm ready to make those calls for Every Little Bit Helps."

Sherie's eyes lit with enthusiasm. "That's awesome." She reached into a cubby and pulled out a list of names and numbers along with the script. "And here's a list of duties and responsibilities. Would you mind looking it over? I started with your ideas and added some things."

"Sure." She glanced at the blackboard of events. "So today's table games?" They usually played checkers and dominoes. Same old thing. "I can't wait until we get those volunteers and get some fun events planned."

"Me, too. Thanks for helping, Carly."

"Jah. You're welcome. I owe you an apology."

"No, you don't. I get it."

Carly nodded with relief, feeling good inside and wishing it hadn't taken so long to push aside her resentment.

Miranda came down the hall, breathless. She whispered, "Mr. Gadget fell. He's back in his wheelchair, and I think he's fine."

Sherie replied, "I'll call the nurse. After she checks him out, I'll call the family. Meanwhile, Miranda, you can finish your rounds. And Carly, you can help the breakfast staff."

Several thunderclaps drowned out further instructions. Placing the volunteer paperwork in her cubby and starting toward the kitchen, Carly knew it was going to be a long day. Behind her she heard Dot's soft refrain: "Water in the gutter, water in the street. Water, water, water wetting people's feet. See how it pours. I'm glad we're indoors."

After breakfast Carly took the newspaper to Martha's room and found her sitting in her flowered recliner, reaching for her inhaler. High humidity always worsened her asthma. Normally all medications were locked in the residents' drawers, but when Martha's family admitted her, they made it clear that while the caregivers could monitor the preventative inhaler, Martha would administer her own emergency inhaler until either they or the staff thought she was unable to use it correctly. A special disclaimer clause had been written into her contract.

She went to the side table, which held an old-fashioned lamp, a tiny devotional book, a Bible, a political magazine, a tissue box, and a nebulizer.

"How about a breathing treatment instead?"

"Good." Martha nodded.

Carly prepared the nebulizer and handed Martha the mask. Then she sat down beside her and started to read from the *New Era*. " 'The annual geranium giveaway was a success. Every year geraniums from the city's median strip are pulled, and the geraniums are given to people who would like them from 1:00 to 3:00 p.m. while supplies last. All the geraniums were given away.' "

Martha pulled her breathing mask aside, "I did that once. They didn't last long."

Continuing, Carly read: "Pumpkin Festival—"

Martha waved her hand, to skip to something else. Then Carly got a sudden hunch. "Summer steelhead return from March through October with peaks of the run occurring during late spring and early February. There are tales of smallmouth bass lurking in the lower Calapooia, and largemouth can be found in ponds throughout the west end of the county." She lay the paper on her lap and got up to turn off Martha's sputtering nebulizer. "You like fishing?"

"Jah. John and I used to go below the dam at Foster Lake. He'd take the boys off the Pleasant Valley Bridge. Wonder if any of the boys will come home for my birthday."

Trying to redirect the conversation, Carly asked, "Did your dad ever take you?"

"No," Martha made a face. "I had too many brothers. Us girls had to stay home with Mom."

"You lived close to the river, didn't you?"

"Well, Jah." Then her eyes lit with amusement. "James Irish tried to teach me to bait a hook. But I wasn't having any part of that. But he did teach me how to fish."

Widow Martha tightened her lips, realizing she'd made a mistake. She hoped nothing came of it. She'd never ever told anybody his surname for fright her parents would find out. And hadn't she done a good job to suppress his memory all the time she'd been married to John? She'd been faithful. So why had it popped out now? Was she losing her mind? *"It's not our fault,"* James had reasoned. *"Fate dealt us a bad hand. If you were older, we'd elope."*

How her heart had soared at his declaration. Only she was too young. "And your folks want you to go into the military."

"We can write," he suggested hopefully.

She remembered her struggle. The pain of letting him go. "Look me up when you get home," she'd said. "If God wants us together, He'll make a way."

"I hope there really is a God," he'd replied.

It had been the clincher that had allowed her to release him.

She wondered if he'd ever found Jesus. Though she often struggled with her sins, she loved the Lord.

Carly's heart pounded. "Was he the boy you liked that one summer?"

Martha's eyes darkened. "We were just friends. So what about you?"

"I like fishing."

"I mean when are you going to get a man?"

Carly sputtered, "Excuse me?"

"You heard me. Men are like stockings, you know. You can't pick up the cheap ones. You have to get the ones that are worthwhile. Like my John. He was an interesting man. Never could outsmart him." Her eyes went to the bookcase across the room, filled with books from all sorts of genres. "We made a good match. Had a good life."

Carly saw she was steering the conversation away from her summer fling. "When are you going to quit with the stockings?"

"Just wanna make sure you learned your lesson. Why don't you date that Lapp fellow from the woodworking class? He's made of quality stuff. Like my John."

"Adam won't be teaching the class until after Christmas. His family owns and operates a Christmas tree farm. Anyway, that's getting a little personal, don't you think?"

"I thought we were friends."

Carly touched Martha's arm. "We are. It's just a touchy topic for me. Dating doesn't seem to agree with me."

"Baloney! The ones who can't handle you aren't worth fretting over.

But that Lapp fellow's different. I can tell."

"You're right about him. But we're friends. Just like you and James Irish were friends."

Martha's face broke into a smile. "I knew it! You like—" Seeing her mistake, she clamped her hands over her mouth. When she pulled them away, she said, "It was a long time ago, and I shouldn't have brought it up because it dishonors John."

Her elderly friend must have loved both men deeply. "I don't mean to be trite or dishonoring. You were a good wife. But now that John's gone, it's all right to think about those childhood memories. People remarry all the time."

"Who are you to talk when you don't even love one man?"

The harsh statement cut her, but she didn't dwell on it. "Of course, you're right." She began to tidy Martha's side table. "Your breathing seems improved, but since it's raining today, we'll give treatments every four hours." Then she remembered what she'd wanted to talk to Martha about in the first place. "Can we talk about Dot?"

Martha nodded. "I worry about her when she's not driving me nuts with those nursery rhymes. It's worse when she's troubled."

Carly suddenly realized that the nursery rhymes could be causing Martha's angry outbursts. "You think reading scripture to her would help?"

"Crusher reads to her every morning when he brings her orange juice at ten o'clock."

"Do you know if it helps?"

"Helps the canary. Dot claims the bird likes it when Crusher reads."

"So it makes Dot happier?"

"Well, jah. I guess I could read to her."

"Why don't you read something from Psalms, verses about overcoming fear?"

"Sure. I can find something like that."

"In fact, if you read the same verse every day, she might be able to remember it." Carly handed Martha the paper. "Thanks, I need to go now."

But Martha shoved the paper back. "I'm done with that. I'll find her a verse now." She took the Bible from her side table and began leafing through it.

Feeling much better, Carly moved down the hall and paused a moment to watch Klepto in her room working on one of the new puzzles Sherie had purchased for her. Carly envisioned Martha accepting a handwritten journal telling her that James Irish made it out of the war alive. She had to make it happen.

Chapter Sixteen

Saturday dawned crisp and clear. After the rain, it had stayed above freezing. Carly was eager to head back to the Crawfordsville Bridge area. Even though the sky was clear, this time she threw her new rain jacket into her wicker basket along with a notebook and pen, her lunch, and her freshly charged phone. Her first stop was the couple who lived at Martha's old home-place. But they'd never heard of James Irish and didn't recognize the surname.

After that, she went to the bridge, using it for a starting point, and rode away from Crawfordsville. She hadn't gone far when she saw an elderly man in jeans and a striped polo shirt walking to his mailbox. She hit the brakes and came to a clean stop.

"You handle that bike like a pro."

"That's because it's my mode of transportation."

"You don't have a horse and buggy?" he asked.

"Oh, I'm not Amish. I'm Conservative Mennonite."

"Is that a fact? Well can't say as I know one from the other."

She fixed her kickstand and offered her hand. "My name's Carly Blosser. I'm on a scouting mission."

"George Street. Nice to meet ya. What kind of mission? Something for your church?"

"No. I work at Sweet Life Retirement Center, and I'm trying to locate one of the resident's old friends. . .for her birthday."

"That's a nice thing you're doing. Let me stick these letters in the mailbox and take you to the house to meet my wife, Rosie."

Carly waited, then walked with him to the back door. "Rosie!" he called. "I'm bringing somebody inside."

The cutest woman met them in the screened porch. Her eyes widened when she saw Carly, her eyes roving, taking in her plain clothing and covering. Carly knew she probably wasn't a good representation, that most likely her hair was messy. But she introduced herself and repeated what she'd told George.

"You drink coffee?"

"Jah. Thanks." Once she was served, she explained, "I was hoping to find somebody who's lived in the area long enough to remember the Irish family."

"You stopped at the right house. My family's lived here since the house was built."

Thank You, Lord, Carly prayed. "The man's name was James Irish."

"Nope, doesn't ring a bell."

"He used to go fishing on the Crawfordsville Covered Bridge."

George chuckled. "People come from miles to fish there."

Carly suddenly wondered if James had ridden his bike or driven. Surely Martha would've mentioned a car.

"I'll make some phone calls if you like," the woman offered.

"Save you from riding all over creation," George added.

"I'd appreciate it. Let me give you my phone number." Carly rattled off the numbers and finished her coffee.

"We've got some friends over at Sweet Life," George said. "In independent living. I don't mean any disrespect, but I was surprised the bathroom isn't even set up for a wheelchair."

Embarrassed, Carly said, "They're remodeling each house as residents—she searched for the right word, not wanting to alarm the elderly couple—"leave."

"Thankfully our family lives close. We should be able to finish our days here in the home we love."

"That's wonderful." Carly rose. "Thanks so much for helping me."

"It's been a pleasure," Rosie replied.

They both saw her to the door and waved until she was headed down the road.

After that, she spoke to three more people who happened to be outside. Nobody had ever heard of the Irish family. Discouraged, she ate her lunch at the bridge. She sat at the picnic table, remembering that stormy day when Adam had rescued her. He'd asked her if she wanted to risk a relationship, and she'd refused. They'd put on the brakes that day. Adam wasn't his flirty self any longer, but more cautious.

Yet he was the closest friend she had. Had they made the right choice? In weak moments, she hoped he'd work out his problems and make the offer again.

She thrust her chin in the air. She'd make do with whatever the Lord's will was in the matter. But one thing was clear. She was going to need Dale's computer expertise because she'd run into a block wall regarding James Irish.

On Sunday after church, everyone rallied around Carly, asking about her recent illness and giving her their good wishes. While she enjoyed the attention, her eyes kept roving, searching for Adam. Finally, she saw him cross the churchyard and head toward the parking lot.

"Adam!"

He turned. His eyes lit with pleasure, and he waited for her to catch up. "Miss me already, huh?"

"Of course I do. Sweet Life needs you."

He arched an eyebrow at her.

"I have his name."

"Martha's old fling?"

"Jah. It's James Irish. Ever hear the name?"

"Nope."

"I canvassed the neighborhood yesterday and found an old couple whose family lived in the area a long time." His eyes lit with hopeful interest. "They never heard of the Irish family, but she's going to make some calls for me."

"That's great!" He touched her arm. His touch lingered there, then dropped to her waist. "Would you like a ride home?"

Tempted, she glanced around the churchyard. Ann was talking to her sisters but shooting a nervous blue gaze at Adam's dad. Then she saw Roman watching them. Her heart nearly stopped at the blatant disapproval on his face. Even when their gazes met, his remained stony. She knew he was part of Adam's problem and was glad Adam's back was turned toward Roman. "No thanks. Not today."

Adam finally withdrew his touch, leaving a burning spot at her waist. He waited, evidently sensing she wasn't finished.

"I could use your help."

"You know I'm here for you."

"Could you call Dale again and see if he can find anything?"

He hesitated.

"What's wrong?"

"Nothing." Adam shook his head. "I'll do it."

"Okay, thanks. Have a good week."

"You, too."

As she rode home, she wondered what she'd said or done that had made him hesitate and grow introspective. Maybe he knew they were being watched and was in a hurry to get rid of her. But then why had he held his hand so long on her waist?

Adam pulled into the home-place, wishing he hadn't accepted his mom's invitation to Sunday dinner. But he went through the back door which led to the kitchen and wrapped his mom in a hug. "Smells awesome."

"Just a roast," she replied. Sissie Lapp was humble but proficient. No matter how his dad harped about female submission, Mom ran the household. Personally, he didn't see anything wrong with it. There was enough estrogen in the house that Dad probably didn't even know. He just stayed out of the way, handling the farm. Adam asked Ann about the children and listened to her contented prattle. Then taking a slice of cheese, he asked Charity about her newborn. She slapped his hand. "Don't ruin your appetite."

"Dad's in the living room," Mom said.

Having delayed going there as long as possible, he took the cue and left the women to their final preparations.

As soon as Adam sat in Mom's recliner, Dad lowered his newspaper.

"Smells good in there, but I couldn't get by with anything but one slice of cheese."

Roman chuckled. "I heard Sissie's screech."

A small herd of grandchildren raced through the room. Two lingered. Ann's blue-eyed Mary with brown ringlets dashed behind Roman's chair. "Hi, Papa."

Brown-eyed Jacob squatted behind Adam's recliner. "We're hiding. Don't tell."

"Act normal," Mary whispered. "Talk about trees."

Roman folded his hands behind his head. "Did you get the quotes on shipping yet?"

"Working on that," Adam replied, playing along as Beth's son Matthew tiptoed through the room, looking for his cousins.

"I said talk about trees. Act normal," Mary whispered.

"I hear you!" Matthew yelled, and all three children dashed out of the room.

Roman's arms lowered. He leaned forward. "From the spectacle you put on at church, I half expected you to bring that Blosser woman to dinner."

Adam rolled his gaze.

"She trying to lure you back to Simon's?"

Though Roman probed, Adam held the Rook card—the highest card in a game many Mennonite families enjoyed. "She asked me to call Dale."

Roman seemed stricken. "Why? Doesn't she know he's happily married?"

Grinning inwardly, Adam kept a straight face. "She knows we keep in touch, and she needs some information from his computer."

"Bah! Why doesn't she go to Simon?"

Adam shot Dad a look that said, *Really?*

"I suppose Dale's still after you?"

"Jah. He's determined."

"Just like his dad," Roman muttered angrily. Then he shook his head. "Watch out for them."

"Who?"

"Si and Dale. The Blosser woman, too. You've got your whole life ahead of you. Don't make any choices you'll regret."

That evening, Adam hauled some wood inside and made a fire in his fireplace. He rested his legs on his footstool and adjusted the throw pillow his sister Ann had given him. Looking around the room, he wondered what Carly would think of his place. How would she transform it? With enticing smells from the kitchen, a rabbit snoring at his feet, and a wife snuggled content at his side? Or would she drag him into countless schemes? If Dad was right, he was doomed. He couldn't get her out of his mind.

He scowled at his phone. The last time he'd talked to Dale, his cousin had reported the house next to his had gone up for sale. That Adam could get it for a good price. It needed fixing, but he'd help. He'd been right when he'd told Dad that Dale was determined. Like every other male Lapp. Like Dad. After Christmas, he'd surely put up a fight about Adam returning to Sweet Life's woodworking shop. If they kept going toe-to-toe, there'd eventually be an explosion. He didn't want to see their relationship end up like Si and Dale's.

Punching in Dale's number, he soon had him on the line. After some small talk, he asked, "Remember that name I wanted you to investigate? Well now I have the last name."

"Great. That'll help."

"It's Irish."

"Never heard the name. But I'll see what I can find."

"Thanks."

"Uh. . .somethin' going on between you and Carly?"

Adam had been waiting for this. "We're friends. Would it offend you if I took it further?"

"Only because we both know how dead set she is about Indiana. She's trouble, you know. Anyway, I've been talking to Jenny, and we'll match your dad's offer. Make you a full partner."

"I'm not holding out to pressure you," Adam said. "Things have been going better with Dad. Except he doesn't like Carly. If I date her, he's likely to toss me out." The other end of the line went quiet. No doubt Dale was remembering how Si had done that to him. Remembering his relationship with Carly. "Sorry. That was inconsiderate."

"That's all right."

"Why don't you guys come out for Christmas? It's the one time Dad and Si pretend to like each other. You can stay at my place."

"Thanks for the offer, but Jenny likes to be with her family. They actually like each other, you know."

"Think about it. I miss you."

"You know how to remedy that. How about you come here after Christmas?" The line grew quiet again. "I'll even buy your ticket."

"I'll think about it. Thanks for doing me this favor."

"Sure. I'll let you know what I kick up."

"All right. Take care." Adam set the phone on his side table and sank into the sofa, allowing his imagination to travel to Indiana. As kids, they got along fine. But would Dale be just as manipulative as Dad? He wondered what the house was like that needed work and imagined the two of them fixing it up. Jenny would probably keep his refrigerator stocked. Dale claimed he'd gained weight because she was such a good cook.

Then his thoughts returned to the day he'd just spent with his family. His sisters adored him, and after Dad's digs, he'd been fairly agreeable. They made a great team at work. And besides that, Carly needed him. He just needed to be firm with Dad and take his time with Carly. He needed some time to wear Dad down, and then he'd set after Carly. She'd probably play hard to get. It would be fun. He fell asleep on the couch with a smile on his face.

Carly curled up on her green-striped sofa and made Sherie's calls. She rewarded herself with hot chocolate, cookies, and play-breaks with Cocoa. Often she had to leave Sherie's scripted message: "This is Carly Blosser, and I'm a caregiver at Sweet Life Assisted Living. We're starting a volunteer program called Little Steps"—she always cringed at this point because they'd changed the title from Every Little Bit Helps—"and it's based on the belief that everybody can do one little thing to stamp out loneliness. We're looking for people who can sing, read, write letters, do clerical work, hand massage, take photos, exercise, be a phone companion or a staff assistant. The list is even longer. If you are interested, please call Sherie at. . ."

Carly was surprised to watch the calls roll in on Monday. Sherie recruited a volunteer named Becca to answer phones and assist with the program's organization details.

"Carly, you did such a great job with that phone list."

"I didn't recognize any of the names. Where did you get them?"

"They were hand-picked people who are involved in the community. Their connections will help spread the word in circles that might generate funds for improvements." For the first time, Carly believed Simon had done the right thing to put Sherie in charge because she had a wider worldview. "But I've been thinking we need more Mennonite volunteers to stay in line with the founding ideals. And your people are such hard workers. Dependable. You did such a wonderful job with the calls. Are you ready now to put one of your own ideas to work?"

"Jah. I'm ready."

"How about passing out fliers to your church people."

Biting back a smile as Sherie set her church apart as a peculiar people, she replied. "Jah. I'd love to do that for you."

"Great. I'll put them in your cubby by the end of the day." Sherie pushed up her glasses and gave a dismissive wave. "That's all."

Carly clocked out and fetched the library cart. A small group, including Martha, Klepto, and Repeater, gathered in the lobby to get first choice of books. After she took down recommendations, she punched in the code and the double glass doors opened. The library was in a separate building. Inside she took the elevator, wondering if the entire retirement center would implement her volunteer program if it was successful in assisted living. She'd ask Jimmy and Auntie to help with the fliers. Adam, too.

Chapter Seventeen

Carly took Adam's hand, but the wind caught some fliers, causing her to stumble out of the back of Jimmy's four-door truck cab.

"Clumsy," she muttered, dusting off her skirt and checking her covering.

"You okay?"

"Jah. I'm fine. Just my pride." She lifted her skirt a bit. At least she hadn't ruined her stockings. And it had been amusing to see the struggle on Adam's face as he chose to help her instead of chasing the fliers.

Jimmy returned to them panting, "Carly!"

She quickly dropped her skirt, her gaze catching Adam's. He shrugged, but his grin said it all. Jimmy handed her the captured fliers, and she divvied them out evenly. Jimmy suggested he and Adam take one side of the country road and she and Auntie the other. They'd use rubber bands to affix the fliers to the outside of the mailboxes. And after they'd canvassed an area, one of the men would run back for the truck.

But when an aggressive dog gave the women trouble, Jimmy motioned them over, eyeing Adam speculatively. "We should split up, for safety's sake." But when Aunt Fannie strode to Jimmy's side, his expression hardened, sending a definite warning to Adam.

"Hey. We're all in plain sight here," Carly joked, trying to ease the tension. But nobody laughed. "I should've grabbed a couple sticks out of the bed of your truck." That brought smiles.

With a shrug, Adam said, "Let's go." Then as if to taunt Jimmy, he leaned close and whispered, "I'm looking forward to that soup you've been bragging about. There's a lot resting on that pot of soup, you know."

"Oh, really." She laughed. "You should've warned me before I added the mushrooms."

"Gross."

She glanced across the street at her brother, but he wasn't watching them. "With the look Jimmy gave you, I'm not so sure it matters. I guess you weren't joking when you said he warned you away from me."

"Nope."

"Actually your dad was shooting daggers at me last week at church when I asked if you'd contact Dale." She shook her head. "At our age, you'd think we could do as we pleased."

"You'd think." But Adam's pleasant demeanor had vanished. "Maybe you misinterpreted Dad. He was probably thinking about Uncle Si or something."

"I don't think so, but it's nice of you to protect me. Is he the part of life you still have to work out?"

"Jah. But it's different than what you're thinking."

"No, I understand." She knew dads warned their sons away from her because of the rumors, but it still hurt. Before he could say something to take away the sting, they were interrupted by a couple of children riding bikes up and down a gravel lane. Carly recognized them from church as the Zook children.

"What you doin'?" Michelle, a girl about twelve inquired.

"Delivering fliers about the need for volunteers at Sweet Life Assisted Living."

"That's the old people?" her younger brother asked.

"Yes. They're lonely and need people to help them." She handed the flier to Michelle. "Will you give this to your mother?"

"Sure." She read it out loud, " 'Everybody can do one little thing to stamp out loneliness.' I suppose I could read to them. I love reading."

The sweet idea brought a smile to Carly's lips. "They'd love it. But your mom would have to agree."

She dumped her bike and started running. "I'll go ask her."

"Wait! Michelle!" The girl came back, panting. "Can I see the flier a second? See there? Have your mom call that number if she'll allow you to read. She'll need time to think it over. Probably have to ask your dad, too."

The girl nodded with disappointment. "Probably."

And she'd need to clear the idea of children volunteers with Sherie. Carly's mind raced. They would need to be chaperoned. The idea rooted itself and inspired her. Entire Sunday school classes of children could visit. Unless they brought too many germs into the facility.

It was a pleasant afternoon for Adam even though Carly turned introspective after her conversation with Michelle Zook. The pleasant aroma inside her cottage was gladly received since he hadn't been sure she could cook. It had even crossed his mind that Ann might have to teach her. He knew Carly could do anything she tried.

Her aunt Fannie stooped to pet Cocoa. "I suppose I'd better go feed this spoiled rabbit."

Jimmy followed Carly into the kitchen. "I'll set the table."

Adam grinned, following his friend. "I'll watch. I've no idea how to set a table."

Sneering, Jimmy asked, "You eat on paper plates?"

"Whenever I can," Adam admitted, his gaze stealing to where Carly worked over the stove. She bent to put rolls in the oven, and he looked away. After that, the conversation turned to Jimmy's trip to the badlands. He had them enraptured until it was time to do the dishes and Aunt Fannie shooed them out of the kitchen.

"Wanna help me restock Carly's stick pile?" Jimmy asked.

Adam grabbed his coat and followed.

"This isn't working. I saw the way she looks at you. How you look at each other," Jimmy clarified. "Did you tell her about Nappanee?"

And he'd thought he'd reined himself in all day.

"So far there's nothing to tell."

"So that's a no." Jimmy threw some sticks on the pile. "I shouldn't have stayed away so long."

"It's not what you're thinking. I've been busy at the farm. I'm not even going to Sweet Life anymore."

"Either you get serious about Carly or you need to stay away."

"*She* invited *me* today."

"You could have said no."

"You're the one who told her she could come to me when she needed help."

"Because I trusted you."

"You still can. Besides, it's not like you've never hurt a girl before."

Jimmy's eyes darkened, and he softened his tone. "You're right. By the way, your sister Faith smiled at me in church today."

Adam bristled, wondering who this stranger was in his best friend's skin.

"Hello! Hello!" Magnificent called as Carly passed by the bird at Sweet Life's assisted-living lobby.

A cheerful face greeted her. "Hi, I'm Becca."

Carly introduced herself, happy to meet Sherie's new volunteer and loving the middle-aged woman's enthusiasm. "We're happy to have you here."

"Thanks. Sherie told me whenever I can't find her, you're next in line to answer any questions."

Carly's brow arched in surprise at the plumpish English woman with a flushed face and short curly hair. "Of course. I'm happy to help you get settled in."

"Just answering phones today and making some calls for Sherie." She picked up a file and fanned herself. "Don't mind me, just having a hot flash." Beads of sweat had popped up on the volunteer's forehead.

"Why don't you bring in a fan?"

"Oh, could I? That'd be great."

The assisted-living alarm went off, and Carly cut off the conversation, hurrying to Nines, who was pushing the double glass doors.

"Why won't it open?"

Carly gently removed the woman's hands, hoping the incident

wasn't going to frighten any of the residents. "What do you need?"

"I need to find my son. I need groceries."

"I heard he visited you yesterday." Since he lived out of state, the visit must have stirred up some confusion. "Did he bring the children?"

Uncertainty colored the woman's expression. "They were here yesterday?"

Carly nodded. "Jah."

"Then why didn't he take me grocery shopping?"

Nines was definitely having an off-kilter day to appear in the lobby in pajamas. "I have an idea. Let's go to your room and write down any items you need on your white board."

"What?"

"Come. I'll show you. Let's use your favorite purple pen."

"I do like purple. Reminds me of wine," she snickered.

About half of the residents weren't Mennonite. Nines was one of them. Carly steered the conversation away from wine, lest she have to listen to her drunken stories again. Giving up wine to enter the facility had been hard for the woman. "You haven't gotten dressed yet. Let's look in your closet for a purple top. Wouldn't that be fun?"

"Okay!" Nines picked up her speed, heading down the hall to her room.

But as they turned the corner, Sherie motioned to Carly. "We need to talk."

Nodding, Carly helped dress and settle Nines, then hurried to the staff room.

"You wanted to see me?"

"Please sit down."

Carly eased onto the chair by the fridge and waited until Sherie spun her chair around. "How did it go with the fliers?"

"Some friends and I canvassed the area along Halsey–Sweet Home and Old Holley Roads, where most of our people live."

"It's still early. I'm sure we'll get some calls."

"I think you will. We made some face-to-face contacts. In fact a twelve-year-old girl got me to thinking. She asked if she could read to the residents."

Sherie's eyes widened. "That's good. She'd need a chaperone, of course."

"That's what I thought. She'd need one to drive her here anyway. What if we organized an entire children's group? They could sing or mingle with the residents."

"What a great idea. Do you want to be in charge of organizing it?"

Feeling a stir of excitement, Carly replied, "I'd love to."

"Great. I'll keep you posted about any calls we get from the fliers."

"Thanks."

"That's all."

Carly stepped out of the room just in time to see Klepto sneaking by and examining something in her pocket. So much for the distraction of the new puzzles. She made a mental note to talk to Kelly's family about providing clothing without pockets. "Kelly, what do you have in your pocket?"

Klepto's expression fell. Knowing what came next, she turned her back to Carly and clamped her hand over her pocket. "Nothing."

Moving to face her, Carly said, "You're so good about helping everyone find their missing items. Someone's going to be excited to see what you've found."

But instead of relinquishing her treasure, she turned aside again and dipped her hand in her pocket and then to her mouth.

"Oh, no!" Carly cried, only getting a glimpse but pretty sure what was happening. To her advantage, Klepto seemed stunned when Repeater's teeth wouldn't fit into her mouth. Carly gently yet firmly clutched both of the woman's wrists and commanded. "You already have nice teeth. Now give those to me."

Klepto stared at Carly for a long moment before she tossed them at Carly. With a yelp, Carly dropped to the floor and caught them in her skirt. She bowed her head with relief as she heard Klepto clattering down the hall. Next she heard the woman's door slam.

Miranda brushed by, then spun back. "Carly? You okay?" Finally able to smile, she showed Miranda what was in her skirt.

"Ew. Yuck."

"I know."

"I'll get you a paper towel." When she returned, she asked. "Is your brother back in town yet?"

Rising, Carly replied, "You do realize Jimmy's Conservative Mennonite?"

"If he's anything like Adam, that's fine by me."

"You'd want to change to a plainer lifestyle?"

Miranda looked stunned. "I don't know. Does dating have to be so serious?"

"What do you think are the odds of dating somebody and falling in love?" Carly asked.

Shrugging, Miranda replied, "Maybe 10 percent?"

Now it was Carly's turn to appear shocked. "For me it's more like 90 percent."

"Well if I was dating Adam, it would be for me, too," Miranda teased. "Is Jimmy just as cute?"

Carly only had to think for a moment. "Jah. Girls like him. But he's not ready to settle down."

"Perfect. Neither am I. I'd love to see your yellow cottage, and I don't have anything to do this weekend. Why don't you hook us up?"

"We'll see. Right now I've got to sterilize these teeth and check on Klepto."

Chapter Eighteen

"How can I help?"

Carly couldn't verbalize the responses that sprang to mind. She was mentally kicking herself for giving in to Miranda's request. She met the other woman's dark, imploring eyes, seemingly guileless. Carly was appalled to discover her true feelings as they arose to the surface. She fought to school her reactions. "There's ice in the freezer. You can fill the glasses if you'd like."

"Sure."

Behind her, Carly heard the gentle *plunk, plunk* of Miranda at task. She drowned her out by fervently mashing the potatoes. Heat from the open oven door enveloped Carly as she brought out a savory roast. Preparing dinner was no big deal. She'd wanted to discuss Sherie's newest assignment with Auntie, anyway. And they usually got together when Jimmy was home. Might as well let Miranda see for herself that Jimmy wasn't her man.

After three quick raps, the door flew open, and the man in her thoughts bound into the room. "Smells great, Sis."

Cocoa hopped out from hiding when he heard Jimmy's voice, and Jimmy knelt to scratch him behind the ears. But his brow lifted with surprise when he saw Miranda. Before he could say anything, Aunt Fannie arrived and plopped a pumpkin pie on the counter.

Miranda giggled and introduced herself as Carly's friend from Sweet Life.

Jimmy wiped his hand on his pants and held it out for Miranda. She gave it a gentle squeeze, then jerked away. "Sorry. I was filling the glasses."

didn't mean to take over here."

"Nothing of the sort!" Auntie chided. "These are marvelous."

"I like this one," Jimmy said, pointing to a design where each square was topped with a ribbon and bow.

Carly tapped a Christmas tree design made from four triangles each tilted playfully.

"This one reminds me of Adam's tree farm."

Jimmy gave her a sharp glance.

Miranda tapped her watch. "I should get back to the house. I'm on for dinner duty tonight." She gave a contrite smile. "The house only has one car, and they dropped me off earlier. I need to call for a ride."

Scooting his chair, Jimmy jumped to his feet. "I'll take you home."

Carly frowned. For a guy used to fending off girls, he was slipping.

Miranda thanked him and then Carly before she told Aunt Fannie, "I'd be happy to help more." She shrugged. "If you like."

"Would you like to look at some material with me? I have to send samples along with my pattern."

"Sure." Miranda scribbled her phone number on one of the pattern pieces. "It was really fun. Thanks so much."

When Jimmy was at the door, Auntie called, "Don't forget to take that pie." Once they were gone, she turned to Carly. "I like that girl. She's a real surprise."

"She certainly is."

"Inspiring. In fact, I've even got an idea for you."

"Jah?"

"I understand Ann's good with the children at church. Why don't you ask her for ideas about incorporating the children."

Carly's eyes lit with excitement. "Of course. She loves children. Maybe she'd even head it up for me."

Later when Carly was alone, she absently stroked Cocoa. She needed to rethink her relationship with Miranda. How quickly the woman had wormed her way into her family's hearts. Why was her own so cold against Miranda? Her thoughts rambled through the afternoon's events. She hadn't even known Miranda was an artist. How easily she'd sketched her ideas. Carly's favorite was still the tree. A quilt like that would make a great gift for Adam. Someday.

She shook aside the thought. Giving Adam gifts was trouble. Then she remembered his sister Ann also helped out at the tree farm. Would she have enough time to help with the volunteer program? Thinking there was only one way to find out, she picked up her phone.

A large wrench held the door to Sweet Life's furnace room ajar. Carly hadn't heard anything was wrong and assumed it was Rocco doing routine maintenance work. She stuck her head inside to give a friendly greeting. It took her eyes a few minutes to adjust to the dimly lit room. The first thing she saw was a battered red toolbox, a familiar box that caused the hairs on the back of her neck to prickle. Her gaze shot to Mr. Gadget, who was slumped over in his wheelchair in front of the heating unit. Her worst fear came true. "Sonny!"

Mr. Gadget flinched, and a screwdriver clunked to the floor beside a discarded hammer. Her eyes lifted and she saw dents all along the unit's protective casing.

"Have it running good as new," he muttered.

She swallowed, quickly assessing the situation. The unit was partly dismantled and wires were precariously exposed. She had no electrical training but assumed since Sonny was still breathing that they weren't in imminent danger. She touched his shoulder. "Good. You can finish after lunch. I'll bet you're hungry."

He rubbed a hand over his balding head. "Guess I could eat."

Careful not to touch any of the wiring, she wheeled him out of the room, closing the door behind them. Catching Miranda in the hall, she pawned Sonny off and hurried to the front desk. "Becca, call Rocco. We need him immediately!"

After conferring with Sherie, she put a call through to Sonny's son, explaining the situation. "It's time to take his toolbox away." She listened to the son's objections. "I know. But it's one thing to dismantle his bed and another to play with live wires. He could have gotten killed today." She blushed when he put the blame on the center's care. "We can't be with him every second." After a lengthy discussion, it was finally determined to place the toolbox under lock and key until the weekend when it would be replaced with plastic tools.

"That's rough," Becca said. Then she turned a cheery smile toward the lobby. "Good morning."

A ray of sunshine filled the room as Ann's four-year-old-daughter, Mary, skipped toward them. "Hi. We're having a picnic lunch."

"You are? How wonderful," Becca replied before turning to answer the phone.

Glancing at the residents gathering for lunch, Ann raised a brow. "Is this a bad time?"

Carly brushed her hand through the air. "No more than usual. Sonny just dismantled the heating element, but Rocco's putting it back together." When Ann's eyes widened, Carly grinned. "I'll go grab my lunch." She was anxious to discuss the volunteer program with Ann.

When she returned from the staff room, she waited while Ann finished conversing with some of the residents who had gathered for the noon meal. Martha was questioning little Mary about her age and when she planned to attend school. Smiles all around, the residents loved having Mary visiting them.

After that, they moved outside to the garden patio and sat on a metal bench. "Thanks for meeting me like this."

"No problem. I feel guilty for not coming more often."

"One person can't do everything," Carly said. "I hear you're really good with children."

Ann dimpled and hugged little Mary. "I love children."

"Did you notice how the residents lit up when Mary entered the room?"

"Jah. It made my heart swell," Ann replied.

As they spread out their lunch items on a metal side table, Carly explained, "That's why I invited you to lunch."

Ann tilted her head. "Really? This isn't about my brother?"

Carly laughed nervously. "No. Sweet Life is starting a volunteer program called Every Little Bit Helps."

Ann nodded. "Adam told me you drafted the entire program and that he was appalled at the way Uncle Si treated you."

"That's water under the bridge. Sherie's been letting me help. In fact, she liked my newest idea and asked me to make it happen." Surprise governed Ann's expression, and Carly could see the other woman was struggling to understand how she was to be involved. She recognized the instant that Ann understood.

"It has something to do with children, doesn't it?"

"Jah. Michelle Zook asked me if she could read to the residents. They would love it. Children could sing and play games." Carly leaned close and whispered. "At this stage in life, the residents have much in common with children. They enjoy the same things."

"That's a wonderful idea. I could bring the church group over."

Carly bit her lip. Then she continued. "I'm single. I don't know much about children."

Ann grinned. "And I do."

"Jah. I know you're busy at the Christmas tree farm right now, and I hate to ask, but you're perfect for the job. Will you head up the children's volunteer program?"

"Mama! Look!"

Carly watched the child's delight as a gray squirrel with a bushy tail skittered along the fence wall and finally climbed high into an oak tree.

Mary clapped her hands. "Again! Again!"

"He's gathering supplies for winter."

"Does he live in that tree, Mama?"

"Jah, I suppose he does."

"Can I go look?'"

"Sure."

They watched the little girl run to the fence and stand gazing up into the tree. The squirrel chattered loudly.

"What's he saying, Mama?"

"He's scolding you for interrupting his work."

"Is he the old people's squirrel?"

"Jah, honey." Her voice faded, "I already teach Sunday school. And like you said, it's November, and I'm busy at the farm. But my main concern is Dad. He's already jealous about Adam's time here at the center."

"I hadn't thought about that." Carly bit her tongue, to keep from saying how unfair and childish it was for Roman to control his adult children and prevent them from helping others. Being the family peacemaker probably made Ann more aware of her dad's feelings.

"Let me talk it over with Ron, and we'll pray about it."

"Of course." She could understand getting a husband's approval. But even that grated her at the moment.

Ann watched Mary skip along the fence, where she was gathering leaves, acorns, and seed pods. "Now I know how Adam feels."

Carly studied her friend.

"Dad's a good man, but stubborn. He doesn't like anybody to cross him."

A catch appeared in Carly's throat. "And he doesn't like me." She fiddled with her napkin. "So he doesn't want your entire family to have anything to do with Sweet Life?"

Ann's hand shot out. "Oh no. No, it's not that. It's Simon. He says he doesn't want us to be led astray by his brother who broke away from our church."

Carly's thoughts drifted. When they'd dated, Dale had attended a more progressive church. When he'd proposed marriage, he told her it wasn't an issue so she'd assumed they'd go to the Conservative Church. Assumptions. In the end, he suggested finding a new church in Indiana, one that would fit both their needs.

"But Adam and I know it's more than that." Carly blinked. Met Ann's gaze.

"He's jealous of Uncle Si. It's just a delicate situation. With nothing to do with you."

Carly found that hard to believe.

"Mama!" Mary skipped to the table and pointed back at the tree. "Is heaven up there in that tree?"

"No honey. Why?"

"Because all those old people are ready to go to heaven."

Ann smiled apologetically.

Carly sighed. "I guess that's one thing children don't have in common with the residents."

"That's why your idea is so good. They'd bring life to this place."

Long after Ann had gone, while Carly was looking for the General's hearing aid, their conversation lingered. It was what Ann hadn't said that hurt the most. Roman Lapp was stubbornly set against Carly because he didn't think she was good enough for his son. And even if Adam went against his father's wishes, would she want to be a part of a family that lived in fear of the dictates of the family head? She didn't think so.

Chapter Nineteen

Snip. Snip. November brought death to Carly's flower garden. As gardening went, it was her least favorite month, and she spent many late afternoons cleaning and mulching. On Saturday, Jimmy promised to come and help rake and compost leaves. Kneeling now, she trimmed her pink coneflowers and chrysanthemums down to four- to six-inch stems and worked the dry heads back into the soil. As her thumb scattered the seeds, little Mary's words came to mind. *"All the old people are ready to go to heaven."*

Hearing the words from one just starting life had initiated the sadness that enveloped her yesterday. Since then, it'd been easy to allow negative thinking to invade her mind. Working the soil, she understood death was inevitable and even a blessing. Wasn't heaven a better place? She should be happy for the release the elderly experienced. Free from pain. Reunited with loved ones. She was too earthly minded. She wanted to change. To trust God with her life and find her own release from the pain her job entailed.

"Hello!" Imogene waved two glasses of sweet tea by invitation.

Carly rose, swiping her brow with the sleeve of her black sweater and crossed the street. "Thanks." She took several satisfying sips of the sweet tea.

"Why so glum? Spring is just around the corner."

"Hardly." Only that was negative thinking, and she'd just chastised herself for that. But she could be honest with Imogene. "It's just that my flowers reflect everything else in my life. Dying."

"Bah! It's all of us old people you hang around with. What about that good-looking fellow with the black truck? He even gets my blood a-pumping, and I'm happily married to Baldy."

Carly laughed. "Adam's a good friend. He runs a Christmas Tree Farm, and he's pretty busy this time of year."

"So that's the problem."

"Some people are meant to remain single," she reminded herself as much as Imogene.

"I probably can't change your mind about that, but I can give you a cutting of my pink camellias. They'd sure look pretty against your yellow cottage."

"Really?" Carly squealed. She bit her lip and looked across the street. "Where?"

"Why not back by your stick pile?"

"You tired of looking at that?"

"Just problem solving."

"I could do more with the back. In fact, it could use a major face-lift."

"Imogene!" A man's voice called from her neighbor's cottage. Imogene sighed. "I'll see what Baldy wants and bring the cutting over in a little bit."

"Okay. Give me enough time to take a shower. And thanks for the tea." Now inspired, Carly set off imagining pink camellia bushes against a short, white picket fence to hide her stick pile.

Adam threw bags of fertilizer into the bed of his truck. He planned to take it home with him and haul it to the farm in the morning. He started his engine, and his eyes automatically scanned the dusky surrounds. Several logging trucks rolled through the heart of town. The last one squealed its brakes, and his heart lurched. His gaze involuntarily shot to the scene.

He saw a woman with a camera and had to shake his head. She obviously hadn't realized that as soon as she stuck her foot onto the crosswalk, all traffic on both sides of the divided road would come to a screeching halt. The trucker motioned her across. They seemed to carry on some kind of argumentative conversation with hand motions. It appeared she'd only meant to go as far as the median to take some photos, but the trucker wasn't moving until she gave in and proceeded across all four lanes of traffic. He waved and stepped on the gas. She stood with her hands on her hips, her camera dangling from a shoulder strap.

Thankfully, the squeal of brakes wasn't caused by Carly. He missed her. There was always the possibility of seeing her when he came to Sweet Home. Generally, he did business in Brownsville, but the fertilizer had been on sale. Anyway, since he wasn't volunteering at Sweet Life, and with Jimmy miffed at him, things had been too quiet where Carly was concerned. And it was driving him crazy. Like a moth drawn to the fire, he hopped in his truck and veered off Main Street, heading toward Hawthorne.

When he drove into Carly's drive, he sat in the truck for a moment, reconsidering. While he'd been lonely, things had also been uneventful and calm. Boring, in fact. Now that he'd cooled off over Jimmy's threat, he didn't take it too seriously. And with Dad—he stiffened his backbone and opened the door.

Carly's lights were on inside the cottage and Adam rapped three times, then remembered that was Jimmy's knock and added one more. She didn't keep him waiting long. But when she opened the door, he blinked. Then froze. Stared.

"Oh!" Her face reddened. What little he could see of it, hiding within the glorious abundance of long blond dancing curls that hung over her shoulders almost to her waist. Her hair made a magnificent golden halo, and she was an angel. And his angel wore no head covering.

His mouth went dry. He stared. And kept staring. His fingers itched to touch it. Of course, he'd seen his sisters like that occasionally. And he'd seen women from outside the church with all sorts of hairstyles, but the shock of seeing those long blond curls on the woman he loved was almost more than he could bear. Yet he couldn't look away. His heart pounded with male excitement. He grinned. "I probably should've called." *So glad I didn't.*

She tried to brush her hair off her shoulders, but it just bounced back.

"It's really curly. How do you get it under your cap?"

She straightened her shoulders. "I thought you were Imogene from across the street. She's bringing me camellia cuttings. I plan to plant them in the backyard, and I'm also putting a little white picket fence around my stick pile."

"I'll build it for you. I'll start right now if you'd like."

Smiling, she stepped away from the door. "You might as well come in before Cocoa gets out."

The rabbit wasn't anywhere in sight, but he wasn't going to point that out to her. Inside she sat on a chair, and he took the lumpy sofa.

"I suppose you're here to check on me since Jimmy's out of town."

Good news. "I didn't even know he was gone."

She raised a curious brow.

He shrugged. "I miss Sweet Life, not knowing what's going on with the residents." Why did he say that? But from the smile on her face, it worked.

"Since it's colder, they're cooped up inside. Sonny, who Miranda calls Mr. Gadget, has more time on his hands, and so he dismantled the heating unit."

Grinning, Adam said, "That's awful. But what about you? Any scrapes I've missed?"

She lifted her chin. "None whatsoever. Um. . .except"—she hesitated, and he braced himself—"I asked Ann if she'd head up a children's volunteer group."

He hadn't expected that. "What'd she say?"

"That she has to take your dad's feelings into account, but that she'd pray about it."

"She'd be good at it." He made a mental note to encourage Ann to do it.

Carly fiddled with a long strand of her hair. "Have you heard from Dale about James Irish?"

"Jah. He's coming up blank."

Her expression fell. She looked so vulnerable that it was all he could do not to sweep her into his arms and kiss away her worries. And run his fingers through her hair while he had her that close. He had plenty of curiosity about it. If he pulled it, would it spring back? Was it as soft as it looked? He licked his lips. Something thumped his shoe. He looked down to see Cocoa acting strangely.

"Better scratch him behind the ear. And you'd better hurry."

Doing as bid, he found himself saying, "Maybe if we went fishing at Crawfordsville bridge, we'd get some inspiration regarding James Irish."

"Are the fish biting now?"

"Does it matter?"

She reddened. "No."

"Great." He straightened and rubbed his pants. "It's a date."

"Well I don't know about that."

He shrugged. "Let's argue about that Sunday afternoon. I'll pick you up around two."

"Jah, okay."

Cocoa thumped twice and Adam quickly scratched him behind the ears again. "How long does this go on?"

"I don't know. I think he likes you."

Just then there was a knock at the door. Carly looked stricken, and Cocoa hopped away, hiding beneath the table.

"You want me to hide, too?" he joked.

"Don't be ridiculous. It's just Imogene. She's been wanting to meet you anyway."

Carly opened the door, and her neighbor stepped inside.

"I saw the truck. Hope I'm not imposing, but I promised you these cuttings."

"Of course not. It's time you met my friend Adam."

He took the cuttings and shook Imogene's hand. He made some small talk as he went to Carly's cupboard and put them in water. When he turned around, both women seemed shell-shocked. "What? I'm a tree farmer. I know what to do with a cutting."

"He's a keeper," Imogene said.

"And he's building me a white picket fence to bring out their pink color." Carly blushed.

Imogene smiled. "Is that a fact?"

Starting to sweat under the collar, Adam took his leave. But driving home all he could do was grin.

Carly lifted her skirt to keep it from catching on blackberry twigs as she followed her fishing-gear-clad companion down an embankment to a rocky but grassy shoreline located between two bridges. To their left was the historic Crawfordsville Covered Bridge. Restored now, its white paint was pure and picturesque against the green tangle that overhung the Calapooia River. To their right was the modern concrete edifice that carried traffic along the Halsey–Sweet Home Road.

Adam leaned his pole against a tree and grinned, unfolding a blanket to a size just big enough for two people to sit upon if they were welded together. Then he patted it invitingly.

"Jah. That's not happening." She scooped it up, gave it a firm shake and watched it settle on the lumpy ground. Even at that, she would be closer than she could probably handle to the man who made her insides tingle. Dale had never made her feel like this.

Throwing his head back with laughter, he gave in and sat cross legged. She watched him ready his gear. "If you change your mind and want to fish, I'll share my pole."

Not knowing if it was helpful Adam speaking or flirty Adam—whom she didn't fully understand yet—she replied, "We'll see." But she joined him on the blanket. The gentle breeze occasionally rustled the leaves, and bright sunlight filtered through the green canopy, dazzling the red-striped bobber.

He explained, "We might see some salmon. Since the Brownsville Dam was removed, a few are finding their way back here again."

"I have no experience with fishing. Is that what we're hunting?"

Adam laughed. "Jah. But I doubt we'll see any."

"Oh ye of little faith."

Stretching out his legs, he yawned. "Jah, that pretty much describes me. I should've brought you down here last summer, when it was warmer."

"I'm warm enough." She smiled. "Why did you bring me here today, Adam?"

"I thought I just explained that. I wanted to see if the salmon are running."

She tilted her head and pouted her lip. "Really?"

"Because I missed that dimple you show when you get mad."

She felt like putty in his hands. Didn't really like it. "I missed you, too. So does this mean you've sorted through those major issues in your life?"

"Partly."

She lowered her gaze, feeling frustrated that he was clear as mud about issues that supposedly were huge enough to keep them apart while she was making her feelings obviously known.

Sensing her frustration, he tried to explain. "Look, when we talked before, I was trying to decide whether I was going to make some changes in my life. Changes that would incur costs, all around. I thought I had to have all the answers, know how it was going to work out before I got close to you. But I'm never going to have all the answers, and I'm tired of waiting." Adam laid aside his pole and took her hand. "Tired of waiting for you. That's all I know. Can't it be enough?"

Carly raised her eyes and nodded, a lump forming in her throat.

"I can't guarantee I won't hurt you."

Irritated by his last remark, she jerked her hand away. "Do people in love talk like that? Do they even think about hurting one another?"

"Well they do when somebody's brother threatens them."

Relaxing, she thought she better understood. But she wasn't worried about Jimmy. And she couldn't see how it would serve any purpose to force Adam to admit that his dad hated her. If he was willing to overcome that obstacle on his own, she'd just have to trust him.

He lay on his back now, staring up at the clouds that peeked through their private canopy. "See those clouds?"

She laid back and nodded.

"They aren't rain clouds. Just clouds. People who serve only themselves are clouds without water carried by the winds. But that's not you. You're the watering, nurturing type. You draw people. I tried to resist at first. But I can't."

"So I'm a rain cloud?"

He rolled on his side. "Jah, you can be kinda stormy." His own gaze grew so dark she wondered if she should take cover. But his touch was gentle on her cheek. She vowed she wasn't going to make the first move *this time*. She didn't have to wait long. His lips found hers. And she allowed it. Enjoyed it.

His hand went to her waist, and he pulled her close. Her hand tentative against his clothed chest, she let herself relax in him.

When they drew apart, he gave her a lopsided grin. But her eyes widened with what she saw taking place behind him. With a giggle, she cried, "Look!"

Behind him his pole was being dragged downstream.

He jumped to his feet, did a little dance at the edge of the stream, and for a while she expected him to go in after it. "Of all the—" He finally stilled and placed his hands on his hips. "What can I say? It was worth it."

"Was that a salmon?"

"It had to be." He shook his head regretfully.

"Oh, the poor fish."

"I'm sure the pole will get snagged someplace. Someone will either cut it loose or have their dinner."

She rose and gazed downstream. "I hope so. Next year I'll know what to get you for your birthday."

"I don't want a pole. Next year, I want a repeat of this year." He grinned. "That was the beginning of all this, you know."

"I suppose you're always going to look back to that night. Always going to blame me for everything."

"No. I'm going to thank you. But I'll probably always have to get you out of your messes." Before she could argue, he snatched her hand. "Let's take this stuff back to the truck and explore."

They walked along the inside of the covered bridge and ran their fingers over the ridges of carved initials that had survived coats of paint. Now they knew that J. H. + M. S. weren't the initials they'd hoped to find. "Somebody was determined," he said, giving her a look of sheer purpose. It thrilled her to her black-clad toes.

She lowered her lashes and moved to one of the latticed openings. "Do you think they fished back there, in our spot?"

"Probably." He grinned. "If Martha was as pretty then as you are now, I'll bet he lost a pole or two."

Feeling happier than she ever had, she twirled and went to the other side. "Or did they stand under that huge tree and kiss?"

"It certainly looks like a kissing tree." He captured her hand. "Let's go find out."

Laughing she allowed him to lead her beneath the huge, droopy evergreen. She looked up. "It's amazing, isn't it? It must be thirty feet in diameter." She ran her hand over the rough, mossy bark. Breathlessly happy, she met his gaze.

"Magnificent." His voice softened. "Beautiful." He touched her lips. "Wildly, delicious."

She smacked him playfully.

But he drew her close, and when she was encased in his arms, she'd never felt so cherished, so in love. So free. When at last they pulled away, she asked, "Is this love?"

"Jah, sweetheart. I'm pretty sure it is." He leaned his back against the tree and backed her up against him so that they could both watch the Calapooia River. His arms around her waist and his chin resting on her shoulder, he whispered, "Why did we wait so long to admit it?"

It was a rhetorical question. They both had good reasons.

"I'm going to be busy the next several weeks. I need to warn you that you probably won't see much of me. But that doesn't mean. . .Ahh!" He pushed her away, and she stumbled over one of the gnarly roots.

Gasping, she watched as he suddenly sprang away from her. "Ants!"

She scrambled up and into the clearing as he proceeded to hop on one foot and then the other, pulling off his shoes and his coat. "Ants," he repeated.

Frantically, she checked her own clothing, but she seemed to be free of them. She moved closer. "Are they biting you?"

"Some, but they're crawling everywhere. Yuck!" He continued swiping and slapping. You'd better look the other way."

Turning around, she crossed her arms and listened to his mumbles and rustling of clothes he must surely be discarding. "There's a restroom over there."

"Good idea."

She heard him moving in that direction, and then the door closed. Her lips curled, though she did feel sorry for him. She went to examine the kissing tree. They should have noticed earlier. Beneath the pine needles were mounds of duff and ants. Poor Adam. With what came out as part sigh and part giggle, she went to wait for him at the picnic table.

When he finally came out, he grinned sheepishly. "I think we need to try out a few more trees, sweetheart. Because that's definitely not going to be my kissing tree." She laughed as he took her hand, his other scratching the back of his neck. "Come on. I gotta get you home and go buy some ant lotion or something."

She could tell he was miserable when at the door his good-bye kiss was brief. He'd left her with the admonition that the following Sunday his family was having a birthday party for his nephew, and he didn't know when he'd be able to see her again.

Chapter Twenty

Humming, Carly placed her bike in Sweet Life's bike rack and waved at Aesop. He purred over on his red scooter, and she stopped to talk to him, noticing his fuzzy, ear-muffed hat. "You're bundled up today."

He slapped his gloves together. "So—so you like my new hat? On sale at the mart. If—if you're gonna ride your bike all winter, you should get one. Might"—he grinned—"might mess up your hair. But it'll keeps you nice and toasty. Worth it."

Her hair. Unbidden she recalled the sight of Adam standing on her stoop the night she'd just washed her hair. She'd recognized the admiration in his eyes. And then he'd asked her out on a date. And on their date, he'd confessed his love. She grinned, realizing Aesop was watching her curiously. "Guess I should get out my winter scarves. But I think Auntie will soon be bringing me to work. She did for a couple months last winter."

"Well—well it's too cold to sit still. Have a good day, miss."

"You, too, Aesop."

She turned the corner and rapped on Rocco's door as she passed.

He popped his head out. "You sure got a bounce in your step this morning."

"Do I?" Carly grinned. "Guess I love my job."

"Wish I could say the same."

"Is there a problem?" she asked.

"Yep. Just found there's a plumbing leak at two of the independent-living houses."

"Uh-oh."

"I'm already over budget this month. I'm hoping this doesn't turn out to be an epidemic. All those houses were built at the same time, and you know how these things run in cycles."

"Well don't fret. Finding the money to pay for repair isn't something that should fall on your shoulders. That's for Simon and the board to worry about."

"Except Simon forces me to cut corners, and I don't like to do that."

"I'm sorry."

"Listen to me. Ruining your good day. Go on now. Don't pay any attention to me."

"One day at a time, Rocco."

"You bet. Thanks for reminding me."

For a few minutes, Carly brewed over Rocco's predicament, but eventually her thoughts returned to Adam, and she couldn't keep from smiling.

Inside her assisted-living building, her heart hummed. At breakfast, Nines asked if she could help her rearrange some things in her apartment. She'd agreed and now found herself listening to Nines's explanation.

"So you see, if my chair was right here"—the older woman stood in the middle of her living area—"closer to the TV, then I could hear it better."

Carly tapped her cheek. "I see your point. But that's in the middle of the room, and you might get tired of walking around it. Why don't I get Miranda to show you how to manage the volume on your remote." They'd gone over this before. More than once.

"No." Nines shook her head. "I can't remember how to do it. And what's the use of watching TV if I can't hear what's going on?" She patted her cat, Teacup's, head. "We'd like it here, wouldn't we?"

"All right. Let's give it a try. Why don't you go sit on the sofa, and you can tell me when I get it right."

Excitement lit the older woman's face. She sat on the sofa with her purse in her lap, leaning forward with anticipation so that Carly felt bad for not giving in to her request sooner. She knew exactly what the outcome would be because they'd done this before, but why not make her happy? Restore her dignity? Today, she wanted everyone to be happy. It took a lot of effort, but Rocco had too many other things on his mind to bother him, and finally she got the heavy recliner dragged into the center of the room. "How's this?"

"It blocks my view of the TV." Nines frowned.

"Come sit in it. Then tell me."

Nines shrugged and moved as if someone was making a big imposition upon her. When she sat in the chair, she used the recline lever and nestled down into the chair. "This is better!" she exclaimed.

"Good."

The woman looked behind her. "But now it looks so bare where the chair used to be. And I'm too far away from Teacup's pillow."

"We can move Teacup closer."

"No, I might stumble." She shook her head, which at the present was adorned with a black hat with black netting. "Can we move the chair back a little?"

"Jah, sure." She helped Nines out of the recliner and back to the sofa. Carly moved it about two feet. "How about here?"

"No, a little more."

Carly moved it another two feet. "How's this?"

The woman gestured, "More."

"Here?"

"A little more."

When the chair rested back in its original carpet imprints, Nines squealed, "There! That's perfect. Should I try it?"

Carly helped her back to the recliner. Teacup leapt into Nines's lap. She grinned. "Perfect. So much better."

"Jah. That should work good for you. Want to rest a bit, while you're in your chair?"

"Yes. Thanks, Carly."

"I'm glad I could help."

Back in the hall, she paused to rub sweat from her temple. Miranda appeared from a resident's room. "Did Jimmy tell you we got together before he went out of town?"

Carly shook her head. She'd been so engrossed in her own weekend with Adam that she'd forgotten about *them.* "I haven't seen him since the other Sunday when we were all together."

Miranda lowered her mascara-painted lashes. "We went out to eat one night. Afterward we talked a long time before he took me inside."

Carly pushed away the image Miranda was creating in her mind. "So what are you trying to say?"

Miranda shrugged, looking hurt. "Nothing. I like him. I just wanted to thank you for setting us up."

She hadn't set them up! Or had she? It wasn't coming out at all like she'd envisioned with Jimmy ignoring Miranda. But why did it matter so much to her? All of them were adults. Still, she didn't want to raise Miranda's hopes. "You're welcome." Carly started to turn away, then thought better of it. She should be honest with Miranda. "You both seemed to click, but be careful with your feelings. I feel responsible now."

"Don't worry. We're just dating. Having some fun."

"Jay, okay. I'm happy for you."

Miranda pursed her red lips, "So what's going on with you and Adam?"

"We're dating, too."

"I thought so. He's super cute. Better take your own advice. You're way more sensitive than me."

Surprised, Carly nodded. "I suppose so."

"Hey. Maybe we can double sometime."

Carly laughed. "Actually, Adam's pretty busy at the tree farm right now. And Jimmy doesn't approve of Adam and me." She shrugged. "But who knows?"

Suddenly the day didn't seem quite as bright. She started toward the receptionist's desk but halted when she heard loud barking.

Mrs. Maloney, one of the new volunteers who brought her pet to the center, had lost control of her normally mellow dog. The basset hound's barks soon turned into a hair-raising howl. Becca scurried to shut off her fan, and when the plastic bag that had been dancing near the receptionist's counter finally deflated, the dog's howl turned back into barking.

Mrs. Maloney half dragged her dog over to the bag to reassure it that everything was all right. Glancing around the room, Carly saw that most of the residents were responding as if it were good entertainment. Only Nines seemed concerned, leaving them to go and check on Teacup.

The dog incident, though minor, had fried Carly's nerves. She shook her head. As she watched Mrs. Maloney work the room, her thoughts returned to Adam, and she pinpointed her frustration. It was Miranda's warning to watch her heart. Adam could have invited her to their family birthday party. But he hadn't. And she was worried that after being around his family, especially his dad, he would withdraw again.

Adam was managing a rough day by whistling away his cares and thinking about Carly. He couldn't wait until he could see her again. But the happier he felt, the more sullen Dad became. After checking one of the noble fir fields and noticing some fungus, he ditched the whistling, and they drove in stony silence to the cut-your-own site where they needed to do some last-minute pruning.

Glancing over, he saw Dad's face remained glum, and he was slumped down in the passenger's seat. Normally, he had an anger problem. This pouting attitude was somewhat new and unpredictable. But whatever kind of snit he was in, it was better just to pretend not to notice. But Dad wasn't having it that way, either. As soon as Adam turned off the ignition and moved to open the door, his arm shot out to stop him.

"There's a rumor going around about you."

Lightly gripping the steering wheel, he tried to be patient and prepare for the worst, and most likely the ridiculous. "I don't know what you're talking about."

"You were seen at the Crawfordsville Bridge with that Blosser woman."

Adam rolled his gaze upward. *Not this conversation again.* "Well that's not a rumor because it's true. I was at the bridge with Carly."

Dad slapped the dashboard with both hands. "Son, what were you thinking?"

Adam gripped the steering wheel tight. "Why is that such a crime?"

"Because they caught you with your clothes off. For Pete's sake, couldn't you have done it someplace private and not out in broad daylight? Good grief, half of the church lives off of Halsey–Sweet Home Road."

For a few futile seconds, his mind tried to figure out who saw what. Half the church? But it didn't matter. Whoever ratted was a gossip and had their own problems. He crossed his arms. "A grown man shouldn't have to explain himself to his dad or half the church."

Dad shook his head. "At least consider the woman. She's already had to live down one set of rumors. Although she probably doesn't have any good chances anymore."

Adam stared, deeply offended.

"For marriage, I mean."

"I don't know why you would say that. I don't believe those things Dale said about her."

"So what are you going to do about this?"

"Look, we kissed behind a big tree where nobody could have seen us, and then I got ants all over me. I was throwing off my clothes because they were eating me alive. I was probably running toward the men's room when"—he raised his hands to make air quotes—" 'half the church' saw me. And you're right. If what you heard was disgusting, then it's nothing but a rumor."

"Thank goodness." Surprisingly, Dad's lip curled. "Ants, huh?"

"Jah. Ants."

"Well that's a relief. At least there's no wedding to be planned?"

"Not yet, anyway."

"So you didn't get your fill of her yet. Well, you will one day. And it'll be too late."

"Carly isn't her aunt. And she didn't lose a little boy."

"What's your point?"

"Maybe Fannie was still mourning."

Dad seemed to consider it. "Is that what Carly told you?"

"Jah. Said she's still afraid to love again."

While Dad was considering that, Adam went on, "Carly's not a clone of her aunt. She's kind and caring. And I believe there's more to the story of what happened between her and Dale. Why don't I invite her to Jacob's birthday party so you can get to know her? Find out for yourself?"

"No, for Pete's sake," Dad huffed, then gave him a sideways glance. "Your mom probably isn't keen on her, either. There was a time she was jealous of Fannie."

"Well there's been a lot of water under the bridge since then. It's time you both forgave Carly for something that wasn't even her fault. You're even members of the same church."

"It's got nothing to do with forgiveness. But I guess if anybody would know what's going on under the bridge, it'd be you. You know I don't approve, but at least be more discreet in the future."

Dad opened the door and climbed out of the truck.

Adam went to the bed for their pruning tools. He wished he could lop off Dad's hard-headed ways as easily as he could shape a tree for those who used it to celebrate the Lord's birthday. But somewhere beneath all that crustiness, he thought he saw glimpses of a vulnerable man. Only, if Dad had never gotten over Fannie, then how did he expect Adam to get over Carly?

Chapter Twenty-One

Early watched Nines conversing with Dot about her missing cat. Teacup was the only residential pet aside from the household bird, Magnificent, and Dot's canary. Teacup must have been named as a kitten, because it was anything but tiny. It was as ancient as its owner and normally didn't do anything but eat, sleep, and use its litter box. As long as Nines could care for the cat, it was allowed to stay at the center.

"I think that barking dog upset Teacup. He got off my bed in the middle of the night, and I haven't seen him since."

That day Martha had needed extra care for her worsening asthma, so the staff hadn't made a search for the missing cat yet.

With a shaky hand, Dot carefully set down her decaf coffee. "He couldn't have gotten far. He's stiff as a board. Looks ready to croak. That's why I'm not worried about him eating Birdie. He's got to be in your room someplace. Did you look under the bed?"

"Of course I looked under the bed." Nines smacked Dot's arm with her spoon. "He could easily take your bird if he wanted to. He's just too civilized. And he's certainly not useless. He can still get on my lap."

Dot pulled on her sleeve. "You got mashed potatoes on me."

"Don't be ridiculous. You're the one without any table manners. You never place your napkin on your lap."

Dot snatched her napkin, dabbed at her sleeve then spread it out on her lap. "I guess I forget sometimes."

"Got this?" Carly asked Miranda. "I need to give Martha her breathing treatment."

"Sure, we're good here."

Carly started toward the hall. They'd been in and out of Martha's room all day, and the resident nurse had even been called in earlier. Usually, Martha's asthma worsened at night. If they didn't get these symptoms under control soon, it would be a rough night.

Hall Patroller stopped wheeling her chair long enough to confront their tallest resident, the General. "Go put your pants on," she scolded.

He seemed undeterred, with his long, Casper-white legs nude up to his paper underwear. "Huh?"

Carly raised her voice. "Put your pants on!"

"Lady. I swim in less than this."

Hall Patroller gasped. She wheeled up to Carly. "He's doing it again."

"Thanks for pointing it out to me," Carly mumbled. She caught his arm. "Jah, but we're not swimming today. It's November, the start of winter." He'd been dressed earlier and had been one of the first ones finished with his breakfast. "What happened to your pants?" she asked, leading him back toward his room.

"I felt like dressing in uniform today."

"You miss the air force, don't you?"

He moved alongside her but cast a disapproving look at the Hall Patroller. "She thinks she's in command," he complained.

"I know. But she's lonely, and it gives her something to do. She was once a high school principal."

After she had the General clothed, Carly went to give Martha her breathing treatment.

She found the older woman in a recliner struggling to breathe. Martha tried to tell Carly something but went into a coughing fit. Seeing the asthma had worsened, Carly pressed the emergency intercom button. "I need the nurse at room 110 right away."

Then she placed meds in the nebulizer and placed the mask on Martha, patting her purple-veined hand. "Don't try to talk, dear. Just relax. You want me to call your daughter?"

Martha nodded vigorously, and Carly made the call. As they waited, she saw a lump moving on Martha's bed. What on earth? She went to investigate. Teacup! No wonder Martha was having an asthma attack.

"Did you know Teacup was in here?"

Martha shook her head.

"Well that's your breathing problem. I'll get her out of here." Snatching up the plump cat, she hurried it out of the room and placed it in Nines's apartment, shutting the door. By the time she'd returned, Linda was taking Martha's vitals.

"I called 911. They're on their way."

With tears welling, Carly knelt beside Martha's chair and placed her hand on her knee. "Don't worry. Once they give you a steroid shot and get you on a ventilator you'll recover quickly and soon be back here good as new."

Martha couldn't talk anymore, but she squeezed her eyes shut as if she didn't want to face the procedures that would soon occur.

Widow Martha felt scared. Torn between fighting for her life and releasing her spirit to go home to the Lord. To John. She hated the struggle of a body that wouldn't cooperate. Her emotions hadn't felt so out of control since she'd been a young wife carrying her first child. Helen had arrived squalling and precious. How she'd enjoyed the challenge that came with motherhood. But nobody had warned her that her own daughter would one day turn against her. Put her away in a home and never visit.

"I'm going to be eighty-five," she'd told Helen.

"Yes, I know. Do you have something special in mind?"

Not if I have to spell it out, she'd thought rebelliously. "Surprise me."

"How about some warm slippers or a cozy blanket with winter coming?" Slippers! Suddenly she felt resentful that she'd been a December baby. "Not slippers, for Pete's sake!" she'd replied. *I want you to take me home. To bring the grandkids more often*. But she was too proud to express her innermost needs. Gasping, she thought maybe it would just be best to end it all today. She sure didn't want to go to the hospital and get all those needles attached and be prodded and poked. It was so much to bear. She closed her eyes and pleaded with the Lord.

When the paramedics arrived, Carly left the room. At the receptionist's desk, she dialed housekeeping. "I need room 110 thoroughly cleaned, the bedding changed, and the filter replaced. Be sure it's an allergy-proof one, whatever they're called. . . Great. Thanks."

By the time Carly was off the phone, Martha's daughter Helen hurried through the lobby. "I was at my granddaughter's school. Luckily it was nearby. How is she?"

"Sounds like they'll take her to the hospital."

"Oh, gracious. Let's see, I'll have to call Steve and see if he can. . ." Her words faded as she hurried down the hall to Martha's room, but the scenario was all too familiar. Helen was always busy, busy, busy. Carly sucked her bottom lip. On the bright side, it would give the family some time together, and that was exactly what Martha desired.

Needing to clear the hallway, Carly coaxed Hall Patroller to follow her to the lobby. "I know you're busy here, but I could really use your help for a minute or two. She situated her at the game table. "Just for one second." Carly went to a bookshelf and brought over a puzzle box. "I need you to get this started. You know how some of the residents struggle, and you're so good at getting those border pieces going."

"I don't know." She gazed back at the hall, longingly.

"Please."

"Oh, all right. You know we have to turn them all over first."

"You get started on that. I'll be right back."

The emergency squad took Martha out through the emergency exit at the end of the hall, and thankfully her departure didn't cause much of a stir. Except in Carly's heart.

One night in the middle of the week, Adam was heating leftover soup Ann had given him when he saw Jimmy pull into his drive. He turned off the stove. Either Jimmy had come to make amends, or he'd heard about his date with Carly and was going to make even more threats.

"Hey. Come in."

Jimmy went to Adam's favorite chair and plopped down in it. He crossed his arms as if daring him to ask him to move, which normally would have happened. But under their strained friendship, Adam let it pass and moved onto the sofa.

"I'm fixing soup. You want to eat with me?"

"Nope. Won't hold you up long."

"You look beat."

"Just pulled into town."

"So what's on your mind?"

"Just wanted to apologize for the way I acted before."

Adam was suddenly glad he'd left the plane ticket in his truck after he'd gotten the mail. Wouldn't have been good for Jimmy to see it when it didn't mean anything. He really needed to send it back to Dale and somehow convince him that he wouldn't be taking him up on his offer. "No problem. I get it."

Jimmy explained, "When I was gone, I was thinking about how much I love being on the road. I understand how a new start would sound good to you. I don't know how you've endured being under your dad's thumb this long. If you go to Indiana, I'll stop in and see you."

"Apology accepted, but I won't be going to Indiana. I'm serious about your sister. I'm just holding back until I get Dad's blessing."

"That could be a long time."

"Believe me, I won't wait forever."

"I'm going to keep my nose out of this, but it would be better for you to tell Carly about Dale's offer before she hears it from somebody else."

"I was going to tell her, but things are going good between us, and I don't want to bring any doubts into her mind."

Jimmy jumped to his feet. "Maybe you're right. I've gotta get home and shower. Hit the sack."

As he watched Jimmy leave, he felt uneasy. It was as if Dale's shadow hung over their budding relationship. Maybe Jimmy was right. Maybe Carly even wanted to talk about Dale. It might clear the air so they could move ahead without any qualms. And if Jimmy let it slip about Indiana, she'd be hurt. It would take forever to penetrate her stubbornness. In that respect she was like her brother. Adam would take her home from church on Sunday and set things straight before he went to the birthday party.

Thursday night, Jimmy stopped by Carly's cottage. He grinned. "Yard looks great."

"No thanks to you." She gave him a bear hug.

"Sorry I skipped out on you. But how about Saturday after next I rake some leaves?"

"That long?" She pulled a face. "It's a date."

"And you'll make me something really great to eat?"

"Don't I always? I have some of Auntie's Texas sheet cake if you want a piece now."

"You don't have to ask me twice." He sat at her table, and Cocoa hopped over and propped his head on Jimmy's shoe. He laughed at the rabbit. "You'll get what you want after I eat."

Carly joined him with the cake, smiling.

His fork paused midair. "You're sure in a good mood."

"Just happy."

"That's good." He licked his fork clean. "Any special reason?"

"I'll tell you, if you promise not to get upset."

"Uh, oh. What are you up to now?"

She felt her cheeks heat. "I had a date with Adam last weekend."

His eyes lit with interest.

"We're seeing each other now."

"Jah, that's what Adam said." He laid down his fork and folded his hands, questioning her in a soft tone. "Just be careful. Sometimes guys don't take things as seriously as women."

Carly bristled. "You mean like with you and Miranda?"

"Jah, like that."

Miranda's happy report of her date with Jimmy struck Carly hard. Could the two relationships be compared? No. "Adam told me he loved me."

Now her brother's face reddened. "He did?"

Blushing, she asked, "Why don't you want us to be together? Don't you want me to be happy?"

"More than anything in the world. But you're my sister. And Adam's just my dumb friend. I don't want you to get hurt."

"I know you're thinking about Dale. But it's different with Adam. You know that. Sometimes I think your reservations are causing Adam to overthink things."

"You're kidding, right? He's always been the brooding type."

"Jah, but—"

He put both hands in the air as if to fend off her accusations. "Sorry, Sis. You're probably right. I'm overly protective."

Carly got up and kissed him on the cheek. "That's why I love you."

On Sunday, Adam pulled into the church parking lot behind Jimmy. When they got out of their trucks, he slapped his friend on the back.

Jimmy flinched. "I know I should stay out of this, but just so you know, Carly's in love."

Adam nodded at another member of their congregation and whispered. "You better mean with me."

Jimmy halted. "It's that serious between you two?"

"Jah, that's what I've been trying to convince you about. I'm taking your advice. Telling her about Indiana today."

Jimmy nodded. "It's the right thing. Good luck."

"Jah, better say a prayer for me."

Adam took his own advice and after church hurried across the parking lot to speak to Carly. "Can I take you home?"

She gave him a melting smile. "Sure. Just let me tell Auntie."

He waited for her in the truck, his heart picking up speed when she returned. "I still have the birthday party today, but I wanted to see you."

She shivered.

"What? I'm that repulsive?"

"Hardly," she grinned. "But it's so cold."

"Move closer."

She moved over, and he reached across her to turn up the heat, surprised when she jerked away.

"What's wrong?"

She rubbed her eye. "Something just flew into my eye. Something from the vent." Tears streamed down.

"There's tissues in the glove box."

Half blinded, she opened it and found the tissues, dabbing at her eye.

He turned onto the next gravel road and parked on the shoulder beside a row of sheltering trees.

Looking at him through watery eyes, she asked, "What's this about?"

He hugged her, pulling her close. "Just want to make sure my girl's all right."

"It's better now."

"Hey, look at this tree. You thinking what I'm thinking?" He pulled her gently into his arms, kissed her wet cheeks and found her lips. When he pulled away, he whispered, "I guess you know I'm falling hard for you."

"Jah. I'm falling for you, too." Her hand flew up to fix her hair.

He caught her hand. "I like it messy."

"Adam, the Beilers live on this road. We can't park here."

Feeling bold from Jimmy's enlightenment, that she was in love with him, he teased, "Where do you want to park?"

Smiling she scooted away, removing a handful of bobby pins and pulling down the visor to fix her hair. And to Adam's horror, the plane ticket floated down and landed right in Carly's lap. Feeling his world collapsing, he watched her pick it up and turn it this way and that.

"Just trash," he tried.

"Are you sure? It looks like a ticket of some sort." Curious, she pulled it close to her face and studied the print. "This isn't trash! It's a plane ticket. To Indiana."

Adam rubbed his hands through his dark hair. "It's not what you're thinking."

Her face tensed. She shoved pins into her hair. "I'm listening."

"We need to talk about Dale."

Instantly she went rigid. Her voice went cold. "You want to know if the rumors about us are true?"

"No." He shook his head, fumbling for words and trying to figure out how her mind had gone there. "I don't care. I mean I don't believe them."

She stared at the cursed ticket as if it was vile.

"Not about *you* and Dale. About *me* and Dale."

She troubled her brow. "You're going to visit him? To talk about us? You going to ask his permission?"

"Ew, no. This isn't about us. Look, Dale wants me to move there. He's offered me a job." When her eyes widened and her mouth slackened, he quickly added, "Of course I'm not going. Sometimes with Dad, it's tempting. . ." He was losing it, attempting to be humorous at such a crucial moment.

"You're considering it?"

"Not anymore." He cupped her cheek. "Not since we started dating."

She dropped her gaze. "Then why do you have this ticket dated January 10?" Her voice sounded small and hopeless.

"Because Dale sent it to me." How could he explain it? "Every time I talk to him, he comes up with some new enticement. He's not taking no for an answer. This ticket is just one of his useless tactics which won't work any better than the others have."

"What kind of enticements?"

Adam shrugged. "Dumb stuff. Completely ineffective."

She placed the ticket back in the visor and snapped it closed.

Watching her neck color, seeing her fury rising, he started to ramble. "Jah, dumb stuff. Like he picked out a house for me. Jenny wants to set me up on a blind date with her friend." He shook his head. "It's surreal. But I'm not having any of it. Because I have everything I need and want right here. It's you I want. You believe me, don't you?"

She dropped her gaze. "I want to, but this is sounding vaguely familiar."

Feeling hurt, Adam snapped, "I'm not Dale."

She looked up, surprised. "I know, but—" She shrugged.

Or maybe he *was* too much like his cousin. Maybe that's why she was attracted to him. But he was smart enough not to tread there. He gave a contrived laugh. "Well I'm glad that's behind us. I knew you'd understand." But his heart hammered in his chest.

"You haven't told him no yet, have you?"

He shrugged. "We both know how hard it is to say no to Dale."

Her eyes turned dark with fury. "You're wrong about that. Regardless of what you've heard, I could say no. And I did."

"Oh, Carly. That's not what I meant."

She pushed him away. "Just take me home."

Chapter Twenty-Two

Carly slammed the door and stumbled to her couch, listening to the fading rumble of Adam's truck. It was happening all over again. Adam would use the tickets to check out Dale's offer. Then he would decide to move and leave her. She gave a bitter laugh. Dale was determined to ruin her life.

She tried to calm herself, replaying the conversation. *I'm falling hard for you, but I need to clear the air.* Then there was all the blathering about Dale. Obviously, Adam was waiting for some kind of confession or denial. While he was weighing his options, he wanted to know the truth about those rumors. Well she'd set him straight on that. Or had she? What exactly had she told him?

Cocoa leapt onto the cushion beside her and snuggled into her side. She shouldn't have demanded he bring her home, but she hadn't been able to handle the shock. Her head ached from the stress of it all. She turned her face into the pillow.

When she awoke, she rose and was cleaning out the litter box when she heard *rap, rap, rap.*

Oh, go away.

Rap. Rap. Rap.

Jimmy wasn't going away. Fine. She jerked the door open. "Oh. I thought it was Jimmy." She backed away as Auntie stepped into the cottage.

"He's a coward. He asked me to check on you. Adam called him pretty distraught."

Carly plopped back on the sofa and hugged a pillow. Auntie sat beside her and pulled her into a hug. "I'm sorry."

"Men are jerks," Carly hiccupped.

"Of course they are."

"Except for Uncle Bob."

"Jah. There's a few good ones out there."

"But not Adam. I thought he was. But I was wrong. Not only is he flying to Nappanee in January to check out his cousin's carpentry business, but he's checking out a house they found for him. It's like history's repeating itself."

"Appears that way."

"But the part that really hurts is they're even setting him up on a blind date."

"He told you he's going to Indiana?"

"No, he denied it. But I saw the plane ticket. It fell down from the visor in his truck. I don't know if he would have told me anything about it if I hadn't found the ticket. He claims he loves me but admitted he hasn't given Dale his answer."

"The man sounds confused."

"I'm confused."

"Well. . ."

Cocoa started thumping. Auntie look worried. "Uh-oh. Did you feed him?"

"Jah. But I've been ignoring him."

"Well I suppose I'll have to humor that old rabbit." She reached down and met his sweet spot. "Did you know Miranda has helped me with some quilt designs?"

"No." Instantly, she remembered what Jimmy had told her about Miranda. "Was she helpful?"

"Jah. The young woman's very talented. She asked me a lot of questions about our faith."

"She acts all nonchalant, but I think she's setting her cap for Jimmy. And he's not serious about her."

"Not yet, anyway," Auntie replied.

Carly's head jerked to the side, not liking where this was heading. "Are you matchmaking?"

"Maybe. She's really sweet and kinda lost." Cocoa nipped and she jerked her hand away. "Ouch!"

With a sheepish shrug, Fannie watched Cocoa hop down the hall to the laundry room. "I sense you don't like her. Is there something I should know about her?"

Carly thought hard. "I'm not sure why we don't click. Unless it's our age difference. She's so young, and she acts even younger than she is. She is good with the residents."

"Jah. But given her past, it's remarkable that she keeps such a great attitude."

Staring at Auntie, she admitted, "She hasn't told me anything."

Auntie patted Carly's knee. "You should try to get to know her."

Giving her aunt a reproachful look, she replied, "That's fine to suggest, but the truth is I don't even know if I can drag myself to work tomorrow."

"You're a fighter. You'll survive. Once we get through today. What can I do for you?"

Carly shrugged. "Just stay awhile."

"There's no place I'd rather be."

On Monday, Carly returned to work. Becca was still flustered from a mistake she'd made over the weekend. "There was a mix-up in scheduling, and I had the guitar musician come the same time as the lady doing the Christmas card craft. And with all that mess going on, we found out that Martha was taken to the care center because she wasn't strong enough to return here after the hospital got her stabilized."

This saddened and worried Carly. She knew how upsetting it must be for Martha not to be able to administer her own inhaler. She was trying to think of something to cheer her up when she would later visit the care center. Thus her mind was partly preoccupied when Nines announced that Teacup was missing again.

Surely not, Carly thought. She'd just had Martha's room disinfected and cleaned, readied for her return. She hurried into the vacant room and saw the familiar lump in Martha's bed again. Angry, she jerked back the covers and gasped at the stiff corpse. She stared a moment, then threw the covers back over Teacup and headed for the receptionist's desk.

On the way, however, she heard Dot crying, so she stopped to see what was happening with her. "Dot?" The small woman sat at her table, her head in her arms. Gently, Carly approached. "What's wrong, sweetheart?" She spent several moments trying with no luck to make sense of Dot's garbled response. She went to her kitchenette and got her a glass of water.

After that, Dot was able to express herself. "Everybody's gone. I'm all alone."

"No you aren't. I'm here."

"Martha's gone."

"Jah, but she's just recuperating and will return to us." She didn't know that for a fact, but Dot wouldn't remember what she'd said long enough to hold her to it. "I'm going to visit her later. Would you like me to say hello for you?"

Dot nodded. "I miss her. She's my best friend. Besides Crusher." Then she started to cry again. "And he forgot my orange juice this morning."

Carly went to the sink where they always kept the dirty glass to prove that he'd brought it. "Look. See this glass. He was here."

Dot took the glass and peered into it. Then she set it on the table with a clink. "Am I going crazy?"

"No. Of course not. Just a little forgetful, but otherwise good as ever."

"I just don't understand why Martha doesn't come to see me."

Then Carly remembered the cat. "Would you like me to turn on the Christian music station?" It had been one of the ways Martha was helping Dot remember her faith.

"Please."

After getting her settled, Carly focused on her earlier purpose, hurrying to the front station to locate Sherie.

She whispered. "Nines's cat died on Martha's bed."

It took a moment for Sherie to recover, but then she quickly responded. "Let the cat alone for now, since Martha's not here. Call Adam and see if he'll make a box. Then we'll tell Nines and have a funeral for it in her room." The sad thing was that Nines didn't have any family in town to help her through times like this. With her son living out of town, they'd have to be her support.

Carly nodded. Except she wasn't calling Adam. Not after she'd ignored six calls from him yesterday. Instead, she found Miranda and asked her to make the call. Just before quitting time, Adam arrived. When he walked into the lobby, Carly turned and headed for the staff room. Minutes ticked by, and finally the door creaked open. His dark eyes peered at her. "Let's go outside and talk."

"I'm busy."

His wore a determined expression. "We can talk privately or here for the entire staff to hear."

"Fine!" She threw the door open and barked at Miranda. "I'll be back in a second." She could feel the woman's curious gaze peering into her back. Outside she crossed her arms. "Thanks for embarrassing me in front of Miranda."

He smirked. "I think you did that to yourself. Did you really think you could hide from me?"

"I wasn't hiding. I was cleaning out the refrigerator." Thankfully, she spoke part of the truth.

"Well the last time I checked. . .on our last date. . .I was a little more interesting than a dirty refrigerator. I'm sorry I didn't tell you about Nappanee, but that's old news. The important thing is our relationship. I should've told you, but I didn't think it mattered anymore. I'm sending back the plane ticket."

"That's nice. In the meantime, I'd like to take a break."

"You mean until I send the ticket back?"

"Until after January 10."

"So you don't trust me. That hurts."

"I'm sorry. This has been a really stressful day. I need to get back inside."

"This isn't over, you know."

She turned away.

"Wait!"

She paused.

"Tell Sherie I'll bring the box in about an hour. And heads up. I'm staying for the cat's funeral."

She nodded as Crusher approached them from assisted living. When he saw them, he hesitated.

"Want to help me make a cat coffin?" Adam asked him.

The older man's eyes lit. "Sure."

CHAPTER TWENTY-THREE

Since they were on a time crunch, the box was a simple, rather crude affair. Adam handed Crusher the sandpaper while he put away the woodworking tools. "I miss this place."

"Me, too. I started doing kits."

"What kind?"

"Miniature cars. Painting them, too."

Knowing such a collection wouldn't be church-approved, Adam replied. "No kidding? My lips are sealed."

"Keeps me busy so I don't have to think about Dot all the time."

Putting the cover on the saw, Adam asked, "How's she doing?"

"She had a rough day. Martha had to go to the hospital, and now she's in the care center."

With shock, Adam instantly realized the impact this would have had on Carly. "Is it serious with Martha?"

"Seems so. And Dot's been crying half the day."

"I'm sorry to hear it."

Crusher put aside the sandpaper. "You and Carly having a spat?"

Adam held up a finger while he used the noisy air compressor to blow dust off the box. Then as Crusher swept, he poured out the entire story about how he'd fallen for Carly when they worked together to hook up Martha with an old boyfriend, mentioning how that part was confidential. He hadn't even got to the part about Nappanee, when Crusher interrupted.

"You've been looking at the wrong bridge."

"What do you mean?"

"That was the summer that Martha's house burned down. Her family moved up toward Scio while they rebuilt. I'll bet it was the Larwood bridge."

Adam realized that Dale hadn't done any research in that area.

"Anyway what caused the spat between you and Carly?"

With a grin, Adam explained, "That's a long story. But the information you just gave me will make a great peace offering."

Crusher chuckled. "Glad to help."

"Now, let's get this box over to assisted living. Sherie gave me the key to the emergency exit so I can sneak it into the hall and into Martha's apartment."

"I doubt you'll get past Patty. She monitors the hall, you know."

"Let's try. The fewer residents who know about it, the less grief it'll cause."

"Hope Sherie knows what she's doing. I'd better go with you. Make sure Dot's okay."

Carly sat with Nines, who'd been given the news. The older woman took it better than Carly had predicted, but then Nines was a private woman and thought it was unseemly to show her emotions in public.

"I couldn't figure out why he kept running away from me. Now I know he was just trying to find a secluded place to rest and go to heaven. And Martha's bed really is a soft setup."

"Jah. I'm sure he went peacefully."

"He won't have to suffer anymore. I think it was pretty painful for him to get around."

It was an issue upon which Carly remained undecided. Could she ever be satisfied to lose a loved one even though their suffering was great? Thankfully, they hadn't needed to make that decision for Teacup. "Do you have his bed or something to put in the box with him?"

Nines stood, and her helpless gaze scoped the room. "No. He slept on my bed. But let's give him that sofa pillow."

Carly widened her eyes. "The one with the pretty needlework?"

"Yep."

"Are you sure?"

"He's the only family I have."

Patricia Smith knew that wasn't the entire truth. She had a son, but he'd moved to California straight from college. At the time, she'd wondered if she'd been too strict on him, always complaining about the dirt he dragged into the house and the way he dressed. She remembered teaching him to iron before he went to college.

He'd hugged her. "Don't worry, Mom. I'll be back."

It was the same thing he'd said when he moved to California. Oh, Patricia knew her memory was slipping, but he was the only family she had left. That's why she always dressed ready to go. When he finally showed up, as he did about once a year, she'd be looking her best. But after her husband died, it was Teacup who kept her company. Poor old, faithful Teacup.

Carly understood Nines's feelings. "You're right. It'll be perfect for him."

Miss Hall Patroller stuck her head inside the apartment. "Adam's here with the box."

"Thanks," Carly replied.

Nines busied herself, gathering up Teacup's toys. A few minutes later, Sherie entered the room. Behind her was Adam with Teacup.

Carly helped Nines back into her chair, and Adam placed the little coffin by her feet.

"How about we step outside for a moment and give you some time alone," Sherie suggested.

Nines didn't reply, and they all left the apartment. In the hall, Sherie said, "Let's give her about fifteen minutes, then go back in and hold the service."

When Sherie left them, Carly's head throbbed from the stress of Adam's gaze. "Thanks for doing that for us."

He nodded, "It's not much."

"It's special to Nines. She's. . ." Her voice trailed off. She wasn't ready to face Adam, especially under stressful circumstances. But he was always a rock when anyone needed him. He could be a godsend—she'd give him that.

As if he was reading her mind, he asked, "Can I take you home later?"

"No." She answered too quickly.

"It'll be too dark for you to ride your bike. I'm good for a ride, right?"

And he claimed she read him like a dog-eared book. She guessed it was mutual. Narrowing her eyes in distrust, she replied, "All right, but don't expect any decent conversation."

Adam was thankful for small victories. It was another hour until Teacup's service was over. Then he loaded the small coffin in the bed of his truck, having offered to bury her at the farm. He'd described an idyllic spot where they'd buried all their family pets. Nines had liked the idea, and he'd even seen appreciation in Carly's eyes.

Next he hoisted her bike into his truck and secured it. She was already inside the truck, shivering. Adjusting the heat control, he started down Long Street. The drive would be short. He needed to make the most of his time with the woman whose mind was set against him.

Her voice sounded far away, but she threw him a bone. "Do you think demented or partially demented people feel grief the way a normal person does?"

"I would imagine they'd get over it quicker, but they probably grieve daily about their memory loss."

She rubbed her lovely temples. Stress lined her apple-cheeked face.

Why hadn't he said something more comforting? "Got a headache?"

"Jah. A doozy."

"I've got news that'll cheer you up."

She looked at him for the first time since she'd gotten in his truck. "Oh, jah? Try me."

"Crusher told me an interesting story about Martha."

"You know she's in the care center?"

"Jah, he told me."

"I meant to go over there tonight." She looked back out the window. "But now I can't."

"Don't worry. She's a fighter. She'll soon be back at Sweet Life." Carly didn't reply, so he continued. "Anyway, the summer she was sixteen, her house burned down."

Her eyes widened, and she involuntarily tucked a stray blond curl behind her ear.

He felt his pulse quicken.

Her voice softened. "Tell me the story."

He pulled into her drive, relieved she wasn't charging out of the truck in a huff. So far so good. He explained all Crusher had revealed, ending with, "He's pretty sure it would be the Larwood bridge."

She sucked her bottom lip. "This changes everything."

"I know. We need to start over." He saw the hesitation in her eyes. "It makes sense because that bridge has a great beach where people fish. So let's go over on Sunday afternoon and poke around a little."

She jerked her gaze away. "No."

He caught her hand. "Carly, please."

But she drew it away, onto her lap. "I wish you'd quit toying with me."

"I understand I hurt your feelings. But if I'd laid everything out, especially as mixed up as my mind was in the beginning, you wouldn't have given me a chance. And I'd never have known I could fall in love with you."

Her eyes held pain, and her dimples flashed. "You even toy around with your words. Could fall in love, I think I might be in love. Jimmy told me about the kinds of tricks you both use with words when talking to women. I wish you would just leave me alone."

"It's called flirting. It's a little dance that helps guys learn about women."

Not amused, she folded her hands. "It hurts to imagine you flirting with your blind date in Nappanee. Are you going to check her out and compare her with me?"

"What? No."

She rolled her gaze toward the night sky.

"Because I'm not going to Indiana. You'll see. I'm staying here and proving to you and Dad and your brother that this is where I want to live and work." He hesitated, then added, "And love."

She studied him with a yearning expression. "I don't have any answers for you tonight, Adam. It's not a good time to be discussing this."

"I understand. Let me walk you to the door."

At her stoop, he tried to take her arm, only intending to kiss her cheek, but she shrugged away. "Thanks for bringing me home. For dealing with my bike."

"Sure. Take something for that headache and think about going over to Larwood bridge on Sunday."

She nodded and closed the door.

The drive home was dark and lonely. The Indiana opportunity had botched his life from the get-go. He wished he'd never gotten that birthday card from Dale. Maybe it had provoked Dad to treat him better, but then he'd offended Jimmy and now Carly. And before this was over, Dale and his family would be offended, too.

When he'd called to politely refuse the plane ticket, Dale had insisted that he keep it until after Christmas. He wouldn't take no for an answer, and now Carly was putting on the brakes. Even being picky over the words he used when he described his feelings. He needed to talk to Ann to see what he was doing wrong. He looked at the clock. She'd still be up. Maybe she could help him come up with an idea to win back Carly's trust. But then he remembered the little coffin in the back of his truck.

Chapter Twenty-Four

The following Sunday at church, Carly's raw emotions steered her away from Adam. She didn't want him to find out she was going to Larwood bridge with Aunt Fannie. But her plans of slipping away without notice went awry went Ann intercepted her outside the church building.

She drew her to a tall evergreen where people habitually clustered. "I'll bet you thought I forgot all about your suggestion."

"What suggestion?" Carly teased, keeping her eye out for Adam.

"Good one." Ann tilted her head expectantly.

"I knew you would get back to me when you were ready."

When Ann clapped her hands like an enthusiastic child, she got Carly's attention. "I'm going to do it! Here's my plan. I'm already taking some children caroling, so I'll take them to Sweet Life. In the meantime, I'll get organized, and the children can begin their visits in January." She beamed.

Adam appeared in Carly's peripheral vision. She touched Ann's arm, thinking to make her exit. "I'm excited. I'll have Sherie call you to work out the details." She noticed a flicker of disappointment in Ann's eyes and hesitated. "Unless you want to tell me more about it now."

Ann followed Carly's nervous glance. "Oh. I get it. You're trying to avoid my pesky brother, aren't you?"

Carly sighed. "Too late for that."

"Sorry."

Carly gave her a genuine smile. "So tell me your plan."

"I'm rounding up adult volunteers, like my sister Faith, to act as chaperones and setting up a reading program. I'm also going to work with the Sunday school team to coordinate a quarterly program for the residents—an extension of what the kids learn in class. Some songs."

Carly caught her excitement. "That's perfect. The reading will be regular, and the programs will witness to the residents who don't have church backgrounds. I knew you'd be good at this."

"Good at what?" Adam placed a hand on Ann's shoulder.

Ignoring him, she told Carly, "I have lots of other ideas, too, but thought we should start with the obvious and easiest to implement." She glanced at Adam. "I was just telling Carly how pesky you can be."

Feigning shock, he replied, "Well that was a waste of time. She already knows that. In fact I came over here to try and convince her otherwise."

"Good luck with that."

Carly's heart sank as Ann waved, leaving them alone together. Her voice was unenthusiastic. "She's agreed to head up the children's volunteer program."

"She'll be good at it. I'm glad you delegated it." He leaned in to whisper, "Gives us more time to locate James Irish."

The heat rushed to Carly's face, and she changed the topic. "Martha's back at assisted living."

"That's great. When's her birthday?"

"December 12."

"Not much time. Want to check out the bridge today?"

"Sorry. I have plans with Aunt Fannie."

"What about tonight? I could come over and get started on that picket fence at your place."

She shook her head. "No, not today."

Aunt Fannie's greeting couldn't have been worse. "I'm ready whenever you are. It's going to be fun checking out that old bridge. Take your time. I'll meet you at the car."

Adam's face, normally tanned year around, suddenly paled. His lips tensed.

"I'm sorry. I. . ." Carly faltered.

He raised his hands to ward off her explanation. "Now I get it." He turned away angrily.

Several heads turned toward them. Blushing furiously, Carly lifted her chin and hurried to her aunt's car. She got in, clenched her jaw, and slammed the door, turning on her aunt. "Why did you tell him we were going to the bridge?"

But Fannie was unaffected by the angry outburst. "I'm baiting him, Honey. Showing him what he's missing."

Carly ground out the words. "I don't want to bait him. I want to forget him."

"Well he looked real mad. So maybe that'll work out for you."

As they drove, Carly sank back in the car seat and poured out her misery. "One happy week, then everything fell apart. Within a few days I lost Adam, Martha went to the hospital, Nines's cat died, and I lost the old black dog." She swiped at her tears. "It was the last straw."

"Oh, now. That old dog was a nuisance, and you know it. What happened?"

"He got old. Don't ever get old, okay?"

Auntie remained silent.

"For a while now, I was delivering the stick to him up on his porch."

Auntie gasped. "You weren't?"

"Friday the porch was empty. He's gone. And I don't even know if he was loved."

Auntie pulled into her driveway and killed the engine. "I'm sorry. You've had it rough, for sure."

Carly nodded.

"But today's going to be different. Let's go put the soup in a thermos and head out." Auntie kept up a steady prattle after that, only pausing when they pulled into the parking lot at Larwood bridge. Then she snapped her mouth shut.

Carly felt the blood drain from her face.

Larwood bridge was under construction. Hurrying out of the car, she got as close as she could to the barricaded signs warning them to keep away.

She didn't hear Aunt Fannie's approach. "Look at all those boards in a stack across the river. I'll bet Martha's initials are on one of them."

Carly looked at the pile of boards, then back at the forbidden construction-site warnings. The bridge's floorboards had large gaps where the river showed through. "How do we get across? Is there a way around?"

"S-sh. Here comes a security guard."

Stomping her foot, Carly let out one of Martha's expletives. "Oh for Pete's sake."

"Sometimes the door just has to smack us in the face," Auntie replied.

The security guard approached, eyeing them warily, but made small talk. Were they from the area?

"Jah," Auntie replied. "Just came to have a little picnic."

He arched a brow. "Cold day for that."

"We brought a couple thermoses of soup. Just takes a small blessing like a hot cup of soup on a cold day to make a person happy, doesn't it? Want to join us?"

He studied Auntie, his gaze lifting to her head covering. "Thanks for the offer, ma'am. But I'll have to decline. I'm on duty now." He tipped his hat. "Enjoy yourselves. Just stay clear of the construction site."

"Sure thing."

After he was gone, Carly shrugged tighter into her coat. "You think this place is guarded 24-7?" Was there a road that led to the other side? Where could she get a boat?

On Monday, Carly watched Martha administer her inhaler and settle back into her recliner. "I'll bet you're glad to have that back."

The older woman coughed and dropped it into her pocket. "It was a nightmare without it. I don't understand why they wouldn't let me have it."

"Anytime you get admitted into a hospital or care center, they take away your meds."

"They think I'm demented?"

"No, of course not. They do that for everybody."

"Well I'm glad to be home. I'll never complain about this place again."

Carly smiled, wondering how long that resolution would last.

"The care center was awful."

"You had me worried. I meant to visit you, but Nines's cat died, and I ended up staying here late."

"Nines'ss cat?" Martha sighed. "I'm sorry for her."

"She's doing pretty good."

"How can you tell? She has such a vacant look, just sitting and waiting for somebody to take her someplace. Nobody ever does." She shook her head and looked Carly in the eyes. "I know you would've come if you could. But my own daughter was too busy to visit. She only came the day I was admitted and the day I was released."

"Now Martha. You weren't in the care center very long."

"Seemed like forever. Thought I was gonna die there. Anyway, Helen's just too busy for her own good."

"We all have to live our own lives."

"You telling me to butt out?"

"Eek!" Hall Patroller's sharp voice rent the air. "Bird's out! Bird's out!"

Carly jumped, and Martha started to get out of her chair. "You'd better stay and rest. I'll go check it out and let you know what's going on."

Slumping back into her seat, Martha crossed her arms.

Out in the corridor, Hall Patroller's wheelchair was up against the far wall with her arms sheltering her head and hissing, "Hate birds! Hate birds!"

Meanwhile Crusher was trying to coax Birdie down off a hall sconce. Carly hurried to Hall Patroller and touched her shoulder. "Shh. Let's not frighten the bird so Crusher can get it."

Hall Patroller lay her head against Carly's side. It was the first moment of weakness she'd ever seen in the woman. She massaged her shoulder. Down the hall, Crusher was able to coax the bird onto his arm and was stiffly walking back toward Dot's apartment when the General bounded out of his room, wearing nothing but his paper underwear. "What's all the fuss?"

"Shh! Shh!" Carly pointed at Crusher and the bird.

The General drew up his arms and made them into a pretend rifle. "Bang!"

The bird flew up off Crusher's arms and circled the hall.

"Missed 'em!" the General shouted, raising his arms and trying to get a bead on the excited bird. Thankfully Crusher took control of the situation, ducked into Dot's apartment, and whistled for the bird. When it flew home, Crusher slammed the door closed. The General stood outside the closed door. "Bang!" Then his voice lowered. "Another one got away."

Miranda came and, giving Carly a knowing glance, guided the General back into his apartment. Carly helped Hall Patroller restore her calm and went back to check on Martha, who stood in her doorway shaking her head. "What's this world coming to? Since when are we allowing birds in here?"

The comment stopped Carly in her tracks, and she softly explained, "Why, it's Dot's canary."

Martha shook her head and crooked her finger for Carly to come closer. She whispered, "Everybody knows Dot doesn't have the ability to take care of a bird. What next?" And she went into her room, leaving Carly standing in the hall with disappointment crashing over her.

Later that evening Carly snuggled on the sofa with Cocoa, who was doing his tooth-clicking purr. She felt convicted over the way she'd treated Adam. She'd never seen him as angry as he was on Sunday. She popped some popcorn and tried to read, but nothing would ease her restless spirit. Finally she picked up her phone and pressed his name.

"Hey." His voice sounded suspicious—or was it disappointment?

"Hi." She tried to sound upbeat, but there was silence on the line. He was definitely still angry. "I'm calling to apologize."

"Mm-hm. So you need my help." He sarcastically added, "What is it this time?"

"I was wrong. I should have let you in on our bridge expedition."

"As in telling me you were going or as in including me?"

He was still mad. "Both. I'm sorry." The silence on the other end cut her deeply. She'd never known him to be cold toward her. Now that the shoe was on the other foot, it made her ashamed of how she'd been treating him. No matter what happened between them, she'd try to at least be civil in the future. "And I treated you unfairly."

Finally, he asked, "Is that all?" She hesitated. He might warm up to her in a few days. Unless he was going to go to Indiana. Then he might never make amends. Maybe she'd pushed him over the edge.

His voice slightly softened, carrying a tone of dread. "Are you crying?"

She gave a strangled laugh. "No. You were right. I need your help."

"Humph."

"I'll understand if you don't want to come." She rubbed Cocoa's ear so hard he bit her. The rabbit hopped to the far end of the couch. "Sorry. Cocoa just bit me, and I dropped the phone." Hearing a bit of a chuckle, she got the nerve to continue, "Larwood bridge is under construction. We saw a pile of old boards on the other side of the river. I wanted to rummage through them, but the security guard chased us away. I'm going to go back there and see what I can find." She grinned, though he couldn't see her, and added, "So can I borrow a flashlight? Or a boat?"

"I'll be right over."

"No! Adam, wait!"

"What?"

"Not tonight."

"When?"

"Tomorrow."

Chapter Twenty-Five

Feeling nervous, Carly glanced at Adam, who'd been glum and brooding ever since she got in his truck. "Would it be easier to find the road that leads to the other side of the bridge?"

He cast her a disparaging look. "We're here now."

The parking lot was empty. As far as she could tell, there was no sign of any security guards anywhere near the bridge. Adam turned off his lights, and the night became pitch black around them. She flinched when he touched her hand.

"You know what happens to trespassers?"

"No. What?"

"I don't know. Thought maybe you did. But in case they take us away and we get separated, I want you to know, I always loved you."

Her eyes now adjusting to the moonlight, she could see his teasing grin. She jerked her hand away. "Stop it."

"Okay, then let's go."

The slam of their doors magnified under the circumstances, causing Carly to scan the area again for self reassurance. They still appeared to be alone. Adam took her hand to cross the footbridge over Roaring Creek. The sounds of its rapids intensified at night, leaving no question of how Crabtree's sister creek got its name.

Following the combined light of moon and flashlight, they passed a large picnic table and bore left, away from the rocky beach of the gentler Crabtree Creek. In the summertime, this side of the bridge was full of activity, including children swimming, dogs chasing Frisbees, and families picnicking. Tonight it was eerily vacant except for the sound of creaking trees and moving water.

With her right hand, Carly tugged her scarf tight against the bitter cold. Moving uphill toward the barricaded area of Larwood Covered Bridge, her blood warmed enough to forget any physical discomfort. They paused outside the orange-and-white barricades and stood beside a large sign: Road Closed. Adam dropped her hand and moved his flashlight, scanning the off-limits area.

To the left was private property, some deep ravines, and the perfect area for fishing. "The old boards are on the other side of the bridge," she whispered.

His masculine rumble reminded, "You don't need to whisper."

She shivered. "Jah, I suppose."

"Let me go first. Stay right behind me and watch for missing floorboards. Test the existing ones. They might be unstable, too, because of the construction." He pushed one of the barricades to the side so they could squeeze through.

Nodding, she followed him, and they reached an area where the road had been demolished. The ground was covered with small bits of debris.

"Careful," he admonished. "Don't want to tear your stockings."

She snapped his ear.

"Ouch!"

"Shh!"

They stepped over some yellow caution ribbon and around scaffolding. Then they hugged the left wall of the bridge. Only the girding remained, but they were able to use it to get hand holds as they stepped from board to board over gaping dark holes where complete sections of floor were missing. It would be a drop of twenty or thirty feet down to Crabtree Creek.

Carly's heart beat wild within her chest as they stealthily made their way across the bridge. When they reached the other side and hit the security of dirt rubble, Adam turned and pulled her into his arms. "Is your heart beating as crazy as mine?"

She slipped her arms around his waist, elated from the adventure and thrill of his arms. "We did it."

He bent and kissed her cheek. "The night's only begun."

She pulled away. "Lead on."

They quickly found the demo piles. "Put on your gloves. I'll move the boards around, and you can examine them. Watch for nails. On the ground, too."

"All right."

They'd worked in sync for a long while when Carly asked, "What time is it?"

He checked his phone. "Two o'clock."

"What? It seems like we've only been here an hour or so."

"Need a break? I've got coffee in the truck."

"No." She shook her head. "I'm not climbing over that bridge again until we're finished."

"I'll go."

"No," she maintained, mostly not wanting to be left alone. "Let's keep working. But what if their initials aren't here?"

"We're only halfway through. We need to finish tonight though, because if they see the lumber's been moved, they'll post a guard from here on out. I'd be happy to take you back to the truck so you can sleep while I finish."

"I'm not quitting."

"Let me know if you change your mind."

After that, Carly fought fatigue and was wondering how long she'd be able to continue, when Adam let out a whoop.

"What?"

"Here it is. Come see."

She scrambled around the lumber pile and felt her dress catch. Giving it a hearty tug, she didn't care that she heard tearing. She knelt beside him and ran her fingers over the aged carving. It couldn't be plainer. James + Martha and beneath it J. I. + M. S. "Wow." In reverence, she sank to her haunches and marveled. "I can't believe he carved out their entire names."

Adam searched her eyes. "They must've been in love."

"It's a shame to leave it here," she whispered.

"Then let's take it."

"That long piece of timber? Anyway, it would be stealing."

Adam frowned. "I should have brought a saw."

"It's enough to know the story's true," she said wistfully.

"Then let's get you home. We both have work tomorrow."

She nodded. The trek back across the partly demolished bridge wasn't as stirring as it had been earlier, but she carried with her a quiet satisfaction of confirming Martha's story. As the moonlight shone on them through the open roof, she willed a happy conclusion for James Irish.

Once they'd made their way safely around the barricade and started downhill, Adam drew her to himself. "What have we here?" His low rumble led her to believe that the security guard had appeared. Frantically her eyes searched the area and returned to his gaze. "It appears to be a kissing tree," he purred.

Her hand fluttered at her coat's lapel. "You scared me."

"Did I? You haven't seen anything yet." Then he drew her to a huge, barren-leafed tree with rough mossy bark and a twisted trunk.

As his arms slipped around her waist, she looked into his eyes. "I thought you learned your lesson last time."

"Didn't you know? Ants sleep at night."

Laughing she fell against him and accepted his kiss. Though her mind remained cautious, her heart couldn't push him away. He deepened the kiss so that she didn't remember they were standing in the bitter cold of night, nor care that her dress was torn and her stockings ruined. Again. All she knew was that she was in the arms of the man who owned her heart. She had no control over what he did—if he went to Nappanee or not—but tonight she didn't care.

When at last they drew apart, he whispered. "I think we found our kissing tree. This one's a keeper. So are you."

Adam was exhausted the next day but sporting a smile. Sweat rolled down his face as he worked the saw to fulfill a big commercial order. Dad was pleased. They were days ahead of schedule. The helicopter would pick up the trees at the end of the week. And the entire Portland order was due to Adam securing the account and handling all the details. Regardless of how the cut-your-own-tree lot fared this year, they'd be in the green.

And Carly had forgiven him. His prayers were answered. The previous night seemed surreal, like a wild adventure. That's exactly what Carly was—a wild adventure. Being an easy-going guy, he understood how he needed her to shake things up for him now and again. To keep life from getting dull.

Turning thirty had been devastating. Someday he hoped to view it as a year of transitions. His mind dwelled on Carly and their kissing tree. She was the godsend, a gift he would learn to cherish and protect. Would Christmas be too early to propose?

January would bring a year of new beginnings. Dad was taking him into the partnership. He'd be able to afford marriage. And they weren't getting any younger. He'd never even discussed children with her.

Dad's grunt reminded him he was getting ahead of himself. Dad was still an obstacle. He could invite Carly to spend Thanksgiving with the family. It would be an ordeal. One step at a time. And hopefully in time for Christmas. . .

"You've been whistling all day. Happy to get this order filled?"

"Jah, you're right about that. Maybe we can take an extra day off at Thanksgiving."

Dad eyed him dubiously. "The farm's open to customers."

"Then I'll rephrase that. Maybe I'll take the day off."

"Maybe. We'll see." Dad's gruff voice carried admiration, spurring Adam to take advantage of the mood.

"Think I'll ask Mom if she can handle three more for Thanksgiving Dinner."

"Oh? Who do you have in mind?" he asked gruffly.

"Jimmy." He hesitated, then added, "His family."

Dad lay down his saw and crossed his arms. "You're the most stubborn Lapp of the lot."

Adam grinned. "Which is great as long as I channel it in the right direction. Right? So I have your blessing?"

Dad's face turned red. "You do not. And it's not a joking matter. My feelings on the matter have not changed and never will." Then he picked up his saw and swore under his breath.

Dropping the matter, they worked in silence until dark. By then Adam's muscles and body sagged with fatigue and lack of sleep. He dragged himself home, showered, warmed up some of Ann's savory-smelling stew, and was ready to fall into bed when his phone rang.

Reclining, he moaned. Not Dale. He almost didn't answer, but an inner stirring made him reach for the phone.

"Hey, buddy."

"Whoa. You sound tired. Did I mess up the time change?"

"No. Just a long day. I was turning in early. What's up?"

"Bad news, I'm afraid." After a moment of silence, Dale continued. "I had an accident. Broke my leg. I'm in a cast from my hip to my foot."

Adam sat up. "What happened?"

Dale explained how he'd fallen off scaffolding and concluded with an appeal. "I need your help. I hate to ask, but I've got this job I need to complete, and you've got a plane ticket."

"I'd like to help, but—" Adam hesitated, trying to word his rejection.

"I can put my other work off, but if you could just come for a couple days to finish this one job for me, I'd be grateful."

Running his hand through his hair, Adam replied, "I'd like to, but we're busy at the farm, and I don't think I can get away. Don't you have any employees who can finish the work for you?"

"Nobody. You know how I'm having trouble with help. My lead guy is going out of town for Thanksgiving. I thought maybe you could come for the holiday. I can put the job off that long."

Adam's mind scrambled over all that would be happening at the farm on Thanksgiving. His sisters and their husbands stepped up to handle the cut-your-own-tree lots. As long as they finished the commercial job, there was really no reason why he couldn't take off some time. In fact, he'd already brought up the topic to Dad. "How many days would it take to finish the job?"

"Probably two days."

"I could take four days max, including travel time."

"I owe you. I'll change your plane tickets and get back to you with the details."

"Good." But he knew it wasn't going to be good when he told Dad his plans.

"One other thing. I got the information you wanted. On James Irish. Got a pen?"

Rummaging in his bedside drawer, Adam mumbled, "Jah, go ahead."

"I couldn't locate him. But he survived the war. And I have contact information for his grandson, Jason Irish."

"Great!" Adam scribbled the information, thinking how happy Carly would be. Then it hit him. His promise to Dale might be hard to explain to her. In fact, she wouldn't like it a bit. Might not trust him again. He told Dale to take care and recuperate, then fell onto his pillow in a sweat. Just when things were going great. But fatigue didn't allow him to overthink it. With foreboding, he fell into a sleep riddled with troubling dreams.

Chapter Twenty-Six

When James Irish's grandson Jason agreed to meet them, Carly and Adam headed to Portland. They hadn't given Jason the entire story, only that old friends were searching for his grandfather. He claimed James was living, but seemed protective of his grandfather and stipulated they meet alone.

Adam's truck ate up the interstate as Carly took in the scenery. An hour and a half away, she didn't get to Portland often. They passed small towns with food and gas exits. In the background green foothills and snow-capped mountains, like those familiar to Sweet Home, graced their travels. She remarked on the vineyards.

"You'll be seeing more of those as ground disease destroys the tree farms," he grimly stated.

"I didn't know there was a problem."

"Jah. It's spreading through the region. We're worried about our nobles, but so far it hasn't reached our farm."

"How does it spread?"

"Usually it comes with seedlings purchased from nurseries."

"Oh."

He changed the topic. "So how was work, the day after?"

He didn't have to elaborate, because their adventure and kisses enveloped them like a bright cloud, never far from either of their thoughts. "It was rough. I had to move Nines's furniture again."

"And put it back?" he grinned.

"Exactly. And Mr. Gadget used a butter knife to remove his headboard again. That man is strong."

"And determined. Seems like you could use a full time handyman just inside assisted living."

"Rocco keeps busy, that's for sure. Which reminds me. Training started for our first batch of volunteers. Your uncle made a gallant speech welcoming them. We talked a little bit, and he complimented me on the idea. Then he says, 'Why didn't we think of this sooner?'"

Adam grinned contritely for his relative. "You know he does that just to see your dimples."

"So that's a Lapp thing?"

"It appears so."

"I'm nervous, Adam."

Her nerves didn't ease when a tall blond man greeted them at the door of his expensive condo, bearing a stony expression. It gentled somewhat as his blue gaze took in their plain clothing and Carly's head covering. He invited them into a great room, impressive with tall ceilings and beams, and they sat on a leather sofa. "Can I get you a beverage?"

"No thanks." Carly squirmed. "I'm sure you're curious so we'll get straight to the point. I work at an assisted-living facility in Sweet Home, and one of my residents is Martha Struder. She told me that the summer she was sixteen, she met your grandfather. They were in love that summer, but because they weren't of the same faith, she had to sneak out to meet him at Larwood Covered Bridge."

Jason remained quiet throughout the explanation, curious but cautious. "And you are telling me this because?"

"Because she's depressed. Her eighty-fifth birthday is coming up, and I thought it would be fun to surprise her with news about James. You see after he enlisted in the military, she never heard from him again. And all these years, she's wondered if he made it out alive. Wondered what happened to him."

"That's quite a story." The broad-shouldered man studied them with a grim expression.

At this point, Adam jumped into the conversation. "According to Martha, your grandfather was in love with her, too. He carved their names and initials on the bridge. We found the old carvings."

Jason tilted his head. "So you came to invite Gramps to the party?"

"He's certainly welcome." Carly smiled. "But I wanted to get his story. How is his health?"

Jason hesitated, then seeming to have made an inner decision, replied, "For his age, he's robust. He doesn't drive anymore. He uses hearing aids and a cane. He has in-home care. What about Martha?"

"She's in assisted living because of her asthma. But she gets around well. She's been sad since her husband died about a year ago, and I got this crazy idea that finding James might bring her some joy. Of course I didn't know what we'd discover." She glanced at Adam fondly. "We even went to the wrong bridge at first. But we found out Martha's house burned down and she was living in a rental the summer she met your grandfather. That information led us to the right bridge. And finding their names and initials confirmed the story." She leaned forward and lowered her voice. "Some of the residents have dementia, you know."

Jason grinned, revealing white, even teeth set in a generous mouth. "You've gone to a lot of trouble for Martha."

"Jah. And I understand your reservations."

Jason folded his hands. "Here's what I'll do. I'll talk to Gramps, ask him about his old girlfriends. If he remembers Martha, I'll ask if he wants to meet you. Is that fair enough?"

"Jah, that's good. Her birthday is December 12."

Jason nodded.

"Oh. Martha said when they met, he was fishing. He asked her if she wanted to bait his hook. He fished regularly by the bridge."

"He does like to fish. So is Martha of your faith?"

"Jah. We're Mennonite."

Jason cracked his knuckles. "This should be interesting. I have a feeling there'll be a birthday party to attend."

Carly rose, and the men followed suit. "Thanks so much for your time."

"It's been my pleasure."

On the way to Adam's truck, Carly let out a long sigh, "Whew! He wasn't very friendly at first."

"Jah, and he thinks we can drive down here on a whim. He's a little uppity for my taste."

"But it's not about him," she reminded. "It's about James Irish."

On the drive home, Adam listened to Carly babble about her hopes regarding James Irish. She envisioned him coming to the center and playing bingo with Martha. She had him pegged as a charming man with amusing stories, who would liven up the center.

Adam had plenty of reservations. If the grandson was any indication of family genes, he would be a disagreeable old codger who falsely raised Martha's hopes then irritated her with his stories of war and commerce.

But there was another annoying problem. It was only a couple of weeks until the party, and he was going to be gone over Thanksgiving. He didn't know when he'd be able to bring Carly back to Portland to meet James. He felt she needed more of a chaperone than her aunt, who sometimes took Carly places. He'd need to forewarn Jimmy. But he didn't relish telling that pessimist about his trip to Indiana.

Worst was breaking the news to Carly. He needed to do it now, because he'd learned the hard way what happened when he procrastinated.

As the truck licked up the miles, he grew restless. But next to him, Carly's cheeks flushed with excitement, and her eyes sparkled with life. Normally, he'd be satisfied to absorb all her goodness. But he had a lifetime for that.

"How about stopping in Salem to get something to eat?"

"Jah, sure."

They pulled into a popular pasta place and parked. Taking her hand, they started toward the restaurant's entrance. "We need to start going on some real dates. Don't you think?"

She squeezed his hand. "I'd love that. Though we've done some fun things."

"You're thinking about the kissing tree, aren't you?" He enjoyed her blush and the fact that he'd rendered her speechless.

Inside, they sat at a round booth that allowed him to scoot close. A few glances lingered on them. While people in Salem were used to seeing Mennonites, many remained curious. Adam ignored them and concentrated on the adoration he saw in Carly's eyes. "I always get lasagna in Italian restaurants."

"I wouldn't have guessed you were a plain guy like that."

"I've been thinking that's one of the reasons I love being around you. It forces me to be more adventurous." She raised a brow, probably waiting for one of his quips, but he didn't tease her about her escapades. Wanted to keep her in a good mood.

"Well there's nothing plain about you," she said.

"That's because I'm a godsend."

"Burr," she corrected, closing her menu. "I'm getting the gnocchi."

"Risky," he teased.

After they ordered, she smiled confidently. "I have something to ask you. It might take you out of your comfort zone, but since that's what you like..."

"Ask away."

"Join us for Thanksgiving? Aunt Fannie invited Miranda, and Jimmy'll be there. And Cocoa, of course. Turkey with all the trimmings, and it's a tradition that we shell nuts. We could use the extra hand," she joked.

Squirming, he stalled. "I didn't know Jimmy's dating Miranda."

"They've had one date that I know of, but Auntie's doing a bit of matchmaking. She really likes Miranda because it turns out she's quite creative. Helps Auntie with her quilt patterns. Auntie wants me to embrace her as a friend."

"Have you?"

"Not really, but Miranda's growing on me."

He'd give anything to watch Jimmy try and squirm out of Miranda's clutches. It would have been more fun than what he had planned. "Actually, I was going to invite you to my family's get together. Only now I can't."

"Why don't you use your charm and try to persuade me? What time is it? Maybe we can do both."

He took a sip of water and cleared his throat. "Here's the deal. As much as I'd love to charm your socks off, I have to make a confession instead."

Her expression fell. "All right. I'm listening."

"Remember I told you that I'm not going to Indiana?"

"Jah," she replied nervously.

He quickly assured, "That's still true. I'm not. I'm staying and becoming Dad's partner on the farm. And I'm dating the prettiest girl in Sweet Home."

"Who just invited you to Thanksgiving and is listening to some sort of confession?"

"Right. And I would have charmed her socks off, only something's come up. You're probably not going to like it." Her eyes grew wide and fearful, and he felt the pulse quickening in his neck. "Dale fell off some scaffolding and broke his leg. He's in a huge cast. Now he wants me to change that ticket and go to Indiana and finish a job for him."

She was stricken quiet. She pushed her glass aside, her eyes darting to the ceiling and back. "Wow." She fastened her gaze on his. "But it's your busy season." She tilted her head, her brow wrinkled. "I thought there was tension between Roman and Simon. Did this cause trouble?"

"I haven't told Dad yet. This time, I wanted you to be the first to know. But he'd already given me some time off at Thanksgiving, which I had planned to spend with you." She didn't smile, but continued to thoughtfully study him. "I'm not going to be gone that long. Only four days, including Thanksgiving."

The waiter brought their meals, and while she was still processing the information he'd given her, they bowed to say a silent grace. He prayed fervently for her understanding. When he looked up the light had gone out of her eyes. He felt like a cad for disappointing her. "I'm sorry."

"For a guy who claims he doesn't like adventure, you like to keep me on my toes."

"How so?"

"Every time I trust you, some new surprise knocks me off my feet. You're a complicated man."

"I like the idea of sweeping you off your feet, but I need you to trust me. All those reservations I had before are gone. I want you to know that."

She nodded and offered a lopsided smile, but Adam could tell she wasn't convinced.

Chapter Twenty-Seven

Ever since Adam's pronouncement, Carly had wanted to crawl out of her skin with worry. She trusted him, but she didn't feel as if she had the nerves to last until he was home safe in her arms. She felt insignificant in comparison to all the enticements that Adam would be encountering. At best she tried to force the issue from her mind.

It was comforting to come home to Aunt Fannie's charming old house. Its age offered a stability that was missing in Carly's life after the death of her parents. A stability challenged since Adam had stolen her heart and taken her from one challenge to another.

The house was as embedded into the hillside as her aunt's influence was on her life. As she approached it now, the thick ground cover on the steep bank hid the house so that only the top portion of the windows and gables were visible from the street below. It gave the air of a place where one could hide away from the world.

As she pushed her bike up the driveway's steep incline, Aunt Fannie's quaint garage came into view. Its twenty-four tiny windows brought back memories—washing them was one of her punishments when Auntie had to discipline her. Now they shone dark. But behind them was the relic that Auntie drove whenever she ventured away from her little haven. Carly took a deep breath, drawing in all the peace the home-place afforded.

Cocoa shifted in the wicker bike basket, and Carly laughed. He'd been snorting most of the ride, his way of letting her know he didn't appreciate sharing his space with the hard container that protected Carly's pumpkin pie. Parking the bike and juggling the rabbit and the pie, she made her way inside.

The dining-room table was dusted and decluttered, set in magazine style with Auntie's old china. She now appeared, wiping her hands on her apron. "Take that pie to the kitchen, and I'll show that old rabbit where I put its Thanksgiving feast."

"You got Cocoa something special?"

"Just trying to keep the thing out of trouble." She shook her head.

Smiling, Carly placed the pie on the counter just as she heard her brother's and Miranda's voices. Jimmy must have given her a ride. Hurrying to the entryway, she took their coats and welcomed her coworker. Today she would try to see Miranda through her aunt's eyes. She needed to focus on something positive.

Soon everyone assembled in the kitchen to help with the last-minute flurry of activities. Auntie mashed potatoes and made the gravy. Carly removed a pan of moist stuffing from the oven and replaced it with the rolls. Carving the turkey was traditionally Jimmy's handiwork. She observed the banter flying back and forth as he and Miranda worked together over the succulent centerpiece. They got along well, Carly mused.

Later when they were enjoying the meal with all its trimmings, Carly sought to engage Miranda. "You missing home?"

"Yes, but they're probably not missing me too much." Carly's heart tripped at the pain that flickered across Miranda's face. She saw Jimmy pat her hand while Auntie's jaw tightened. "I did some things I'm not proud of. When the court assigned me community service or jail time, my folks arranged for me to go into V. S."

Astonished to silence, Carly quickly ascertained this was news only to herself. She fought against the heat creeping up her neck. "I'm sorry," she sputtered. "But they should be proud of you now. You're good with the residents."

Miranda beamed. "Thanks. That means a lot."

Carly remained on the hot seat when Jimmy remarked, "I thought you'd invite Adam over today. I heard from him the two of you were seeing each other again. I know you guys had a misunderstanding about Indiana. But when he told me he plans to stay, I believed him. He's crazy about you."

Miranda's head whipped from Jimmy to Carly, who could read the other woman's surprise. Though she wanted to avoid the topic, she was too miserable to carry her misgivings on her own. "I guess we'll eventually see how it plays out." Feeling all eyes on her, she stared at her plate. "I did invite him, but he couldn't come."

"Why not?" Auntie asked.

"He went to Indiana because Dale broke his leg and wants Adam to finish a job for him. He's going to be in Nappanee for four days." She raised her gaze to her brother's disbelieving expression. "He asked me to trust him. Said it had nothing to do with moving out there. He just needed to help Dale."

Auntie's fork clattered against her plate. "I don't like it."

Jimmy shook his head. "No, wait. If he asked us to trust him, then that's what we should do. If he betrays you, Sis, then he's betraying our friendship, too. And after I catch up to him, he'll wish he hadn't. But honestly, I don't think he'll do that."

"Sometimes things aren't as they appear," Miranda said. "I don't know the details here, but I know I got blamed for a lot that I didn't do. Adam seems like a great catch."

Carly laughed. "Uh, obviously. You were after him yourself."

"I'm sorry about that. I honestly didn't think you were interested."

"I know."

Miranda batted her eyes at Jimmy. "Anyway, that was before I met your brother."

Auntie's anger had dissipated, and now she beamed. "Dessert now or later?"

Jimmy grinned. "How about both?"

The afternoon was ideal, and Carly couldn't tell if Jimmy was interested in Miranda or if he was just appeasing Aunt Fannie. But they sure seemed cozy when they started the wood fireplace and cracked hazelnuts. As she watched them, she tried to view Miranda with more acceptance. The girl could use a friendly, steady influence in her life.

With Cocoa curled beside her, it would have been the perfect afternoon if not for the occasional wild thought that struck Carly at random: *Is Adam having dinner with Dale's family and that other woman? Is he having second thoughts about his promise to me?*

Adam hit the ground working. After his plane landed in Fort Wayne, Indiana, Dale and Jenny picked him up and drove seventy miles to their home, where Adam put on his tool belt and hopped in Dale's truck. He'd work all night if need be to get the job done. Nobody would understand if he needed to stay in Indiana longer than the four days he'd scheduled.

"Makes me feel like an invalid, not being able to drive," Dale complained as he gave him directions to his woodworking shop.

Adam glanced at his cousin. He hadn't changed much since he'd last seen him. A little heavier, and his hairline was receding. Other than that, they could be taken for brothers. "How long until the cast comes off?"

"The doc said I might get a walking cast in three or four weeks."

Grimacing, Adam replied, "Let's hope for three."

When they arrived at the shop, Dale hobbled on his crutches to a side door and handed Adam the keys. What Adam saw inside made his mouth drool. In the center of the room was a table saw on a large wheeled workbench. As his gaze meandered, he saw other saws, tools, and lumber racks. The walls were fixed to hold clamps and various tools, all organized impeccably. "This is amazing."

"It's my life. I love it." Dale lowered himself to a stool. "Say the word, and it's yours to share."

Adam inhaled the pleasant sawdust smell. "It's real nice. But you know I'm just here to help."

Dale shrugged. "Had to give it a try."

They worked until 1:00 a.m. that night. When they returned to the house, they snacked on leftover turkey before retiring. On Friday, they rose at 5:00 a.m. and grabbed lunches that Jenny had prepared and headed back to the shop. The project was a large entertainment center that would be installed in sections. Thankfully, under the circumstances, they were only doing the woodworking. The homeowner wanted her painter to do the finishing. They were done by 5:00 p.m., scheduling the installation for Saturday.

Jenny had dinner waiting for them when Adam got out of the shower. She laid a hand on her pregnant belly and swept the other through the air, "I suppose Dale hobbled around after you with a broom and dustpan?"

"No, but he did put the tools away as I finished with them."

"Mm-hm. Not too much of a perfectionist. It's good for you to work with him before you think about moving here. He's just a tad organized."

"She complains because I enjoy using a shop vac."

She laughed. "And I'd like to see you manipulate that with your crutches."

"The vac system is pretty amazing," Adam remarked. "At Sweet Life, it's all done the old-fashioned way. His shop is definitely first class."

"Dale misses you," she said. "I'm sorry it took an injury to get you here, but I'm glad we can spend time with you."

"Me, too." And he meant it. Jenny was not only pretty, but she was upbeat and knew just how to handle Dale. He could imagine himself living here if only he didn't already have a good life in Oregon. And while he enjoyed woodworking, he couldn't say he liked it more than tree farming. They were both in his blood.

Just then the doorbell rang, and Jenny jumped up. "I'll get it."

"No kidding," Dale teased beneath his breath.

Adam chuckled.

When feminine voices filtered into the kitchen, Dale groaned. "Sounds like her friend. I guess Jenny hasn't given up on her matchmaking scheme. She thinks it's the best way to convince you to stay."

Adam's heart sank, and his high opinion of Jenny dropped a notch. But he was taken back when a strikingly stunning woman followed her into the kitchen. Cynthia Clark's hair was smooth ebony, like Miranda's only longer and shinier, and pulled back in a ponytail. While she wasn't Conservative Mennonite, she was dressed modestly in jeans and a T-shirt. She smiled. "I was invited for pie. Am I too late?"

"Of course not," Jenny replied, moving awkwardly, with her big belly, to bring her a slice. While she was up, she refilled all their coffee mugs.

"So how's my entertainment center coming?" Cynthia asked.

Adam's mouth went slack, and he jerked his gaze to Dale, who wore a sheepish smile. "Installation's still on for tomorrow."

Instantly Adam's mind was filled with possible scenarios of what tomorrow held for him. As the evening wore on, he realized that Cynthia was naive about the matchmaking. She couldn't help it if she was a feast to the eyes and her voice was sweet to the ears. But it miffed him that Dale would go so far as to pull this trick on him. Obviously, the woman was good enough friends with them that this job hadn't needed to be fulfilled, like Dale had claimed.

Adam pushed up from the table. "Dinner was great. The pie, too. But I'm still having jet lag and think I'll retire. See you all tomorrow."

In the hall, he heard Dale's crutches clunking behind him. "Wait up."

Adam stepped into the guestroom and Dale closed the door behind them.

"It was Jenny's idea. But before you grumble, let me tell you that it really was necessary to finish her job. She has company coming for Christmas. And the income will be handy since I can't work for a while. If we hadn't finished her job, it would've stalled her remodel and her painter."

Adam nodded. "I'm dating Carly."

Dale's eyes narrowed. "So is she going to come between us?"

"I hope not. You seem happy with Jenny."

"I am." Dale hesitated, looked down at his crutches, and back up again. "You know those rumors about Carly weren't true."

Adam had known, yet it felt good to hear it from Dale. "You want to tell me what happened?"

"I was hurt. Saying I couldn't believe she'd dump me after everything between us. One of my friends took it to mean we'd been intimate, and I never set him straight. I should have. I've regretted it since."

Adam shook his head, appalled. "How could you? It's followed her, you know."

"I've a lot of regrets. Not just about her, but about Dad, too."

"It's not too late to make things right."

"Maybe, I don't know."

"I can't force you to make amends with Simon. Though I know he's lonely and ready. But I probably will ask you to apologize to Carly at some point."

Dale sighed. "If the time is right. Sleep good, Cuz."

Once Dale was gone, Adam sank onto the edge of his bed. He was glad they'd talked about Carly. It made the trip worthwhile. But he knew Dale wasn't convinced he'd turned down his offer. He thought about the stunning brunette in the kitchen. He supposed tomorrow they'd tour the house they'd picked out for him, too. If he still needed to get away from Sweet Home, the enticements his cousin offered might be too great for him to resist.

Chapter Twenty-Eight

On Thanksgiving evening, Carly was refrigerating leftovers Auntie had sent home with her when the phone rang. Her heart sped, but it wasn't Adam.

"Hi. Jason Irish here."

An image formed of a serious, broad-shouldered blond sitting in an expensive condo.

"I spent the day with Gramps. It didn't take much nudging to get him talking about Martha."

Carly stepped over Cocoa and perched on the edge of her couch. "Really? What'd he say about them?"

"Said she was his first love. He taught her how to fish, and she taught him about God."

"She didn't tell me that. I wonder if she was hoping to convert him."

"She did actually. Not to her faith. Their beliefs clashed when it came to the military. But God helped him get through the war. When he returned, he looked for her and discovered she'd gotten married."

"How romantic."

Jason laughed.

Carly found the deep, pleasant sound hard to associate with the stern face she remembered. "Did you mention the party?"

"No. I'll let you handle that."

"All right."

"I don't work Saturday. Are you available to meet him then?"

Carly's mind scanned her options. "Let me think. Adam's out of town, but my Aunt might be able to drive me to Portland."

"You don't have a car?"

"No, I ride a bike."

"No kidding? So do I."

Remembering his fancy home, Carly tried to imagine his tall, lanky body on a bike. "You ride for sport?"

"No. To work."

"Really?" She stretched her legs out on the couch and plumped a pillow. "Where do you work?"

"I do a couple of things, but I was talking about the Homeless Shelter I manage."

"Seems like we have some things in common."

"What kind of bike do you ride?"

"A pink beachcomber with a wicker basket."

He laughed again, and the sound grew on her. "I wasn't expecting that."

"I do get criticism for my choice, but it's my one splurge. If I owned a car, I wouldn't be able to give to the assisted-living facility where I work. Oh, it's piddling. But it's the right thing to do. Especially since my family can help with my transportation."

"I do it just because I love riding."

"Oh, I do, too. What kind of bike do you have?" She imagined a speed bike with all the bells and whistles.

"An old green clunker. One that's not so tempting to steal since it's not a safe area." In her astonishment that Jason wasn't the stiff caricature her mind had created, they shared a brief silence.

Then he offered, "Listen, I don't mind picking you up."

"I don't know. It's out of your way."

"I'd like to get to know you better. For Gramp's sake."

"Jah. All right."

"Adam's not going to get jealous and come after me with a ball bat is he?"

She thought about the possibility that he was entertaining his own blind date, and for an instant, she wanted to get even. But she quickly discarded the idea. They needed to trust each other. "No, he understands how much this means to me."

On Saturday, Carly stared at the blue BMW convertible and wondered how Jason would fit into it. "You don't want to see what will happen to my hair in this."

"No worries. I'll keep the top up." Jason studied her curiously. "How long is your hair?" Carly cringed, suddenly wondering if she should be getting in the car with a man who was little more than a stranger.

"Sorry. That was out of line. I was just curious if you have to cut it short like nuns or how you get it up in that cap."

"You always say whatever pops into your mind?" she asked, getting in and fastening her seatbelt.

He started the engine, and they pulled onto the road. "No, but my curiosity does sometimes get me in trouble."

"I can imagine. But I can also sympathize."

"Oh?"

"My aunt says trouble follows me like bees to honey."

He laughed. Laughter that emanated from his wide mouth and extended to his eyes.

"You have a sense of humor. I didn't sense that the first time we met."

"Protecting Gramps and his fortune is a job I take seriously."

"Well nobody's after his money. I can assure you of that." She grinned. "Unless you'd like to make a contribution to Sweet Life Assisted Living."

"And what would Sweet Life do with it?"

"Probably get a new roof and repair"—she faltered—"I don't know because everything there is old."

"You must really take an interest in the residents."

"Of course. I've dedicated my life to them."

"So how does Adam fit into that scenario?"

She shrugged. "He knows me pretty well. It's just my aunt, my brother, and me. Jimmy goes out of town to work, so he asked his best friend, Adam, to take care of me when he's gone."

"So he's like a brother figure?"

"It started that way. He's continually getting me out of scrapes. Lately, it's more."

"Then you aren't engaged or anything?"

She felt heat climbing her neck. "No. We're trying to work through a few obstacles. Why?"

"Just getting to know you."

She glanced at him but couldn't read his expression. "Besides your grandpa, what's your family like?"

"It's just me, a sister, and Gramps."

"Is your sister married?"

He flashed perfect teeth. "Yup. I have two little nephews."

"My brother isn't married."

"So tell me about your faith. Your church."

"We believe like most Protestant faiths when it comes to Jesus, but we have a few differences that set us apart." His eyes glanced at her head covering. "As you already know, we are peace loving and don't believe in going to war or taking civil jobs."

"You think the world would be better without government?"

"No. But we can't do anything that would require carrying arms or making laws that go against our faith."

He nodded, glancing back at the road. "All right. What else?"

"We live a plain lifestyle."

"Do you mind describing what that's like?"

She tried to compare it to his own lifestyle. "We don't have televisions, and our cars are plain-looking. We use phones and computers for work but try to refrain from getting involved in technology."

"Why?"

Remaining patient, she replied, "Though we live in the world, we are not to be of the world."

"You have a Bible reference for that?"

"Sure. John 17:16: 'They are not of the world, even as I am not of the world.' And Romans 12:2 says, 'Be not conformed to this world.'"

"Thanks for explaining it. So your people wouldn't approve of my car?"

She smiled. "No, not really."

"But you have a pink bike?"

"Jah. And a bright yellow cottage."

"You a rebel?"

"No." She considered his remark. "Maybe a bit. I just don't see why we can't enjoy beautiful colors."

"I agree wholeheartedly." He smiled. "You think Gramps and Martha had talks like this?"

Carly grinned, "I suppose they did."

"It's sad, isn't it?"

Carly nodded.

"But romantic."

"I was hoping they could at least enjoy a friendship. I imagined your grandpa coming to play bingo with Martha." She shook her head. "I had no idea they would live this far apart."

"It's not so far. We're already on the outskirts of the city."

Although the streets were filled with lovely estates, Carly gawked as Jason turned into a long winding drive that led to a white, multiple-gabled mansion. Jason pointed past pristine lawns to a smaller house. "That's where Betty, Bree, and Paul live. Betty's Grandpa's caregiver. Bree, the daughter, manages the inside housekeeping, and Paul takes care of the outside property. We're fortunate to have them."

"I'm embarrassed now, thinking your grandpa would enjoy playing bingo at Sweet Life."

"Nonsense. Don't make any judgments until you meet him."

He led her in a side door, down a long hall with gleaming wood and plush rugs, and into a room where light flooded from a bank of bay windows. "Hey, Gramps. Thought I'd find you in here."

"Trying to soak up some sunshine." James was an older version of Jason. Upon seeing Carly, he struggled to rise from his chair.

Quickly, she crossed the room. "Please, don't get up on my account."

His bottom plunked back onto his chair. "Just give me another try."

She steadied his arm as he rose and leaned on his cane. "See, I can still stand when I see a pretty girl." He glanced at Jason questioningly.

Jason stepped forward. "Gramps, this is my friend Carly Blosser.

She works at an assisted-living facility."

"Heh?"

Jason raised his voice, "Assisted-living facility."

With that, he plopped back in the chair. "Don't even think about it."

She laughed while Jason explained in a loud voice, "I'm not. Now don't be rude."

James shrugged. "My apologies. So are you a long-lost daughter or something?"

"Gramps!"

Carly raised her voice. "Hardly at my age." She poked her finger at his arm. "Now quit sassing me, and I'll tell you a story you might find interesting."

He caught her finger. "You have my interest, little lady."

Pulling free, Carly crouched beside him and spoke close to his ear. "An old friend of yours lives at the facility where I work. Her name is Martha."

His eyes widened. "When I saw you, I had to think of her. She dressed like you." Then he motioned with his hand, "Get up. Get up. Jason, bring her a chair. And get me my hearing aids, too."

After they were both settled, she explained how she'd been reading a news report about a covered-bridge festival when Martha told her about that summer. James's eyes took on a faraway gaze that touched Carly's heart. "She's a widow now."

"Did she have a happy life?"

"Jah. She married a good man and has children and grandchildren. She loved John, but I can tell she never forgot about you, wished things could have been different."

"I knew John was after her. Figured he'd marry her while I was away. Of course we had no commitments. She wouldn't leave her faith for me. I came from a military family, and she couldn't abide that."

"I'm sorry. Would you like to be her friend now?"

He dipped his head, and at first Carly thought he'd fallen asleep. She glanced at Jason, who shook his head. So she waited. Finally he raised his head. "The Lord is my Shepherd now. It's always best to consult Him before making decisions. Yes, I'd like to see her again."

"Sweet Life is run-down compared to your home."

"She looks dumpy, eh?"

"No, no," Carly exclaimed. "The assisted-living facility."

He shook his head. "That's not important. I know Jason and I are spoiled, but we're not snooty."

"Good! Martha's daughter is planning a surprise birthday party for her. Would you like to come?"

"I won't give her a heart attack, will I?"

"No. Her heart's strong. She suffers from asthma, though."

"I remember. Poor thing. Jason. Find out what kind of gift she'd like."

After a gentle tap, a pleasant woman entered the room. "Time for your meds, Gramps."

They took their leave then, and Carly couldn't contain her excitement. She squeezed Jason's arm. "Thank you so much. I'm thrilled. I can't even express how I feel."

Laughing, he gave her a one-armed hug. Releasing her, he said, "You're really good with the elderly. Thanks for giving Gramps something to anticipate."

"You're welcome." She couldn't wait to tell Adam. He'd promised to call. Maybe tonight?

Chapter Twenty-Nine

The anticipated phone call didn't come until Sunday afternoon when Adam should've been sitting on a plane to return home.

"I miss you," he said.

"Miss you, too. But I thought you should be in the air about now."

"I changed my flight."

Carly's stomach clenched. "What's going on?"

"I got the job finished, but Dale had forgotten about a lumber order that would arrive on Monday. It needs to be stacked in his shop. He's got a small forklift, but it still takes hands on to get the job done. By staying a couple extra days, I can get him all caught up and feel better about leaving him, helpless as he is."

Carly paced and stared out her kitchen window. "You're a good friend, but isn't there someone at his church who can help him?"

"That's another thing. They fell out of the habit of attending church. I think he needs encouragement in that direction. I'm hoping for an opportunity to talk more about it."

Her stomach churned. But it didn't surprise her. "I'm sorry to hear that."

"Have you heard from Jason Irish?"

"Oh, jah. He took me to meet his gramps."

"You mean he came to Sweet Home to get you?" Adam asked, his tone incredulous.

"Jah. Pretty sweet of him, huh?"

His voice screeched. "You allowed a stranger to haul you to Portland and back?"

A squirrel scampered across the yard and out of Carly's view. She turned away from the window. "He's not a stranger. He's a compassionate individual who works at a homeless shelter. Even though he has a ton of money, he drives an old bike to work. The reason he seemed cold when we first met him was because he's responsible for protecting Gramps from people who are after his fortune."

"That may or may not be true. You only have his word on it. But you still shouldn't have gone with him."

She sighed and sank onto her sofa. "If you would have met Gramps, you'd know. It gets tiresome having you and Jimmy telling me what I shouldn't be doing."

"Sorry." But his tone was anything but agreeable.

The line went awkwardly silent, and Carly knew she couldn't allow him to hang up before she asked the question so heavy on her heart. "So did they set you up with Jenny's friend?" Silence lingered. Disappointment enveloped her. "They did."

"Not like you're imagining. But the job I did was for Cynthia. She was there for the install, and she's pretty much a part of the family. She told me she's concerned for Jenny, hoping she'll start going to church again."

Cocoa hopped onto her lap and stretched to lick her salty cheek. "Why don't they go to church?"

"There was a dispute about bringing instruments into the worship service. You know they attend a liberal church similar to Uncle Si's. Guess they were sickened by the church split and thought they'd stay away and heal. Only they aren't going anyplace now."

Pushing Cocoa down, she replied, "That's so sad."

"For my conscience' sake, I really needed to stay and do what I can to help them. Dad didn't like it much, but like you said, it's tiresome to have people trying to change my mind about things."

"Jah. I get that." *Guess I had that coming.*

"Well I need to hop in the shower."

"I appreciate the call."

"Miss you."

"You, too."

The next day as Carly flew down the hill at the end of her street, cold air burned her red swollen eyes. Into the wee hours, she'd wrestled between believing Adam or reading more into his actions. If he decided to move to Indiana, she'd be devastated. In her misery, she discovered a deeper root for her distress. She was lacking God's peace. Once she was able to cast aside her own wishes and offer God her future, His peace filled her. She closed her eyes now, relishing the Holy Spirit's presence.

And that's why she was blinded to the skateboarder who darted out from a side street. The collision sent them both skidding across asphalt. Something hard crashed into her face and blackness followed. Moments later, she stirred to find the concerned features of a teenage boy hovering over her.

"You all right?"

"I think so." She raised on one elbow. The kid's backpack was in the ditch alongside her bike. "Are you? I'm sorry. I didn't see you."

"My fault." He explained, "When I saw we were going to hit, I ditched my board. It hit your front tire and bounced up and hit your face. It's all bloody. Looks like your nose is broke. And you already have a shiner."

"Help me up? See if I can stand?" The boy pulled, and she was able to rise, pretty sure nothing else was broken. She straightened her skirt, noticing it was stained, her stockings torn.

"You skidded quite a ways."

"Wow." She tenderly touched her nose, then her eye, and withdrew a bloody hand. She felt queasy. "I'd better go home."

"I've seen you before. You live up the hill." He retrieved his backpack and skateboard. "I'm gonna be late for school if I don't get going. But you look bad. You should go to the doctor."

She smiled, and her whole face throbbed. "Go on. I'm fine."

"You sure?" he asked, slipping into his backpack.

"Jah."

The kid snatched up his skateboard and sped down the hill. Carly started toward the ditch, wincing with pain. She groaned when she saw her back fender was dented. *The worst yet,* she mumbled walking it up the hill. *Wonder if this ever happens to Jason.*

At home, she'd barely made it into the house when there was a rap and the door opened. "Look at you," Imogene exclaimed. "I couldn't believe it when I saw you out my kitchen window. You got a first aid kit?"

"Jah, in the bathroom."

"Sit down, honey. Let me take care of you."

Carly sat at the table and called Sweet Life. "I had an accident on my bike. I'm not going to be able to come in today." She shook her head, "No, I'm okay. Just banged up. My face collided with a skateboard." Imogene returned with the first aid kit and a hand mirror for Carly to see her face. "I'll keep in touch. Bye." She clicked off the phone and looked into the mirror. With a gasp, she said, "I look like a monster."

"Let me clean it up. You need to go to the doctor." Imogene worked, clucking over her like a mother hen. "You're going to need stitches on your temple. Change your clothes, and I'll go get the car."

As Carly moved to the bedroom, every muscle ached. When she got home, she was going to crawl into bed for a week.

During her three-day convalescence, Carly was convicted about her outburst to Adam. *I'm tired of people telling me what I shouldn't do.* Though she didn't like people interfering with her plans, her recent spill reminded her that she needed caring people in her life. Between her neighbor's concern and Aunt Fannie's tongue lashing, she felt loved. She'd spent time reading the scriptures and praying for renewal.

Her body was battered. While her clothing covered the bruises, her broken nose—though set by the attending physician under anesthesia—was swollen and purple. Her shiner had turned yellow, but she could cover her stitches by carefully swooping her hair over the area in a ridiculous manner, compared to her normal style.

Her first day back at work, the residents stared at her as she gazed at the beautifully decorated Christmas tree gracing the lobby.

Becca nodded with pride. "Volunteers and residents. Ain't it gorgeous?"

While Old Holley Fellowship didn't decorate trees for Christmas, she couldn't deny it provided a wondrous touch.

"Wait till you see it at night."

Dot looked at the tree, then at Carly. "What happened? You look like a freak show."

"Freak show," Repeater said, seeming pleased with himself.

The residents didn't want to talk about the tree. They wanted to talk about Carly. They managed to get the entire story of her accident during breakfast.

"I was going down this long hill by my home so I'd picked up quite a bit of speed. Then a skateboarder darted out of a side street, and we collided."

Dot's eyes widened. "You ran over a kid? Did you kill him?"

Martha shook her head. "She doesn't drive a car. She was on a bike."

"He saw the collision coming before I did and ditched the skateboard. It hit my tire and bounced up at my face."

"You used to be so pretty." Dot's eyes softened and distanced. "*Jack fell down and broke his crown*."

Crusher patted her hand and looked sympathetically at Carly, mouthing, "Sorry."

Carly smiled, glad that Crusher seemed happier these days, now that he had his new model-car-kit hobby to keep his mind occupied.

"She's still pretty," Martha defended.

"Thanks. Now let's change the subject. Tell me what kind of birthday cake you want me to bake. Red Velvet or German Chocolate?"

"It's my birthday?" Martha asked.

Carly's heart filled with sadness. Ever since Martha's trip to the care center, she'd been having frightening memory lapses.

The General, who'd been fiddling with his hearing aids, piped in, "Scars just add character." Standing, he started to unbutton his shirt. "Wanna see my war scars?"

"No," the women squealed in unison.

After that, forgetful as many of the residents were, they continued to question her all day long. Each time, Carly's explanations grew shorter until she quipped, "Just a biking accident." And her frustration increased with their childlike insults.

Miranda, who'd watched the breakfast scene unfold, later drew Carly aside. "Sorry about the accident. I wanted to visit you. To help. But I don't have a car."

"You did help by carrying the extra load here."

"You're right about that. It takes two people to replace you, and of course, we only had one. Plus Becca. A new guy, Brett, is starting a computer class. He even got some people to donate two computers."

"That's great."

"Crusher's his first enrollee."

"Really?" Carly was stunned. She imagined him too conservative-minded to learn computer but wouldn't judge him.

"And with the new companion volunteers coming in and out. . .it all helps."

Carly grinned. "Exactly."

"But I'm glad you're back."

Feeling Miranda's sympathetic gaze, Carly replied, "Thanks. The doctor said I won't have any war scars."

Miranda laughed. "Good to know." She whispered, "Don't let the General hear you."

"No kidding."

"I suppose Jimmy and Fannie both want to take your bike away."

Normally that would've raised Carly's ire. But since her prayers, the old defensiveness was diminishing. "Guess we're in the same boat. Neither of us have cars. With you in Albany and me in Sweet Home, it's hard to develop a friendship outside of work."

"If I stay here, I'll get a car. Or maybe a cute scooter like Aesop drives. It's hard to live on the smidgen I get from V. S." One of Miranda's eyebrows lifted. "I don't mean to be nosey, but you get a pretty good salary here, right?"

"It's plenty. I could afford a car, but I choose to live with less." No need to tell Miranda how much of her paycheck poured back into Sweet Life. "So you're thinking about staying after your V. S. term is over?"

Miranda nodded. "I like it here."

"I hope you stay."

Miranda pulled her into a bear hug.

"Ah-h. Careful."

"Oh, sorry. Maybe we can beat fate. A couple of us from the house are going to a Christmas craft festival. We could swing by and pick you up."

"In case you haven't noticed, I don't look so great to meet new people right now."

"They'll love you. Think you're brave. If you like, I can put some makeup on you."

"I don't know about that. But I do need to find a gift for Aunt Fannie."

But further planning was shelved when Nines came crying, "My picture of Teacup is missing. And I know who took it."

"Before we accuse anybody, let's go check your room. Maybe the cleaning lady moved it."

CHAPTER THIRTY

After work, Carly soaked in her tub, laughing at Cocoa's antics visible through the open door. The rabbit scurried from room to room, leaping and twisting in the air as if to lure Carly to join his play. "Sorry, but I'm not so energetic. You probably slept all day." Cocoa, made another leap and scraped the wall. "Uh, oh. You okay?" He scampered away in embarrassment.

When the phone rang, she stepped onto a bath mat and snatched her robe from the back of the door.

"Hi. It's me, Jason."

"Oh. Hi." Carly sank onto her yellow quilt and lay back against the pillow.

"Gramps is excited about the party. Keeps asking me what to get Martha for a present. Any ideas?"

"A book? She's an intellectual. Loves to talk about current events. Unfortunately since John died, she doesn't have anyone to talk politics. I read the paper with her whenever I can."

"No wonder they clicked. I'm sure Gramps can find a good book."

There was a moment of silence, and Carly ventured, "I thought of you this week."

"You did? I've been thinking about you, too."

She felt her cheeks sizzle, realizing he'd taken it wrong. "When I dumped my bike."

"Whoa. What happened?"

"You know the hill at the end of my street?"

"Mm-hm."

"I collided with a skateboarder."

"Ouch."

"Exactly. I broke my nose."

His voice held concern. "I'm sorry. Hope everything's reparable?"

"I look nasty, but I'll heal. The kid got off with minor scrapes. Am I the only one who takes spills?"

"Hardly. I crashed into a tree one time when I was looking the other way. That stopped me in my tracks. Another time, I was passing a car and a man opened the rear door and I slid halfway under his car."

She laughed, easily picturing herself doing similar things, only it seemed funnier to imagine his tall, lean body taking the hits.

"Laughing at me? Now you owe me. And I've got the perfect way to collect."

"Jah? How's that?"

"I'm coming to Albany this weekend for a charity event for the homeless. It's called Super City Event. We set up a clinic and barber shop. There's free food and employment agencies for those seeking employment."

"I'll bet that's something to see."

"I was hoping you'd say that. The clinic could use help, and since you're a caregiver. . ."

"But not a nurse," she reminded him.

"I understand. But they need extra hands. And hey, if you look a little beat up, you'll fit right in at the clinic."

She laughed. "Ha. Ha. Sorry, but I already made plans for Saturday."

"How about Sunday? I can pick you up."

She wasn't sure how others in her church would feel about skipping the service, but she had no qualms when it was for a good cause. "Jah I'd like that." She heard an engine pull into her drive and pulled back her curtain. "Jason. I've got to go. Adam just pulled into my drive."

"Okay, tell him hi. Talk to ya later."

She pulled her robe tight and went to the door. When he rapped, she opened it just a crack and peeked out at him with a grin. "Hi. I'm glad you're home."

"Carly? What happened to you?"

"Just a bike accident."

He started to push the door open.

"Wait! Give me a minute to dress, and I'll be right back." She shut the door and hurried into a dress and stockings before she returned. "Sorry about that."

"No problem." He took her hand and massaged her thumb. "What happened?"

For the umpteenth time that day, she repeated the story. Earlier with Jason, it seemed funny, but with Adam's concerned eyes peering into hers and his brows arched in that judgmental *V*, she felt embarrassed.

"A skateboarder?" He shook his head and perched on the edge of her sofa, patting the cushion. Pulling her into his embrace, he whispered, "It's good to be back. You need somebody to take care of you."

She tensed, pulling out of the embrace. "It's embarrassing. Can we just drop it?"

His hand dropped to his lap. "Jah, sure."

She fought the lump in her throat and forged ahead with the question that was foremost in her mind. "Did you get your work finished in Indiana? Or do you need to return?"

"I'm done. Home to stay."

Relief flooded through her, but she studied him thoughtfully, searching for sincerity.

He kissed her cheek. "I hope that was a spot that wasn't bruised."

While it was good to have him back, things felt tense between them. "It was my first day back to work. I'm pretty exhausted."

His expression fell with disappointment. "Can we get together this weekend? I'd like to take you to the Point, the restaurant that overlooks Foster Lake. Then I'm available if you need help going to Portland or—"

She shook her head, and he looked puzzled. "No?"

"I'm sorry, but I didn't know when you'd be back, and I booked my weekend already."

With frustration, he repeated, "Booked?"

"Saturday I'm going to a Christmas craft show with Miranda and some of her friends. I don't know what time we'll get back."

"How about Sunday?"

She shook her head. "I'm sorry, but I can't. I'm going to Albany with Jason."

His voice exploded. "On a date? What is this? Revenge over Cynthia?"

"Of course not. I'm helping him with a homeless project called Super City Event. I'm working in a free health clinic."

He slumped and crossed his arms.

"Like I said, I didn't know when you'd be home."

"I told you I was only staying a few extra days."

"Actually, you didn't share much about your plans. And you only called me once." If he'd really missed her, he'd have called more often. The grating sound of Cocoa's nose pushing his water dish across the floor drove her to her feet. She took it to the kitchen to refill. Then she stared out the kitchen window. Darkness met her eyes and filled her heart. Why was everything with Adam becoming so difficult?

She was aware that her single status partly stemmed from her take-charge, nonsubmissive attitude. She'd thought he liked that about her, but now she wondered if they were always going to clash. She'd been focusing on why he wasn't ready for a relationship, but maybe she should have been focusing on her own heart. Could she give up her free will for him?

He followed, touched her shoulder. "I didn't call because I worked late hours. I fell into bed exhausted each night and rose before daylight. So I could get home again. But I didn't realize that Jason would move in on you while I was gone."

She turned to face him. "It's not like that. We're just friends. We have a lot in common, working in social services." She raised her chin. "He rides a bike to work, and. . .he understands. . .me."

Looking stricken, Adam replied, "In a few short days, he understands you? It's taken me a lifetime, and I still don't understand you."

That's my point.

She started to rub her temple, but felt her stitches and let her hand drop. "Look. I'd love to see you, but I've made a commitment to work at the clinic. Now it's your turn to trust me."

His jaw hardened.

It felt liberating to throw back his favorite line at him. Until the

Holy Spirit checked her motives. She urged softly, "Adam?"

"I do. It's him I don't trust."

"He said Gramps is looking forward to Martha's party."

"I'm sorry I wasn't here to finish what we started."

She touched his arm. "I know."

He placed his thumb under her chin. "We're both tired. And I don't want to fight." She nodded.

"I'm going to be swamped at the farm this week." He grinned then, and she got her first glimpse of her godsend. "We've been through worse. We'll survive this. So you want to book me for the following weekend?"

Biting her bottom lip, she replied, "Sunday afternoon is Martha's birthday party."

"I'll take you."

She smiled. "I'd like that."

He kissed the top of her head.

"It's a date."

She watched him drive away. *He's right. We're just too tired to think clearly.* "Come on, Cocoa, let's go to bed."

Despite the age differences, Miranda's roommates accepted Carly as one of the gang. Since they all had to pinch pennies—given their voluntary positions—they accepted her mode of transportation as reasonable and her bruises as marks of honor. She was surprised to discover how much they knew about her. Seemingly, Miranda often spoke about Sweet Life.

Still she was relieved when they dispersed at the craft show. Inside a large building, booths were decorated with greenery and twinkly lights to create a Christmas theme.

Miranda smiled. "Told you you'd fit in."

"They're great. Thanks for inviting me."

They stopped at a stationery booth. Fingering a ladybug paperclip, Carly asked, "Are you going out with Jimmy tonight?"

"Nope. I'll be washing my hair and doing my nails. Tomorrow I'm in charge of devotions, and I still need to prepare." Carly sensed something was bothering Miranda. They moved to a booth displaying candles and fragrant soaps. "Everything okay, then?"

"I do need to ask you something."

Carly nodded. "Sure."

"Is our friendship based on my relationship with Jimmy?"

"Of course not. Actually, Aunt Fannie is responsible for pointing out all your good qualities. Guess I was stuck in my own little world, not seeing." She shrugged. "I mean, we don't look like we go together, do we?"

"Assumptions. They've plagued me all my life. I try to avoid them." Miranda picked up a bar of cellophane-wrapped soap and sniffed. "This reminds me of Mom."

"Is that good or bad?"

"Both. I miss her."

"Let me buy it for you." At first Miranda objected, but eventually she accepted Carly's gift. "I like volunteering, but I'll be happy when I actually get paid for working at Sweet Life. My term's about over. Sherie said they'd keep me on if I stay."

"That's great! I hope you do." They skirted around a line of rowdy children waiting to get their faces painted.

"Last weekend Jimmy and I came to an understanding. We like each other as friends, but he's not ready to settle down, and I'm not willing to live a plainer lifestyle so. . ." She shrugged.

Carly slipped an arm around Miranda. "I understand. But you probably need to have this talk with Aunt Fannie. She's the matchmaker."

"I hope I'll still be able to hang with you guys. You're starting to feel like family."

"You won't be able to get rid of us. Oh look!" She hurried to a booth of art supplies and chose a white leather portfolio with a clear pocket in the front where Auntie could place a colorful quilt pattern. "It's perfect."

As they left the booth, Miranda urged, "Before we meet up with the others again, tell me what's going on between you and Adam."

Carly shared as honestly as she could about their fragile relationship and their most recent obstacle—that Adam didn't trust Jason. It felt good to have a sympathetic ear.

When Carly grew quiet, Miranda reasoned, "Jason might be the push Adam needs to get his act together."

Chapter Thirty-One

Here he comes! Wow, what a looker. And his car's amazing."

"Stop! He's going to see you," Carly warned.

Miranda released the curtain and jumped away from the window. "If you don't want him, you can hook me up."

"You don't think he's too old?"

"I usually date older guys."

True, but Carly still couldn't imagine them as a couple.

Aunt Fannie crossed her arms. "Such talk. Just like that, you're tossing Jimmy aside?"

"We both know he's not ready to settle down."

"That man. What'd he say to you?"

Miranda sought Carly's eyes for support. "I'm not ready either, Fannie."

It had been Miranda's idea to have Jason pick Carly up at Fannie's. She'd planned to attend church with Fannie and work on their patterns afterward. She told Carly she was going to break the news that Fannie's matchmaking efforts had been a wash. Carly supposed this was one way to do it.

"Now behave yourselves." Carly went to the door and invited Jason inside.

After the introductions were made—including Cocoa—they took time for a cup of coffee. Seeing the patterns scattered on the dining-room table, Jason asked Fannie about her project.

"I create quilt patterns. Miranda can take what's in my mind and put it on paper."

"You were doing fine with that before I came along," Miranda replied.

"You're good inspiration for me. Anyway, it's just an old woman's dream."

Carly explained, "Auntie wants to get a pattern book published. She's had some appointments with publishers and come close but hasn't closed a deal yet."

Jason examined some of the patterns on the table. "I think your dream is valid. These are beautiful. Once they're copyrighted, they'd make awesome framed artwork and calendars. Even stationery."

Aunt Fannie's face beamed, gazing at Jason as if he were better than Texas sheet cake. He also praised Miranda, reminding Carly how wrong her first opinion of him had been. He was generous with acknowledging other people's gifts and encouraging them. His real personality was upbeat. As he and Miranda bent their heads over a design, the stars in her friend's eyes almost made her chuckle.

"Thanks for sharing Carly with me today." She broke from her musing to find him gazing at her with admiration. "She's going to be a hit at the clinic."

"Everybody adores her at Sweet Life," Miranda affirmed.

"Jah, you don't need to talk about me like I'm not here."

They laughed, and he regretfully admitted they needed to scoot to get to the clinic on time. Cocoa hopped after Carly. At the door, she knelt and patted his head. "Be good." Then she told Auntie, "Don't forget to close your bedroom doors and put the chairs up tight against the dining-room table. And remember, he'll obey his bell."

"That old rabbit doesn't know how to behave. Now skedaddle before I change my mind about keeping it today."

In the car, Jason smiled warmly at Carly. "I'm glad I got to meet your aunt. I can tell she's a character. Like Gramps. And I mean that in a good way."

"I'm used to her scolds. She means well. And for the record, she adores Cocoa."

"That's what I figured." He pulled onto Route 20, headed west toward the freeway and Albany. "I didn't want to say anything that might get Fannie's hopes up, but I have a good friend who's in publishing. I could get Tom to check out her patterns. What do you think? He works for a secular publisher, but there's a large group of people eating this stuff up right now, dreaming of days when life was simpler."

Astonished, Carly could hardly contain her excitement. "Are you kidding me? That would be wonderful. She's had her dream for a long time. If it wouldn't be too much trouble?"

"No trouble for you, Carly." She squirmed a bit under his warm smile. This man was so magnanimous it was hard to read him. She couldn't imagine that he was appreciating her as a woman he might pursue—given her plain lifestyle—yet his attentiveness was hard to explain away. "Better not tell her until I talk to Tom and get his opinion."

"All right. Thanks again." She was thrilled for Auntie. And amazed how her life was changing just by allowing a few new friendships to develop.

"And?" He flashed her a white smile. "There seems to be more on your mind."

"I was thinking that until the last few months, most of my friendships were with elderly people. It feels good to be around people who still dream and want to make dreams come true."

"Everybody needs a dream."

"Mine all seem to involve the residents at Sweet Life."

"I understand. I feel the same about the homeless. Gramps wanted me to join the military, but I guess I took after Mom's side. I like what I do. Don't you have any personal dreams?"

Adam came to mind, but she wasn't going to share about him. "I don't know."

"I get it, if you don't want to share."

"What about you?" she asked.

"I have dreams about settling down. Having a family."

She nodded, feeling heat sear her neck. That was her dream, too.

"It's hard to find the right person. I thought I had it all figured out, had met the right woman." He laughed harshly. "Sorry if I sound bitter, but I'm still recovering from a broken relationship." He gripped the steering wheel. "Anyway, money draws the wrong people. I'm looking for somebody with a heart like yours."

She laughed nervously. "You barely know me."

"That's why I invited you today."

"I thought you needed help at the clinic."

"God works in mysterious ways."

"Jah." She'd been praying more lately, willing to follow God's plan for her life, but didn't know how Jason fit into the overall plan. She understood he was part of creating Martha's surprise, but it seemed as though more was happening.

By the end of the day, however, Jason's intentions became clearer. He'd watched as she told stories while the children were being administered shots. His blue eyes glimmered with admiration when she washed a homeless man's feet in a sudsy tub so that a doctor could examine them.

For a multitude of reasons, she needed to set him straight. She was plain, and he was worldly. While they both loved and served the Lord, their doctrinal beliefs were light-years apart, and she'd never compromise. She'd preached this very thing to Miranda when she'd first shown interest in Jimmy. But with Jason, things became complicated so fast that it was hard to discern God's will—a problem that often got Carly into one predicament or another.

But the biggest reason she should thwart Jason's interest was Adam. No matter how handsome, kind, and generous a man Jason was, she loved Adam. Quiet and brooding, her dark-haired hero awakened desires in her that were incomparable to any other. Her godsend—so steadfast—well, until lately. Her burr—he'd be furious if he discovered the situation she'd put herself in and what was occupying Jason's mind.

Adam whistled, proud of himself for securing time both Saturday and Sunday to spend with his suddenly social butterfly. Sunday afternoon was the big birthday party. After Carly's protestations regarding

Saturday—she was baking a cake for Martha's birthday—he'd volunteered to help. To his delight, she'd agreed. Not that he knew anything about cakes except his favorite was chocolate, but he loved any previews of Carly's domestic abilities.

He rapped on her cottage door, and she answered, looking somewhat disheveled, which had nothing to do with her accident because it appeared she'd had her stitches removed and the bruises were disappearing, too. He'd seen this particular look before, probably more often than not. She wore it well. He wondered if she actually cut those little wisps of curls that always seemed to escape her covering and dance around her face. Did she do it on purpose, knowing it allured him? With flushed face, she invited him inside.

"You look adorable." *Adorably frazzled.*

"Thanks. Want some coffee?"

"Sure."

After he tossed his coat over a kitchen chair, she handed him a steaming cup and sank down beside him with a sigh. "What a morning! I was housecleaning and left the door open to shake out some rugs on the stoop, and somehow Cocoa got out. Which I don't understand because he's never done that before. And I didn't miss him right away. Then I had to search. I was worried sick and so frantic I forgot to use his bell. Finally I remembered. As soon as I rang it, Cocoa's head popped up in Imogene's garden. So I had to tell my neighbor in case he ruined anything. She threw a big fuss because Cocoa dug up some of her bulbs. And now he's got a taste for them."

"Whoa. That's not good."

"Anyway, all's well now."

He looked away from her frazzled face and sipped his coffee, imagining what life would be like at his place if Carly and Cocoa moved in. It'd never occurred to him he'd be living with a willful rabbit. "Does Cocoa get jealous of you?"

"Huh?"

"Never mind. I brought you something." He went to the sofa and retrieved a bag he'd slipped there on his way inside. He placed it on the table in front of her and settled in to watch her reaction.

Glancing at him with curiosity, she pulled it onto her lap and reached inside. When her hands touched the smooth wood, she hesitated, and he could read her puzzlement. She pulled his offering out and laid it on the table. Her mouth opened adorably, and her eyes misted. "Oh! Oh, my!" She ran her fingers over the carvings of Martha and James's endearments and swiped the tears rolling down her cheeks. "This is beautiful. How?"

"I went back that night."

Looking both amused and accusing, she asked, "You went back and stole it?"

"Let's just say I made an anonymous contribution to the Larwood bridge's restoration fund."

"This is amazing. I love the way you shaped and finished it. Thank you. When we first started searching the bridges, I didn't know what we were even looking for, but this is it." She stood, and the empty bag fell to the ground. When she started toward him, he rose, eager to accept whatever show of thanks she had in mind. He stilled when she placed her hands on the sides of his face and studied him with unveiled adoration.

"You're amazing. That's the most precious gift I've ever received. Thank you." He wanted to sweep her in his arms and kiss her senseless but the moment was too dear to spoil. She dropped her hands and raised them in animation. "Martha's going to cherish this."

"I hope she enjoys a good adventure story."

"And she thinks nobody cares about her. This is perfect proof we do. And speaking of proof, should we get started with that cake?"

The opportunity to kiss her senseless passed, but Adam cherished the pleasure he'd brought her. He hoped nobody would catch him in Carly's apron. He wondered how many other men stooped so low to please women—behind closed doors, of course.

"You want to measure ingredients or beat?"

"Beat." He snatched up the mixer with a wicked grin.

"First we cream the sugar and eggs." She cracked two eggs into the bowl, fingering out a bit of shell, then moved to the sink to wash her hands. When she returned, she measured the sugar. Even though she dressed more conservatively than most of the women in their church, she couldn't disguise her pleasant curves. Some might call it pleasantly plump, but he knew from holding her in his arms that she had a tiny waist and a perfect, curvy form. He stood spellbound. "So beat."

"Oh. Jah."

When they got to the flour, she patted his cheeks white. In retaliation, he pulled a pin from her hair.

"That's playing dirty."

He shrugged.

"Put these on." She handed him oven mitts and motioned for him to put the pans in the oven.

"Not fair," he complained. But in truth, the afternoon sped by, and when they were finished, they had a beautiful, two-layered chocolate cake and Carly's hair was in disarray. Staring at their masterpiece, he remarked, "I didn't know baking was this complicated. Or messy. But is this going to be enough?"

"No. Martha's daughter's bringing the real cake. This just fulfills a promise I made to Martha."

Admiring her thoughtfulness, he pulled her close. "I made a promise to you, and I mean to fulfill it."

"What promise?" she asked breathless.

"Us." He found her lips, and when she yielded, he deepened their kiss, unaware at first why she pulled away. Drat, her phone was buzzing.

"Bad timing," she said, moving to retrieve it from the kitchen counter. Casting him a breathless smile, she tried to right her hair as she answered. "Hi. Jah, a little busy." She flashed him an intimate smile. He grinned, moved closer, and pulled one of her curls, but she swept his hand away, whispering. "Stop. It's Jason."

With disappointment he moved to the sofa, intent now on following the conversation. While he didn't know what lines the cad was feeding her, it was an earful, given her muttered responses. Jealousy twisted his gut and ignited when suddenly her face became animated. "That's wonderful!" she burst out. "I don't know how to thank you." His heart sank. Why so grateful to a stranger? Then to his increased frustration, she started pacing, happily forgetting he was even there.

Burning now, he rose, went to the kitchen, and tilted his head in a silent plea. *Hey, remember me?*

"Oh, Jason. I forgot. Adam's here."

Forgot?

"I should probably go, but I don't know how to thank you. Auntie's going to be thrilled." Whatever he said on the other end made her face blush, and Adam wanted to smash the man's gleaming teeth. "Jah, bye." She gently put her phone on the counter and turned. "Sorry about that. But you'll never believe what he did."

"You're right," Adam said sarcastically.

"He's found an editor from a major publishing house that wants to look at Auntie's quilt patterns. She's going to be thrilled. Isn't that wonderful?"

Stunned, Adam nodded. "Jah. I'm happy for her." How on earth had Jason wiggled his way into Carly's family life so quickly?

"He said her designs are so unique they'll probably make some into art prints and maybe stationery, too. She could make a lot of money."

"He saw them?"

"Jah."

He watched her discern his mounting anger and downplay her explanation. She shrugged. "He picked me up at Auntie's last week when we worked at the clinic. Miranda was there, too."

"At the clinic?"

"No, at Aunt Fannie's."

He knew he was glaring, but he didn't know how to process this information. An outsider moving in on his girl. If he stuck around, he was sure to say something offensive that would spoil their entire weekend. It would be useless to fall into the same repeated argument over Jason. Frustrated, he stared at the beautiful cake inside the glass stand and didn't say anything for several strained moments. Finally he managed, "I'm happy for Aunt Fannie."

"Thanks." She smiled.

Then for once, Cocoa's interruption was timed perfectly. While

Carly went to feed the impatient rabbit, he got Jason's number from her phone.

Adam paced down the nap of Ann's carpet. "I feel like driving to Portland tonight and facing off with him. But I'd probably get all the way out there and he wouldn't be home or answer the door. But I have his phone number."

"You mean. . .to fight him?"

"Jah. If that what it takes."

"I can't believe my ears." She bit her lip, wishing she was the one upstairs putting the kids to bed, not Ron. What Adam needed was another man to talk some sense into him. She'd never seen him so furious. "You know violence isn't the answer. Carly wouldn't like it."

"I don't understand why she's encouraging him."

"Maybe you haven't noticed, but she's kind to everyone."

"The way Carly talks about Mr. Magnanimous, he sounds like a male version of her—like they're soul mates. Only he's got the money to back up his plans. He's loaded."

"It's just a friendship based on their desire to help others. Remember, it's opposites who usually attract."

"I help others."

"Of course you do; I didn't mean that. She's spontaneous, and you're steady. She's blond, and you're dark." Ann grinned hopefully, but he wasn't buying it.

"I know she's *attracted* to me. If Jason hadn't come along, I'd have no doubts about winning her over. But it's like he's spinning a web and she's too naive to see it."

"Carly's not naive."

"Oh, jah? Then why am I always getting her out of scrapes?"

"Because you're just what she needs. She knows that."

"What you say sounds good, but you'd have to witness how she acts to believe it. He's pulling the wool over her eyes. I can't take it. I'm driving to Portland tonight."

"You can't do that."

He pulled out his phone. "Then I'm calling him."

"Have you considered the difference in their faith? Do you really think she'd abandon her beliefs? You know she's strong-willed and independent."

He put his phone in his pocket and sank onto the sofa.

"Mission accomplished," Ron piped, coming down the stairs. While easing into his recliner, he swept his gaze across Ann and Adam.

"Thanks, honey. I think Adam could use some advice. While I make a pot of coffee, tell Ron what's going on."

Adam shrugged. "Just jealous and trying to decide if I'm going to take the other guy's teeth out."

Ron chuckled. "I remember that feeling. But our women hate that kind of thing. It'll set you back months with her."

"That's the thing. Carly doesn't like it when I try to run interference. She's sensitive when it comes to criticism."

"Aren't we all? Something to consider, though, before you marry her."

"Marry?" Ann asked, returning to the room and serving coffee. "Of course! That's it! Just propose to her so she has to make her decision before he sinks in his claws. You'll be her hero, her knight in shining armor."

"Uh, I was just advising him to *think* about how serious he is about her, not advising him to marry her. Not when she's acting all fickle."

"She's not fickle. Honestly, don't you guys know Carly at all?"

Ron's advice echoed Dad's, stereotyping Carly as inappropriate wife material. Sure she wasn't like his mom or Ann, and maybe he didn't understand her like Ann claimed to, but he knew she was right for him. "I can't even get dating right. How would I manage a proposal?"

Ron shook his head and watched the siblings skirt around his well-placed advice.

"I know!" Ann squealed, then covered her mouth and looked at the stairway to see if she'd awakened her children. Lowering her voice, she said, "Take her to one of those covered bridges. It's kind of your thing now, right?"

"The kissing tree," Adam murmured, almost forgetting he wasn't alone.

"There! Your problem is solved."

With his new plan, his anger toward Jason faded so that he almost pitied the guy. After all, what kind of competition was a newcomer with somebody who had a kissing tree with Carly?

On his way home that night, however, Adam's hands still itched to call Jason—he'd been too embarrassed to admit to his sister how he'd gotten the number—and then his phone buzzed. Dale. Disappointment fell over him as he pulled over. "Jah, what's up?"

"Bad news. I guess I overdid it and messed up my leg again. They're talking surgery now. I'm going to be laid up for a long time. I was hoping you could come out and help me again, you know, after Christmas."

Adam's heart thudded.

"I just expanded the business, you know. I can't carry this forever without getting some income going."

Slapping the steering wheel, Adam listened to his cousin's explanation with growing frustration.

CHAPTER THIRTY-TWO

The Family's Sweet Room, where groups of people could congregate for special occasions for Sweet Life's residents, was made festive with white tablecloths, flowers, balloons, crepe ribbon bows, and birthday banners.

Carly wore her newest blue dress and was in a celebratory mood. "I can't wait to see her expression," she told Adam as they took their cake to a table and set it off to the side of the family's centerpiece cake.

"How'd they do this?" she marveled. Somehow photos of all Martha's children and grandchildren had been transferred to the icing. Words edged the entire rectangle: "We love you and wish you a happy year."

"It's just what she needs. But it makes ours look plain."

He touched her lip. "Not to me."

Her heart melted. Adam looked especially handsome in his Sunday white shirt that complimented his dark features. She was pleased how he'd controlled his jealousy over Jason. His steady presence at her side made her hopeful there wouldn't be any scenes at the party. This was all about Martha's happiness, and she was going to enjoy every moment of it.

By the door, Martha's daughter Helen greeted Jason and James, looking perplexed. Carly hastened over to make the introductions, explaining, "James is the old friend I told you I'd invited. Martha's childhood friend."

Frowning thoughtfully, Helen waved them in. "Well, find a place. I just got a text that she's on her way." She moved to the center of the room. "She's coming. Everybody get ready."

Carly helped find a chair for James, and he slowly lowered himself into it moments before Martha stepped into the room.

"Surprise!" everyone shouted.

The startled woman stumbled back and placed her hand at her breast. "What on earth?"

"Happy Birthday!" Helen exclaimed, and the family rushed forward to give their greetings. Carly's heart soared as she watched Martha's happy expression while her family led her around the room, pointing out the cake and decorations. They eventually settled her in a chair next to a huge pile of presents.

James chuckled. "She never did like surprises. Always liked to be in control of things, only that didn't work out for us because circumstances were against us. She's still pretty as ever."

"She'll like one surprise. When she notices you."

"Give her time to enjoy her family. Then I'll make my way over and knock her socks off."

Watching everything transpire around her, Carly wondered if the occasion would create an awkward reunion. She began to fret, regretting the public setting with grandkids tugging Martha's arms and climbing onto her lap.

"The right moment will come," Jason assured. "Hey, sweets, can I get you some punch? How about you Gramps?"

"Jah, I'll help you," Carly replied, inadvertently playing the role of an assisted-living caregiver.

"I'll get my own coffee," Adam muttered, trailing behind.

"I've never seen Gramps so excited," Jason whispered. "Since I met you, he acts ten years younger." He placed his hand on the small of her back. "Thanks."

But Carly's nerves were on edge. She filled a punch glass and handed it to Jason. "I just hope this works."

Returning with his coffee in time to hear her remark, Adam assured, "It will. But if it doesn't, I'll help you pick up the pieces." He winked, then cast Jason a smirk.

"Don't joke," she said. Her heart suddenly beat wildly. "She's looking this way. She sees him."

Martha gripped her armrests, her complexion paling. Then with a brush of her hand, she moved aside her hovering grandchildren and started out of her chair toward them. Carly hurried to meet her in the center of the room. "There's an old friend who wants to meet you."

But Martha batted her aside like a pesky fly. "I see him."

Hurrying to keep up with Martha's determined pace, she almost ran into her when the older woman stopped abruptly in front of Jason. "Who are you, young man?"

"Jason Irish, ma'am."

"No." Martha's hand went to her breast and she wheezed, "It can't be you."

Widow Martha thought she was hallucinating. Most likely losing her mind. She knew she'd been confused ever since her hospital stay. But if James was a hallucination, she was going to take a long hard gander, one that would last her the rest of her days. She pinched her arm. It hurt.

She poked his chest. He felt real.

He grinned at her, that familiar grin that warmed her insides. He looked older than the last time they were together, but not old enough to match her age. Then it hit her. He was a ghost.

"Why did you come?"

"To bring Gramps to your party."

"Over here, darling." An older man slowly stood and leaned upon his cane.

Her heart pounding, she fished in her pocket for her inhaler. She turned away from both apparitions and took a couple quick puffs. When she turned back they were still there. And Carly and Adam wore grins the size of the Grand Canyon.

Narrowing her eyes, she studied the one with the cane and dawning prevailed. "James?"

"Wanna bait my hook, baby?"

Momentarily clamping her hand over her mouth, she squealed with delight, "It is you. Glory be. You're alive! Come here so I can see you."

He stepped close. "Of course I am. I promised you that before I left." As her long-lost love drew her aside, she swept one lingering look over Jason. "Now don't be falling for my grandson. That'll hurt my feelings."

Carly giggled. "I've never seen her so befuddled. After tonight, she's going to have a lot to think about."

Adam sidled up to her. "And she didn't even see our cake yet." He placed his hand at her waist. "You did good."

Jason rubbed his chin. "It was tempting to let her go on believing I was Gramps. To steal his girl. He's so ornery, he deserved a good setdown."

"I saw your struggle," Carly replied.

He smiled at her and sent a warning glance Adam's way. "But regardless of my own preferences, I wouldn't do anything to spoil your party. Not tonight."

Adam warned, "No, but somebody else might." He nodded toward Helen who was shooting Carly daggers from across the room. Helen pointed at the pile of presents. Feigning ignorance, Carly looked the other way, not wanting to spoil the happy reunion taking place in the back corner of the room. When she looked back, however, Helen was headed to personally interrupt the conversation. After what appeared to be some emotional banter, she led Martha back to her chair and placed a gift on her lap.

Gramps hobbled back to them, and Carly and the others watched the birthday girl open her gifts. When she opened the bag from Carly and Adam, Helen asked, "What's that?"

Martha steepled trembling hands to her mouth. Then rubbing her initials over the carving, she met James's eyes. Carly could see Helen putting the pieces together. Martha looked right at Carly and mouthed, *Thank you*, and Carly felt more satisfied than she had in months. Peace flooded her soul.

For at least five minutes. That is until Helen approached her with pinched lips, snatching her arm. "A moment, please."

Carly shrugged at the men and allowed Helen to draw her aside.

"I see what you're doing. Bringing that old flame to her party and stirring up foolish romantic notions. I had no idea spinsters like you entertained such thoughts."

The words stung deep, and she didn't know how to explain her actions.

"How do you think this will affect the family? Her children and grandchildren? Have you thought about that? My dad's probably rolling in his grave. If you don't nip this thing in the bud, I'm going to get you fired. You understand? I'll not have you messing with my mom. That's emotional abuse."

"I was just trying to help with her depression."

"There's no way Mom can have a relationship. Not with the way her memory's failing. Surely you've seen something's snapped inside her since her last hospital stay?"

Another slap. Why hadn't she taken Martha's recent confusion more seriously and reconsidered bringing an entirely new element into the fragile medical mix. "But everybody needs friendship and hope."

"Hope!" Helen dashed away angry tears. "You'll be the one dashing those hopes. I'm going to Simon Lapp with this. You had no right. I wouldn't be surprised if you've been the one poisoning her with ideas about her family not caring. How could you?"

Stunned, she watched Helen march away. Carly retreated, rushing to the ladies' room. Gripping the counter, she closed her eyes. Silent tears rolled down her cheeks. The door creaked open, and covering her face, she dashed into the nearest stall and plopped down on the toilet lid. How low her life had sunk. Moaning, she sobbed. *Fired? Would Simon fire her? Worse, had she orchestrated another sad ending for James and Martha?*

"She called me a spinster!"

Adam's heart broke, and he couldn't wait to get Carly home and comfort her in his arms. "Cruel woman. Well you're not." Not if he could help it. It was all he could do not to blurt out a proposal on the spot.

She moaned, "She's going to Simon. Wants me fired."

Adam's thumbs tapped the steering wheel. "Don't worry. I'll talk to Uncle Si. Wait, I thought he knew about it."

"Jah, so did Helen. But I only told them it was an old friend. Men and women can be friends, right?" She gave him a sheepish smile. "Fine. I was matchmaking. And I should've told them the truth, but I just hoped it would work out the way I imagined."

"It still can. I'll talk to Si," he repeated.

"No." She looked at him through misty eyes. "Not this time. You can't keep doing this for me. I need to face my own consequences."

"Old hothead will probably back down, once she cools off. Probably just spouting threats."

"It's selfish of her, don't you think?"

"Jah. Your heart's in the right place. That's all that matters."

She raised her chin. "Is it enough? She thinks I've been feeding Martha the notion that her family doesn't care about her anymore. She can't see that I've been doing the opposite, making excuses for her."

Adam shook his head with frustration.

"I tried to keep up a good face in front of James and Jason. They've no idea what's about to happen. Jason told me that Gramp's book had some kind of special meaning, and the gift seemed to seal the deal for him. That Gramps had his foot in the door, and she'd already invited him to play bingo on Tuesdays." She moaned. "And he's already agreed. But Helen claimed I'm the one responsible for dashing their hopes." She rubbed her forehead. "That's what hurts most."

"Why don't I call Jason and explain a few things, see if they'll just hold off for a bit and see how things settle? Surely Gramps will understand if it takes the family a little bit of time to accept him."

"No," she maintained. "I'll tell Jason when I see him next week."

"Oh?" *What were they planning now?*

"Didn't I tell you? He's bringing that editor around to see Aunt Fannie's designs."

Discouraged that Carly seemed determined to refuse his help, he pulled the truck into her driveway and killed the engine. He walked her to the door, sheltering her from the cold with his arm. "Nothing can take away the joy you gave Martha tonight. She knows he's alive. And she has that carving to remember it."

She looked up at him with admiration. "You always know how to make things better."

He kissed her forehead. "Because we're good together. Got your key?"

She fiddled in her purse and unlocked the door. "I know it's early, but I wouldn't be good company."

His heart sank with disappointment, but he squeezed her hand. "Sure, I understand."

He left, wondering how to help her. How to propose. And with the night's catastrophic conclusion, he didn't want to think about what would happen if he needed to go to Indiana to help Dale again. Christmas was at the door. Everything was closing in on Adam at the same time. And with Jason in the picture, he couldn't afford to delay or make any mistakes.

Chapter Thirty-Three

Monday morning, Carly awoke to frigid weather. Dark clouds rolled in from northern skies. She considered calling someone for a ride, but stress gnawed her because she faced a day of reckoning, so she opted for the exercise. Making sure the thermostat was set to keep Cocoa snug for the day, she bundled up in her heaviest hooded coat, thick gloves, and boots. And as she coasted downhill, a furtive skyward glance told her she was fortunate the hill wasn't already slick with snow.

When she passed the home where the old dog once lived, discouragement threatened to hitch a ride. Determined to remain strong, she focused her thoughts on her plan. After Adam dropped her off Sunday evening, she'd decided to report to Si first thing Monday morning, rather than wait for trouble to trickle down to her.

Once at Sweet Life, Rocco stored her bike, and she dragged herself to Si's office. He looked up surprised. "Well if it isn't the abominable snowman."

Peeling off her outerwear, she pointed to a chair. "May I?"

"Sure." He studied her curiously. His good mood indicated Helen hadn't talked to him yet. Too bad she would ruin his day so early in the morning.

"There's been an incident."

He frowned.

"At Martha Struder's birthday party on Sunday."

He shook his head. "I hadn't heard."

Taking a deep breath, she explained. "I located an old friend of Martha's, and there was a reunion of sorts that took place at the party."

"I remember something about inviting some old friends. What happened? Weren't they friends after all?"

"Oh, they were happy to see each other, all right. But Martha's daughter Helen was angry at me for bringing James."

"Who's James?"

Carly wet her lips. "Martha's old friend."

"You were matchmaking?" He placed his head in his hands as if warding off a migraine.

She shook her head. "It's not like I was trying to get them hitched. Martha needs interesting companionship. Most of our residents have dementia. James provides a pleasant diversion." The explanation danced around the truth, and she felt guilty for it.

"What exactly did Helen say?"

"She wants me fired."

"Fired!" He rapped the desk. "She wants me to fire my best caregiver? Does she have some kind of evidence against you? Besides matchmaking?"

Carly's mind got stuck on *best caregiver.*

"Well?"

Nodding, Carly replied, "She mentioned emotional damages. Or abuse."

"You did the right thing to come to me."

A dry sponge, she soaked up his praise.

"I'll call her and try to downplay the ordeal." He studied her. "Your volunteer program is doing great. I like the way you're plugging in with Sherie and delegating work. Lately, I've felt an attitude change in you. But I have to be honest. I'd hoped we'd gotten past these kinds of situations."

At that moment, she realized she'd forgiven him. Wasn't even sure when it had happened, but all her resentment was gone. And it seemed he'd also forgiven her. "Thanks. Me too."

"You're a valuable employee, but if Helen threatens to sue us, I'll have to let you go."

Her heart sank. "I understand. I hadn't thought about her suing you."

"That's the thing with you. If you'd think things through before you go off on your tangents, then maybe you wouldn't drag Sweet Life into so many scrapes."

"I'm sorry. I prayed about it. And I sought advice. I thought I was doing the right thing. In fact, I still believe it was the right thing."

"You're stubborn. That's a blessing and a curse. I can't keep picking up the pieces. But on the other hand, I can't afford to lose you. So you see my dilemma?"

She nodded with humiliation. Blessing and a curse. She understood. It sounded a lot like what she always told Adam—godsend and a burr.

Although she hadn't gotten fired—yet—she left his office feeling disappointed and low. But when the snow began to fall, the residents gathered in front of the lobby's glass doors to watch the garden turn white, and a peaceful awe settled over Sweet Life. A sweet respite from what might yet occur, but she was happy to snatch at the little bit of happiness.

Another pleasant moment was when Miranda reported that her parents had sent her a plane ticket to go home for Christmas. She was ecstatic, and Carly hoped her new friend could find healing.

Later in the day, however, the storm intensified, and she knew the roads would become too hazardous for Aunt Fannie. Even before she went to Rocco for help, Adam called. "You need a ride?"

"Jah! I do."

"I'll try to be there when your shift ends."

"Thanks."

Adam had already loaded Carly's bike into his truck before he came for her. Thankful for her boots, they trudged through unplowed snow to his vehicle.

Inside, he grinned. "Cozy?" He patted the bench seat, and she moved closer then leaned her head on his shoulder. He started the heater, but stayed parked. "Did you talk to Si?"

She nodded. "First thing this morning."

"Good girl."

Raising her head, she said, "He seemed more angry at Helen than at me. He even said some good things about my work before he lectured me. He said he'd call her. That if she threatened to sue, he'd have to let me go, but he was going to try to smooth it over. So now I wait."

"Sue?"

"I know."

"Don't worry about it now. Let's enjoy the snow."

She leaned back and watched white swirl outside their snug cocoon. "Jah, it's blissful, cut off from the world like this."

"Let's just enjoy it. I've nowhere to go. I can't work, and there won't be anybody at the tree lot tonight. From here on out, there'll only be a few stragglers buying from our small stock of cut trees." His arm draped over her shoulders. "The lot becomes more of a family party than anything else. My sisters bring board games and baked goodies. Everybody winds down, and it's like the start of our own Christmas traditions."

"Sounds wonderful. What's Christmas Day like at your house?"

"Lots of food, presents for the grandkids. More games. Did I mention the singing? What about you?"

"The same except no kids and we don't sing. We exchange gifts. I already have Aunt Fannie's. Any ideas for Jimmy?"

"An atlas." They both laughed.

"Before I take you home, I need to tell you something."

Carly hoped it was an invitation to Christmas or even an evening to spend with his family at the tree lot party, but something in his tone warned her it wouldn't be. "Jah?"

"Dale called again."

Dread traipsed up her spine. When would she be able to shake his ghost?

"He's going to have surgery on his leg. He asked me to go back and help him out after Christmas. I haven't exactly agreed, but I might have to go."

"Oh." She edged out of his embrace to better examine his face.

"It doesn't change anything between us."

"How can you promise that? What if it's your fate. And you can't fight it?"

"Trust me. It's not. Things are going good with Dad. I have you. Why would I want to leave?" He toyed with one of the curls at her temple. "Cynthia told me Jenny went to church last Sunday, so that's good news. And Dale's bringing the family home for Christmas. Staying at my place. We'll sort it out then."

Panic choked her throat. So much to absorb. "You're staying in touch with that woman? *Cynthia* gave her your phone number? You're talking?"

"No. She must've gotten it from Jenny. And it's not like you're thinking. You don't have to worry about her. Everything's going to work out. You'll see."

Though skeptical, she nodded, thinking about Dale's arrival. Wondering how she would face him after three long years. Wondering if it would stir up all the rumors. If his arrival would ruin things with Adam. If he'd go back with him to Indiana. Feeling Adam's concerned gaze, she asked, "Do you have Christmas with Simon's family?"

"No, but we get together sometime over the holiday." She was considering this when he added, "I know there's contention between Dad and Si, but we're still family and know how to act civil on occasions. It means a lot to the women. And us cousins."

She removed her gloves and fiddled with them, and he turned down the heater.

"How do you want to celebrate?" he asked.

"Us?"

He nodded expectantly.

There was still an *us*? She realized they were both trying so hard. She couldn't be the first one to give up, could she?

"Carly?"

"For Christmas?"

He nodded. He wasn't offering to take her home like she'd hoped. She didn't want to abandon Auntie and Jimmy anyway. Didn't want to see Dale and Jenny. She couldn't ask him to abandon his family, either. What a mess. Yet her mind sought for something to hold him close.

"Would you like me to cook?"

"An intimate dinner at your place?"

She nodded.

His grinned. "Just say when."

"How about Christmas Eve?"

"It's a date."

With relief, she asked, "What about your Christmas list? Anything I should know about?"

"I think you know the answer to that. More of this." He drew her close, and she melted into his kiss. That is, until a rapping on the window startled them apart. Pushing away from his embrace, she flinched to see Aesop's snowy features peering through the frosty window at them.

Adam lowered his window and blinked against the snow that swirled into the truck and stung their faces. Aseop brushed the window sill with his red gloves and blew the snow off his bare fingertips. "You—you all right in there?"

"Jah." Adam gave him a sheepish grin.

Aesop peered inside, his blue eyes bright from the cold and hooded with snow-dusted brows. They widened protectively when he saw Carly. He tugged his furry cap and looked accusingly at Adam. "I—I saw Carly's bike on the back. Was—was worried about her."

"I'm fine," she chirped, embarrassed over his concern.

"The—the roads aren't getting any better."

Adam nodded. "You're right. We'll go. You should take cover, too."

"For—for a while. It's gonna be a long night." Normally, his shift ended at 1:00 a.m. "I'm—I'm gonna sleep in the maintenance room, just in case. Take—take care then." Carly watched him leave, bent against the blizzard for it was too nasty to use his scooter.

"Poor guy. It's sweet how he watches out for me."

"Jah, well I feel like I just got my hand slapped. But he's right. We'd better go."

The drive home was slow-going and silent while Adam concentrated on his driving. They passed several vacated cars stuck in ditches. She tried to relax her heightened nerves, trusting his driving. Trusting in his promises, even when Dale was actively pursuing him. Trusting that she'd have a job in the morning. That Martha and James would find happiness. Mostly just trusting God.

Tuesday brought a slight break in the snow, and the plows began, but Carly would've had to miss work if Adam hadn't taken her. When she arrived, the night caregivers were happy to see her.

"We thought we'd have to do a double shift," one of them remarked. "Miranda can't make it in."

Knowing the voluntary house was in Albany, Carly replied, "Jah the roads are probably bad between here and the interstate."

Sherie arrived late and sent those home who could manage the snow. But a nightshift V. S. employee stayed. It was one of Miranda's friends. "Go take a nap," Sherie told her. "I'll fill in."

When Carly went into Mr. Gadget's room, he was already in his wheelchair command center. She noticed his chair was more stocked than normal. "What all you got in there?"

"Packets of jelly and butter and newspaper. Underwear. All good for camping."

"So it's camping today?"

He shook his head. "In case you haven't noticed, we're in the middle of a blizzard here. Gotta be prepared for the worst."

She glanced at his window and saw it was snowing again. "Jah. You're right."

Convincing Hall Patroller to take a break long enough to eat breakfast, Carly checked to see if Repeater had his dentures.

"Wow!" Dot marveled. "When did it start snowing?"

"I suppose bingo will be cancelled," Martha stated glumly. But then she brightened, showing Carly a card she'd gotten from Ruth Stucky explaining why she hadn't made it to her party. "Says she wants to visit sometime."

"That's special," Carly exclaimed just before Rocco burst into the room, tracking snow onto the floor. It clung heavy to his coat and gloves.

"Where's Simon?"

"I don't know. Not in his office?"

He shook his head. "He's not answering his phone. And the roof's collapsed over the maintenance building."

Carly gasped.

Sherie flashed a warning glance her way, then led him into the staff room. Carly couldn't remember when she'd seen Rocco so rattled. But quickly recovering, she smiled at the residents whose eyes had widened in fright. "Don't worry, they've got it under control."

"The roof's going to cave in," Martha stated grimly.

Dot jumped up in confusion and ran down the hall. "Crusher!"

"Our roof's fine," Carly reassured. "Maintenance is a separate building." But given Rocco's agitation, she wasn't so sure things would be fine. Glancing tentatively at the ceiling, she breathed a prayer.

Klepto's hand snaked out and swiped a salt shaker. Carly calmly moved to her side and forced it from her clenched fingers, replacing it in the center of the table. It seemed forever until Sherie returned alone, Rocco having taken a side exit.

She motioned to Carly, then quietly explained, "We've contacted a crew to come and remove the snow from all the roofs. It was hard to find someone willing to come during the storm. Simon's trying to get his driveway plowed, but he authorized the work."

Sweet Life's budget would take another hit. With Christmas around the corner, Carly's own donation to the Sweet Life fund would be smaller. But suddenly she remembered something more important than money. "What about Aesop? He was sleeping in the maintenance room last night."

"I don't know anything about that."

Carly nodded glumly. "I need to check on Dot."

Hall Patroller wheeled by them. "She went to her room."

"Thanks." Carly opened Dot's door, and the canary chirped a greeting, but the elderly woman was nowhere in sight. The curtains were open, revealing a picturesque vision of drifting snow, if not ominous given the present situation. "Dot," she called. "Dot?" Each time she called, the canary whistled back. Otherwise, the room remained silent.

She moved around the pristine room and saw a foot sticking out from beneath the bed. *Not again!* Compassion swept over her as she knelt and peered beneath. "Dot. It's me, Carly. It's all safe now."

"Shush! I'm hiding."

"No need. Come out, and I'll sit with you."

"I want Crusher."

"It's too nasty for him to come right now. But he'll come soon."

"But he knows how to make it stay away."

She tried a more authoritative tone. "It's safe. Now crawl out from under there."

"It's back, you know."

"What, honey?"

"The Death Angel. It was here last night, leering at me."

Carly assumed Dot's mind was tangling its circuits. She'd run to hide from the collapsing roof, but once she'd gotten under the bed, those earlier memories returned to frighten her. Carly took the Bible verse Martha had written and read Psalm 118:6, " 'The LORD is on my side, I will not fear.' So you see, God's watching over you."

"I know," Dot sobbed. Surprising Carly, she repeated the verse. "I say that verse all the time. It helps."

"Then come." Slowly the woman crawled out, and Carly helped her onto the bed, where she hugged her tight with both arms. "You don't have to fear death," she whispered. "It's when we get to see God. He loves you and has prepared a lovely place for you in heaven. Your body will be young and you won't forget things anymore."

Dot began to rock. "I know. But why do I see that ugly face? It hates me." Carly wished she knew. Felt angry that something evil was tormenting the little woman who had been a churchgoer all her life. "The next time you see it, tell it to go away because you are Jesus' little lamb."

Dot began to sing, "*Mary had a little lamb.*"

Chapter Thirty-Four

By the end of Carly's shift, they were officially snowed in with assisted living operating on a small core of personnel: Sherie, Carly, the night shift V. S. worker, Linda the nurse, and Rocco. As far as she knew, Aesop was still missing. Simon couldn't make it to the center so Sherie took charge. She planned to let them use one of the empty apartments to take naps after the residents were asleep. And she kept the coffee pot filled.

Carly worried about Cocoa. He might be hungry, but he should be warm as long as the electricity didn't go out. Surely if that happened, Imogene would check on him. She knew where the extra key was hidden. Carly prayed the electricity would stay on. Assisted living had a backup generator, but the residents in independent living didn't. She'd overheard Sherie on the phone, giving someone instructions to call in rescue units if that happened. It was too soon to report Aesop.

The night was uneventful except for the General streaking down the hall naked and Nines's stubborn refusal to dress for bed. With all the snow, Nines had transported herself back in time to a Christmas of long ago and was determined her husband would be there any moment to take her home. But once those fires were diffused, the center settled into a peaceful quiet. Carly slept soundly during her four-hour break.

She awoke to sunshine. With relief, she freshened up and hurried to the front desk.

A frazzled looking Sherie beamed at her. "It's over."

"Thank God." Carly's prayers would be fully answered when everyone could be accounted for once again.

"The snowplows are busy at work. And that crew is working on the roofs again. Go ahead and make your rounds. We'll have cereal for breakfast, and I've got soup we can make for lunch if the kitchen crew doesn't make it in by then."

Carly nodded, taking one side of the hall while the weary V. S. worker took the opposite.

Nines was already dressed in her black net hat, waiting for Carly to administer meds. Repeater had on his coat, claimed he was going to shovel them out of the blizzard. After she convinced him to go to breakfast first, she checked on Mr. Gadget. He was digging caulking out from around his window with a butter knife.

Flying across the room, she stilled his hand. "What are you doing?"

"Gettin' rid of this snow."

"If you take your meds, I'll let you eat your breakfast in front of the garden window. It'll be fun to watch the squirrels in the snow. Would you like that?" He agreed, and she had just stepped into the hall when she heard Aesop's one-of-a-kind stammer. Ecstatic that he was all right, she hurried toward him. Crusher was there, too. She snapped one of Aesop's suspenders and hugged the sinewy security guard. "I'm so glad to see you. I was worried about you."

"I—I found Crusher out in the storm. We—we holed up at his place."

She turned to the older man. "Crusher," she admonished.

"I would've come, but Aesop threatened me with his gun." After that, he started down the hall with his customary glass of juice for Dot.

Aesop shrugged. "I heard about the maintenance room."

"I'm so glad you weren't in there."

They spoke more about the storm, and then Carly motioned toward the kitchen. "Get some coffee. Stay for breakfast and warm up. I've gotta finish my rounds." She started down the hall and froze when a loud eerie moan erupted from Dot's room.

A man's groan. Crusher's. Her heart leapt with fright. She hurried toward the room and entered to find him embracing his wife's rigid body. Whipping her phone out, she called the nurse's station and talked to Linda's volunteer. Next she called Adam. Then she shrank against the wall and watched Crusher release his grief over the woman he had adored.

By noon, Dot's body had been confirmed dead and removed to a funeral home. Adam took Crusher home and helped him make a list of people he wanted to notify. Once Miranda and a relief caregiver arrived, Carly carried the canary's cage out beside Magnificent.

Shrugging into her coat, she left the building. First she trudged to the destroyed maintenance room. A sign indicated maintenance was temporarily headquartered around the corner in an adjoining closet-sized room containing the center's communication equipment. Inside, Rocco was helping Aesop use the emergency intercom to check up on all those in independent living.

Outside, the world was sparkling with snow jewels, and various Sweet Life workers were scurrying around. A friend had passed, but life continued.

She pounded her boots against Crusher's porch and let herself in. "How is he?"

Adam's face said it all. "He's resting. His daughter's coming in from Texas. She's renting a car in Portland and should arrive late tonight. Think I'll stay with him until then."

"That's good."

"But now would be a good time for me to take you home."

She nodded. "If you give me Crusher's list, I'll make the calls."

Relief flooded his face. In the truck, she told him about Dot claiming the Death Angel had returned. "What do you make of that?"

"We know she was a Christian. In spite of her dementia, God knows her heart. I think the evil one used her weakness to torment her."

"That's what I was thinking. But she seemed peaceful, as if she'd died in her sleep." Carly wondered if she could have done more to help the woman endure her last lonely months. Dot had seemed to enjoy the Bible study with Martha. But she couldn't always pull up the verses on her own. Was it like Auntie had claimed? Her fears worsened in the end because she'd never overcome them when she was of strong body and mind? That lifelong character traits exaggerated in the elderly?

As if reading her mind, he consoled, "You did everything you could. She's in a better place. Even Crusher admits that."

Adam walked her to the door, and she was relieved to see Cocoa lively and well. He didn't thump, scratch, or bite, but just licked snow from her boots. She swept up the rabbit and gave him a squeeze.

"I gotta go."

"All right. Tell Crusher, I'm making his calls." Adam kissed her and left.

After she fed Cocoa, she sat at her table with Crusher's list in front of her. But before she could make any calls, she would allow herself to mourn her friend.

Already feeling vulnerable from grief and lack of rest, Carly returned to Sweet Life Thursday morning to find Helen engrossed in deep conversation with Sherie at the front desk. Dread trickled down her spine, and with head dipped, she hurried past them. She placed her coat in the staff room and glanced at Helen's back, rushing down the hall to start her rounds.

A fresh wave of grief hit her when she saw Dot's closed door. Swiping her eyes with her sleeve, she gripped the handle to Nines's room when Martha popped her head into the hall and motioned her over. "I could use some help."

Hastening across the hall, she followed Martha into her room. The elderly woman was struggling to breathe, so Carly readied her breathing machine. "Your daughter's here."

"Not a good time."

"It's hard losing Dot, isn't it?" Carly asked.

Martha nodded and pulled her mask aside to speak. "I'm glad I started that Bible study with her."

"You were good friends. And you'll meet again someday."

She sank back against the recliner's headrest, her shoulders slumped, and allowed the medicated air to help her breathe. When the treatment was finished, Martha closed her eyes. "I'm so tired. Can you help me back to bed?"

Carly rose and placed her palm against Martha's forehead. No temp. But she understood. "Sure. Unless you want to wait for Helen?"

"Nope."

So Carly removed Martha's shoes and helped her into bed. She removed her covering and tucked the covers under her chin. Martha turned onto her side, facing the wall.

Widow Martha stared at the wall, entertaining all kinds of evil thoughts. Why had she been born with asthma? Why was it getting worse? If only she could breathe well enough to rest. She was so tired, she just wanted to sleep and never wake up. It hurt bad that Dot was gone. Oh, the real Dot had been gone a long time, but losing her felt even worse.

Her friend's death reminded her that her own time was shortening. And she didn't think she had the strength to see it through. She should pray or read scripture, but she just didn't have the strength. Maybe if she fell asleep, her daughter would leave, and she wouldn't have to talk and be reminded she was growing forgetful. Anyway, she'd been having some delicious dreams lately. She felt someone kiss her check and flinched. Carly. God's special gift.

Carly turned to leave. But Helen was blocking the door from where she'd been observing them. She summoned her with a crook of her finger.

With dread, Carly stepped into the hall. "Do you want to go someplace private to talk?"

Helen shook her head. "I just want to apologize."

With a wave of relief, Carly replied, "No need."

"Yes, there is. I was so frightened when Mom got snowed in. And then when I learned about Dot, I saw things more clearly. It's my own fault Mom's lonely. She's taking this hard and I don't know how to help her."

"Just walk through it with her. We'll help her together."

"But I said such terrible things to you. They weren't true. I knew it when they were spewing out of my mouth. I just haven't known how to cope with Mom's situation."

"I understand. I've been thinking, too. It wasn't fair I didn't warn you about James."

Helen gave a harsh laugh. "For months Mom's been obsessing over her birthday. Now she's obsessing about playing bingo with James. Well, she was before Dot's death. And I don't have the strength to fight it. Maybe we need to let her have her way. It might cheer her, letting James come to bingo. But you will make sure they're chaperoned when he's here? I don't trust that old geezer."

"I'll make it a personal point to chaperone them. But his grandson, Jason, will always be with him."

"Good." Helen sighed. "It's rough. But I'm going to try to do better. I don't know what I'll cut out of my schedule, but something's got to go. I don't want any regrets when it's Mom's time to pass."

Carly didn't want to think about that day. Of all the residents, Martha had wiggled her way right into the center of her heart. Maybe because she was a little tough like Aunt Fannie.

Later that morning, she found a few minutes to slip away to Simon's office. He was happy to hear the report that Helen was no longer holding a grudge. He claimed they'd had a good talk on the phone. His fatherly pat lifted her spirits.

During the afternoon, Carly had a sudden inspiration. Sherie affirmed her suggestion because the storm had cancelled some of their scheduled weekly programs. It only took one phone call. And with the schools closed, Ann was able to round up a helper and bring several children to the facility.

They gathered the residents in the lobby by the Christmas tree to sing carols. Helen managed to convince Martha to come and listen. Even the Hall Patroller left her station. Klepto's hands touched only the children, and the General was fully clothed.

The angelic faces, so earnest and radiant, sent positive feelings throughout the center. Everyone laughed when the birds joined in with the singing. Miranda seemed happy. And for at least that hour, Carly was completely content.

CHAPTER THIRTY-FIVE

By Friday, all the roads were plowed, so Shirley decided that since so many activities had been cancelled during the week, they would hold their regular Thursday bingo a day late. Knowing that she now had Helen's permission, Carly called Jason and arranged for him to bring his grandfather down for the afternoon.

When Martha wouldn't come to breakfast, Carly thought it might be because of her excitement about bingo. When she went to check on her, however, she was shocked to discover Martha still clothed in her nightgown, rocking in her chair and staring at the wall.

"Hi, sweetie." Carly sat on the edge of Martha's sofa. "Did you remember what today is?"

Martha turned a vacant stare at her. "The days are so long. At one time I thought they sped by. Now they just drag on and on."

"Not today. Today's going to be fun."

"Why?" Martha grunted. "You come to give me a breathing treatment?"

"No. Did you remember that today's bingo?"

Instantly a spark of interest lit Martha's eyes, but she argued, "Today isn't Thursday."

"No, it's Friday. But Sherie's organized it for today to make up for all the other activities we missed because of the snow. And James Irish is coming to join in the game."

"Don't be ridiculous. I had a dream about him though. He was at my party. The silly part—you know how dreams can be—he was there both as a young version and an old version of himself."

Feeling as if she'd fallen into some kind of sci-fi zone, Carly managed a smile. "That wasn't a dream, honey. It's real. His grandson brought him to your birthday party."

Martha's mouth gaped. Carly watched her put the pieces together. "And Dot died?"

"Jah. She's gone to heaven."

Nodding, Martha said, "I'm having trouble thinking straight, I guess."

Carly watched the woman's struggle as she tried to convince herself that she wasn't losing her mental faculties. "So let's put on your best dress and get you ready for bingo."

"But I don't want him to see me this way."

"He won't, we have time."

"No. I mean. . .old like this."

Carly smiled. "But, he's old, too."

Her eyes sparkled. "Oh."

Martha presented herself at the game table early, announcing to everyone who came to join, "I'm saving this seat for a friend."

"Saving for a friend," Repeater mimicked. "Ain't we friends?"

"Shush! There he is."

Carly turned to see Jason and James crossing the lobby. Jason wore a gray sweater and tight jeans.

Widow Martha glanced at James with delight. After Carly convinced her she hadn't been dreaming about him or the birthday party, she'd found the book of poetry he'd given her. Helen had stashed it, along with the carvings, inside the linen closet. Hurrying across the lobby, she greeted him.

"It's like a wonderful dream that you're here."

"Life is a vapor, my dear. But I'm all yours today."

Giddy with the emotions of young love, she hooked her arm through his. "I missed you."

He squeezed her arm. "We still have things that'll keep us apart, but I don't see why we can't enjoy each other's friendship. Do you?"

"Certainly not!" she said, breathless.

His eyes teased, "You're a lot easier than when you were young."

"No, just wiser." Wise enough to realize that she would live one day at a time. She would enjoy James. Have a little bit of heaven on earth before she moved on to the more glorious land. Meanwhile, she'd thank God for the blessing of friendship and trust Him to provide the strength she needed.

Carly watched the joy on the elderly couple's faces and heard Martha say, "It's like a wonderful dream you're here."

Beside her, Jason said, "Gramps was really stewing about the storm."

"Martha's best friend passed away this week. She's struggling."

"I'm sorry. Hopefully this will do them both some good. Say, what's going on outside? They have that smaller building barricaded off."

"The roof collapsed in the storm. We had to hire a crew to remove snow from all the buildings. We need a new roof so bad." She shrugged. "I don't know if that has anything to do with why it collapsed. But we're constantly fixing leaks. Simon, the director of the board, hasn't been able to get funding to do the repairs that are necessary. At one time, Sweet Life was the darling of the Mennonite community. Now that it's old and needs repair, they've lost interest in it. You know the modern mentality, pitch it and get something new."

"If Gramps and I are going to be spending time here, we may have to make a donation toward the roof fund. Wouldn't want the sky to fall on us."

Carly could only stare at their benefactor.

Adam conveniently checked on Crusher right before bingo.

Hello! Hello!

Chirp. Chirp. Both birds called for his attention.

"G-49" Shirley called. "G-49, folks."

But from the moment Adam stepped into the lobby, all his senses went numb except for his eyesight. Carly was hugging Jason in full view of the entire room.

Jealousy narrowed his vision and faltered his step. They were so engrossed with each other, they hadn't even seen him. Clenching his jaw, he strode toward them. As they drew apart, he overheard Jason's words.

"You're welcome. After your aunt meets with the publisher, let's celebrate. Let me take you out to dinner."

Once again, Adam's fingers twitched with the desire to smash Jason's perfect teeth.

"You mean with Auntie?"

Adam gleefully watched the disappointment cross Jason's expression. "Sure."

When Carly finally saw him, she stepped away from Jason. "Adam."

He forced a smile. "Hey." Nodded at Jason. "I was checking on Crusher. Thought I'd see how you were doing."

"Good." She nodded toward the game table. "I have so much to tell you."

He glanced at Jason. "Can you excuse us a moment?"

Jason shrugged and moved to lean against a wall where he could watch the ensuing game.

"But now's not really a good time," Carly explained. "I should be helping Shirley with the game."

"The funeral's set for Saturday afternoon. Can I take you?"

"Oh, no. That's when we're meeting with the publisher."

Finally something was going his way. "Do you have to be there for that?"

"No." She shook her head. "Jah, thanks for the offer."

He followed her gaze to the bingo table. "They look happy."

"Jason and James are donating money to fix all the roofs."

"How nice." Adam gritted his teeth and glanced over at Jason, longing to ask him to go outside to discuss some things. But Jason moved toward the game table. Joining the game. Clever.

"Isn't it amazing? How God brought them into our lives? Not only are they blessing Martha, but now they're blessing the entire center. It's like they're an answer to prayer."

It irked Adam that Jason was filling his *godsend* shoes. And if he did have to go to Indiana again, the guy would probably make his move on Carly.

Carly's gaze followed the game, and he knew at the slightest provocation, she'd be across the room, swiping tokens from Klepto's hand or keeping the General from drawing battle plans on the cards.

"How's Crusher doing?"

"Good as can be expected."

She touched his arm. "Thanks for dropping by. I'll see you on Saturday."

So easily dismissed, he fought to contain his anger and jealousy. He'd go, but there was no law that said he couldn't linger around in the parking lot.

Adam sat in his cab, growing more irritated by the minute as he kept his eye on Jason's car. The game should be over. Irish was probably trying to confirm his dinner date with Carly. When he found out she was already engaged on Saturday, he'd probably change the whole appointment with the publisher. It seemed he could magically make anything happen. Who couldn't, with his funds and networking?

When he finally spotted them making their way down the walk, he felt an instant of chagrin to see James leaning heavily on his cane. Skirting the yellow taped maintenance building, Jason used hand gestures and James nodded enthusiastically. Though donating money to the center was a wonderful thing, Adam's gut wrenched with loathing.

He timed his appearance so that when Jason turned from helping James into the car, he saw Adam. But the intruder quickly covered his surprise with a smirk.

"I'd like a word with you."

"Sure." Jason eyed him cautiously. "Let me start the heater for Gramps first."

Adam waited. When Jason returned, he nonchalantly stuffed his hands into the pockets of a coat that probably cost half a year of Adam's wages.

"What's up?"

"I thought you might need reminding that Carly's my girl."

An eyebrow shot upward, but he quickly recovered. "Funny, she hasn't mentioned that to me."

"Probably because she doesn't realize you're pursuing her."

He brought his hands up and tugged at the collar of his coat. "Then maybe it's time I made myself plainer."

Adam shrugged. "If you want a setdown."

"Let's let her decide."

"Why? Can't you see we're different. We live a plain lifestyle compared to yours. Surely you can't be serious about her. And I won't have you trifling with her, throwing your money and influence around for a one-night stand."

Jason shrugged. "Can't fight romance. Don't you get it? It's Gramps and Martha's story all over again. Only ours will have a happier ending."

"Over my dead body."

"Then you'll have nothing to worry about."

Adam grabbed the front of the snob's shirt.

Jason straightened but didn't flinch. "Maybe you don't follow your church's teachings as faithfully as you claim."

Unable to contain himself any longer, Adam swung. But the moment his hand connected with the other man's eye, he felt regret. Backing away, he raised both hands in the air as if to disavow what had just occurred.

He watched Jason stagger and recover.

"Thankfully, there's such a thing as repentance," Adam mumbled.

Jason climbed into the car and sank into the leather seat, not surprised to hear his grandfather's deep chuckling.

"I saw that coming. The way he glared at you during bingo."

Yanking the rearview mirror down to look at his throbbing eye, Jason replied, "Well thanks for the warning. I didn't think you saw anything in there but your beloved Martha."

"You're right. But I felt his vibes. He reminds me of John."

"Martha's husband?"

"He found out about us. Threatened me like that. Only I gave him the shiner. Wonder if Martha ever found out John knew about us?" He tilted his head. "You're not going to ruin this for me, are you?"

"I hope not, but you wouldn't want me to roll over and play dead, would you?"

"What's going on with you and Carly?"

Jason put the car in gear and started out of the parking lot. "She's amazing. We've got so much in common."

James released a mild oath, which was unusual for him, these days. "The differences aren't going to vaporize. Anyway, what about Karen? You sure this isn't a rebound thing?"

"Maybe. But I'd regret it if I didn't try. We're going to be seeing her every Thursday anyway, right?"

"You young people never learn from history."

"Sure we do. Only we try to change it. Hindsight and all that."

"Better pray about it." James chuckled again. "Bingo's going to be mighty entertaining."

Chapter Thirty-Six

Saturday, the weather turned bitter cold and windy for Dot's funeral. Somberness settled over Carly as they neared the church. Funerals reminded Carly of her parents' deaths. Today the same old question haunted her. Why had God allowed it?

Oh she'd heard the Adam and Eve explanation. Eve ate the fruit, and now mankind dies. But why her parents? And why did Dot have to suffer with dementia for so many years? Letting her mind follow the same old circles brought her near despair—as if nothing at Sweet Life mattered because they were all on this road toward pain and death.

Adam turned into the parking lot. "You're quiet."

"Just praying I'll be able to endure the service. It reminds me of when my parents died."

"You want to talk about that?"

"Mom and Dad had been arguing. My dad had quite a temper and used it to get his way. He wanted to go into town that day, but Mom was worried about the bad roads. Like usual, she gave in to him. And then they had the accident."

"You blame him?"

"Not anymore. I know they loved each other. But it made me vow to never marry a man who would control me like that. Dale had those tendencies."

She saw Adam's head snap up. Didn't know why she was telling him this. But once she started talking about it, she couldn't seem to stop. "Oh, he didn't have Dad's temper. But he didn't like to take no for an answer. When he decided to move to Indiana, he wouldn't budge. Didn't want to hear how I felt about it."

"I'm sorry. I know I told you that going to Indiana wasn't about us, but while I was there we did talk some. He's real sorry about the way he treated you."

Her lips trembled. "But today is about Dot. And Crusher." She tore her mind away from the memory of the accident to focus on the upcoming ordeal. She especially dreaded the graveside service afterward. But that wasn't even the end of it. Later that night, she had to deal with Jason. She needed time to regroup before she could face him. "I'm not good at funerals. I was hoping to skip the meal afterward."

Adam turned off the ignition and glanced over with surprise. "I'd like to go for Crusher's sake, but I can take you home first."

"Thanks."

"I'm sorry this is so hard for you."

She nodded and gazed unseeing at the plain architecture of Old Holley Mennonite Fellowship Church. Its steep, gray-shingled roof bore no cross or steeple. The church contained no stained glass but reflected the plain lifestyle of its congregation. Such a lifestyle was based heavily on faith and tradition. At this moment, her faith became an undergirding source of strength.

Still, she prayed. *Lord, help us. Give us strength.* With the Holy Spirit's presence and the support she felt from seeing an entire throng of dark-colored vehicles, comfort enveloped her like a blanket. When hardships struck, it was good to belong to a fellowship that banded together.

They sat in the truck, its tailgate up against a snow bank. The turnout had to be more than Old Holley's 125 members.

"Ready?"

"Jah."

As they walked toward the church, she bent against the harsh wind. Adam squeezed her hand, providing a bit of warmth. Women who normally wore small floral prints were dressed in dark colors and moved together as one dark cloud toward the little white church.

In the vestibule, Carly removed her coat and tossed it over her arm as she left Adam and solemnly moved to the left, the women's side of the church.

Inside the sanctuary, the lines moved up the aisle and past the casket so that everyone could say their good-byes. Dot didn't look natural, but she looked peaceful. Carly kissed her finger and placed it on Dot's cold forehead. Then struggling to hold back a sob, she moved back into the line.

She took a seat beside Aunt Fannie and Miranda—the latter stuck out with her short skirt and bare head. But funerals were open to all so it was not an issue. While the wind shook the single-paned windows, a male song leader opened the service with a hymn. One of the ministers gave the eulogy, and a sextet presented two a cappella songs that were followed by a sermon.

Regardless of the harsh weather, she'd never been so glad to leave the sanctuary. Outside they hugged their coats and scarves tight as they trudged to the neighboring cemetery.

Miranda shouted over the howling wind. "Poor Crusher."

Carly nodded, remaining silent from her inner suffering.

"I'm thankful we have something good to look forward to, the editor that's coming tomorrow."

"It was good of Jason to change the appointment," Carly agreed.

"I'm on pins and needles," Aunt Fannie admitted. "Like a girl waiting for her date."

Smiling, Carly said, "And not just any date, but the one that's *the one.*" Her heart felt a moment of peace, thinking of all the good things that had happened recently. Like the verse the minister had used from the familiar Twenty-third Psalm: *"Yea, though I walk through the valley of the shadow of death, I will fear no evil: for thou art with me."* She could see God's handiwork all around her.

So many of her prayers were being answered—many brought about by her new Irish friends. That's why facing Jason later would be so difficult.

She found herself moving into a line again as only two at a time could fit on the path that had been shoveled into the large snow banks edging the parking lot. The graveside service was short on two accounts, the cold and the fact that the ground was frozen. Normally, they waited while some of their men shoveled dirt onto the lowered coffin, but because of the weather, Crusher had opted to let the funeral home handle everything.

After the service, Adam located Carly. "You all right?"

"Jah, except I look like a scarecrow and feel like a popsicle."

He laughed. "You look beautiful, and I'll see what we can do to get you warm." Draping his arm across her shoulders, he sheltered her as they made their way to his truck. Inside he tucked a blanket around her.

On the ride home, he envisioned just how else he'd warm her. Comfort her. After Crusher's dinner, he'd come and start a fire in her fireplace. He'd bring his popcorn popper and cuddle on the couch. Then he'd ask her if he could take her on a surprise excursion Sunday afternoon. He intended to take her to the bridge and propose. His gut now squirmed with anxiety and anticipation.

"Can I drop by later? I'll start a fire and bring popcorn."

She looked at him with disappointment in her eyes. "Oh, not tonight. I need to deal with some things."

He took her hand. "Sure you couldn't use the company? I know I could. You don't have to do this alone."

"I'm sorry. Another time."

"Tomorrow? I was hoping to take you someplace special."

He saw the longing in her gaze, but also discouragement. "I've got church and then that editor's meeting at Aunt Fannie's. We changed it to Sunday because of the funeral."

"I wondered about that." If they were going to announce their engagement at Christmas, he had to propose this weekend. "After that? I really want to see you."

She smiled with relief. "Jah, that sounds good."

"So don't wash your hair or anything. Count on seeing me. Actually, if you want to wash it, that's fine by me. I'll even brush it for you."

"You'll do nothing of the kind, Adam Lapp."

He shrugged and grinned. "Just trying to be helpful."

She giggled and seemed to relax. He was disappointed he had to wait until the next day to see her, but it would give him time to break the news to Dad. He was thinking about what he'd say when her cottage came into view. Carly instantly stiffened, her face agitated.

Then he saw the reason. He pulled in behind Jason's car and put the gear in Park. "Did you know he'd be here?"

She nodded.

Anger rose in him like a beast, narrowing his vision. "I can't believe I missed part of Crusher's dinner to bring you home to meet him. I'm a fool. You told me you weren't up to seeing me tonight." He waited for some kind of assurance that their relationship wasn't falling apart and miles from the road to commitment and marriage.

She placed her hand on his. "I said I had to deal with some things."

He jerked his hand away. "A carefully worded lie. You know what? I'm done here. Just go. Have your fling."

She turned to fully face him. "Now, Adam. Let me explain. I'm only going to dinner with him so that—"

"I know. So you can drool your thanks all over the little rich boy who's making all your dreams come true. Jason told me you hadn't even told him about us. He said it was your choice. Looks like you've already chosen."

"But I choose you."

"Only. I'm not willing to share. So go."

"Adam. You're being unreasonable. Whatever happened to trusting each other? Does that only work one way?"

The beast inside was uncontrollable, and he didn't know what he would do next if he didn't leave. Give Irish another black eye? He ground out the words, "Just. Get. Out. . . of my truck."

Her eyes widened, shimmering with tears. "Fine!" She threw the blanket at him and climbed out of the truck, slamming the door. He watched her march toward Jason's car, and the only victory he felt was when her covering blew off her head and sailed across the lawn. She ran after it, her hair losing its pins and blowing wild.

Jason jumped out of his car to help her. Jealousy raged. Biting his lip, Adam looked away. Yanked the truck in reverse. Bitter and hurt, he resolved, *Let her new godsend pick up the pieces from now on. See how that goes.* He needed to calm down so that he could fulfill his obligation to Crusher. At least he was a man of his word.

Chapter Thirty-Seven

Although Adam's jealousy was deeply embedded, his anger dissolved almost as soon as he'd joined the gathering for Dot's funeral dinner where he was able to focus on Crusher's needs. But as soon as he was able, he left. His route took him past Jimmy's place, and he noticed his friend's truck parked outside his apartment. Missing Jimmy and thinking he was the perfect guy to give him some advice, he pulled into his drive.

Jimmy was surprised to see him and invited him inside. Things hadn't changed much at the bachelor pad. He walked up to Jimmy's desk and looked at a wall map. "Got a bunch more pins in there since I was last here."

"Jah. Went the southern route last week as far as Birmingham. Can I get you a pop?"

"Sure." Adam slouched into an arm chair and waited for Jimmy to bring his drink. "Thanks."

"Where you been all dressed up?"

"Dot's funeral. I got to be friends with Crusher, working at Sweet Life."

"Oh. Guess I was out of the loop on that."

"Talked to Carly lately?

Jimmy shook his head. "Nope. I was thinking about going over tonight."

"Don't bother. She won't be there. She's on a date."

Jimmy tilted his head. "With you?"

"Nope. Her new benefactor. Jason Irish."

Looking concerned, Jimmy asked, "Who? Look, I'm really out of the loop. What's going on?"

Adam filled him in on everything he knew about Irish, watching Jimmy react with suspicion. "Guess I'll drop by tomorrow while they're having their meeting and see for myself what's going on with this guy."

"That'd be good. I can't do this anymore, you know."

"What do you mean?"

"Watch out for her while you're gone. I'm done. She's driving me crazy."

Jimmy's brows furrowed. "You going to Indiana?"

"No!" Adam stood. Ran his hands through his hair. "Why does everyone keep assuming that?"

Throwing up his hands, Jimmy worked to calm him. "Easy, now."

Adam plopped back down on the chair. "Dale's having surgery, and I might have to help out after Christmas. Nothing definite yet, but I'm not moving there. Dad's been great lately. I'm happy here."

"Jah. You sound real happy."

"I would be if your sister didn't drive me crazy."

"You mad at her or that Irish fella?"

"Both."

"Sounds like you're jealous."

"Well, jah."

"Thought you loved her."

"I do."

"Then why aren't you fighting for her?"

Adam grinned. "You didn't see the shiner I gave him."

Jimmy burst into laughter. "I wish I could've seen the king of easy-going get riled. I was always the one with the temper. You're supposed to be the one keeping us out of trouble."

Discouragement pressed Adam's shoulders. "She didn't even tell Jason we were dating. This guy connects with her in ways I can't. They both work in social services. They both ride bikes to work. He's funding renovations at Sweet Life. He can make her dreams come true."

Jimmy shook his head. "You need to get a grip. He's not Mennonite, and Carly won't compromise. Don't let your feelings get in the way of reality."

"You had to be there."

"So I'll go scope him out and give you my take on the situation."

"Thanks." Adam relaxed. "Got any plans for tonight?"

"Nope. You can stick around if you want. We can order pizza later."

"Great." He figured it'd help him keep his mind off Carly's dinner date—off Jason seeing her hair that way. "Hey, are you dating Miranda?"

Jimmy laughed. "Not anymore. But Aunt Fannie's adopted her so we're friends. She plans to stay after her V. S. term is over."

"You think a guy can be just friends with a woman? It didn't work that good for me."

Shrugging, Jimmy replied, "Keep the faith. I'm pretty sure you and Carly are meant to be together."

"I'll never speak to him again," Carly vowed as she chased her prayer cap across the frozen lawn. His squealing tires humiliated her. He'd tossed her out of his truck! Still in disbelief, she halted and turned to watch his black tailgate disappear at the end of Hawthorne. Not only had he rejected her, he'd broken up with her. And yelled at her!

"I'm done here. Go have your little fling. Just get out of my truck." Her pain intensified. She'd never dreamed it would end this way. She'd waited patiently while he dallied with the Indiana woman. After all that, he'd broken up with her for no good reason. If he'd only let her explain. What a temper. Worse than their last argument. She had no idea he could be such a pigheaded. . .

"This what you're after?" Jason grinned, waving her prayer cap.

She gave him a sheepish smile, embarrassed he'd witnessed the incident. "Jah, it got away from me." Her hair flew wild around her face so she couldn't see, much less think. "Let's go inside. I've been frozen all day." She fiddled with her key.

"Let me."

Inside, she told him to make himself at home while she repaired her appearance. In her bathroom, she leaned against the closed door for support. She could hear his low voice, probably talking to Cocoa. She slid down against the door to the floor and placed her head in her hands. She'd had a lot of rough days, but this contended for worst ever.

Adam's furious face filled her vision. What had happened to the easy-going man she'd grown to love and trust? If today was a preview of their future, she was fortunate it was over between them. For the second time that day, memories of her dad's angry outbursts flooded over her. Men!

And Jason was no saint, either! Her anger expanded to include him. If he hadn't come early, she could have spared Adam the pain. She'd only accepted Jason's dinner invitation to talk about his misguided idea of pursuing her. Because she loved Adam. But what would she tell Jason now that he'd witnessed Adam's temper tantrum? It would make her look and feel like a fool.

Groaning for what still awaited, she pulled herself up off the floor. The mirror didn't lie. Definitely contender for worst day ever, if not worst hair. This would take starting from scratch. But then it was Jason's own fault if she kept him waiting. He'd arrived early. He was to blame for the entire episode.

When she finally emerged, the aroma of freshly brewed coffee met her in the hall. It was hard to remain angry at Jason when she saw him sipping coffee and scratching the chocolate-and-white lop-eared puddle stretched out on his lap. After all, Cocoa was a good judge of character. The fact that he wasn't in hiding mode warmed her heart.

"I see you made yourself at home," she teased, pouring herself a cup.

"That's what you told me to do." His eyes lit. "Wow. You look great. How do you do it?"

"A Mennonite secret." She knew she didn't look great. She'd pulled her hair so tight her eyes nearly slanted, hoping to make herself unappealing to lessen the pain of the rejection she meant to deliver. Especially after the way Dale's rejection had backfired on her. But his lopsided smile warmed her. It was the type that went all the way to the crinkles of his eyes. Bruised eye. "What on earth happened to your eye? You wreck your bike?"

"We're bookends, you and me. Destiny."

This wasn't going to be easy. "Tell me the entire story."

"Actually, it didn't have anything to do with my bike. Your hotheaded protector was waiting in the parking lot for me after bingo."

Her mouth gaped. She snapped it closed. "Adam?"

"One and the same."

"I don't believe it."

"Believe it. Right in front of Gramps, too. Ask him."

She tried to recall what would have set him off at bingo. Shaking her head, she said, "I've never seen him behave like this before. He's always been such a gentle guy."

Jason's lips thinned. "Guess I haven't seen that side of him yet. Did he threaten you today?"

She sighed. "No. Nothing like that. He's just. . ."

"Jealous." He gave her that lopsided grin. "So am I, but I don't act like that."

If this was a personal vendetta between the men, that meant Jason had intentionally provoked Adam by coming earlier than planned. He wasn't as innocent as he let on, but even so she felt like it was her fault. "If anyone's to blame, it's me. I should have told you up front I was dating Adam."

"There must be a reason you didn't. Such as. . .he's not right for you?"

She frowned. "We were working on some issues when I met you."

"Were?"

She smiled. "Jah. Okay. Still working on some issues." She studied him as everything started to make sense. "So that's what Adam meant about making a choice."

"He forced you to choose?"

"No, but he accused me of choosing you, just before he drove away in a huff." She saw the light in Jason's eyes and knew she was giving him false hope. "That doesn't matter. Thing is, I like you a lot, but I love Adam. Even if he is acting bad."

"Is that wise?" The side of his mouth twitched. "But leave him out of the picture for a minute, and let's talk about us. Love takes time. Time to get over, too."

"You still love the woman you told me about?"

"Karen? I guess when I'm feeling weak, I do. That's why I understand your struggle."

She nodded.

"Let's just start with getting to know each other. Doing some of the things together we both enjoy." He shrugged. "Who knows where that might take us?"

She shook her head and set her coffee on the side table. "Even if Adam and Karen weren't in the picture—"

"Believe me, Karen's not. But go on."

"I'd never date someone outside the church."

"But I'm a Christian."

"I understand. But not Mennonite. We have traditions."

"I'm not asking you to leave your faith. Lots of couples have mixed faiths. Think of all the other things we have in common. Of all the good we could do together." He nodded enthusiastically. "We could make our own traditions, too. It's romantic." He tilted his head. "Come on. I know you're a romantic."

She couldn't deny it. "You're wonderful and generous, but all I can offer is friendship."

"I'll take it. Glad that's settled." Before she could object, he reached across the table and took her hand. "I've been inconsiderate asking you to dinner. I can see it's been a rough day with the funeral and all." He shrugged his brows toward the door to remind her about Adam's behavior. "So while you were in the bathroom, I ordered pizza."

"You did?" She'd never felt so grateful. "Thanks. That's so thoughtful." He really did get her. He caressed her hand in a comforting sort of way.

"While we're waiting, you can open my Christmas gift." He jumped up and went to fish something out of his coat pocket.

"But it's not even Christmas."

"I know. I can't wait."

"Oh, Jason. I can't accept—"

"Please. Let's celebrate friendship."

She nodded with hesitation. Maybe he did understand. "Okay, thanks."

She tore away the wrappings and burst into laughter at the bell he'd gotten her for her bike. "This is perfect. I love it!"

"Then, I'm jealous. Seriously, use it when skateboarders are around."

She laughed.

Jason pointed at the window. "I see headlights. Pizza's here."

Afterward, they moved to the sofa. He kept a respectable distance between them, and she was able to relax and enjoy the companionship. He knew just when to crack a joke, how to listen, and when to leave. But before he did, she found herself telling him all about Dale and Adam. He asked some questions but never gave her any advice. Never made her feel uncomfortable or foolish.

At the door, he took her hand. "I'd never treat you like those men have. You're so special. I will cherish your friendship and whatever else you allow to develop between us."

It had been like a healing balm washing away a bad day, and she didn't have the heart or energy to remind him that friendship was all she would ever offer him. If Adam hadn't exploded, she would have clarified things with Jason. But the way things turned out, she couldn't bring herself to turn him away.

Once he was gone, she sank into a bubble bath with great relish. Closing her eyes, the day's events paraded through her mind. The conversation she'd had in the truck about her parents. It reminded her how much she still missed them. Then the funeral and Crusher's sad countenance. Love was painful. Maybe not even worth the bother. She should have stayed friends with Adam. That first kiss was her downfall. She wouldn't make the same mistake with Jason. He would make someone a wonderful boyfriend or husband. But not her. She wished he hadn't provoked Adam past his boiling point. She couldn't forget his angry snarl, how he'd ordered her to get out of the truck. *"I'm done here. Go have your little fling. Just get out of my truck."* Hurt and anger rose in her. Worst day ever. But it felt good to have spent the evening with a friend who understood.

Adam squirmed. It wasn't easy to sit through a church service, feeling convicted over his recent outbursts of anger. But he wasn't entirely convinced he was wrong. Passive-aggressive, Carly had once deemed him. He'd been passive for too long. When he'd confronted Dad, things got worse but started healing.

Those who attended Old Holley adhered to a lifestyle of nonresistance. He'd been taught it from birth. But they swept under the carpet the messy way Mennonites sometimes handled things. It was what drove Dale away from church. Dealing honestly seemed the better way. Especially when the other guy got the shiner. Only it felt crummy when Jason hadn't fought back.

He glanced at Carly's pew. She sat straight and serene. Not the disheveled, distraught woman he'd last seen. Jason had probably comforted her. The idea grinded his gut. His own actions had played right into the other guy's hand. He'd been so jealous at the time that now he couldn't even remember what he'd told Carly. It was all one black blur. But he was pretty sure tonight's date was off now.

Spending Saturday evening with Jimmy had helped him realize he wasn't ready to give up on Carly, after all. But he'd lost a lot of ground and would need to keep a cool head if he wanted to win her back. She must have felt his gaze because she glanced over. He gave her a lopsided grin. She glared and turned away.

Jah, she was mad.

Late the previous night, he and Jimmy came up with a plan. He'd scope out the scene at Aunt Fannie's and report back to Adam. If he gave him the go-ahead, then he might soon be an engaged man.

Feeling Adam's stare, Carly finally gave in and looked over. Expecting to see the dark, stormy expression she remembered, she was shocked when he grinned back as if nothing unpleasant had happened between them. It was a pleading, flirty smile. Insufferable! Casting him the dirtiest look she could muster, she glanced back at the preacher, trying in vain to concentrate on the sermon.

Was Adam turning into a jealous maniac? Remembering Jason's bruised eye, she decided that he would have to prove himself before he wiggled back into her good graces. But inside, a tiny, traitorous hope sprang to life in her heart.

Beside her, Auntie bowed her head. Probably praying for her meeting with the editor. Carly vowed not to let her own problems ruin anything for Auntie's big day.

Chapter Thirty-Eight

After church, Adam went to his parents' home for lunch and a family farm meeting. With Christmas only a week away, it was more celebratory than anything else. The adults assembled in the living room. While they didn't have a tree, the fireplace was decorated with an evergreen swag and candles. Some wrapped gifts waited in the corner for the grandchildren. They weren't taught that Santa was real, only the story of the Savior. The coffee table held a manger scene and a Bible opened to the Christmas story. The piano was decorated with more greenery and hymnals opened to the familiar Christmas carols. And the side tables were laden with plates of home-baked goodies that made Adam's mouth drool.

During family meetings, Faith—who had been a surprise baby born long after her other siblings—usually supervised the grandchildren. His sisters and the brother-in-laws who pitched in at the farm were included in the meeting.

Dad cleared his throat, and the conversation ebbed. He gave a little spiel about what a great year they'd had and thanked everyone, handing out bonus checks. Adam placed his in his shirt pocket and snatched a lemon bar. It was partway to his mouth when Dad said, "I've an announcement to make regarding Adam. Since I'm not getting any younger, I'm making him a partner. In January, we're drawing up the paperwork to make it legal. I hope you girls don't feel slighted. You know that Adam and I take a salary, just like you. The profit gets put back in the farm, except for the annual bonuses."

Instantly the room lit with chatter, Adam set the lemon bar back on his napkin. The congratulatory remarks seemed sincere to him. There didn't appear to be any objections. It wasn't really news. Just a formality.

After that, Dad talked about his goals for the upcoming year. He assigned one of Adam's sisters the task of getting involved at the university that was doing research on the ground disease attacking noble firs and ruining some of the county's tree farms.

Pride swelled in Adam's chest in part because Dad was thinking progressively, but mostly because he was keeping his word about the partnership. When the business discussion waned, Adam saw his chance to tell them about Dale.

"I think you've all heard our cousin Dale had an operation on his leg? The operation went well, but there'll be a substantial recovery time. So he's bringing the family to Sweet Home for Christmas. Staying at my place."

"When's he coming?" Sissie asked.

"I pick them up at the airport on Tuesday."

"Think he'll make up with Simon?"

"I hope so."

Later when he was alone with Ann, he confided, "I might be bringing Carly home for Christmas." He shrugged. "She's mad at me right now, but I'm hopeful."

"I'll pray," she said with a grin.

He popped a piece of Mom's famous peanut butter fudge into his mouth, as delicious as he'd remembered and watched the activities bustling around them. Hope burgeoned. Yet so much depended on the call Jimmy would soon make to report his observations. Adam needed to know what he was up against and if Carly was interested in Jason. Either way, he and Jimmy had come up with a plan, and he was willing to risk everything to make his dream come true. He didn't want this to drag out. His nerves couldn't take it.

Sunday afternoon was sunny but brisk as Carly biked to Aunt Fannie's. Only Cocoa's twitching nose was visible from the bundled wicker nest.

The sun cast glints on her shiny new bell. She wasn't able to try it out with Cocoa on board as she didn't know how he would respond since he was trained to come at the sound of a bell. But the gift tickled Carly and she wanted Jason to see she liked it.

Parking her bike on Auntie's porch, she carried Cocoa inside and was met with the smell of chocolate chip cookies.

"Oh. You brought that rabbit." Aunt Fannie made a face that appeared to show genuine displeasure. She clasped and unclasped her hands. "Think we could cage it for the meeting?"

Carly swept her gaze across the dining-room table. Auntie's patterns were neatly organized and cookies on china served as a centerpiece. "Sure. I'll put Cocoa down for a nap. Looks like you're ready."

"I'm a nervous wreck," Auntie replied.

Kissing her on the cheek, Carly took care of Cocoa. When she returned, Jason was standing in the entryway, introducing his editor friend Tom. She also saw Miranda and hurried to get in on the introductions.

"Jason gave me a ride," Miranda whispered. "You aunt set it up."

Carly's eyes widened. "That works. When's your flight again?"

"Tonight."

Jason introduced Tom. The editor was tall with reddish-blond hair and freckles. Younger than she'd imagined, maybe he just had one of those baby faces. He wore a button-down shirt and jeans, and his finger sported a wedding ring. "It smells good in here."

"Bribery," Auntie replied. "Let's all go to the table, shall we?"

"It's kind of you to give up part of your weekend," Carly acknowledged.

"Not a problem. The wife and kids are at her mom's today. I'll join them later."

They settled around the table, where Jason settled in beside Carly and whispered, "Don't get jealous over Miranda. Your aunt asked me to pick her up."

Carly feigned a smile, hating to admit she had felt a prick of jealousy. How foolish. "It's fine."

Tom flipped through designs and questioned Aunt Fannie about her work.

"I see you attached the bell," Jason whispered.

"I love it. Did you know Cocoa's trained to come to me at the sound of a bell?"

"No way. What—" Jason's next question stuck in his throat when a stranger strode into the house.

"Hey, everybody. Having a party without me?"

Carly jumped up to greet her brother. "Auntie's showing her patterns to an editor. Come join us." She introduced him, and he settled in next to Miranda. Grinning at Jason, he helped himself to a cookie.

Jason whispered, "Do he and Miranda have a thing?"

"Not anymore, why?"

"Just didn't want to end up with another shiner."

Carly giggled. She looked across the table to see Jimmy's curious gaze resting upon her.

She quieted when Tom suddenly raised his voice. "I'm glad you brought me here, Jason. I think we've got a winner. I did a little research before I came, since I'm not an expert on quilts, but these seem unique."

Carly watched Auntie's eyes light. "Thanks so much."

Tom turned toward Aunt Fannie. "I'll have to take it to committee, of course, but if I get my way, you'll be getting a contract."

With a triumphant whoop, Auntie pumped her hands in the air. Everybody laughed, and the older woman jumped up. "This calls for a drink."

Jason arched his eyebrow, glancing questioningly at Carly.

"Make mine straight, as usual," Jimmy said.

"So what will you have, Tom? Coffee, tea, or milk?"

He chuckled. "You had me there." He glanced at the cookies. "Milk. And this is all going in my report."

When the party started to wind down, Jason pulled Carly aside. "Think Miranda would mind hitching a ride back with Tom so I can take you and Cocoa home? I have some photos I want to show you of

Gramps and Martha and some of the other residents."

Carly glanced across the room where Miranda and Jimmy were laughing. "What about my bike?"

"I've got a rack on my car."

"I don't think Jimmy will mind taking her home."

Adam snatched his phone to his ear the second it vibrated. "Hold on." He headed to the hall bathroom for privacy. "Okay. Let me have it."

"Auntie impressed the editor. He's a nice guy and seems to think he can convince the publishing committee to give her a book contract. He even mentioned art prints and stationery."

"That's great."

"Jah, everybody's pretty excited. Auntie was ecstatic. This place was a real mess. Everybody hugging everybody."

The picture that came to Adam's mind of how Carly would thank Jason wasn't pleasant. His voice hardened. "So what's your take on him?"

"Mm. Good looking. Polite. Big smile. Big Teeth. Black eye's fading. You sure you gave him one? Oh, and I hear he's loaded and generous."

Impatient, Adam said glumly, "Jah, I already knew all that."

"Oh"—Jimmy milked it for all it was worth—"you wanted my take on Tom? I think he was right about Auntie's designs."

"Jah, very funny."

"All right. You sitting down?"

Adam frowned. "No. I'm closeted in the bathroom, waiting for my friend to quit joking around. And from what I can see in the mirror, I'm getting ticked."

"Ticked at me? After I went out of my way to help you? Though the chocolate chip cookies were worth it."

"Should've been here. Lemon bars and peanut butter fudge."

"Jah, you win."

"Come on. Just tell me what you saw."

"You're right. I should cut this short because Miranda's waiting for me to give her a ride home. They're tight. There's no denying it. And your plan won't work tonight, because she just left with him.

Something about showing her some pictures he took at Sweet Life of the residents."

Adam felt as though he'd taken a fist to the stomach. Guess there was more than one way for a guy to fight back. If anyone was passive-aggressive, it was Irish.

"Hey, you still there?"

"Jah."

Jimmy's voice took on a serious tone. "If it's any consolation, she doesn't look at him the same way she looks at you. But you'd better move fast. I don't trust this guy. Don't want him lurking around my sister. And if you're not going to do something about it, I will."

"I'm going to do something, all right. But we've got to regroup. Does tomorrow night work?"

"Nah, thunderstorms heading in. How about Tuesday?"

"Nope. Dale and Jenny get in that afternoon. Wednesday?" Adam asked.

"I'll make Wednesday happen. Good luck."

Chapter Thirty-Nine

Adam lifted the lid off the slow cooker and sniffed the aromatic stew.

Ann smacked his hand, gazing around the sparkling kitchen to make sure everything was set for his guests who would arrive at any moment.

"Hey, I'm starved. My mouth's been watering all day."

"And you can wait a little bit longer." She put on a mitt and pulled piping hot corn bread from the oven.

He watched her place it on Mom's old table set for dinner with her old dishes. "Looks great. I couldn't host without your help, you know."

She removed her apron and hung it on a hook in the pantry. "It was time this place had another good cleaning, and it was my turn. But don't forget to thank Ron for taking care of the kids today."

"Nah, you deserve the thanks, getting the beds ready."

She placed her hand on her hip. "One of these days you won't need us anymore. You'll have Carly taking care of you."

"I'm trying not to think about that right now. Makes me nervous."

"Sorry," she said with a grin that belied her words. "The wheelchair ramp was a good idea."

"Dale's, actually."

The doorbell cut off their small talk. Adam threw open the door and his gaze fell on Dale, appearing out of place in the wheelchair. His leg was in a cast, and he was grinning from ear to ear. Behind him, helping with the chair, was Jenny—looking even more pregnant than before. But it was the other woman that made Adam's jaw drop.

"Cynthia?"

"Surprise!" she said, waving her hand.

He didn't know how long he stood there with his mouth hanging open, but finally he felt Ann pulling him aside. "It's cold out there. Let them in, Brother."

Coming to himself, he jumped back. "Sure, come in."

Jenny pushed Dale over the threshold, and then he was able to wheel the chair around himself. "Nice place."

"Is that stew I smell?" Cynthia asked, moving toward the slow cooker. "I didn't expect this kind of hospitality from a bachelor. Figured Jenny and I would have to do the cooking."

"You will," Adam replied. "Ann's responsible for dinner and getting this place presentable."

Ann rushed forward to introduce herself to Jenny and Cynthia. Then Ron and the children arrived, and Adam didn't have a moment alone with his sister until he walked her to the car. "You handled that without so much as a blink," he accused. "You didn't know about her, did you?"

"Of course not. But I'm glad you had some extra sheets in the linen closet."

"That's all you can say?" he demanded.

"You think they brought her to snare you?"

"Of course they did!" He sounded panicked in his own ears. He leaned close. "In Indiana I didn't think she knew about the matchmaking scheme. But she's called me a few times, and she's acting predatory."

"Jah, I thought so, too. I'll call the sisters. We'll all pray."

Wednesday the morning sun glistened on lingering patches of snow and warmed Carly's cheeks as she peddled through Sweet Home and veered off her normal route. Imogene had once had her mail stolen from her mailbox and had since instilled in Carly that whenever she paid bills, she needed to drop her mail off at the post office. But when she peddled around the corner, she saw something that made her heart somersault. Adam's truck.

Slowing, she watched him hop out and go to the passenger's side. He opened the door. Out popped a pretty pregnant woman. Instinctively, she knew this must be Dale's wife. She braked and moved her bike behind a large bush to watch what would happen next. She rather expected Dale to appear. But Adam leaned back inside and assisted another woman. A long-legged brunette who clutched his arm far too long for Carly's liking. She wore jeans and a pretty scarf at her neck. Her hair was long and straight. She was stunning. Cynthia!

Disbelief and anger washed over her. Jenny glanced her way, and Carly ducked behind the bush. Her heart slamming inside her chest, she waited a moment, then stole another look. Jenny hopped back into the truck on the driver's side. Adam and Cynthia's backs were turned, and they walked toward a restaurant. The brunette laughed and clung to him, but she couldn't see Adam's face. Then they disappeared inside.

Carly clasped her hands over her heart and stood frozen. No wonder he'd stopped calling. She thought she was going to be sick. The truck drove away, leaving her bereft and angry. Fighting not to cry, she mounted her bike and peddled furiously. She was so buried in her miserable thoughts when she reached Sweet Life Retirement Center that she didn't see Adam's truck again until it was too late.

She jumped off her bike, pausing momentarily while her brain scrambled to find a way to avoid meeting its passengers. But it was too late. A wheelchair appeared from behind the truck. From bad to worse, her emotions plummeted when she recognized Dale.

"Carly?" He wheeled toward her, laughing. "On a pink bike?"

She lowered the kickstand and placed her hands on her hips. "The way rumors fly, I would have thought you'd heard about it."

"It suits you."

Just then Jenny appeared and strode toward them.

"Jenny, this is Carly."

The pregnant woman smiled. "I've heard so much about you."

Reluctantly, Carly feigned a smile. "It's nice to meet you."

An awkward silence prevailed until Jenny said, "If you'll point me to a restroom, I'll let you two catch up."

With surprise, Carly acquiesced. "Sure," she said and gave brief directions. Turning back to Dale, she asked, "You here to see Simon?"

"Yup. Hope he's here."

"Jah, that's his car." For all the times she'd practiced what she'd say if she ever saw Dale again, words escaped her. "Jenny seems nice."

"She's a jewel." He gave a mischievous grin much like Adam's. "Jealous?"

"Really?"

"Guess I was a little bit when I heard you were seeing Adam. Don't get me wrong, I'm happy with Jenny."

"Was seeing Adam, while you were trying to lure him to Indiana."

"Look, we could go on slamming each other, but Jenny left us because she knew I hoped to make amends with you on this trip."

Carly's eyebrows shot up. "Let me get this right. So you came to scoop up Adam and hoped to leave everybody on better terms this time? Including your dad?"

"That hurts, Carly. The truth, if you'll allow yourself to admit it, is that we didn't love each other enough. That was the real issue."

It hurt to hear him blurt out the very thing she'd been telling herself for the past three years. She sighed. "I know."

"But it was cruel of me to allow those rumors to circulate. I'm going to set that matter right while I'm here." He gave a contrite grin. "If I don't, Adam will break my neck."

"I don't know if it will make a difference for me at this point, but I appreciate it."

"I'm real sorry about everything."

"Jah, me too." She gave him a genuine smile. "Your wife's lurking around the corner over there. Maybe you should call her back. I've got to get to work, anyway."

"Okay. It's been good seeing you. You look good on that bike."

She toed the kickstand and started to walk it past him, then hesitated. "It's crazy, but I think right this second I just forgave you. And don't worry about Simon. He's softened a lot the last couple of months. He'll be glad to see you."

"That means a lot." The silence stretched between them again. "Hey, regarding Adam. . . May the best man win."

"Don't push it," she replied. But as she walked away, she felt as though the competition was already over. Yet she was wrong in thinking the day couldn't get any worse. Crusher was waiting for her at the bike rack.

"Will you humor an old man?"

"Of course. How are you doing?"

"Don't worry about me. Dot left me a long time ago. I had a dream she passed peaceful, reciting that Bible verse she'd memorized." His voice broke. "And don't be sad for me, either. I'm moving to Houston to live with my daughter."

"You are?" Carly felt tears sting her eyes. "I'll miss you."

"Before I go, can I give you a little advice?"

"Of course."

"I've been watching you for a long time. You're good to everybody at Sweet Life but hard on yourself. Quit pouring everything into a bunch of old folks and save some of that affection for Adam. You two are meant to be together. Remember, there's enough of God's love to go around."

She nodded, unwilling to dash his hopes about Adam. "Does he know you're leaving?"

"Jah."

"I'll try to remember your advice," she replied, clutching him by his suspenders and then hugging him tight.

Chapter Forty

Cocoa raced around Auntie's house while Carly rested her head on the sofa armrest.

"That's quite a story," Auntie said, working the rocker. "I'm glad you were able to forgive Dale."

Jimmy pestered her with his stocking feet, trying to crowd her and usurping more than his share of the couch. "I'm sure Adam didn't invite Cynthia."

"At this point, it doesn't matter. It's over between us, and they've set their trap for him."

Jimmy poked her with his toe. "It's not like you to give up so easily."

She kicked his leg. "Thanks for taking Miranda home."

"Took her to the airport, too."

Auntie winked at Carly.

"Don't give me that look. You know I'm not ready to settle down. But I don't mind having Miranda's pretty face around to look at. You two get pretty boring."

"Pooh!" Auntie said. "Carly that rabbit's getting ready to scratch the sofa."

Reaching down and lifting Cocoa, she nestled her face in his plump wrinkles. Speaking to the rabbit, she said, "Should we ask Jimmy for a ride home?"

"Already, what's the rush? Got any popcorn, Auntie?"

Carly nudged her brother with her toe. "Well scoot over then and quit hogging the couch. I think I'll take a nap."

Unfortunately for her, the doorbell chimed.

"Get that," Jimmy demanded.

"You get it." When she saw he wasn't going to budge, she shot him a dirty look, repositioned Cocoa, and shuffled to the door in her stocking feet. "Jason?"

"Jason?" Jimmy echoed, embarrassing her.

"Could we talk?"

"Come in."

He eyed the porch. "Out here?"

"Sure, let me get my shoes and coat." She shrugged at her relatives' inquisitive gazes and quickly rejoined him.

He brushed off Auntie's porch swing, and she joined him.

"Auntie's still talking about Tom and her contract."

"I'm glad it turned out well for her." He took her hand. "I have something I need to tell you."

Growing worried, Carly asked, "Is Gramps all right?"

"He's fine. But I'm going out of town for Christmas." He hesitated, searching her eyes.

"All right," she replied, growing increasingly concerned over his fretful behavior.

"Karen called. She invited me."

"Oh," she gasped. "That's great. Really, I'm happy for you."

He massaged her hand. "Friends?"

She drew her hand away. "Absolutely. Don't worry about me. I'll see you the next time you bring Gramps to bingo."

"Thanks for understanding. I hope things work out for you and Adam, too."

Carly stood. "It was kind of you to drive all the way out here. Tell Gramps hi for me."

He stood, watching her with concern.

She gave a small wave and went inside. She smiled at Jimmy and forced a cheerful, "I smell popcorn."

"What did he want?"

She gave a small wave. "Nothing important." Starting toward the kitchen, she halted at the sound of the doorbell again. With exasperation, she turned to see what else Jason wanted. But when she opened it, she stared dumfounded.

Adam thrust flowers in her face. "Peace offering?"

Surprising herself, she slammed the door. "Men!" she spat at Jimmy and stomped to the kitchen. But she heard her brother let Adam in and afterward some male murmurings. Then it grew quiet.

She jumped at Adam's voice. "Something smells good in here. Carly knows I love popcorn."

"I could care less what you love."

"Carly!" Auntie chided, then gave her an arched look. "Finish up in here?" she asked and left them alone.

Carly snatched the flowers out of his hand and started rummaging through Fannie's cupboards for a vase. "You've got a lot of nerve showing up here."

"I have a knack for being at the right place at the right time."

He'd surely seen Jason leaving. "You rub me like a burr. Did you know that? It's my private nickname for you. Burr."

"Wow. That's harsh. Does it mean anything to you that you're driving me mad with jealousy?"

She ran water into the vase and stuffed the flowers into it. "I get the mad part. I saw Jason's eye. How often does your angry side surface?"

"Hardly ever. Ask any of my sisters."

"If I cared, I would. You also need to learn a few things about communication. It really hurt me when you wouldn't listen. That you threw me out of your truck. Flowers don't make that right."

"But I know what will."

"Oh, jah?"

"Come with me. I'll show you."

"You don't get it. I'm not going anywhere with you. Right now you're on my blacklist."

He tried to touch her dimple, but she slapped his hand away.

"Listen. If it was any other time of the year, I'd let you take all the time you needed to forgive me. But Christmas is only a few days away, and I don't want to spoil it for us."

"Sorry, Adam." She used the words that had been tumbling in her mind ever since his rejection. Ever since she'd seen him with

Cynthia. "It's over. Just go."

"Well I tried to handle this the easy way. But you asked for it."

Before she knew what had happened, he'd swept her up into his arms and was carrying her through the house. She tried to wiggle out of his hold, but he'd clamped her tight. "Let me go! Are you insane?" As he strode through the living room, she cried. "Jimmy!"

But her brother hopped up and opened the door for Adam.

"Wait!" Auntie shouted, then ran toward them with Carly's coat.

Carly twisted. "Aren't you going to help me?"

"Sure, honey. I'll watch that old rabbit." Then she shooed Adam out and shut the door.

On the porch, Carly spewed, "You drive me crazy."

"Ditto."

"Where are you taking me?"

"Us. Taking us someplace special." When he got to the truck, he didn't release her. "How many times have I either helped you with your projects or come to your rescue?"

"A few, but—"

"I know you're mad, but you owe me at least one last favor. Can you agree that you owe me one favor?"

"Maybe."

"So will you please promise to stay in the truck and hear me out?"

She rolled her gaze upward. He made a good point, and her rebellious heart really wanted to give him a chance. "Jah, I suppose."

"Good, because I won't let you get away, even if you try."

He placed her inside, helped her into her coat, and fastened her seatbelt. Then giving her an impish grin, he ran around to the driver's side and started the truck, wasting no time in putting it in gear. *Probably thinks if the truck's moving, I won't get out*. But by now she was far too curious and a tad entertained. Yet there was no need to let him know that. "I'm still mad at you. I can't believe you ambushed Jason in the parking lot."

"But I'm getting better because I let him leave peacefully a moment ago."

"Humph!"

"You told me I didn't know how to communicate. But I'm going to try to explain. Normally I'm pretty laid back, but Uncle Simon pointed out that I was letting Dad run my life. I guess because it was a pretty good life, I hadn't let it bother me much. About that time Dale made his offer, and I was trying to figure out what I should do. But the real straw that broke the camel's back was when Dad and Si both started telling me how to handle my love life."

He looked at her so that she understood he was referring to them. "After you told me I was passive-aggressive, I knew I had to confront both of them. Honestly, they can be so childish at times. Anyway, they both backed down when they saw me taking control of my own life. Confrontation is not always a bad thing."

Carly had to acknowledge it was something she did all the time, and she admired him for the way he'd taken charge. "But fighting?"

The truck suddenly hit an icy patch and started to slide toward a snowy ditch. She clasped the armrest and was thankful when Adam brought it back under control. She saw they were on Route 20 headed north toward the country.

"Sorry about that."

She relaxed her grip on the armrest. "It just doesn't seem like you to clobber somebody."

"I know you have issues with your dad's anger, but you know I'm not like that. The man I dealt with is not the same one you know. Irish provoked it. But I regret my actions. Just so you know, it takes a lot to make me angry."

She knew it was true. Adam's anger wasn't easily tripped like her father's had been. If she was honest with herself, she shouldn't even be comparing them.

"Still, I won't let anyone take my girl. I know I hurt you when I asked you to get out of the truck. But I needed to leave before I did something dumb again. I needed space."

"Your girl?" She asked sarcastically although she felt tingly with delight. "What about Cynthia?"

Surprise lit his eyes. "She's nothing to me. You stole my heart that first night you kissed me. And I plan to steal yours back in a few minutes."

"Throwing the kiss in my face again."

"You bet." He winked.

"What exactly did your dad and uncle say about me?"

"It's probably better if you don't know."

"I need to know."

Adam studied her, and she matched his gaze with pleading eyes. "At the time Uncle Si was aggravated at you, and he wanted me to date you because he thought I'd keep you happy and occupied."

"That's awful." She didn't put it past Si, though. Following Adam's earlier remarks to its logical conclusion, she asked, "So your dad doesn't want us together? I knew he didn't like me."

"Keep in mind how controlling he is. Mom's easygoing like me. He thinks you're too much of a handful for me."

"Is that so?" She arched a brow. "He's obviously underestimated you. You're a stubborn man."

"And underestimated you."

She smiled.

"Once he gets to know you, he's going to adore you. You're so irresistible."

He was doing a pretty good job communicating now, saying all the things that made it easy to forgive him. "We're going to the bridge, aren't we?"

He ignored her question. "It seemed like everybody had an opinion about us. Jimmy didn't help matters when he threatened me."

He'd obviously changed his mind, the way he'd opened the door for Adam to sweep her away. "We had a rough start."

"So let's start over."

"Jah, I'd like that."

When they got to the Larwood bridge, he gave her a mischievous grin. "I kinda liked holding you in my arms. Want me to carry you over the walking bridge?"

"No, I do not."

"Your loss."

And she knew it was, but she wasn't ready to throw all propriety to the wind. He helped her out of the truck, and memories flooded over her. How they'd snuck onto the bridge and how he'd rummaged through the lumber. How he'd come back for that piece and fashioned it into something lovely for Martha. He might not be much of a communicator, but his romantic bent would make up for it.

"Careful, it might be slick."

She paused at the center of the footbridge and looked down at the river. "It sounds different from the last time we were here. More of a creaking than a roar."

"That's because it's partly frozen. We're going to have to come back in the spring when we can enjoy this without freezing off our toes."

She nodded, wondering why he had brought them. Larwood bridge was still under construction, but even through its snowy blanket, she could see progress. "Martha hung that carving of her initials on the wall in her apartment. Have I thanked you for that?"

"Jah, but you can do so again." He bent and captured her lips. Breathless, she matched his fervor. When he drew back, he whispered, "I love you."

"I love you, too."

"Then let's seal it." He took her hand and led her across the footbridge toward the large old tree that grew on Crabtree Creek. "I wanted to make this day special for you so I brought you to our kissing tree."

"This is special," she breathed, feeling her heart race in anticipation.

But he didn't embrace her. Rather, he dropped her hand and stood askance with crossed arms, staring behind her. "It's a nice old tree, don't you think?"

What a funny thing to say. If he'd bothered to bring her all this way, why was he talking instead of kissing?

Her heart still racing, she replied, "Jah, it's big."

"I love the twisted mossy trunk, don't you?"

She laughed. "Thinking of becoming an arborist?"

"If that's what it takes to get you to turn around and examine the tree."

Shrugging, she turned. And stared. At eye level was a beautiful carving of a large heart with—"That's our initials!"

"Uh-huh. Because I'm making a lifetime commitment to you."

Delighted, she ran her fingers over the carving. "When did you do this?"

"About a week ago, and I've been trying to get you out here ever since."

She recalled how on the way home from Dot's funeral, he'd told her he wanted to do something special on Sunday, but she'd told him about meeting with the editor. Then making it worse, Jason had been waiting for them. Turning back to him, she said, "I'm sorry. You must have been so disappointed."

"You're worth the wait."

Though he hadn't asked about Jason, she wanted to clear the air. "Jason and I are only friends. He even has a girlfriend."

"I'm sorry. It seemed like you were falling under his spell."

"I never did. I was already under yours. And I'm afraid I always will be. But I saw you with Cynthia. Is she staying at your house?"

"Not anymore. They're at Simon's now. And I won't be going to Indiana with them. When I convinced them I was crazy about you, Jenny said she'd get one of her brothers to help Dale out instead."

Thinking of her recent conversation with Dale, she replied, "So they've really given up?"

"Jah. Because I told them I was going to marry you—if you'd have me. Will you?" His dark, pleading eyes penetrated to her very soul.

She cupped her hands over her mouth and shook her head.

"No?" Worry instantly clouded his dark features.

She'd never thought such a day would happen. Wetting her lips, she murmured, "I just can't believe my dreams are coming true."

"Does that mean ”

"Jah, I'll marry you. You're my godsend. How could I not?"

He swept her into his arms. They confessed their love again, and Adam whispered, "I told the family I was bringing you home for Christmas."

"I thought you were coming to my place on Christmas Eve."

"We can do both. I just want to be with you. Let's invite Jimmy and Fannie, too. Think they'll go for it?"

"It seemed like they were in on this little plot of yours."

He shrugged contritely.

"I'm sure they will."

"Good." He smiled at her, his eyes filled with love. "Well if this is our kissing tree, we'd better do some kissing."

Epilogue

"Ach!"

Adam looked up from his paperwork. Dad tugged a hanky from his pocket and dabbed at the coffee he'd sloshed onto his shirt. Adam bit back a smile, thinking it wasn't always his fault. Though sometimes he did hit ruts on purpose. "Maybe you should just give up the habit."

"Maybe you should mind your own business." Pulling a chair over to Adam's paper-littered desk, he spilled more on his boots. Swiping the toes of his boots onto his pants' legs, he looked at the stacks of paperwork. "With such a good year, I suppose we're going to owe a lot of taxes."

Adam leaned back and folded his hands. "I'm just getting started here."

"You could say that. Dale's way ahead of you."

"Jah, I know."

"Something you probably don't know: when a couple gets engaged, they set a date."

"Thought you didn't like the idea of me marrying Carly." He thought of Carly's latest motto: Rome wasn't built in a day. She called Dad her Roman project. He didn't know who he was up against, didn't stand a chance against her charm.

"I don't. But I like the idea of grandkids. Especially those who will carry on the name and the business." As if a new thought suddenly struck him, he set his coffee on the desk and leaned forward. "Since you wouldn't take my advice, there's only one thing I ask of this whole Blosser-woman thing. One little favor."

Now he was calling his stipulations favors. Possible softening?

"Oh, jah? What's that?"

"You're going to have to produce a son."

While he loved everything about that idea and would do everything possible to make it happen, he replied, "You know that God's in control."

"Better start praying, unless you want a whole passel of kids."

"That's probably not going to happen at our age."

"So quit wasting time. Someday I'd like to see my grandson sitting at this desk."

Shaking his head, Adam humored him and listened to his ramblings until his phone rang.

"Hello."

On the other end, "Hi, good looking. Thought you'd like to know about a little problem. We've got rats in the attic."

"What?"

"Not really. The workers are putting on the new roof, but the residents think we have rats in the attic."

"That's why you're calling?"

"No, there's another problem."

"Concerning Carly?"

"Yep."

Dread traipsed up Adam's spine.

"What's she gotten herself into this time?" Dad demanded. "Is that Simon?"

Shaking his head, Adam whispered, "Miranda."

"Who's Miranda?" he shouted.

"Shush!" Growing impatient, Adam said, "No not you. What's happening? Is she all right?"

"She's stuck in that old elevator again."

Adam glanced at his dad's angry expression and the stacks of tax preparations. "Anybody with her?"

"Mm-hm. The General, Nines, and Repeater."

"I'll be right there." He hung up the phone and looked his dad straight in the eyes. "She's stuck in an elevator. This kind of stuff happens all the time with Carly, so if you want that grandson, you'd better get used to it." Then grinning, he left to rescue her.

Other books by Dianne Christner

The Plain City Bridesmaids Series

Something Old

Something New

Something Blue

Dianne Christner's first book was published in 1994, and she now writes full time. She has written more than a dozen novels including several historical fiction titles and writes contemporary fiction from her experience of being raised in the Mennonite church. Dianne lives in Phoenix, Arizona, where she enjoys the beauty of her desert surroundings and life sizzles in the summer when temperatures soar above 100 degrees. Dianne and her husband have two married children and five grandchildren. Readers are invited to connect with Dianne at www.diannechristner.net.